Spí Web

By Robert J Franks©

ISBN 978-1479341320

Copyright © 2011 Robert J Franks

First published in 2011 by Robert J Franks via Lulu.com
Text copyright © Robert J Franks 2011

The Author has asserted his moral right

No part or whole of this book may be reproduced in any form, or by any means, without prior permission from the author

Printed and bound by Createspace.com
Cover artwork and illustrations by Robert J Franks ©

Chapter Headings by Colin Franks ©

For Valerie and Colin, my parents who never gave up hope, no matter how much I messed up.
For Alison, my sister, and her entire brood, who share my love of silly things.
For Denise, Cheryl and Colin, loyal friends who have stood by me through thick and thin

Prologue

When their mother is killed in a car accident, Jason, 12, who was injured in the crash himself, becomes embittered and angry. After the will is read, he finds that he and his sisters Kylie, 10, and Anna, 4, are to be taken in by their grandfather, Ethelbert Gobswistle.

Initially daunted by his bizarre looks and behaviour, the children quickly warm to the dotty old man. And magic enters their life. At their new home, they meet Etain, once a black celtic warrior, she is now in the form of an ethnic plastic Christmas fairy, much to her chagrin. Outspoken and opinionated, she brooks no nonsense from either Gobswistle or the children.

As the mismatched group slowly becomes a family, they find they are pursued by the mythical Medb, an ancient witch who wants the source of Gobswistle's magic, the Anguinum, a magical crystal fashioned into the shape of a green glass apple.

They flee their home, taken by Gobswistle to meet a group of ancient Seers, who tell them they must find the three Books of Huddour, three magical texts, to save themselves from the Medb. But the books lie hidden in the past.

As they leave the Seers, the Medb attacks, and the group find themselves cast back in time and separated from each other; Jason and Anna land in Argyllshire. Gobswistle, Kylie and Etain, now returned to her original form of warrior, land on the Isle of Mull. Their stories separate, but run side by side.

Jason and Anna land near Kilneuair, where they are befriended by Aiken Drum, a bizarre looking but simple and friendly creature. Hearing of their quest, he is terrified, for Huddour killed his wife and children, but he offers to take them as far as he can. He takes them to Kilneuair, where they meet Aiken's friend, a short round bad tempered woman called Gaira. Secretly in love with Aiken, she has spent many years selling surrounding villages to the Vikings to prevent attack on Kilneuair, thus keeping Aiken safe. When she realises Jason is taking Aiken from her, she plans to stop him.

Jason meets Cináed Mac Alpain, king of Argyllshire, and his advisor, Myrrdin. Jason is astounded to recognise Myrrdin as a much younger Gobswistle. Myrrdin tells of a prophecy that hints Jason himself may turn the tide of the Viking invasion, but at a cost. Realising his fate is somehow bound up with the Vikings, Jason agrees to help.

Omnust Ossian, the captain of the army, is set to train Jason. Jason was gifted by the Seers with a magical knife; one night after training, Jason discovers just what this magic is when he sees the entire invasion of Kilneuair played out in the mirror like blade. He tells both Myrrdin and Cináed what he sees.

Gaira, still seeking a way to rid herself of Jason, hides a scrying mirror under the king's bed; the twin of the mirror is held by Ragnar, leader of the Vikings.

On a training session on Gorlach hill, Jason is kidnapped by an unknown attacker, and his story ends here in the first book.

Unaware they are on an island, Gobswistle, Kylie and Etain head south. Gobswistle's fragmented memory hints that Jason lies in that direction. They come across a burned out monastery, and inside find an empty box that had held the Three Books they seek.

Goblins attack them while they are in the monastery; Kylie is elfshot, and she begins changing into a goblin herself. After a protracted battle to escape, the threesome set out to find help. In a dream, Kylie meets Herne the Hunter, who tells her not to head south, for she may kill Jason.

They find help in the form of Athdara, a selkie trapped in human form, held prisoner by her brutal and devout husband, Tearlach. At great cost to herself, Athdara is able to expunge the goblin spirit from Kylie, but cannot remove the magic that will make her change form. Kylie will become a Cait Sidhe, a giant cat, at full moon. That first transformation will take her into the Rage, where she will attack anyone, but after that she will be able to change at will.

Furious at what he considers his wife's betrayal by the use of pagan magic, Tearlach sets out to kill her, only to be confronted by Etain. After an epic swordfight, Etain is the victor. Athdara transforms once more into a selkie, and returns to the sea. Kylie, Etain and Gobswistle discover that an army sent to aid the king of Scotland seek shelter in the monastery that Kylie was attacked in. They vow to stop them.

Chapter One

Kylie couldn't help staring at Etain. Even though the warrior sidhe had been wearing the fighting leathers a day now, it was still a slight shock to the system. Gone was the camouflage jacket, all the padding, all the zips. The fighting leathers, worn and supple, clung to every muscle in Etain's body. And she had *lots* of muscle. Her braided hair was now tied loosely at the bottom with a leather strap, and where Tearlach once had his sword, Etain had tied a small leather pouch, filled with the nails she found around the abandoned Tigh Dubh. She looked, now, as if she belonged in this time.

Gobswistle followed behind, the old jacket now hanging off his shoulders, his hands thrust deep in his pockets as he stared intently at the ground. The pockets bulged with the innumerable packets of herbs he'd shoved into them. Etain had criticised him for bringing things he no longer remembered the use of.

"I forget what I remember and remember what I forget," he'd retorted. Etain hadn't pursued the matter.

The morning sun, wonderfully warm now after the bitterness of their first few days, beat down an them as they walked. The rolling landscape around them was familiar; they'd covered it only days previous, only heading in the opposite direction. The sea lapped against the shores beside them, and Kylie kept casting furtive glances at it. Was Athdara down there now? Did she swim with Daileass? And Firtha, was she old enough to transform? Did the selkie, Athdara's first children, swim with them?

Kylie brought her attention to the path before them. Before, when they had been journeying south, the tracks were muddy but almost unused. She remembered seeing only animal tracks. A badger, maybe, or a wildcat's, occasionally a deer's. Now the half dried mud held the shape of scores of booted feet, all marching resolutely north.

Towards the monastery.

She should be scared. She'd *expected* to be scared, when she found out where they were headed. To return to the place where she'd been injured, where she'd been cursed, should have filled her with dread. Instead, she felt almost exited. Almost happy.

"We're gettin' close," said Etain a short while later, looking at the tracks, startling Kylie out of her reverie. "See? Where the mud's gone dry – there's no footprints. They've been here less than a day ago."

"I still don't understand why you won't let me use the Anguinum," muttered Gobswistle.

"'Cos Ah don't want splattin' into no monastery wall," replied Etain. "You gonna tell me you remembered how to use that thing now?"

"Doesn't mean we can't try," replied Gobswistle.

"Actually," said Etain, "yes it *does.*"

"Have you *no* faith in me, wench?"

"Since you ask, nope, none. And don't *wench* me."

Gobswistle stomped on in silence.

Kylie looked at her grandfather. "Granddad?"

"Wot."

"How-how..." she took a nervous breath. She'd never seen Gobswistle this angry. Not so continuously. "How're you going to stop them? This army? From going into the monastery?"

"I don't get you," said Gobswistle. "What do you mean, *how do we stop them?* We tell them not to go in!"

"Yes, but...what are you going to tell them?"

"That's a good question, actually," said Etain. "You gonna tell a bunch of hardened soldiers that the monastery's full of goblins? Spriggans?"

"And why shouldn't I, pray?"

"Hmm, yeah," nodded Etain mockingly, "after all, at the worst they'll only laugh at you. Or chop your head off. They're *soldiers*, old man, preparing for battle. What d'you think they'll make of an old man, a woman and a child prattlin' on about monsters from a fairy tale?"

"I'll tell them who I am!" said Gobswistle forcefully. "I'll tell them I'm Myrrdin!"

"Oh, so you remember being him now, do you?" Etain stopped walking, turning to look at her friend.

"...Sort of," said Gobswistle, not meeting her gaze.

"Oh *really?*" said Etain. "So what you doin' now then? Today, this very minute?"

"Braiding my beard for all I know!" snapped back Gobswistle. "You tell me then! You tell me how I stop those men marching to their death because I told them to go there! Because I'll tell you now, I'll not make that mistake twice!"

8

Kylie expected Etain to snap back, as she had so many times in the past. She'd got used to their bickering, and had come to realise it meant nothing. These two were the closest of friends.

But Etain didn't snap back. She reached out, taking the old man's hand. "Wondered when you'd remember," she said quietly.

Gobswistle blinked at her, his eyes watery. "Remember what?"

The faintest of frowns crossed Etain's brow, vanishing as quickly as it appeared. She patted his hand, then released it. "Nothin'. C'mon, old man, we're catchin' up. Time to up the pace."

"Etain?" Kylie jogged up to Etain's side.

"Yes, child?"

"What was that about?" she asked, double-timing her walking to match Etain's long strides. "Back there. When you said about his remembering?"

"Nothin'," said Etain. She didn't look at Kylie. "Don't matter none."

"I saw your face," persisted Kylie. "He upset you."

Etain looked back at Gobswistle. He seemed oblivious to them, muttering to himself as he studied the footprints in the ground. "Oh...hell. Okay." She turned back to Kylie. "When him an' me first met. Ah just thought he'd remember, is all. Near Strathclyde. It was a battle. Cain't even remember what it was about – guess Ah'm gettin' as fool headed as him – but..." She sighed. "He'd just been and come back from *your* time. Somehow. Mebbies he'd been reading history books, Ah dunno, but he thought he knew how the battle'd go. An' he was important, then. Like a Laird, or a prince, with an army to order around. Lailoken, he wuz called back then. He got it wrong. Ah mean *really* wrong. All his army, his friends...you've seen how soft hearted he is."

"What happened?" said Kylie quietly. "What did he do?"

"He...went fruitloop. Crackers. Not like he is now, no *that's* old age. He was grieving, and he couldn't cope with the guilt. Ran off into the forests. Started talkin' to damn pigs." She sighed. "Took him years, centuries mebbies, to recover. Wild man of the woods, he was called."

"You think him running after these soldiers, it has something to do with that?"

Etain shrugged. "Consciously? Ah think *he* thinks he's correcting a mistake he made as Myrrdin. But yeah, whether he remembers or not, Ah think he's trying to make amends."

Two hundred didn't really sound that much. Two hundred pounds could get you a basic computer, maybe a holiday. Or a good day out for the family.

Seeing the figure represented by two hundred soldiers, marching in four columns of fifty, heading without wavering towards the monastery that sat like a cancerous growth on the distant horizon, made Kylie realise just how many people it actually was. And how *intimidating*.

They stood on a slight bank, looking down onto the path the army trod. The army was about two hundred yards in front, the monastery maybe a further third of a mile.

They were running out of time.

"What do we do?" she said to Etain.

"Beats me," replied Etain. She sounded worried, almost scared. "This was your granddad's idea. Ah said Ah'd help though. Hey, old fool?"

"Less of the old," muttered Gobswistle, one hand to his brow as he peered down the slight incline.

"There's your army. They're minutes away, man! We need to act *now* if we're to stop them!" She'd already pulled a small nail from the pouch by her side, the ironfire licking around her fingers.

"Dear lady, unless you intend scorching them, please put that away!" Gobswistle was rummaging through the numerous pockets of the jacket. "Where the devil is...*Aha!*" He pulled out the small glass apple bowl.

"You gotta be kidding!" hissed Etain, backing away. "What're you gonna do with *that?!*"

Gobswistle was already trotting down the slope, waving the glass apple above his head. "I say! Hey!" he called out to the figures in front. "You need to stop! There's spriggans in there!"

"Oh guh-*reat,*" hissed Etain. "C'mon, we'd best keep up." She took Kylie by the hand, and the two of them ran after Gobswistle. "Hey wait! You cain't go in there!" she added her voice to Gobswistle's, and the men at the very back turned to look at the three people pelting down the track towards them. One of them unslung a bow from his back, notching an arrow.

"Yipes," yelped Etain, "No wait, we're on your side! You cain't go in there – you'll get killed!"

Another soldier notched an arrow, staring down its length at them.

Etain skidded to a halt, her ironfire lengthening. "Aw crap, this was a bad idea." She pushed Kylie behind her. "Stay there," she growled.

"No wait, *don't!*" shouted Gobswistle. "We're here because of Myrrdin! We have a message from him!"

An arrow bit into the dirt an inch from his left big toe.

"State yuir business," said one of the soldiers. Only the rearmost men had stopped, six or seven at most. The rest still marched to the monastery, with its gaping doorway, its scarred courtyard.

"Our business is stopping you!" shouted Gobswistle. "Myrrdin sent us!"

"Captain says it were him that *sent* us," said the soldier. He notched another arrow, as did the men around him. "Be on yuir way, old man. T'is no place to bring a child."

The rest of the army were drawing ever closer to the monastery, and panic began to fill Gobswistle. He began marching forward, the Anguinum held high. "You cannot enter! Listen to me, please! There's death in that monastery! We've seen it – we nearly died! The child, my granddaughter, she was elf shot..."

"Lower yuir weapon," ordered the nearest soldier.

"What?" Gobswistle looked at him uncertainly, then lowered his hand. "No! No, this isn't a weapon – I mean well it *can* be – but no, it's an anguinum, a Druid's Stone..."

"Ah dinnae care what it is," said the soldier. "Put it on the ground."

Gobswistle, staring at the tip of the numerous arrows pointed at him, quickly complied, shrugging helplessly. "You can't go in that place!" he repeated.

Etain grabbed his arm urgently, pointing at the men in front. "We're too late," she said.

The leading soldiers where crossing the cratered flagstones of the monastery's courtyard, approaching the remains of the gated entrance. Even from this distance, Gobswistle could see them speeding up, their voices filled with concern, as they discovered the total dereliction of the old monastery.

With a cry, Gobswistle lunged at the anguinum on the ground before him. Even as the soldiers leapt forward, he sprawled in the half dry mud, holding the glass apple bowl up in front of him. "*Save them!*" he shouted.

Etain threw Kylie to the ground, covering her with her own body as green fire flared up from the old man's hands. The soldiers, startled by the eldritch light, followed the sidhe warrior's example, throwing themselves to the ground.

Gobswistle's body was lifted from the ground, almost snatched, so quick was the movement. Green fire spiralled around his form, roaring and spitting, and he vanished from sight.

"Devilry!" shouted one of the soldiers. "T'is the work of the devil!"

The fire died. Gobswistle hung horizontally in the air, his wide eyes staring sightlessly at the blue sky above. Slowly, rotated by an unseen hand, he turned upright. He was gently lowered to the ground, his battered silver boots sinking slightly into the mud.

Wide eyes searched out Etain. "Well, that worked really well, I think, personally." he said conversationally. Then he passed out.

The nearest soldier poked him with his foot, then turned to the remaining men behind him. "Bind them."

*

Kylie, Etain and the unconscious Gobswistle sat tied together in a rough triangle. They'd been dragged unceremoniously across the ground and thrown into one of the blackened craters that covered the courtyard. Two soldiers remained on guard, the youngest of the army. They looked no more than fifteen or sixteen, and their leather armour hung badly from bodies not yet old enough to fill them. They sat now on a couple of fallen pillars a few feet from the crater's rim, nervously looking at Gobswistle as his head rolled from side to side.

"Why did you let them tie us?" whispered Kylie to Etain. "Surely your ironfire..."

"They're on our side," whispered Etain, "whether they realise it or not. Ain't gonna go burning our allies. 'Sides, Ah c'n still reach mah pouch. Ah c'n get us out o' here any moment you like."

"Be silent," said one of the captors, trying to sound menacing.

Gobswistle's eyes popped open, and he glared at the youth who had spoken. "Madame Pompadour was a painted personification of preposterous pretentiousness," he declared angrily, before slumping forward unconscious.

There was a long silence then. It was Kylie who broke it. "What did the anguinum do?"

"Ah...." Etain was staring at the back of the old man's head. "Ah..erm...that better not be who Ah think it is..."

"He sounded *English,*" said Kylie. Indeed, the faint southern American accent had appeared, in those few bizarre words, to have been replaced with an almost public school accent.

Gobswistle's head swung round, and he leant forward as far as the ropes would allow to look at his Granddaughter. "Madame de Pompadour était une incarnation peinte de prétention l'irrationnelle," he insisted. "Oh bugger," he added, and his head rolled forward.

Etain rocked her head back, staring at the sky for a few seconds before screwing her eyes closed. "We're *screwed,*" she muttered.

"What's wi' him?" called over the other youth. He held the anguinum in his hands, turning it over as he studied it.

"He's *old,*" replied Etain. "He used to know magic, he got old, it backfired. You may wanna be careful with that. You saw what it did to *him.*"

The youth rapidly placed the glass apple on the paving underfoot. "Wh-why were ye shoutin' at us no' to go in there?" he jerked his thumb at the ruins behind him. "There's no danger in there – we'd a' heard by now."

"Or just maybe," said Etain, "the total silence means everyone's been killed by those damn spriggans."

Gobswistle's head came up, looking at the soldiers. "Les monstres de fées changent les gens, vous savez."

"That's French," said Kylie. "He's speaking *French.*"

Gobswistle turned to look at Kylie. "Bonjour, petite-fille. Et pourquoi je ne devrais pas parler le français ? C'est une langue si passionnée!" He lolled forward. Before his head reached his chest though, he raised it abruptly, still looking at Kylie. "Fairy monsters change people you know. Hello, granddaughter. Why shouldn't I speak French? It's such a *passionate* language!" He leant back a bit, turning so that he could see Etain. "Well hel-*lo* and bonjour! And aren't you a delight for the eyes?"

Etain didn't look at him. "We're *so* screwed," she muttered.

Gobswistle was looking around him nervously yet curiously. "I say...this is that...that monastery thingy, isn't it? Where all those spriggans are? Kylie, Kylie, have you become the Cait Sidhe yet?"

Kylie looked at him in bafflement, not replying.

"You're younger than I last saw you," he continued. "What are you? Nine? Ten?"

"She's ten, she becomes the Cait Sidhe at the next full moon," and now she did turn to look at Gobswistle, "and how long do we have to put up with *you?*"

"Granddad," said Kylie, "Etain, what's going on? He's Gobswistle!"

"I bloody am not," said Gobswistle. "What on earth sort of childish name for that for one of the three most *powerful* alchemists?!" With the ease of taking off a jumper, he lifted the ropes that bound them over his head, standing up and brushing himself down. The ropes that had bound his wrists simply fell away. "When on earth are we, anyway?" He ignored the two soldiers as they leapt up, swords drawn. "And what on *earth* have I got on my feet?" He stared at his silver boots with something akin to horror.

"Eighth or Ninth century Ah guess," said Etain. "*You* brought us here. To save the army from entering that monastery."

"Did we?" said Gobswistle, tapping a finger to his chin. "Did we? Surely they're *meant* to change though, from what I remember..." he paused, his fingers exploring both his beard and his hair. "What on earth..?"

"You outgrew yer dandified ways," said Etain. She snorted. "What, don't you like them?"

"So unkempt, undignified...." muttered Gobswistle, trying to smooth down the hair. He cocked his head on one side, regarding Etain. "You're old."

"Watch it."

"Older then. Still beautiful though. Thought you said you'd never..." and his fingers made 'ditto' marks in the air, " 'delve into the silvery threads of time.'"

The two soldiers stepped up to Gobswistle, their swords raised. "Now listen," began one of them.

A withered finger touched the tip of each sword and with a yelp, both soldiers dropped their blades, both swords bursting into a red flame. "Do behave," muttered Gobswistle.

"It's my first foray," said Etain.

"Via America presumably," grinned Gobswistle. "Loving the accent."

The ropes now loose, Etain got busy removing the remaining constraints from herself and Kylie. She paused to look at the old man. "Ah repeat, *how long do we have to put up with you?*"

"Granddad," said Kylie as she got up, "what's happened? What did the anguinum do to you?"

"The anguinum!" yelped the old man. "Of course! Where is it? Ah!" He saw it on the ground where the two soldiers had been sitting, and bent as though to lift it.

The two soldiers, daggers now in hands, moved in front of him, if a little nervously, to block his way. "Let's not be silly," smiled Gobswistle, and invisible hands lifted the two soldiers into the air, depositing them ten feet or more away. He lifted the glass apple, then turned back to his granddaughter.

"What was the last thing I said?" he said, smiling gently. That *So that's alright then* smile that Kylie knew so well. "Qu'ai-je dit ?"

"You-you told the glass apple to save them," she said nervously. It was weird and creepy. He *looked* like Gobswistle, but the mannerisms, the accent, the *intelligence*, were all foreign to her. And, it seemed, *his* magic *worked.* "You're not my granddad, are you?"

"OY!" bellowed a voice beside them, making them both jump. Etain was looking over at the two soldiers, who had been edging towards the broken entrance to the monastery. They halted, looking sheepishly at each other like two naughty little boys. "You even *think* about goin' in there," she bellowed, "It'll be me tyin' you up!" She drew a nail out of the pouch, and her ironfire blade grew forth. "You seriously wanna try me? Come 'ere!"

"...And back to me," grinned Gobswistle. "I am indeed your granddad. Always have been, therefore always will be."

"You sound different."

"Because I am not yet the Granddad you know."

"More's the pity," muttered Etain.

"Scorn, thy name is Etain," replied the old man. "The body may be this...Gobswistle?" and as Kylie nodded, he shuddered. "Well I'm sure I had a good...*reason...* but *my* name is The Comte De Saint Germaine!" His hands came up in a theatrical flourish.

Kylie looked at him. "...Who?"

Gobswistle's smile faded. "Count Saint Germaine? The talk of Versailles?"

Kylie shook her head.

"I put Catherine the Great on the Throne! I created dyes worth fortunes! I serenaded Royalty with my violin concertos!"

Kylie looked over at Etain, who was hustling the two young soldiers, baffled by their sudden reversal in fortunes, back to the little group. "He's an alchemist, sorta like Athdara."

"*He's an alchemist like Athdara,*" mimicked Gobswistle, sounding almost petulant that his name had meant nothing to the little girl. "Who's this Athdara, anyway? Her name rings a bell..."

"She's a Selkie," said Kylie.

"You compare *me* to a bloody – a bloody circus act?!"

"She saved me, took the-the Unseelie spirit out of me," said Kylie defensively. "She was brave! Bravest woman I've met!"

"You two, *sit,*" said Etain, leaving the two youths by the pillars and not looking round to see if they'd obeyed. They had. "Enough with your posturing," she snapped at the old man. "There's one hundred ninety eight men in there." She pointed at the monastery. "Gobswistle wanted to save their lives. He called on the anguinum to help. It kicked him out of his own body and summoned *you* from his past. Why? And for *how long?*"

Before he could respond, the monastery exploded.

Chapter Two

"Duck and cover!" yelled Etain as wood and brick began showering down around them. From the centre of the monastery, a giant fireball roared its way into the sky, smoke and ash following in its wake.

The two young soldiers ducked down behind the fallen pillar they'd sat on; Etain and Kylie took shelter in the nearest old crater.

Gobswistle stood upright, his arm brought up to fend off the worst of the heat from the fireball. A look of horror settled over his face as he watched the fragments of ancient brickwork and shards of wood bounce and ricochet off the ground around him. There were blue flashes of light around his body as various pieces of debris were blocked by his own magic.

One hand came up, catching a sliver of smouldering wood as it flew towards him.

"Gobswistle!" bellowed Etain. "What the *hell* are you doing?"

Gobswistle ignored her, turning the splinter over in his hands. Threads of green fire, almost invisible, ran up and down its length. "il est juré." He muttered to himself, scarcely audible over the roar of the flames. " Un juron diabolique ancient..." He passed his hand over the palmed splinter; in a blue flash it disintegrated, becoming ash that Gobswistle rubbed away on his jeans.

"Gobswistle!" shouted Etain. "The men! The army!"

Gobswistle gestured for her to join him, his arm waving madly at her.

"Stay low," said Etain to Kylie, who nodded, ducking down below the rim of the crater as Etain clambered out to join the old man.

"What is it?" she shouted over the sound of falling masonry and the roaring fire. "What happened? What *was* that? They don't *have* blackpowder, they can't have...!"

"It was no *compound* explosion, ma belle fée," he replied. "The very timbers of the monastery, they were cursed! Booby trapped!"

"But-but, *we* were here! *We were here!*" she stared at the fireball, dimming now, becoming a giant mushroom cloud of smoke and dust. "Why didn't – why..."

"Not enough of us," said the old man. "We weren't a threat. We were...we were three people. We should have been an easy target for the spriggans, if we'd been mortal. Un repas facile pour les anciens."

"The army..?" she was looking at the vast and ragged crater where the monastery had been. "Are they..."

"Dead?" Gobswistle shook his head. "Je ne pense pas ainsi. I think not. And I think..." the mushroom cloud was dissipating now, and the clatter of falling debris was lessening. "I think," he said slowly, "I understand why the Comte de Saint Germaine is needed."

The two young soldiers were nervously peering over the top of the pillar, and as one of them eased himself up, he dislodged a fragment of brick from its surface, sending it clattering to the ground. He flinched visibly as the old man rounded on him.

"Are you hurt?" he shouted over. By his side, Etain had returned to Kylie, helping her out of the crater.

The young man shook his head. "No." He stared over at the vast crater. "My – my regiment, the captain..?"

By his side, his companion was standing himself.

"They're dead," he half shouted, half sobbed. "They're all dead!"

"No they are *not*," said Gobswistle/Germaine. His face was hard, determined, and the young soldier, recognising his authority, stifled his emotions. "That's better. I think...I think they *all* survived. But they are in terrible danger. Horrendous danger."

"The spriggans?" said Kylie. Her face was pale and shocked.

"No," said Gobswistle, "The spriggans, I suspect, are no more. They served their purpose."

A tear rolled down Kylie's cheek, unnoticed by either of her companions. Why should she feel such grief for them? They had cursed her, turned her into a changeling, a monster; why did she feel so sad for them, yet almost nothing for the soldiers now missing? As she stared at the vast crater, a hand went to her shoulder, to where the wound had been only two days before. The gift from her family.

Etain saw the gesture, and misinterpreted it. "You're thinking your bolt was made from the timbers of this place?" she looked at Gobswistle. "Is that possible?"

"Possible? Of course it's possible!" snapped the old man. "In fact I'd guarantee it! You two! Here!"

The two soldiers, accustomed perhaps to following orders,

immediately falling in, in front of Gobswistle and his companions. "Oh don't be ridiculous – *I'm* not your captain – oh damn it men, *fall out!*"

With a nervous sideways look at each other, the two relaxed, but only a little.

"Names?" snapped the old man. "Come on, names! What are you called? *Dites-moi vos noms!*"

"Sir, m-my name is Cathal," said the taller of the two. Mousy brown hair fell to his shoulders, and his chin and upper lip were covered in what Kylie's mum would have called *bum fluff.*

"Don't *sir* me, my name's the Compte de..."

"It's *Gobswistle,*" corrected Etain fiercely. "We don't have time for that damn mouthful. And you? *Your* name?"

"F-Fionnlagh, sir," said the blonde, freckly youth, directing his reply to Gobswistle.

"*Ne moi l'appelez pas!*" bellowed Gobswistle, and the youth flinched in confusion. "How long have you both been soldiers?"

"Two weeks," said Cathal at the same time as Fionnlagh said "three months."

"Seen battle? *Either* of you?" Gobswistle was rummaging in his pockets.

Both silently shook their heads, naughty schoolboys in front of a fearsome headmaster.

"Do you understand what's happened? To your company?" He brought out his ball of string.

"They're...*not* dead?" said Cathal.

"No. Well...maybe some, through falling masonry." He measured a length of string, then snapped the length off, returning the remaining ball to his pocket.

"Is the – I mean do they – are their wounds..." Fionnlagh looked from Etain, to Kylie, to the old man. "Are their wounds cursed?"

"Shrewd man." With a quick sweep of his hands, his unruly hair was layered back over his head and quickly tied into a short pony tail with the string. It looked for all the world like an eighteenth century Frenchman's bouffant wig. "Best we go find out then."

"I don't like him," whispered Kylie as they crossed the courtyard behind Gobswistle and the two soldiers.

Etain looked down at the little girl whose hand she held. "Cain't say he's *mah* favourite version of Gobswistle either. He's a letch."

"He's good at magic though." She thought about the ease in which he'd disarmed Cathal and Fionnlagh. "Better than Granddad." She felt vaguely guilty for saying that; it felt like a betrayal of the old man who'd taken them in. A thought struck her. "He's not always been called Gobswistle?"

"no, you *know* that." They'd reached the outer rim of the crater. "Watch your footing – it's loose round the edge. No, he changed his name to that when he got booted out of America."

As they gingerly made their way over the edge, Kylie persisted with her thought. "So what did he change it *from?*"

"Ah didn't ask," said Etain, peering down into the pit below them. It was like a massive bowl, filled with planks of smouldering wood and shattered blocks of granite set against the blackest of soils. Yet no bodies could be seen. "Ah wuz in a toolkit in a cupboard. Remember?"

"But you knew him with other names?"

Etain, clambering down over boulders, simply grunted.

Kylie followed, her tiny feet finding footholds where Etain's had slipped and twisted.

She jumped daintily onto the next boulder below, bouncing off smaller stones and planks as though she weighed nothing. "So which is his real name?"

Etain slid gracelessly through the dirt to arrive at Kylie's side. "Whatever name he's goin' with at the time." She looked up at where the little girl had jumped from, the precarious route she had taken without effort. "How did you just *do* that?"

Kylie shrugged. "I dunno. Just sort of ...*did.* I'm going to catch up with Granddad." She bounced away before Etain could say anything, as light and agile as a dandelion seed dancing in the wind.

Etain's eyes narrowed. Seven days until full moon, and already it showed on Kylie. Gobswistle, the two youths, even Etain herself, were wary, *scared* of this vast pit, what it may hold.

Kylie seemed totally at home.

The crater was vast; so vast that the other side was still partially obscured by smoke and ash. The footing was treacherous, with jagged bricks hidden under loose soil and gravel. Slowly the little group made their way down into the belly of the crater.

One of the soldiers turned to Gobswistle. "Where are they?" he hissed. "Where's me regiment?"

Gobswistle leaned breathlessly against a large fragment of stone work, regarding the youth. "Vous appelle Fionnlagh, n'est-ce pas ?" He sighed heavily, stretching his aching back. "I do not know. I...thought they'd be down here."

The crater, cast into shadows and half darkness by its depth, debris, smoke and ash, was devoid of any signs of either the spriggans or the regiment that had entered the monastery.

"Fion, Gobswistle," called Cathal, a few yards away. He'd lifted an old oak cell-door, still intact, to look beneath. "Please – Ah think ye'd best see this!"

Gobswistle made an *after you* gesture to the young soldier, and Fionnlagh headed over, steadying himself against the shattered pieces of brick and woodwork. With a quick nervous look around him, Gobswistle followed.

It was a round tunnel, new looking and fresh in the loamy soil, plunging almost vertically down into utter darkness. As Etain and Kylie joined them, the old man held his hand out over the center.

"What is it?" said Etain. "Are the men, are they down there?" By her side, young Cathal made a wimpering noise.

Gobswistle frowned briefly at the soldier. "Yes. Yes, they are down there. There is some sort of... caverne souterraine, erm... underground cavern. Vast. And it's new. Feel that?" and he gestured for Etain to hold her hand over the pit. "That *cold?* That is not local magic. It is European. Bretanic."

"Huddour?" asked Etain. Gobswistle nodded silently. Etain withdrew her hand, wiping it with obvious distain on her leg. "What do we do, then?"

"We go down," said the old man simply, standing up.

"Sir..." began Cathal.

"*Gobswistle,*" scowled Gobswistle.

"Gobswistle," corrected the youth, picking nervously at a splinter in his hand, "th' tunnel, it's near straight down, sir. How dae we..?"

Before Gobswistle could answer, Kylie had leapt past him, diving into the tunnel headfirst, as though she were diving into a pool.

"*Kylie!!*" yelled Etain, lunging for the little girl, her fingers skimming Kylie's heels as she shot like a projectile down into darkness.

"Damn!" shouted Gobswistle, on his knees by the side of the pit. "Que pensait-elle ?! Has she no sense?" He quickly rummaged through his pockets, dragging out the Glass Apple.

"You wanna make it *worse?*" said Etain, staring at him.

"Despite your predilection for calling me by that ostentatious name," snapped Gobswistle, clambering to his feet, "I am *not* Gobswistle. I *know* how to use this création merveilleuse." Even as he spoke, green fire was circling from the Anguinum to encompass his hand and wrists. "Now," and again his voice became commanding, "Rassemblez-vous autour de moi! Faites-vous dans un cercle!" The two soldiers stared at him, eager to respond but not comprehending.

"Form a circle and hold hands!" said Etain. She glared at Gobswistle. "Will you *drop* the damn French?" They quickly encircled the tunnel's opening, all holding hands. Etain held the wrist if the old man's hand as he held the fiery Anguinum.

"Jump," instructed Gobswistle, "on my mark. One...two...*three!*"

With only the slightest of hesitations, the soldiers jumped with Etain and Gobswistle. The walls were illuminated by the light from the

Anguinum as they sped down into the darkness. Cathal and Fionnlagh had their eyes screwed shut as the walls sped by and wind ripped at their clothes and hair.

"You sure this is gonna work?" bellowed Etain over the roar of the wind.

"You're beautiful when you're frightened," shouted back the old man, grinning broadly.

They shot out of the bottom of the tunnel like a cork out of a bottle. A hundred feet below them, the ground rushed hungrily up to greet them. Both soldiers screamed as they plummeted. But ten feet above the ground they stopped, bouncing up a little way as though on elastic bands, then gently descended to the group.

"Are we...are we dead?" whispered Cathal, his eyes still tight shut.

Fionnlagh opened one eye. "Nope. We're...we're..." he looked around, both eyes open. "Blessed Bridhe and Mary..." He released his grip on Cathal and Etain, turning to take in all that he saw.

Gobswistle smiled slowly at Etain. "your hands are as gentle as ever," he said softly.

Etain took her hand from his wrist. "You weird little *creep!* Don't *touch* me!" She looked around. "Kylie? Kylie!" But at the moment, there was no sign of the little girl.

Only the bodies. Five were visible in the green light from the anguinum, and the shadows in the depths beyond hinted at more.

Fionnlagh was kneeling by one, the blade of his dagger held under the body's nose. "He – he's alive, sir," he said to Gobswistle. He held his knife up to show the mist that had condensed on the blade. "Shall Ah check the others?"

"Yes," said Gobwistle. "No, Wait." With a quick wink at Etain, he launched the glowing anguinum into the air. It shot roof-wards, stopping only a few feet below the mouth of the tunnel. It pulsed an emerald green for a split second, then dimmed. Then a brilliant blue-white light filled the chamber.

It was like being inside a hollow gemstone. The chamber was ovoid, the floor curving up to meet the roof as it curved down. Floor and ceiling were as shiny and reflective as a piece of polished obsidian, and just as black.

The still forms of the regiment lay around the chamber, scattered and jumbled like trees fallen in a storm. But they lay with their feet pointing to the centre of the chamber, as though some sepulchral central explosion had felled them. Various wounds and injuries were visible, though none appeared fatal; a splinter of wood embedded in an arm, a piece of metal embedded in a leg. Some of the wounds seemed so minor that the men surely should be awake and moving, but all the men lay unconscious and unmoving on the glassy floor.

"Sir, look," said Cathal, pointing. "Isn't that yeh granddaughter?"

All eyes looked to where he pointed.

At the axis of the chamber, incongruous in her modern clothing, stood Kylie, her hood up and her face lost in shadows.

"Kylie!" shouted Etain, already making her way towards her. "Girl, get over here! What do you..."

The hooded figure looked up at the sound of the voice, and two piercing yellow eyes regarded Etain impassively.

Etain stopped, unsure. "Kylie?"

Gobswistle came to her side. "Leave her," he said quietly, trying to guide her back to the others.

She twisted her arm free. "Get your hands offa me," she growled. "She's your grandchild! Somethin's wrong, cain't you see that?"

"Again you address me as someone I am not," replied Gobswistle. "I see more than you give me credit for. The spirits of the changelings, the Unseelie court, the ones who will fill the vessels of these soldiers; they sense a difference in Kylie. They *hold* her, they *call* to her. They've *been* calling to her since the moment we returned. Maybe even as we approached. Un enfant de deux mondes. A changeling not under their control. See."

One wrinkled hand passed in front of Etain's eyes, and the scene before her rippled and changed. Ghostly, vaporous forms whipped around the figure of Kylie; forms of vicious, long snouted beasts, of short, squat tumorous beasts, recognisable animals and creatures from the nightmares of children. All of them circled Kylie, hands gently stroking her, caressing her avariciously. Occasionally one would shoot out to a body, fingers probing the wound, and the body would twitch and moan.

"Can they...can they still claim her?" asked Etain.

"They try," said Gobswistle, "She is like a beacon to them, even more so than the injured men. they try, but Athdara, she knew. She knew the ancient ways. The best they can do now is bring on the *Rage*."

"It's too soon!" hissed Etain. "The full moon is days away! It could *kill* her!"

"Again, you just think of the girl," breathed Gobswistle. He was gently going through each of his pockets, opening pouches of herbs and sniffing them.

"What d'you mean?!"

"There are two hundred and two other people trapped down here with her, most of them unconscious." said Gobswistle gently. "If she changes, if she goes in the *Rage*, what do you suppose happens to them? Ce serait un massacre!"

As Gobswistle/Germaine's magic faded, Etain stared at Kylie. Cold yellow eyes stared back. She was silent for a while as the old man's words burnt their meaning into her mind. She turned to Gobswistle. "Can you help her?"

"I can help *us.*" Gobswistle lifted his nose from a herb pouch, and a grin spread across his face. "The selkie are not the only ones who know the ancient ways."

"What's the' doin'?" whispered Cathal to his friend. Etain and Gobswistle stood a few yards from them, pouring out small piles of herbs.

"Dunno," whispered back Fionnlagh. "Th' old man, reckons he c'n help oor lot."

"He mebbies can," said Cathal, scratching at his hand. "Ye've seen his magic, an-an' he's got this air aboot him..."

"Aye, he bossy a'reet. Reckon he's fro' the south though. He keeps sayin' them funny words, like from overseas. Me Dah tol' me 'boot them." Fionnlagh looked at his friend. "What yer frettin' with yer hand for?"

Cathal shrugged. "Had a splinter. Think Ah got it. Can't see it now." He looked over to where the old man and the black woman were. They could hear the two of them arguing quietly as they worked the perimeter of the circle they were creating. "She sounds funny an'all."

"Ah've heard legends o' her type. Fierce like. Loyal, if ye dinnae cross her." Fionnlagh shuddered. "See t'muscles on her though?"

"She'd make a haggis o' yer innards!"

"Glad she's on our side," muttered Fionnlagh.

"Why'd the' want us tae stay outside o' the circle?" wondered Cathal.

"Mebbies the' don't want us gettin' caught in the magic?" replied Fionnlagh.

"Aye," said Cathal, scratching his itching palm against his thigh. "Wouldnae want that."

"This had better work," said Etain, pouring out yet another handful of herbs.

"Faithless female," grinned Gobswistle. "The magic is reliable. It is but what Athdara did for Kylie."

"These herbs aren't the same."

"I have had to factor in the fact that the demonsouls are not yet in residence in the cadavers." He trotted past Etain, then turned to count how many piles of herbs had already been built. "We're getting there."

"They are *not* cad..." Etain paused, straightening. "But Kylie is a changeling," she said.

"Caused by the cursed bolt, yes." He stooped, pouring out a little orange pile of herbs.

Etain looked around the vast chamber, at all the men who lay prone on the ground, their bodies pointing accusingly at the unmoving Kylie. "So these men, they're all..."

"Yes, yes, ils sont toutes les créatures de fees. Changelings." He glared at Etain. "What would you have me do, then?"

"Ah thought...Ah thought you were gonna save them."

"The magic of Huddour matches my own," said the old man. He returned the herb pouch to his pockets, removing another in its place. "I cannot reverse it. They *will* change. But as Athdara did with Kylie, I hope to leave their minds and spirits intact."

"You *knew* this would happen, didn't you?" said Etain. She stopped pouring out the herbs, straightening and drawing the string closed on the little pouch.

"Don't stop!" snapped Gobswistle. "We've nearly completed the circumference!"

"*Didn't you?*" insisted Etain, not moving. "Up there, you said they *were supposed to change!*"

"Alors, devrais-je les quitter?" shouted Gobswistle. "Let them change into what Huddour intended? To spread terror across the north?"

A scream silenced any response Etain may have had. It was a keening, high pitched scream, half human and half feline. It came from Kylie. Her padded coat lay in shreds on the ground, and she was shredding her remaining clothes from her body. Blue fire lapped round her body as she twisted and writhed, her skin pulsing and bulging, globular pustules breaking out across her skin; blisters of liquid blue fire.

"Dépêchez-vous!" shouted Gobswistle as he ran to the next point of the circle. "Nous avons seulement des minutes!"

"But Kylie..."

"Cannot be helped before we help these men!" A gesture in the air, and the Anguinum plummeted from the ceiling, landing in Gobswistle's outstretched hand and plunging the chamber into semi darkness. Only the fire from Kylie's body now illuminated the area. Gobswistle withdrew a small bottle and broke the wax seal, pouring the oily contents into the anguinum. "The last votive! Place it!"

Kylie screamed again, more guttural this time, more animalistic. Etain flinched at the raw power of the child's voice, and ran to the final empty point in the circle, rapidly emptying her herb pouch. "It's done!" she shouted over to the old man.

Gobswistle closed his eyes. "Aya Aya Cernunnos, Aya Aya Kerridwyn, Aya aya..."

Etain stepped back as a ribbon of powder shot up from the pile of herbs in front of her, shimmering snake-like to where the old man stood. All around the chamber, similar ribbons of powder glistened and wove their way to Gobswistle, twelve streamers from the twelve equidistant piles. Each ribbon touched the top of the Anguinum, merging with the oil within.

As the last ribbon touched the glass apple, blue white light exploded out from it. Long tongues of flame shot forth, almost white in their light, one flame for each of the unconscious men, each flame spreading the length of his body as it touched him.

The chamber became a matrix of white light, burning brighter and brighter. Etain brought an arm up, shielding her eyes, but still she was blinded by the brilliance.

In the centre of the matrix, almost unheard over the roar of the flames, Kylie screamed.

Utter darkness.

Utter silence.

An orange light flared in the darkness; Etain had drawn her ironfire. "Gobswistle?" she called, staring into the darkness. "Kylie?"

"...Etain?" it was Kylie's voice, soft and frightened.

Etain swung her blade round, trying to see her.

Kylie lay in the middle of the chamber still, most of her clothes shredded around her, leaving her in only a vest and tattered jeans. With a wimper, Etain leapt over the stirring figures on the glassy ground, scooping up the little girl. She hugged her close. "Child, are you alright? You had me so scared!"

Kylie hugged her back, holding her fiercely tight, stifling sobs.

"Let's get you out of here," whispered Etain. She made her way over to where she'd last seen Gobswistle. He was still there, the anguinum held out in front of him, his eyes closed and his brow creased in a frown. "Gobswistle?"

The old man didn't respond. His frown deepened.

"*Germaine!*" snapped Etain. He seemed in some sort of trance.

One eye popped open, regarding Etain with a watery eyeball.

"You did it," said Etain. She risked a gentle smile. "Look around – they're all beginnin' to wake."

Both eyes opened. "Did I?" he said. "Did I really? Dear lady, how wonderful!" Trembling hands lowered the Anguinum, and he looked around, a look of bemused bafflement on his face.

All around, the soldiers were beginning to stir, and the sound of low questioning voices began echoing round the chamber.

Cathal and Fionnlagh were helping the nearest men to their feet, whispering urgently at them, pointing over at Gobswistle and Etain in something akin to awe.

"Ah hope you get us out o' here," said Etain, stroking the quietly crying girl's hair.

"Me? But-but...how did we get here?" said Gobswistle, his gentle south American accent causing his friend's eyes to open wide in alarm. "Where are we anyway? Did I – did I...last I remember was asking this damn contraption to help them! It worked?" he peered quizzically at the now dark Anguinum.

Etain looked up at the tunnel, a hundred feet out of reach above their heads.

"We are so *screwed.*"

Chapter Three

Jason pelted down the darkened path, his feet kicking up mud and stones that splashed and bounced off the budding bushes that lined the path. Behind him, Eigyr disappeared into the blackness of the woodland. He was vaguely aware of a torchlight moving towards her, and of Aiken calling his name.

He couldn't stay.

What he'd seen in his knife filled him with terror. Danger surrounded him on all sides now, and to stay with Aiken, with Omnust, only brought death to them. As his feet beat a rhythm to the abandoned village, his mind raced, appalled and sickened with the images that still burned in his mind's eye, mocking him, taunting him.

He'd seen his friends, lying dead in the forest above, torn and bloody, the moon as it was now, a quarter moon. And the Vikings in Kilneuair – the unsuspected spy working with them – he had to warn Myrrdin, but he'd also seen his return to the village, the death that had followed.

As he entered the village, he became aware of an argument between Aiken and the pregnant woman. His hearing was so acute now that he could even hear the lapping of the distant sea against the shore. He paid it no heed. He stood now in the deserted market square. He felt utterably lost and alone. He stood there gasping for breath, half sobbing, totally lost now as to what to do.

There was a flash of blue to his left.

He span. "Who's there?" he demanded, one hand on Carnwennan's hilt.

In the doorway of the house opposite stood a small figure, its face hooded and in darkness. The clothes were, oh they were *wrong*. Jeans, a padded brilliant blue hooded jacket, white tennis shoes. The two small figures stood observing each other.

"Who-who are you?" said Jason. He took a few steps forward. "Your clothes – how..?"

The figure silently turned, entering the first room.

"No, no wait!" Jason ran into the house, his blade drawn, his heart pounding in his chest.

The room was empty. There was no other exit for the figure to have left through, but all that was in the room was a small battered worktable and a chair.

"Hello?" called Jason. "Anyone here? Hey!" He was about to leave the room when something on the table caught his eye – a pile of linen, ten or more squares, piled atop each other in the middle of the ancient table. Next to it was a stick of charcoal and a small ball of string. Jason moved closer to the table.

He stared in astonishment at the string, his mind racing. On the string, small and insignificant yet totally incongruous, was a sticker saying '99p'. Jason gave a laughing hiccup, spinning on the spot, half expecting to see someone behind him, someone who could explain...*what?*

Was it the Medb? She was somewhere here, he knew that, she *had* to be. Was it some sort of trap set by her?

He edged closer to the table. There was *writing* on the uppermost square of linen. As he leant over to read it, his jaw dropped.

Jason

It's not the Medb. You don't have much time before he gets here. Everything you just saw is written down here. Use Carnwennan to deliver it. Read it if you want, but you won't find any mistakes. Act quickly. He's coming.

Ambrosius.

Who was coming? Who was nearly here? The attacker from his vision of his friends in the forest outside? Jason had not seen him. Only the devastation that had followed, the carnage. His stomach churned as he studied the cloth.

The writing was childlike and rushed, as though scribbled in a hurry. Jason looked to the next square. It was a letter to Myrrdin, again in the same child-like writing.

Myrrdin.

This is not for Cinded. Read this yourself, then do what you have to. It's Jason's final visions. He's on his own quest now. But don't forget your agreement with him. And don't run away this time!. Look out for the traitors. And protect the woman who delivers this to you. She is mum and grandma to legends. You-know-who and his dad. But

you know that, don't you?
Sorry.
Ambrosius.

The syntax was modern, like Jason himself might have used. He leafed through the rest of the pages. As promised, in the same childlike, hurried hand, was a word-for-word description of everything Jason had seen in the blade of Carnwennan of the events in Kilneuair. Goosebumps raced up and down his arms as he read. Who had done this? And how? Who *was* Ambrosius? How had he been able to transcribe what Jason himself had seen only minutes ago?

The last page:

He's in the village now, Jason. Hurry.

It took only an instant for Jason to reach a decision. This information *needed* to get to Myrrdin. How and why it was there, and the identity of its author, was unimportant. Discarding the top page and last page, he quickly rolled the linen squares up, using the string to tie them to the handle of his knife. He ran outside, the knife ready for throwing in his hand.

In the distance he could hear Aiken and the woman, still talking, but more quietly. Without hesitation, Carnwennan flew through the air. He knew she found her mark; he could hear the woman's vitriolic complaints. *"Return."* His hand opened at his side, ready to receive the hilt of his knife as she whistled through the night air to return to him.

The panic he'd felt when he'd fled from his friends began to fade. Myrrdin would know what he'd seen. He'd know to keep it from Cináed, whatever the consequences. And he'd kept Aiken and Omnust, Anna and all those people in the forest, *safe*.

But if this mysterious stranger, this Ambrosius, were to be trusted, whoever had been hunting him and his friends in the small forest was now in the village. And was *still* hunting him. The few days training he'd received had taught him what his body could do, how quickly he'd picked up fighting skills. A few days ago, he would have been terrified. *Had* been terrified. Now, he was ready.

So the large brick that bounced off the side of his head caught him totally by surprise.

A shadow scurried from between the houses.

"Oooh, stabbetty sticketty thing," cackled the creature, jumping on top of the unconscious boy, "not so flippin' tough now, are ya?"

Chapter Four

Anna bounced on the bed as she looked out through the unshuttered window, the flimsy frame complaining loudly. "Gaira, Gaira *look!*"

With a grumble, Gaira dunked the scrubbing brush back into the bucket, before scrubbing once more at the floor. "Ah'm working, child," she said. "Yuir supposed tae be strippin' that bed, not brekkin' it."

"But it's *people!*" said Anna delightedly. "Gaira, it's people! Do you think Jason's gonna be with them?"

"Oh what now?" Gaira hauled herself up on the bed frame next to her, waddling across the floor to clamber on the bed beside Anna. "What people?"

Anna pointed down into the street below. Outside the barracks window, the townsfolk were lining the streets, a corridor of moving forms through which a small group of haggard looking old men and young women and children made their processional way, some on horseback, some in carts, too infirm to walk.

Gaira quickly scoured the faces, then grunted. "*More* villagers. An' awd too." She clambered down off the bed. "Yer brother's no wi' them. Back tae work, wee Anna." She knelt once more by her bucket. "More mouths tae feed," she grumbled, "more cleanin', an' no a fighter among them." Her brush slammed angrily against the floorboards.

Anna remained at the window, staring down at the unfamiliar faces. "Where's Jason?" she asked plaintively.

Myrrdin stood outside the king's chambers, his fist ready to knock on the door. Beside him, the guard stood nervously, a sheen of sweat across his brow.

Myrrdin studied him. "The king is out of sorts this morning?" he asked quietly. The guard had the look of someone recently harangued.

The soldier smiled wanly. "Aye, sir. He's been up since afore sunrise."

"Doing?"

"Ah....Ah dinnae know. Shoutin', lot's o' shoutin'." He tugged nervously at his leathers. "Had me wake Morven, too, for an early break of his fast."

"And I guess she shouted at you too?" Myrrdin smiled.

"'Til she heard who it were for. Aye."

"And what was he shouting?"

"God's Breath!" The shout came from the other side of the door, the king's rich, deep voice vibrating the wooden door.

Myrrdin put his hand on the door handle. "Do me a favour," he said to the guard. "Go to Morven again. Bring me some bread and wine."

"But...but Ah cannae leave my post..." the guard looked half fearful, half hopeful.

"You have *my* permission."

"Aye, sir," said the guard. He set off down the long corridor to the kitchen, his pace quickening with obvious relief.

Cináed stared at the sheets of vellum as they fell scattered on the floor around the table. The models on the table itself were knocked over in disarray, tiny little houses sent a tumbling by a giant's hand. With a scowl and a curse he began righting the little houses once more.

"Is it safe to enter?"

Cináed looked to the door. Myrrdin stood in the doorway, only his black hair and beard peeping round the vast bulk of the door.

"Has he returned yet?" was the first question from Cináed's lips.

"More villagers are arriving as we speak. Neither Jason nor his companions are with them." If there was concern in the druid's voice over the boy's absence, his face did not show it. Myrrdin came fully into the room, closing the door behind him. He stared at the table, at the sheets of vellum on the floor. "How goes the war plan?"

"Ach, it makes no sense!" said Cináed. One model house was flung across the room, smashing into splinters against the wall. "All night I've been at this, deciphering Yellowblade's writing, trying to form a battle plan, *all night,* and still I'm as clueless as-as a newborn lamb!" He sighed, rocking back in his chair. "I need the boy. His visions."

"You've planned far more complex, and *sustained,* strategies than this." Myrrdin seated himself opposite Cináed, retrieving the nearer sheets of writing from the floor.

know why I was there?"

Myrrdin looked up at her. "Have you read any of these?"

"I don't...no, no it said it was for you only!" She blushed, flustered. "Don't you care why I was there?"

"Probably because you ran away from your husband," replied Myrrdin, his eyes reading once more. "Again."

"He put me in a monastery! In Winchester!"

Myrrdin did not respond.

"He's kidnapped my son! Constans is-is to be a *monk!"*

Myrrdin looked up. "You and he were both in the same monastery under the care of Archbishop Guithelin . You could have brought him with you."

"You-you *knew?"*

"It was my idea." Myrrdin rolled the squares up, the last sheets as yet unread, retying them tightly. He didn't look at Eigyr, his face deep in thought.

"Yours?!" Eigyr was incensed. "You dared interfere with my life? *You?* Myrrdin or-or Lailoken, whoever you think you are! I was – I was happy, I was comfortable, and as soon as he has me acting like his brood mare once more, *you* have me sent away?" She glowered at him, her eyes ablaze. "Pig! Imbecile! Do you know what it's like in a monastery?!"

"Safe," said the druid simply. "Your husband..."

"Is probably having every farmgirl within a hundred leagues, louse that he is!"

"Is fighting a war to keep your country safe," replied Myrrdin, as though Eigyr hadn't spoken.

"He daren't even look out from under his father's shadow," mocked Eigyr disdainfully.

"Your children are heirs all to the throne of Scotland. Possibly more. But not if you're killed in border skirmishes."

"Yes, and about that," snapped Eigyr, pacing the room, "what's this Ambrosius mean, I'm mother and grandmother to legends? And since when do I need *your* protection? And just who is this Ambrosius?"

Myrrdin, not rising from the bed, caught her wrist. "You have not changed, have you?" he said, his eyes holding hers. "Still everything has to revolve around you, without thought or consideration of the cares and concerns of others."

"Do you know how hard it was for me to gain my position? To escape from that *dreary* village..."

"With your tales of being the daughter of King Bran, with your father sending you away in disgust because of them..." Myrrdin smiled. "I remember. You married your husband for his position. Didn't you?"

"Why should you care!" Eigyr sat on the bed next him, her face red.

"You love him no more than he loves you."

"What was I supposed to do?" demanded Eigyr, turning to him. "The one man, the *one man*, I ever really loved, and he turned his back on me! *This land comes first, saving lives comes first, I cannot afford to love you!* He was more concerned in serving the *king* than me!" She turned away. "I did what I had to."

The two sat silently on the bed, neither looking at the other. After a while, Myrrdin brought up a hand, gently resting it on Eigyr's belly. "These two are our future," he whispered. "You *are* the mother of legends. Which is why I must protect you."

"It...it's twins?" said Eigyr, turning to Myrrdin. "How-how do you know?"

Myrrdin smiled. "I've always known you'd be great one day." He leaned forward, gently kissing her. "*That's* why I couldn't love you."

Chapter Five

Morven wheeled the next casket in on a small barrow, weaving through the tables of the mess hall to where one of the young girls was fighting off some of the more amorous soldiers as she tried to wheel the old casket away. Morven scowled. Leave it to a man to celebrate the swelling of their numbers by getting off his face on barley ale. She was already tired from a long day spent cooking meals, cleaning, polishing, and various other unwelcome but essential duties.

A casket hammer hung from her waist on a piece of string. In two deft moves she had removed it and clouted the nearest soldier over the head with it. "Get out of it, ye daft beggars!" she shouted. "Go on, shift!"

The soldier whom she'd struck span round, one hand to his head, ready to do battle. "What the hell yer playin' at woman?!" he growled.

Morven squared her shoulders, not about to be intimidated by him or his friends. "Ah said, '*shift*', man. Did Ah no speak clear enough?" She glowered up at him. "And leave mah girruls alone!"

"Yeh dinnae speak tae me like that..." growled the soldier, his grizzled beard still damp with beer.

"Ah'll speak te ye's how Ah like if ye's don't leave mah girruls alone." Snapped Morven. "What, yeh wannae tek me on, bunch o' brave men yeh are?"

One of the other soldiers pulled at his arm, trying to move him away. "Leave her be, Vortigern..!" He shrugged it off with a grunt, an evil leer spreading across his face. Behind him, the serving maid was frozen in place, her eyes wide like a rabbit's.

Morven, seeing the glint in the drunken soldier's eye, clutched the hammer tight. Lord, why did she always get the ones who felt they had to prove their heroism by being drunken *bullies*? Well, she was tough. She grew up with seven brothers. Let him *try!*

An empty leather flagon of ale shot from the darkness, striking the soldier on his brow. With a yell, the drew his sword, one hand to his eye, Morven forgotten.

Omnust stood by the fireplace, his throwing dagger in one hand as he gazed at the soldier, his expression somehow uncaring. Dead, almost. "Ah'm as good a shot wi' a dirk as wi' a vessel," he growled. Around him, the room fell silent, men slowly shuffling away from both the soldier and his captain. "Yeh c'n pay fer yeh manners here an' now, or yeh c'n see sunrise tomorrow and pay fer yeh manners on the field." He shrugged. "Up tae you."

"*Girl,*" hissed Morven, "*Move!*" As the two men stared at each other, the girl suddenly came to life, wheeling the empty ale casket away as quickly as she could.

The soldiers, the same men who'd been making their advances on her, parted like a silent sea before her. Many of them chose that moment to leave themselves.

The soldier looked nervously about him, his alcohol soaked brain gradually soaking in the fact that he was about to challenge his captain. His friends had backed away, meeting neither his nor their captain's gaze.

"Ah'd put yuir sword away, man," said Omnust gently. He made no move to put his own knife away, and the quietness of his voice belied the implicit threat it contained. "Ah'd do it *now.*"

The man didn't even hesitate. The sword was slipped back into its scabbard, and with a curt nod to Morven and Omnust, he turned to leave.

"On the field, six sharp," called Omnust after him. "Bring yuir halberd an' shield."

The man hesitated, not turning, before giving a quick nod of his head, leaving the mess hall. Around him, the few remaining men began muttering, retaking their seats around the room.

Omnust sank down into the chair he'd been sitting in, to one side of the fire, a small round table and empty chair next to it.

"A draught for my hero," said a voice. Omnust looked up, his tired eyes focussing on Morven's smiling face. She held a large flagon of ale in one hand, two leather tankards in the other. "May Ah join yeh?"

Omnust frowned. "Ah'm no much company at the moment." He sighed, rubbing a hand across his forehead. "Aye, then, go on." He gestured to the chair.

Morven seated herself, silently thankful for a chance to sit down after

39

a full day on her feet. "Have yeh eaten since yeh got back?"

When he shook his head, she gestured for another of the serving girls, giving instructions to bring stew and bread. She turned back to Omnust. "It's no mah place tae say mebbies," she said, "but yeh look like yeh've gontea battle an' lost t'war." She poured two drinks, shoving one over the the scarried warrior. "Drink, sir."

"It's Morven, isn't it?"

Morven felt herself blush. She'd been unaware the captain knew her name! "Aye, Captain Ossian."

"My men speak of ye's in awe, ye ken."

"Ah'm...Ah'm no one tae bite me tongue," she admitted, a rueful smile on her face. "Ah've two dozen young girls buzzin' around these lads like bees around honey."

"And you protect them?" He took a long pull of his ale.

"Try tae," she said. "But yon lads," and she gestured at some of the rest of the men, "like stags on rut. An' all o' them eggin' each other on..."

She paused as she belatedly realised she was bordering on belittling the soldiers in front of their own captain. "Ah-Ah dinnae mean they're *bad* though, they're good men, *fierce...*"

"They're *lads*," said Omnust. "Who're like as not headed tae the Blessed Lands wi'in days. They'll vent their steam in whate'er way the' can. With awny me an' thee tae stop them doin' things common decency says the' shouldn't." He smiled at her. It was the briefest of smiles, but it reached his eyes, and for a moment he looked almost...

Morven looked away, blushing. "Aye well, lads or lasses, young 'uns need a firm hand." They sat in silence for a few moments, both twisting their tankards. The serving girl was almost a welcome diversion as she returned with the food.

"Smells good," said the Captain, breathing in the steam from the bowl as it was placed in front of him. He looked up at the serving girl. "Thankyou."

"Made it mahself, captain," said Morven unthinkingly, glaring at the comely girl, then found herself blushing furiously. At her age, she was trying to curry favour with the captain, like some fawning country girl? Utterly mortified, she tore at the bread, dunking it into the bowl of stew, not looking at the soldier before her.

Omnust nodded, chewing on a piece of meat. "Thought yeh must have," he said, unaware of her embarrassment. "T'is no only yuir temper the men talk about." After only a couple of mouthfuls however, he pushed the bowl and the bread away. "Ah'm sorry, woman, the fuid is good...but Ah have nae appetite."

Uncertain now, Morven made as though to stand. "If ye'd rather be left..."

"Sit, woman, stay," said Omnust, almost irritably. "T'is no you that..." he took a deep breath, not looking at Morven, his brow creased not in anger but in some other emotion.

Morven's tongue kicked in before she could stop it. "Ah'll thank yeh if yui'll address me as Morven, not *woman.*" Inwardly she cringed, but she kept her face calm as she seated herself.

Omnust looked at her, and there was neither surprise nor anger on his face. "So be it. And Ah'm Omnust."

"Captain, I-I..."

"We both command our own armies, yui with your army o' brooms 'n' brushes, me with swords and arrers," said Omnust. "Ah speak tae either the king, the druid, or soldiers. Ah'm either spoken down tae, or treated with fear. Ah..." he looked directly into Morven's eyes. "Ah need someone who c'n speak tae *me*. On the same level. As a friend."

Inwardly, Morven was profoundly touched. There was a wound, a *humanity,* in his voice that she never heard since his arrival. Suddenly her blushes seemed almost childish.

"You need someone tae talk tae." She topped up both their tankards. "Here, then. Drink. It'll loosen yuir soldier's reserve."

With a snort, Omnust raised his drink. "To Equals, then, Morven."

Morven lifted hers. "To equals." She smiled. "Omnust."

"You remind me of him," said Omnust, his words only slightly slurred. Five flagons, all empty, lay scattered either across the table or on the floor. By Omnust's side, the fire guttered low in the grate. Only small groups of soldiers remained in the mess hall now, most having staggered either to the barracks, or to the bedchambers of some willing maid.

Morven looked up. "Who?" she frowned. Mercy, but the room was spinning. How much had she had to drink? More to the point, what was the hour? She'd be in no fit state for work in the morning.

"Yellowblade."

"The boy?" she thought for a few moments, trying to organise the soaked jumble of thoughts between her eyes. "How?"

"no," muttered Omnust, "no offence. But he wasnae scared of me. Like *yuir* not."

"He was rude tae yeh then."

"No, Ah didnae mean..." he took a deep breath. "He *listened*. And he took on all that he heard. He never called me *Captain* or *Sir*, unless as an afterthought. It's like...he saw...*me.*"

"You speak as though he's dead," said Morven, staring at him. "Is he no' in the barracks?"

Omnust shook his head silently, not meeting her gaze.

An icy hand clasped hold of Morven's heart, and she stared at the captain. "Where – where is he?"

"He left us," said the captain.

"*Jason ran away?!*" The feeling of dread solidified into fear. One of the soldiers at the other tables turned to look at her.

"Keep yuir voice down, woman!" hissed Omnust. He stared at the soldier until he turned back to his friends.

"He is the *King's Banner*!" said Morven. "He's – he's what's given us hope, kept us together, *brought* us together – all the prophecies – why..?"

"He left a note," said Omnust. "Eigyr, the Lady Ivory, she's taken it tae Myrrdin."

"What's it say?"

"She said it weren't fer my eyes," he said. "Said he was followin' his *own* quest. We searched for him. All night, half the day. All we found were blood."

"*Blood?*"

"In mah sister's village. T'weren't there earlier. Tracks suggested two people. An'...summat else. A Spriggan mebbies. Looked like a trap."

"You think he's been captured? Who by?"

"I meant tae keep him safe," said Omnust, staring into the embers of the fire. "If Ah knew, Ah'd've gone after them."

"Have yeh told the king this?"

Omnust shook his head. "The Druid is the king's councillor. Ah didnae know what tae say. He'll deal wi' it."

"And the bairn's sister?" She thought of the little girl, giggling round all day with either Aiken or his friend Gaira. Sometimes even together, the most bizarre of families. "Does she know?"

"Druid's her kin, not me," said Omnust.

"He was supposed to lead us..." said Morven.

Omnust said nothing.

The whispers started only moments later. The soldier who'd been listening told his friend. The friend told it to the barmaid as they stood outside, kissing in the moonlight. The maid told the girls with whom she boarded, who in turn told the soldiers they went to woo.

And, as is the way with gossip, as the story spread, it grew.

Gaira stood outside the back of her ramshackle home, staring up at the moon, her shawls pulled tight around against the bitter frost. The moon was swollen, more than half full, insolently taunting her of the future yet to come.

She took a long pull from the mug in her hand, the watery broth warming her as she drank. Five more days before the full moon. In the village, work was rife. Hidden fire-pits were being excavated, filled with innumerable containers of lamp oil; skins, clay jugs, covered bowls, all ready for the invasion, ready to burn the Berserkers as they entered the village. Stores of arrows were being lofted into trees around the villages, hidden places from which to attack with no need of replenishment. Volunteers were being sought to man the look-out posts, to be placed at strategic points all the way from the coast in eight furlong increments from the coast up to the village. Each one would be equipped with siege mangonels, huge catapults that could launch either rocks or pitch soaked flaming logs into the sky to strike at their enemy. Even now the carpenters and ironsmiths could be heard pounding and hammering away, oblivious to their tiredness, each blow of the hammer another strike for their freedom.

The vikings knew every move.

These preparations, these defences, the extra men who'd arrived over the last couple of days, all were useless.

Thanks to Gaira's actions, each carefully planned secret defence, created through assumed knowledge of the Viking's invasion plan, were known by Ragnar and his men even as they were being drawn up by the King and the Druid.

She didn't regret her actions. She already had blood on her hands from many previous years. Men slaughtered, women and children from surrounding villages and parishes sold into slavery. She didn't know them, and cared for them even less. She knew the people of *this* village. She cared for them, as they cared for her. And she could not, *would not*, risk Aiken. She'd learnt her scrying skills from her mother, and had managed to make contact with the Viking Chief. Oh how'd she played down the prosperity of Kilneuair, to sing instead the praises of other villages, filled with people she'd never met and who would have treated her with contempt even if they had.

She'd meant what she'd said. She would fight as fiercely as her fellow villages. She'd made her deal with the Devil. So long as they got the cursed boy. They would have attacked anyway. She *knew* that. She'd kept her home and hearth safe as long as she could. The Vikings may think themselves one step ahead, but they underestimated her.

"Gaira..."

Startled, the little woman turned, seeking out the intruder. It was one of the girls she'd seen a few days earlier, working with Morven in the kitchens.

"What?" she growled. "What you doin' out here this time o' night? Morven'll skin ye's alive."

"It's all over the village!" gasped the girl, clearly out of breath. "Ye'd best come!"

"What nonsense now?" grumbled Gaira. She opened the door, throwing her mug in through the door. She heard it bouncing across the planks, and belately hoped it didn't wake little Anna.

"It's the boy!" said the girl. "Come on. Ye'd best hurry..."

"Boy, what boy? And don't manhandle me!" She shrugged off the hand placed on her shoulder.

"Yellowblade! Surely ye've heard the commotion?"

Gaira's eyes widened. "Jason?" a small flutter of hope blossomed in her chest. "What's happened? Quickly!"

"Cap'n Omnust, he's come back wi'out him!" The girl sounded a curious mixture of both terrified and thrilled. "Says he's been killed by a gang of spriggans!" She turned round, looking out into the darkness beyond. "All the army, all the people, they're gatherin', they're off tae see the king!"

*

Gaira tucked the rough blankets in around the sleeping child, gently stroking her blonde hair. Let the girl sleep. Someone else could tell her of her brother's death tomorrow. It would not be Gaira. The child would need solace, some understanding of her grief. All Gaira could feel was joy. And utter relief. She'd sent the girl back to join the procession through the village to where Cináed was barracked. Said she needed to attend to things.

Happy now that Anna was sleeping, Gaira went through to the large room at the back, to her table.

Shaking hands made three piles of powder; burgundy, white and yellow, and fingers made clumsy through the rush of adrenaline tightened the drawstrings on the pouches. Within seconds a sulphurous smoke rose above the low table, and the obsidian mirror slowly began to awake.

Something moved in the next room, and Gaira paused, her hands either side of the mirror. Nothing. Anna, most likely, turning in her sleep. She turned back to the mirror.

"Halr Ragnar, Koma

"Halr Ragar, Tala

"Halr Ragnar, Heyra

"Halr Ragnar, Sitja."

As the echoes of her voice died, the ancient helmet rippled into view.

"It is late, wisewoman."

"Ah know, Ah know," said Gaira nervously, "but Ah had tae...Ah had tae *contact* yeh."

"We have no need of you anymore. You have served us well. Your treachery of your fellow man knows no bounds." There was contempt in his voice, almost mocking her.

She paid it no heed. "Ah wanted tae thank ye's."

There was a pause. Ragnar's voice, when he spoke again, was filled with obvious amusement. *"To thank us? For destroying your home, your loved ones?"*

"Fer gettin' the Yellowblade!" Her joy at Jason's demise was more than enough to make her overlook the mocking tone of the viking. "He's gone! Killed by spriggans, they're sayin'! There's no spriggans roond here, no fer years! You must've sent them!"

There was silence from the mirror. Something moved again in the next room. Gaira ignored it. She'd check on Anna again in a moment.

"It was you, wasn't it?" She insisted. "You have him, you kept yer side o' the bargain!"

"You forget your place, wisewoman. We agreed to no bargain. That you demanded one shows your arrogance!"

"My Lord, Ah'm sorry..."

"The...boy... has been removed from the approaching festivities. It has no bearing on any 'bargain' you imagine was made. His visions no longer affect our plans. That is all."

"Yes, my lord..." mumbled Gaira, cowed.

"There is but one obstacle left to remove." All humour suddenly vanished from Ragnar's voice.

"M-my Lord?"

"You said you'd fight us with all your might yourself. To protect the boggart."

The movement behind her grew louder. And Gaira knew, now, that it was not Anna.

"I wonder how far you would go to protect him?" And for the first time, Gaira caught a glimpse of eyes under the helm of the helmet. Steely blue, cold and emotionless. *"Would you tell your king of the scrying mirror you placed? Even if it meant your life?"*

Footsteps approached, quiet and slow. Gaira closed her eyes.

"Fortuitous your contacting me, little heathen witch," said Ragnar. *"It saves the hunt."*

Ragnar replaced the mirror into its velvet sack, resisting the urge to smash it against the abaft of the ship where he sat.

"Ragnar?"

He turned at the sound of the familiar voice, his temper still high. Lathgertha stood on the deck, her long blonde hair streaming around her in the wind. Her small frame and her almost elfin features belied her vicious nature. She looked like a child's doll, yet would rip an opponent's throat out with her bare hands. "The boy is gone."

"But that is good, surely?" She moved closer, and Ragnar could smell her scent. "We *have* the witch woman, and the Seer Boy is gone. That bodes well. Better than we could have hoped."

"The wisewoman thought it was us."

"Really, Ragnar, what difference does it...?"

"Someone has the boy! The boy who can see the future!" He stood, leaning over the side of the ship to look towards land. "The witch said he had been killed by spriggans."

Lathgertha placed a small hand on his shoulder. "If he is dead, then he is no longer a worry. Really, husband, why does this rile you so?"

"She said there are no spriggans in this area. She assumed *we* sent them." He turned to the childlike figure by his side. "There is only one man can create spriggans."

Saucer shaped eyes stared at him. "Huddour," she said quietly. "But-but even if that *is* the case, even if Lord Huddour has him, it still works in our favour." She hugged him, resting her head against the furs covering his shoulders. "Come. Come to bed."

"He stole our gold. Our payment, because I dared mock him over the boy!" He scowled into the night. "And gave it to that damned *Blashie* creature..." and then he paused, his eyes narrowing. "I'll bet," he said quietly, turning to his wife, "I'll bet it was no spriggan. He'll have sent his *pet* after the boy!"

"I would rather have you whole, without gold," said Lathgertha, still hugging him, "than in pieces *with* gold. We dare not go up against *Huddour!* Five more days, Ragnar, then we can return home! I grow weary of the sea."

"The boy could be a bargaining tool," said Ragnar. "Don't you see?"

"I see only a man whose pride has been wounded by the loss of some trinkets," said Lathgertha sourly. "Let it *lie.*"

"Huddour *wants* this Yellowblade, that much I know," said Ragnar. "If we had him, we could use him to bargain for our gold. A fair exchange, Lathgertha. The witchwoman can tell us the boy's whereabouts when he vanished."

"And then what?" demanded Lathgertha. "We have no men to spare! Who would you send?"

Ragnar smiled at her. "My best tracker," he said quietly. He reached out, placing his hands on her shoulders. "And my most trusted warrior."

"I'll cut your throat in your sleep!" hissed Lathgertha. "You dare send me away *now?!"* She threw his hands off her.

"Five days," said Ragnar quietly. "Five days for you to track him down and bring him to me. You should be back in time to slake your lust for blood."

Chapter Six

Anna frowned, only half awake. She could hear voices in the next room, hushed and angry , but it was only interrupting her dreams. They'd been such *happy* dreams, too. She'd been chasing fairies through a forest, a lush green forest, the sounds of a nearby river tinkling through the air. It had been so *real!* And this strange man that she couldn't quite *see*, with funny branches on his head, running beside her, laughing. Telling her not to forget the clover. She wanted to go back there. She didn't want to wake up. She pulled the blankets up over her head, burying her head in the rough pillow, waiting for sleep to reclaim her.

The sudden cessation of the voices, seemingly cut off midsentence, finally roused her. She looked round, rubbing at one eye. "Gaira?" she called quietly. There was no response. She wasn't scared – there were always some strange noises in Gaira's home – but she was curious. There was a candle by her bed, nearly burnt out. Pushing back the covers, she dropped barefoot to the floor, lifting the candle on its holder.

"Gaira, you there?"

She was still half asleep, and the strange man's insistent voice whispered in her ear. Without really thinking about it, she lifted a handful of the wilted clover leaves she'd been collecting from the little bedside table. The voice still whispered at her, and she spat into the leaves, grinning to herself at the nastiness of it, mushing up the leaves in one hand as she walked across the cluttered room, candle held high. She stifled a yawn. Almost without thinking, or perhaps guided by another's hand, she dropped the handful of mashed up leaves, leaving copious amounts of green stain on her palm and fingers. She blotted her

47

eyes with her palm, leaving large green rings over both eyes.

There was a *thump* from the next room, then a louder one.

The last vestiges of sleep were driven from the little's body, and fear began to creep in.

"G-Gaira?" she called quietly. "Gaira, are – are you in there?"

"*We have her,*" hissed a rough male voice. "*Go.*"

"*But the child...*" said another.

"*Go!*"

There was a crash, loud and ferocious, and a sudden breeze blew down the corridor, extinguishing Anna's candle. With a whimper, she froze. The corridor to the back room was plunged into utter darkness for an instant, then a myriad of colour filled it as innumerable tiny glowing figures raced from the room, fast and fleeting as mayflies. They swarmed around Anna, diving at her face, their tiny faces filled with panic and fear.

"No, leave me alone," whimpered Anna – they'd never acted like this before, as though they could *see* her – and a tiny hand swept through the air, trying to shoo them away, "what is it, what do you want?"

The tiny figures seemed to be trying to direct her away from Gaira's store room. Anna didn't move, her eyes fixed on the black doorway beyond, and after a few seconds most of the fairies had gone, out into Anna's room, then disappearing beyond. Only a handful remained, darting round Anna's head like angry but ineffectual wasps.

Anna braced her shoulders, her bottom lip sticking out. "Gaira's in trouble," she whispered to the fairies. "I'm going in."

The fairies momentarily increased their efforts to turn her, diving at her face, their whole bodies speaking of the utmost fear. Anna ignored them, her tiny feet silent on the wood as she moved forward. The fairies banded together in front of her, almost like a protective shield, as she entered the room.

The back wall was destroyed, a huge hole in its centre, fragments of planking scattered around the floor. Moonlight streamed in through the hole, and Loch Awe glinted in the far distance. There was movement outside, only a few yards from the hole; two large shadowy figures, with a smaller, round figure held between them, struggling wildly.

"...Gaira..." whispered Anna. She ran silently up to the ragged hole, staring out at the figures. It *was* Gaira, held between the two figures, struggling wildly, what appeared to be a small sack over her head. She could hear the diminutive woman's muffled screams.

Anna's hands clamped over her mouth in fear. What should she do? She instantly thought of Jason, but he hadn't come back yet. She thought of Aiken, but she hadn't seen him either. Her grandfather, Myrrdin? No, he wasn't her grandfather, he was *cold.*

No. No, she would follow, see where they were taking Gaira. She could find someone then, get them to rescue her. One foot left the confines of the room, resting lightly on the grass outside.

She froze, staring at Gaira. As Gaira was carried away, something was forming around her, like a – a ghost, half obscuring the screaming woman's form. No, not forming around her; growing *out* of her. Like it was part of her. A cancerous growth hidden from view until now, this minute.

Anna's jaw hung limply open as she stared at this eldritch supernatural form, her eyes not wanting to accept what she saw. What she knew it to be. She was dimly aware of a high pitched scream filling the night air. Belatedly she realised it was *her*.

The figures stopped, Gaira dropping to the ground. A brief flash of movement from one of them, and a dagger flew through the air, silent and deadly, heading for Anna's head, too fast for her to duck from.

The fairies launched themselves at the knife, surrounding it, clinging to it, blocking it, their fairy lights burning momentarily bright as a star.

Knife and fairies fell to the ground, and the light faded. Just tiny bodies now, the fairies vanished, soaking into the earth below like water into a sponge.

Anna ran screaming through Gaira's house and out into the night.

Myrrdin sat at the table, re-reading the squares of hastily written text for what seemed to be the hundredth time, his face pale and drawn even by candle light, dark circles under his eyes.

On the bed next to him, Eigyr slept fitfully, moaning in her sleep. She'd not wanted to sleep in the barracks. She was not yet ready to face her father-in-law.

He'd not slept. Though the night was aging now, and the moon growing low in the sky, he'd sat up, taking the opportunity now to read in more details the writings of the mysterious Ambrosius. What worried him more than the contents of the writing was the writing itself. In an unknown hand. Were these really the final visions of Jason? If so, why was the writing not his? Myrrdin knew Jason's writing well, had seen page after page of his writings on the vellum held by Cináed.

Were these, then, a trap? If he followed the visions set down before him, would he be leading his men to death? Or would he be victorious?

Would it be a repeat of Strathclyde?

And why had Jason fled, so close now to battle?

He rubbed his eyes. He couldn't think any longer. He needed *sleep*.

On the floor behind the table were numerous blankets, laid out in a makeshift bed, so that Eigyr could have his bed. It called to him now, beckoning him to rest his head, if only for a few hours.

He leaned forward, nipping out the candle. He made to rise, then paused.

Torchlight leaked in between the shutters on his window, numerous orange glows that bobbed and danced in the darkness. He became aware of numerous voices, both outside the window and in the corridor behind him. He quickly unshuttered the window, looking out into the street beyond.

"What's going on?"

He jumped slightly at the sound of Eigyr's voice. "I did not mean to disturb you," he said quietly.

"I'm a light sleeper these days," said Eigyr, swinging her feet to the floor. "Two brats fighting for room, *you* try getting a good night's rest." She stood, moving to look over Myrrdin's shoulder. "What's going on?"

*

Cináed started, looking around him in confusion. He still sat at his table, empty plates and mugs scattered between the model houses, one of the miniature homes still held in one hand.

What had awoken him?

A loud pounding on his door gave him the answer. Rubbing angrily at his face, trying to restore some semblance of consciousness, he got up. Staggering slightly from lack of sleep, he went over to the door, wrenching it open.

Myrrdin stood there, his face as tired and unkempt as the king's own.

"Myrrdin, what on earth..?" he looked past Myrrdin, at the corridor lined with both soldiers and villages, all staring at their king, their faces afraid and questioning.

"I wished to tell you in the morning," said Myrrdin quietly, "to let you get some rest. It seems that choice has been usurped."

"Tell me *what?*"

"...Jason is gone."

The training field behind the barracks swarmed with people. More people than the king would have thought possible given the size of Kilneuair. Men, women and children filled the field to capacity, and many more stood outside the fence, as close to the gathering as they could get. Questions assailed him as the crowd parted before him, their torches held high.

"Is the boy dead?"

"Has he run away?"

"Did the spriggans kill him?"

"Has he abandoned us?"

Cináed ignored them, his eyes focussed on the makeshift stand constructed for him at the upper edge of the field; two planks of wood laid across two empty crates. Behind him followed the druid, his face drawn and worried, Omnust by his side, staggering slightly and stinking of ale.

An expectant hush settled over the gathering as Cináed mounted the little platform, raising him a couple of feet above his audience. Cináed stared out at the sea of faces, at the poorly dressed people, half of them in their nightclothes, scant protection against the biting spring frost. Their fear washed over him like a wave of the iciest winds as he looked dismally across them.

"You..." his voice came out in a quiet croak, a combination of stress and tiredness. He cleared his throat. "You have all heard rumours of the disappearance of Crowanhawk Yellowblade. It is...with a heavy conscience... I must confirm these rumours."

A rumble ran through the villagers and soldiers, an ever growing avalanche of fear. Cináed held up his hands. "I will give you the facts as they have been related to me by Captain Omnust and the Druid. Yes, the boy left his company yesterday. He was not initially attacked – he left a note saying he followed...he followed his own quest. In their search for him, Omnust, the boggart, and some villagers who were travelling to join us, found signs of a struggle, and a small amount of blood." As the ripple of whispered fear spread once more, Cináed raised his voice, drowning it out. "I do NOT believe the boy to be dead, nor do I have it in my heart to believe he ran away. It is my belief that he was taken by force, and that the letter ascribed to him was written under duress.

"It seems his legend is known to more than just our people. I believed in him them, I believe in him now, that he was sent to save us, to protect us, to teach us how to plan an effective defence, a defence that will turn the blades of the invaders.

"It seemed others believed this too. It cannot be mere coincidence that he was taken while outside the protection of Kilneuair. Someone sought to silence him.

"They failed. In the days before his abduction, Jason spoke with me and with the Druid at great length. The boy was a *Seer.* In his visions, he saw the attack of the vikings, he saw the timing, the placement and the number of our attackers." Cináed held up the vellum sheets he'd brought with him. "This then is what was foretold to us; these are the predictions that have indeed proved costly. I have in my hand the key to our victory! It is Yellowblade's legacy to us!

"Put aside your fear that the boy is needed to ensure our victory. *He* has *upheld* the prophecy, has perhaps paid dearly for it. Now we must play our part. Continue your work on the mangonels, on the pits. Continue to sharpen your blades, to string your bows. We have the knowledge, and we have the *skills*, to write *history* in the coming days!"

He shoved his hand high into the air, the vellum fluttering wildly. *"What say you!"*

The cheers started at the back of the field, then spread forward and outward like some unstoppable fire of noise, some chanting the king's name, some chanting Yellowblade, so loud that it echoed through the empty streets and houses of the village, stirring the nightcreatures that scuttled through the woodwork and gutters of the house.

The king let them cheer for a while, letting them vent their emotions in an outrush of noise. It was only when the cheering had started to die down that he held up his hands for silence.

"One thing. The boy was taken, therefore his whereabouts were known. Someone in this village *betrayed* him. Someone works towards the destruction, the very death of this village and everyone in it.

"Be alert, and be warned. Should the traitor be discovered, *there will be no mercy."* His voice was hard, implacable. The crowd fell into a nervous silence. "Return to your beds."

Cináed stepped down to stand in front of Myrrdin and Omnust.

"In my chambers. *Now."*

The king slammed the door shut, spinning on the two men. "A drunk!" he bellowed. "And a liar! Both of you, *you* are the cause of that-that panic!" He glared at both men. "My most trusted captain, my oldest of friends, and they are either stirring the drunkest of tales or keeping things I should have been made aware of *immediately* from me!"

"With respect, Sire..." began Myrrdin, but a gloved hand struck him across the face.

Cináed stood in front of him, quivering with rage, one finger pointing at the druid's nose, almost touching it. "...BE...*still...*" His finger hovered in front of Myrrdin's startled face, his face red with anger. With a visible effort, he lowered his hand. "You planned on telling me of Yellowblade's abduction *once I'd slept?"*

"We-we have no proof..."

"Proof?" yelped the king. "We have blood! We have tracks! And you *kept* this from me, as though I was some village simpleton who needs rest in order to work? We are preparing for *war!* And yet this man," and he pointed at Omnust, *"this man* sees fit to tell the whole god bedamned mess hall, while he drinks himself into a stupor!" He stepped in front of the captain, staring at the man's downturned face. *"Look at me!"*

Omnust lifted his head, his face a picture of misery. "My lord, Ah meant nay harm..."

"You panicked...the entire...*village!"* So angry was the king that spittle sprayed the captain's face. "They live with fear as their daily companion and now you bring it into their nights! The only reason you're not being publicly lashed is because I cannot afford your men to lose their respect for you as I now have!"

He turned away from them both, facing the door, his fists clenching by his sides. "Is there anything else I should know?"

"Sire..." began Myrrdin, "my lord..."

Cináed did not turn. "Druid."

"The...the visions you have with you..."

"What of them?" The king's voice was quiet, icy cold.

"They are not the final visions of Jason." He reached into his robes, pulling out the role of notes.

Cináed turned. "There are more? And you planned on telling me when?"

Myrrdin held out the bundle. All were there, save the top note. Cináed stared at him, then snatched the bundle off him, untying its string.

"This is not Jason's hand," he said, looking up at Myrrdin.

"It is the hand of Ambrosius," replied the Druid.

"And who is this...Ambrosius?"

Myrrdin forced himself to meet the king's cold glance. "It is a name I have not come across before. It does not detract from the validity of the visions, my lord."

"Does it not?" said Cináed quietly. "Does it not? I'll tell you, shall I, oh *wise* forestman, what *I* see? I see the childish attempt of his abductors to detract from his *true* visions. To *make* us change our plans from the course Jason himself has already set us on." He thrust the notes back to Myrddin, unread.

Myrrdin took them, his hands shaking. "Sire, I believe these to be *truthful*..."

"Then you are as *blind* as you are useless!" bellowed the king. "They are the manipulations of a traitorous hand, yet because they tell you what you want to hear, you believe them!"

"Cináed, they do not tell me what I want to *hear...*"

"I will hear no more of them," said the king, his voice final. "It is the boy's council I need, not an impotent druid. And that," he said, holding up the sheets of vellum, "I have. You, *old friend,* are no longer needed. We stay on the path Jason has plotted for us."

Myrrdin gently inclined his head, putting the squares of material back into his robe. "As my lord commands."

"Is there anything else?" asked Cináed.

"Sire?"

"Is there anything else that has happened I should be made aware of?"

Myrrdin hesitated, thinking of the pregnant woman in his room, then shook his head. The king needed to calm down, to clear his head. If Myrrdin told him of Eigyr's arrival, of her abandonment of her son in the monastery, his mood would not be improved. Whatever damage had been caused to their friendship, it could still be repaired. Or at least, so Myrrdin fervently hoped.

The king stepped to the door, opening it. "Out, both of you. Go on, get out."

Omnust was staring at the open door. "Sire..."

Cináed turned to look at what his captain saw.

A woman and child stood there, hand in hand, the woman in a hooded while robe, the hood up and her face obscured. The child was an ashen faced Anna, green smudges around her eyes bright against her pale skin. She looked from the king, to Omnust, to Myrrdin.

"Where's Jason?" she almost screamed. "I want my brother, *where is he?*"

Cináed stared at her, before slowly turning to Myrrdin. "You didn't even have the decency to tell your own granddaughter?" As Myrrdin opened his mouth, Cináed held up one hand. "No. There is no excuse." He turned to the woman. "Where did you find her?"

The woman seemed nervous. "She...she ran by my window, screaming for Jason. I thought... I thought it best if I brought her here. She was crying, terrified, something about the Wise Woman being taken..." By her side, Anna had moved, half hiding behind the robes.

Cináed was staring at her. "That is one of Myrrdin's robes..." he breathed.

"Myrrdin...was kind enough to accommodate me for the night..."

"Lower your hood."

Slowly, her eyes darting between the king and the druid, Eigyr lowered her hood.

"Lady Ivory..." breathed Cináed.

Myrrdin closed his eyes.

Chapter Seven

Something was roaring. Howling in fact. Some kind of animal? *Lots* of some kind of animal? Jason tried to open his eyes. Vague shadowy shapes danced around him, darkness above him and light below. Jason blinked slowly, his head fuzzy and his thoughts in disarray. Where was he? What had happened? He remembered standing in the village....

Something struck his head and shoulders. "Ow..." His head began to spin. No, his entire body was spinning. Had something hit him? Was it this strange roaring animal? The spinning slowed, but something was striking repeatedly at Jason; his shoulders, his head, his chest, his legs, and one particularly vicious blow to his face. "Ye-*ow!*" Warm brightness filled one eye.

"Oh yes?" said a voice below him. "Flippin' woken up, 'ave ya? Blooding about time, an'all! Bleeding liability, dragging you through the forest an all! All them people, they coulda *hurt* me! *Made* me come down 'ere, you did!"

Jason shook his head. "What..?" The warm brightness turned out to be sunlight, filtering through the new tear in the cloth sack tied over his head. He tried to bring a hand up to remove the sack, only to discover them tied behind his back. The roar grew particularly loud, and salty spray washed over his head.

With a yelp, Jason realised he was upside down. The darkness 'above' was the shoreline below, jagged rocks and boulders cringing below him as the tumultuous waves pounded them into submission. The blue sky benignly watched the battle between land and sea from its vantage point, still and passive.

Something crashed into Jason's back, eliciting another yelp from him and he found himself spinning in the air like a child's top. His one free eye finally made sense of where he was.

Which unfortunately appeared to be half way down a vast rugged cliff face, hanging like a cocooned fly on a length of rope from the tiny grumbling figure above. Gulls and puffins circled lazily overhead, perhaps waiting for these two juicy morsels to fall crashing into the boulders below.

"Sod off, ya feathered *gits*!" shouted the tiny little figure above. "We ain't no lunch for you, alright?" Shaggy brown hair danced back and forth as the creature scurried along the cliff side, seemingly without effort, Jason bobbing precariously below him. Yellow eyes turned to look down at Jason, and a huge mouth gaped into a toothy grin. "'Avin' fun down there?" Though even smaller than his sister Anna, the creature was amazingly strong, grabbing the rope and bouncing Jason up and down like a yo-yo. "You awake now, Not gonna be falling sleepyhead again?"

"I'm awake I'm awake I'm awake!" shouted Jason, his stomach lurching. "You threw a rock at me!"

"'Ow else woz I gonna knock you out!" The creature giggled. "'course, might have hit ya a li'l bit..." it paused, leaping between a particularly large split in the cliff face, "...*hard!*" It looked down as Jason swung yet again into the cliff wall. "Oooo, that's gonna 'urt!"

Jason furiously twisted in the air, trying to lessen the impacts and to get a better look at the creature. "Who are you?" he shouted. "Why'd you attack me? What do you *want* with me?"

"Glorious Blashie," giggled the creature, "wet and windy, love of the ladies, envy of the men!" It started heading up towards the top of the cliff. "Me, I couldn't care less about you, snivelling little snot-faced boyman bogeyman thing. Lunch, is all you is." It leapt over a large outcropping, clinging to the rock face like an agile spider, before looking back to make sure Jason struck the outcrop. "Oops. Sorry! An' it's me master wants you, not me."

His knife! Where was his knife? Jason twisted mid-air, ignoring his spinning head as he looked up at the Blashie creature. It had a large bundle on its back, lumpy and stained, and at the top of it, he could just see the glint of yellow. At least it was *safe*. That was something. Jason stopped twisting. "Who's your master?"

"Wot *is* it with you lot?" grumbled the creature. "Deadly peril, that's what you're in, an' all you do is ask questions! *What do you...*" it paused to leap another gap, "*...want, who's your master, are you gonna...*" and it leapt another gap with a grunt, "*eat me!*" It grabbed the rope, swinging it out as far from the rock face as it could before yanking it back it. "There!" shouted the creature. "Happy now? See wot you made poor old Blashie do?" It grinned; the *hungriest* grin Jason had ever seen, and he curled his body into a ball, trying to reduce the impact of the cliff wall as it rushed towards him. Even so, the wind was still knocked from his body in a loud bark. Above him, Blashie laughed delightedly. "Do it again! That sounded *funny!* Do it again!" And he swung the rope out again, pulling it back even harder. "Huddour said 'ee wanted you alive, didn't say nuthin' none nowt about flippin' undamaged!"

The cliff face rushed out to greet him, and his world exploded into darkness.

Something was washing over Jason's face. Something warm, wet and salty. A fresh cut above his left eye throbbed as the liquid drenched it. With a startled yell, Jason awakened once more. The first thing he noticed, with relief, was that the sack had been removed from his head.

The second thing he noticed, with a lot *less* relief, was the giggling Blashie creature re-adjusting his lower garments as he stood above Jason's head. He shook his head madly in revulsion, yellow droplets flying everywhere.

"Did you just *pee* on me?!"

The creature shrugged. "Wot if I did?" Its tongue slopped out of its mouth, winding up snakelike to probe one nostril as it stared challengingly at Jason.

"You're revolting..." growled Jason, looking around him. They were back on terra firma, long grass and a few stunted shrubs surrounding them. The cliffs were only a few feet away though, and the sea could be heard roaring hungrily below them. Jason was still tied hand and foot, the lengthy rope that had tied him to Blashie now holding him close to a nearby rock, Blashie having lifted the massive rock then throwing the rope beneath it.

The sun was low in the western sky, and the sky was a fearsome vivid mixture of reds, oranges and purples, long fingers of reflections dancing on the sea below.

But the sunset, stunning though it was, was not what caught Jason's eye. It was the moon, further round the horizon. Still pale, and only just visible in the evening sky, it was nonetheless swollen, nearly two thirds full; an eye in the sky opened wide in astonishment.

"How hard did you hit me?!" The accusatory words were out of Jason's mouth before he could stop them. He shouldn't underestimate this tiny little creature, yet his words were hardly respectful. This little creature had captured him, bound him and carried him without effort along the side of a cliff. Jason had no doubts this creature could easily kill him, and would probably enjoy doing so. And in the mirror surface of his knife, Jason had *seen* what Blashie would have done had he remained with his friends.

Blashie however seemed totally unconcerned. "Huddour wants ya. Didn't fancy arguing with ya, specials with that sodding knifey sticky thing of yours." He shrugged. "So I hit ya. Couple o' days peace 'n' quiet like." He was unwrapping the bundle on his back, rummaging through its contents, and Jason's knife, still in its sheath, fell onto the ground.

Jason's whole body tensed, and the leather strips that bound him creaked gently.

Blashie looked over, his hands still buried in his bundle, and his eyes narrowed. He followed Jason's gaze to the blade and grinned. "Yeah, betchew want that an' all, doncha?" He stretched out one foot, actually sliding the knife closer to where Jason was tied. "Go on then! Go ferit!" Laughing to himself, confident that the knife was way beyond the boy's reach, the trowe turned back to his bag.

Jason wasn't trying to reach it. He already knew it was well beyond his reach. He twisted on the ground, trying to bring his bound hands round to one side of his body. With a few grunts, he succeeded. Watching Blashie closely, Jason forced open the semi-numbed fingers of one hand. *"Return,"* he whispered.

The knife twitched, then slid a couple of inches towards Jason.

Jason closed his hand, and the knife stopped moving. He knew, now, that he *could* get the knife. Regardless of how tightly he was tied, regardless of how much the little trowe abused him, the knife would come to him.

When needed.

He leant back against the rock, doing his best to dry his face on his shoulder. Blashie wanted to take him to Huddour. How Huddour had heard of him he wasn't sure, but he suspected that Gaira was somehow involved. But *he* wanted to get to *Huddour.* Now that he felt safer, now he knew he could call his knife when needed, it wouldn't hurt to play the prisoner, at least for the time being.

With a cackle, Blashie dragged a large joint of cloth-wrapped meat from the bag.

"'Ere we go, nosh time, food time, eat and go fart time!" He picked up the knife, oblivious to the drag marks through the grass and dirt, shoving it into his tunic. He waddled over to Jason. "Yew start a fire?"

"What?"

A leathery foot kicked him. "Fire, boy, hot burny cooky fire!" He shook the wrapped meat at him, and globs of blood sprayed over Jason's legs. "Don't know 'bout yew, but I likes *hot* meat!"

"Yeah," yelped Jason, "yeah okay, yes I know how to start a fire." He suppressed the groan that threatened to escape – the kick had been so hard that he thought his shin must be shattered.

"I untie ya, yew behave?"

Jason flexed his ankle. Surprisingly it still moved despite the throbbing. "Yeah, I'll behave."

"Dew *promise?*" He sounded like a schoolyard bully.

"I promise, yes," said Jason.

"Cos yew know," said Blashie happily, "if yew *did* run, just sayin' like, if yew *did*.... I'd eat yer *feet*."

"Do you want a fire or not?" said Jason. "you have my promise. I'm not gonna run off!"

"Cocky little sparrer," grinned Blashie. He placed the joint of meat on the ground, then wrenched Jason's hands round. Ignoring the yelps and moans from Jason, he grasped the leather thongs between both hands, snapping them like tissue paper.

He lifted Jason's feet, and Jason couldn't hold back the scream this time as the creature put his hands between his ankles, pushing them apart until Jason's own ankle bones snapped the thongs. "Go on then, go get wood!" he made a shoo-ing motion at Jason as he sat massaging his ankles.

"Aren't you going to remove this?" said Jason, holding up the rope tied round his middle. "How'm I supposed to collect wood if I can't move?" One hand still massaged his ankles. Only the thick leather of his boots had stopped the skin from being shredded.

Blashie glared at him through narrowed yellow eyes. He leaned over to the rock, and one leathery claw pushed the rock over, the other hand pulling out several yards of the rope before the rock was dropped once more, a good yard still trapped under it.

"Go." The bored and annoyed tone was clear.

Jason got to his feet. "Right, I'll er..." he began walking backwards, away from the creature as it unwrapped the joint of meat. "I'll go get some wood shall I?"

Blashie waved at him with the meat. "Yeah, and hurry up, or I might not save you none."

Jason's heart went cold.

Blashie was waving at him with a human arm.

A few hours earlier

How dare he, raged Lathgertha to herself as she hauled at the oars of her little boat. How *dare* he! Sending her away, only days before the invasion, some fool's errand to catch a little boy who may or may not enable her husband to bargain for the gold Huddour had stolen. It seemed like a fool's errand to her.

What cared she for the hunt for gold? Let some other axe wielding behemoth of a man do the hunting for shiny trinkets for trading. She was a shieldmaiden! A warrior! Not some comely wench for the hunting down of errant boys who were the subject of ancient fairy stories.

She finally reached shore, the bottom of her boat grating against the gravelled beach. She leapt out, dragging the little boat well up the beach, past the tide mark so she could be sure it would not wash out should she need to return.

She leant into the boat, pulling out her chainmail shirt, her sword belt, and her shield. She pulled on the chainmail, adjusting it over her shoulders and pulling her long hair free, then buckled her sword belt around. Its hilt and sheath were worn, dark leather, and were undecorated.

She didn't care much for decorative things. A pretty carving could not turn an enemy's blade. A well sharpened sword could.

Her shield was the only item that bore some form of decoration. Large and round, its diameter matched the length of her arm. The linden wood disc was etched with the ornate shape of a dragon's head, the iron boss in its centre forming the eye of the dragon. She deftly hung it over her back, and set off up the beach to the grassy banks beyond.

Her mood had improved somewhat by the time she reached the abandoned village. She no longer wanted to murder her husband in his sleep. Maybe just maim him a little. Or feed him to the bears! She smiled to herself. Like *that* would work; when he'd come awooing, not so many years gone, she'd used bears to guard her dwelling. She'd thought herself safe from his advances. She'd been proven *wrong*. Although she had to admit, anyone who could kill two bears in his pursuit of a chosen spouse had to be admired!

The sun was shining down directly from above as she entered the tiny village square. So this was where Gaira, that vicious little Wisewoman, had told her captors the boy had vanished from. Lathgertha felt a grudging respect for the little witch, who even now was being dragged across land and sea to where Ragnar awaited her. She'd betrayed nearly every village around her for the sake of the love of a *boggart*. She and her husband had done well out of it, and out of the resulting trades, but if the roles had been reversed, if Lathgertha had the choice between the lives of her fellow people or her husband...well, she could always remarry.

She looked around her. The houses were ancient and weatherworn but sturdy. Most of the doors hung open, and from the footprints around each door Lathgertha guessed it was the original party Yellowblade had travelled with, looking for their lost charge. Footprints and horse tracks filled the little square, obliterating or scarring any other tracks that may have been there, the search party having doubled back many times, covering their own tracks. Lathgertha raised a dainty eyebrow. So the boy was important to them. This had been an intense search. Maybe Ragnar *was* right; maybe they could use this boy as bargaining tool against Huddour.

There was a concentration of imprints in front of one particular house. Lathgertha wandered up to this little circle, crouching down by its side. In the centre of this little patination was a small pool of dried blood, already flaking around the edges. The boy's, she guessed, from when he'd been taken. She smiled as she looked at the tracks. Intense the search may have been, but they'd found nothing because they were looking in the wrong place.

She stood, walking down the side of the house behind. Like the rest of the houses, it was a one storey, stone block house, with a roof of thatched reed. Her hands and feet easily found traction in the side wall, and within seconds she was on the roof.

Here was what she looked for.

In the centre of the roof the thatch was twisted and snapped, as though something heavy had spent some time up there. Blood, more blood than below, gleamed in the sunlight, the tar-soaked thatch keeping it tacky even now.

She walked easily to the broken reeds, her light weight hardly disturbing the slim reeds beneath her feet, and crouched by the damaged thatch. One finger trailed through a clear sticky liquid, and she brought it to her nose.

"Blashie."

She scowled, wiping the vile stink off her finger onto her leg. She'd hoped Ragnar had been wrong. Blashie, cowardly little killer, complicated the retrieval of the boy. She knew of the creature's reputation. So afraid of attack, it would kill without hesitation if it had the chance.

But it also suggested strongly that Huddour *wanted* this boy.

Which meant of course that *she* did.

She stood by the ashes of the pyre, looking at the trampled ground all around. Twenty nine, maybe thirty men had sat and eaten here not more than three nights previous. And a woman. And...

"Well well well, little witch," she muttered to herself, "seems like the boggart was here too..." She traced her finger around the circumference of the brick-like footprint. She'd found the remains of a target on the hill above, and three lots of indiscernible tracks. Was one set the boggart's? Were they *training* the boggart? "A strong adversary..." she muttered. And grinned. "And a good challenge!"

She stood, looking into the trees, peering up the lengths of the trunks. There, hidden amongst the pine needles and branches, totally miss-able unless she looked closely, were the telltale signs of Blashie's passing.

The scuffmarks in the thick bark from his claws, the shower of pine needles on the ground beneath, where something large had been dragged through the trees, either on Blashie's back or suspended below him.

She picked up a handful of the fallen needles. They were still green, but had begun to dry. Two days then. Two days head start. She set off between the trees, her pace set at a maintainable jog.

The hunt was on.

"I'm not hungry," said Jason, bound once more, his back to the small fire as it hissed and snapped behind him.

"Don't care," said Blashie from behind him. "More for Glorious Blashie, innit?" The sound of slurping, chewing and belching filled the night air.

Jason wished he could have put his hands over his ears. Any hunger that he may have felt after having not eaten for two days was chased away by Blashie's food and his obvious enjoyment of it. "Can't you go over there?!" he hissed, his stomach roiling.

Blashie stared at him, a ribbon of cooked meat hanging from one corner of his mouth. "Wot?"

"I don't want to hear you eating!" shouted Jason, no longer caring if he offended the little creature.

"Aww, bless, precious little girl, incha?" said Blashie. He leant to one side; the smell of rotten eggs filled the air. "It's awny meat! Them fellas, in that pile, in that killded little village, them's not go no use for 'em, 'ave they?" He snorted as he tore another chunk from the bone in his hand. "Wot they gonna do, eh? Magically rise from the ashes – 'scuse me mate, can I 'ave me arm back?'"

"You *took* them from the *bodies*?!" Somehow that didn't make Jason feel any better.

"Wooda got more too, if you nosy do-gooders hadn't come along, cindering good fresh meat." He tore the last bit of gristle from the bone, then chucked it onto the fire. He stared at the boy's back. "'Ere. Yew not gonna drop dead, are ya?"

"What?" Jason turned to look at him.

"From 'unger! You ain't gonna drop dead from 'unger?"

Jason turned away in disgust. "No, no I'm not going to *drop dead from hunger.*" He stared out into the fast-darkening horizon. "Why? You worried you might not be able to eat *me?*"

"Don't wanna eachu," muttered Blashie. "Don't want septic pustule of pus shoutin' at me, is all. Wicked temper, 'im. 'Specially with Alban Eiler coming up."

"What's Alban Eiler?" said Jason.

"Lawd, where wuz you brought up?" laughed Blashie. "Sabbat, innit?

Unseelie Court, they ride out."

"What do you mean, ride out?" said Jason, turning back to look at the little demon. "From where? What for?"

Blashie glared at him with all the air of a little boy caught telling tales. "Never you mind," he muttered. He turned away, all the mocking joviality gone, replaced by a nervous sullenness. "You lot, you ask too many blooding questions. Shut up."

Alban Eiler. Jason had heard the phrase before, but couldn't remember when. When he first met Aiken? When he went into Kilneuair? It had been a throwaway comment, something about an upcoming celebration.

But Blashie's reaction to Jason's questioning, and the mention of the Unseelie Court, a name he'd heard two months and a hundred lifetimes ago, surely meant *something*.

A thought struck him. "When is Alban Eiler?"

Blashie grunted. "Shut it. Sleep time now."

"It's full moon, isn't it?"

"So what?" said Blashie. "I gotta bash you again?"

The Unseelie Court. The full moon. The Vikings. *Alban Eiler.*

Did the Sabbat link the others?

Jason *wished* he was back in Kilneuair. For the first time, he wished he was able to speak to Myrrdin.

As he stared out at the horizon, his mind full of questions and the faces of friends, something to the northwest caught his eye. A tiny thing, so small that if he hadn't been looking at the horizon he would never have seen it. "What ...?"

"Wot?" said Blashie instantly. "Wot yew seen? Wotizit?"

A tiny green dot of light was rising into the air, like a tiny firework or flare. Only Jason was sure they had neither in this time. Even as he watched, the dot of light slowed, then began plunging back towards the ocean. Or wherever it had originated from.

"Is-is there land out there?" he said.

"Mull. It's an Island." Blashie was squinting into the distance. "Be magic, that."

"Yeah," breathed Jason. "But whose?" He recognised that green colour. It could have, it *may* have been...

It looked like the Glass Apple.

"Dunno," shrugged Blashie, pausing to force out a particularly loud fart. "Don't care. Sleep."

"But..."

A fist flashed out, catching him on his temple, and Jason fell sideways. Blashie snorted. "Too many questions, innit?"

Chapter eight

The sun was setting low in the sky, swaddling blankets of purple, red, amber and blue comforting the sun as it sank.

Bricks and broken wood cast long shadows into the night; the fragmented remains of the once vast monastery. The crater now filled most of the area where the monastery had sat, deep and blank. White dots filled the lower part of this crater, the occasional one moving a few feet, before settling down once more.

The gulls had found the crater midafternoon. Filled as it was with earthworms and fragments of unidentifiable meat, they'd found their own private larder, and they'd quickly set up home. The afternoon air had filled with raucous arguments over territory rights, until rank, age and strength finally began to assert its authority.

The cold of the early evening hadn't reached the depths of the crater, and the gulls roosted happily, occasionally shifting position to find a warmer patch of earth, or to be closer to their mate.

One or two roosted around the perimeter of the tunnel at the base of the crater, the warm air rising out of it drying the earth around it to a crumbly dark grey. One bird sat right on the very edge, its feathers occasionally ruffled by a blast of warm air, its beak buried in the feathers of its shoulder as it dozed.

A particularly strong blast of warm air rocked the gull, and a black beady eye opened wide in surprise, its head snapping round to regard the pit. An even stronger blast bowled the gull onto its side, one webbed foot wavering briefly in the air. The bird righted itself, hopping back a few steps, its simple mind curious, and more than a little annoyed at the disturbance. Cawing gently to itself, it waddled up to the edge of the pit, peering down into its vertical depths.

A green light was rushing up towards it, driving the wind upwards, an animalistic cry following it. The gull scarcely had time to take flight before something burning with a brilliant green fire exploded like a giant cannonball from the mouth of the tunnel, screaming and yelling, filling the silence with what sounded like utter delight.

"*YEEEE*-HAAA! Wooohooo!"

A giant rat's tail followed the rapidly rising fiery green figure, trailing way back into the darkness without any sign of an end.

At the unexpected explosion of noise and light most of the gulls took flight, cawing in indignation, and a cacophony of noise filled the crater.

The ovoid sphere of shimmering green fire reached its zenith, then began its descent towards the ground. A voice rang out from somewhere within its centre.

"Oh botheration forgot about the doowwW*WN!*"

Two metres above the ground the green fire vanished, and Gobswistle plummeted backward into the soft earth, the Glass Apple clutched firmly in both hands. The rope that had followed him up out of the tunnel began coiling itself around his face as it fell, one end tied round his ankle, the other still lost somewhere in the depths of the tunnel.

Gobswistle shoved the coils of rope off his face, spluttering and coughing, shoving the anguinum into a pocket. He began feeling around his body. "Nose, head, ears – my lord they're big – legs, hands..." eyes that had been tightly closed popped open in delighted surprise. "I'm in one piece!" He scrabbled to the edge of the tunnel. "I'm in one piece! You see! I *told* you it would work, you – you – doubting wench!" He sat back, laughing in relief. "I knew I could do it, I knew I could, I knew I could...!" He stared up at the multihued sky, grinning broadly. "I've *got* to do that again sometime!" He stared at the moon, pale and swollen. Oh, now why did that send a pang of anxiety through his belly? Was there something significant linked with it?

He frowned, the ancient gears of his brain clanking and thumping, totally failing to connect with anything. With a mental shrug he looked away, untying the rope from around his ankles. He needed something to tie it to. Squinting into the half darkness he saw the massive root ball of some ancient tree, the tree itself destroyed in the blast. Each root was thicker than a man's leg, and most of the root was still buried underground.

That would do nicely. He stood up, immediately sinking nearly to his ankles in the soft earth, then strode through the dirt to the roots, the rope wrapped tightly around one hand. Honestly, the amount of complaining Etain had done, and where had it got them? If she'd just let him try the anguinum when he'd first thought of it, but no, she had to point out all his shortcomings, what could happen if he got it wrong, *again*, and trying to reason with two hundred dazed and frightened soldiers, well...!

The rope tried to wrench itself out of his hand, and Gobswistle went flying through the air again, this time not of his own volition. He was dragged through the soil towards the tunnel, his hand forced out above his head, his head ploughing a furrow.

"Not yet, you damn fool woman!" he bellowed.

There was a muffled reply from down below. It didn't sound too happy.

"Just give me a minute and stop your infernal whinging!" Gobswistle angrily got up, brushing clots of what he hoped was only soil out of his hair. "Damned impatient women, be the death of me yet," he mumbled, crossing for the second time to the root ball. "Hoiking me through the air like a damn fish on a line, and don't she know I'm old?"

A few deft knots attached the rope to the thickest root, and he wandered back to the edge of the tunnel. "Right, try it now!"

A female voice shouted some unintelligible words, and the rope went taut. Satisfied, Gobswistle sat by the side of the tunnel, looking up at the moon. Four days until the moon was full. It would look beautiful in this as yet unpolluted sky. He wished he had a camera. He also wished he could remember why the thought of the full moon filled him with so much dread.

After what seemed an eternity, but in reality more like half an hour, Etain finally hauled herself up over the rim of the tunnel. "Ah'm...*never*...doin' that again," she said, flopping backwards.

She hardly had time to get her breath back before cold hands were pulling her to her feet. She angrily shook the hands off. "What you doin', you old fool?!"

"How far behind you are they?" hissed Gobswistle, peering down the tunnel beside her.

"What?"

"The soldiers! *Kylie!*" he tooked back at Etain, the moonlight washing his face with blue-white light. "How far?"

"Ah dunno...what...about twenny minutes, the first one?" she saw the worried look on the old man's face. "Ethelbert, what...?"

He dragged her away from the pit. "The moon, woman, the *moon.*"

She looked up at it. "Yeah, Ah c'n see. Ethelbert, *chill.* We still got four more days before full moon..."

"And where do we go during those four days?" muttered the old man, pulling at his beard. He sounded more as though he was talking to himself. "Can't go to Kilneuar, no, too dangerous, can't stay on the island, too...well, too *trapped...*" he looked at Etain. "So what do we do?"

"Well...we head for Huddour," said Etain. "Stick to the plan, old man."

"How, though?" said Gobswistle. He kept darting looks over at the tunnel, as though expecting some sort of demon to come leaping out of the shadows. "You, me, Kylie, we could have built a raft, found a sealer's curragh, crossed to the mainland easily. You know how much water we have to cross? In *four* days?"

Etain stared at him. "Damn," she said quietly, as she realised what he was saying. She turned to look at the tunnel, where the rope was pulled tight over the edge, dancing slightly as people below climbed its length. "Two hundred men...." she turned back to the old man. "So we find some way. You managed to use the anguinum..."

"By luck! By fluke and guesswork! You said it yourself – one day I'll splat us against a wall..." Gobswistle paced through the dirt, agitated and angry.

"You did a good thing," said Etain. "You saved their lives. And Jason, he's got his own friends, you said. A younger you, and an army. And a king! He might not even need us! We'll get off here eventually."

"No, you miss the point!" snapped Gobswistle. "You're not thinking!"

"Fine, so you tell me then," said Etain, keeping her voice calm. "You tell me, what am I missing?"

"The full moon!" almost shouted Gobswistle.

"Yeah, ok, and what about...?"

"Us! On an island! With a hundred ninety nine changelings who enter the Rage at full moon!"

Etain felt her face pale. "Oh my god..."

Gobswistle nodded. "You see it now. We're trapped on an island with an army of werewolves, werecats and – and *werecamels* for all I know. Goddess knows what else. They're gonna be hungry."

"Yeah, point taken," said Etain. She crouched, and grasped the bouncing rope in one strong hand, the other drawing a small nail from her pouch. The nail grew into a small fiery dagger.

Gobswistle caught her wrist. "What're you doing?"

"Cutting the rope," said Etain. "You, you've worked out the Anguinum, or how to travel by it at least. You go down, get Kylie, the two soldiers – Cathal and Fionnlagh – the rest stay down there."

"But – but – no! They'll kill each other!" Gobswistle shook his head. "No, no , we didn't go through all this just to sacrifice them now, there has to be a way..."

"Gobswistle," said Etain, "*Ethelbert,* they will kill us!" She still held the rope in her hand, but didn't make any move to cut it. "Now I agreed to help ya, and yes, Ah would love to save these men, *all* these men, but unless you can come up with a *how..?*"

"I don't know!" admitted Gobswistle in exasperation and obvious distress. "I don't know, but we can't just – we can't just let them kill each other! The rage lasts one night! *One night,* Etain! Then they can control it! We just have to keep them safe one night!"

"No, Gobswistle," said Etain quietly. "We have to keep *us* safe one night."

"You said yourself, there's *four days* before full moon! We could work something out, *I* could figure something out, my memory, it comes and goes – I might remember something I can do, *have* done..."

"Gobswistle..."

"No, dear lady, think about it!" pleaded the old man. He paused mid-pace, a look of dawning comprehension on his face. "The anguinum, every time I've used it, it's done what I wanted. Hasn't it?"

Etain lowered the rope to the ground. "Ah call that *luck.* You just said yourself...*"*

"Really? Once or twice is luck. It led us through the maze, it saved us in the monastery, it led us to Athdara, it brought us Germaine to save these men, it got us out of the pit! I may not remember how to use it, but it sure as hellfire remembers how to use me!"

He grasped both her hands. "Please, Etain, please just trust me, or at least the anguinum. I cannot let these men die!"

Etain peered down into the tunnel. In the depths of the darkness she could just make out movement. "So what do we do then? While we wait for the magic to use you? Where do we go?"

"I don't know, hell, I..." Gobswistle held his head in his hands, squeezing it tightly. "I just don't know! How the hell we're gonna get over two hundred people off the island..."

As Etain watched the old man, it was as though someone had flipped a switch inside his head. One minute a frightened, confused old man stood in front of her. Then there was the briefest flash of green fire behind his eyes. The shoulders straightened, the eyes became calm, and a strangely young, confident face stared back at Etain through the wrinkles. "Go to Seilchcladach," said Gobswistle. Even his voice sounded stronger. "There's something you can use there, or there will be by the eve of the fourth day. And you, beloved daughter of Lir, will have your skills cut out to get it useable."

"Gobswistle..?" said Etain, her eyes narrowed.

The old man blinked, his shoulders slumping. "...Yes?" The switch had flipped back.

"Do you remember what you just said to me?"

Gobswistle nodded. "The Seelie Court ... they let me remember." He looked almost angry now. "It...it's a *bloody* game to them! They let me see glimpses of things, people I've been, things I've bloody done..."

"What's gonna be at Seilchcladach?"

"And just as quick, they snatch it back!" said Gobswistle, as though Etain had never spoken. "I'm left with shadows within shadows within mirrors, all bloody useless!"

"You gave us a pointer," said Etain. "We go to Seilchcladach. Something's waiting for us."

"Don't trust me," said Gobswistle sulkily. "I made that mistake once. I trusted me. Ended up hanging by my feet from a tree, with my head in a river."

Kylie clung tightly to Cathal's neck as he climbed the rope. The tunnel was almost impenetrably dark, the faint light from the setting sun now gone. Only a tiny orange light hung in the entrance to the tunnel, dozens of feet above their head. Etain, maybe, her ironfire in her hand. Below them, green light flashed from the gemlike chamber beneath their feet, random flashes that varied both in intensity and duration.

The men below, the men who were all changelings in the making, had changed in their demeanour as the day had worn on, becoming quieter, calmer somehow. Gobswistle had said it was something to do with the moon.

But as the evening had drawn in, as her grandfather and Etain had stood arguing under the entrance to the pit, Kylie had noticed something else.

As they stood in the chamber, growing quieter and calmer, a magical thing had started to happen. Green fire, so dim that if they'd been in daylight would not even have been visible, had begun shooting across their bodies. Not all at once, though. Not encompassing them. Just a tongue of fire, here and there, shooting up one arm, across a face, ruffling close cropped hair. But the fire wasn't outlining the men. It was the outline of some hidden form that hung around them. As she and the two soldiers had stared, they could make out one man who had a giant ghostly bear surrounding him; another had what looked like a gorilla with leathery wings, each wraithlike shape only revealed in fragments; a 3D puzzle being assembled before their eyes. And the men themselves seemed unaware of them.

As were Gobswistle and Etain. It was only when Kylie had half-fearfully and half-excitedly pointed out the sepulchral lights that Gobswistle had finally persuaded Etain to let him try the Anguinum.

Cathal and Fionnlagh had volunteered to be next up the ropes after Etain. Their captain, a wiry brute of a man called Uilleam, had only nodded dumbly to their request, his eyes focussed on some invisible point on the other side of the chamber.

As first Gobswistle, and then Etain, had vanished upwards, the fire around the men had brightened. A sinister dull green flickering glow lit the camber, bouncing off the gemstone walls like dangerous promises of things yet to come. It was with some relief that Cathal had volunteered to carry Kylie piggyback to her freedom.

As Kylie had climbed onto his back, she'd felt a jolt from him, a sense of almost familiarity, as though he was somehow...related to her? It sounded bizarre and she couldn't explain it, but that feeling of family did not fade as the young man began to climb, his skinny body belying a surprising strength that carried them both upwards faster than Kylie would have imagined possible. He certainly outstripped Etain, who begun climbing nearly half an hour before.

As she looked down at the rapidly shrinking green light below, she realised something. She was a changeling, just like the men below. Shouldn't she have a magical fire dancing over her form, delineating what sort of changeling creature she would become? Her arms were bare now, as were her legs from the knee down. But there was no fire, no hint of the huge bobcat she knew she'd become.

Cathal yelped. "Stop yer twistin'!"

"Sorry," stammered Kylie, "I didn't mean..."

"S'aright," breathed Cathal. "Not yuir fault. Ah think Ah've done sumthin' tae me left arm. Been twingin' since we ended up down there." He paused, gasping for breath, bracing his feet against the walls of the tunnel.

"you alright?"

"Yeah," said Cathal after a while. "Yeah, it's gone off now." He flexed his shoulder a couple of times, then began to climb once more.

Night was almost over; in the far eastern horizon, the skyline was beginning to glow with early morning fire. The stars above, their energy spent illuminating the night sky, thankfully began to dim. Uilleam, now seemingly once more himself, helped the final soldier out from the pit. Most of the other men now waited around the perimeter of the pit, some of them, the ones who had emerged first, sleeping fitfully. The green fingers of pale fire were gone, and the men themselves seemed to be *awake* once more.

Etain hadn't slept. She'd sent the old man up to the perimeter with Kylie and Cathal, told them to get some rest. She'd stayed by the side of the pit all night, helping and encouraging the men as they emerged. Now, as the captain directed the last of his men up the sloping sides of the crater, she leant against a large fragment of wall, her eyes closed.

"Ye need some rest, mistress."

Etain suppressed her jump. "Captain Uilleam." She eased her shoulders backwards, trying to ease some of the stiffness. "Are all the men out?"

"Aye, ev'ry last one. Thanks to you and yeh friend." He looked around him, and the vast crater, and the men collapsed around it. "The' say ye tried tae stop us goin' in."

"Tried. Didn't succeed." Etain shrugged.

"Wish Ah'd heard ye," said the captain quietly. He leant on the wall next to Etain. "Wish Ah'd no been at the front o' the phalanx."

Etain turned to him. "And would you have listened?" she asked. "The men at the back, just saw an old man and a woman screaming at them. Tied us up. Would you have done any different? If you'd heard us shouting about spriggans?"

"Mebbies," said Uilleam. "Or mebbies it's just t'power of hindsight, makin' me *think* Ah'd listen. Either way, thankee. But now we need rest. *You* need rest."

"Ah could sleep a hundred years, it feels like," grinned Etain. "Lead on, Captain. I shall be right behind you."

As the rest of the surrounding areas began twitching and groaning their way into the start of another new day, the Men of Dun Ghallain rested.

And waited.

Chapter Nine

Fionnlagh awoke with a start, looking around him. The sun was at its zenith, unencumbered by cloud, and the smell of stew wafted across the ruins towards him. On the other side of the crater he could see the dark woman and the odd old man standing by a large cauldron, the old man dropping some sort of herb into the bubbling mass below. Their captain stood with them, deep in some sort of conversation.

What had awoken him?

By his side, Cathal twisted and turned in his sleep, whimpering like a small puppy. His friend's face was damp with sweat, and his skin had a greyish tinge to it. As he twisted and turned, he kept holding and rubbing his left arm, as though even in sleep it pained him.

Around him, other soldiers were beginning to stir, Cathal's moaning rousing them.

Oh great. Fionnlagh really didn't need another day of being ribbed by the older soldiers for his and his friend's lack of experience. The past three months, the daily training, the mock battles, had only just become bearable, and Cathal's recruitment and subsequent befriending of Fionnlagh, as welcome as it had been, seemed to have put him back all those weeks' work.

He reached over, grasping Cathal's shoulder. "Oi!" he hissed. "Cathal! Wake up, yeh soft eejit!" If anything, Cathal's moaning became louder. "Cathal!" said Fionnlagh urgently. "Wake up now!"

Cathal's eyes shot open, and his left hand flew round, grasping Fionnlagh savagely by his wrist.

Fionnlagh stifled a yelp. "Ow! What are yeh doin'?"

There was a red flash behind his friend's eyes. Fionnlagh stared. He hadn't imagined it; for the briefest of seconds, the soulful brown eyes had become miniature versions of the fiery pits of hell. Then Cathal blinked, and he was himself once more, releasing Fionnlagh and looking around blearily.

"What...what's happening?"

He'd imagined it. With all he'd seen the past two days, no wonder his mind was plying tricks. "You were waking the others, yeh soft bairn! Shoutin' an' hollerin' in yer sleep!"

Cathal scratched at his head. "...Sorry." He looked over to where his captain and the others stood. "Are they cookin'? Ah'm starvin'!"

"Aye," muttered Fionnlagh, rubbing at his wrist. "Not as you deserve any. That damned hurt!"

Cathal shrugged. "Sorry. You startled me. Come on – let's go eat." He set off round the crater.

"That bluidy hurt," repeated Fionnlagh, pushing up his sleeve. Cathal had broken the skin with his nails, five puncture marks slowly seeping blood. Fionnlagh glared after his friend. "Eejit boy."

Etain stared at Uilleam. "You have horses?"

"Aye, milady. And chariots." He smiled. "An' glad I am we left 'em in the midland. Didnae want the monastery thinking it were under attack, so we tethered them up, plannin' tae get them when we were settled." He looked round at the desolation around them. "They'd've bolted sure as fog on the sea if we'd brought them."

"And you've supplies on the chariots?"

Uilleam nodded. He stared into the large cauldron. "Aye, an' better than seagull stew Ah reckons." He looked up as Gobswistle glowered at him. "No offence, Sir."

"Gimme a break," muttered the old man. "I'm trying my best to make it palatable. Goddess herself only knows how old this cauldron is." He delved into another pocket, pulling out and sniffing at a pouch of herbs. "Bayleaf, I think." He crumbled a couple into the stew.

"Ah thought them were magical herbs," said Uilleam warily.

"Herbs are just herbs," said Gobswistle. "Their combination, the incantations said with them, that's the magic. They go just as well in a stew." He lifted the barkless stick he was stirring with, taking a little of the gravy onto his finger and tasting it. He grimaced. "Usually."

"Beggars can't be choosers," said Etain. She turned back to the captain. "So how far away are they?"

"A day's march, maybe less. We could reach them late evening today."

"Were they near any villages? Farmhouses?"

Uilleam laughed. "An' risk having them gone by the time we go for them? Naw, milady, no living souls a good hour in either direction.

Why? Is that a problem?"

"No," smiled Etain. "No, that's ideal. How's your leg?"

Uilleam rubbed at his thigh. The day previously he'd had a gaping wound where a large fragment of wood had torn into it, vanishing into the middle of the wound. Now there was only the faintest red mark, and no pain at all. "It's good, milady. You have a healer's hand, Sir," he added, nodding deferentially at Gobswistle.

"Can't take the credit unfortunately," said Gobswistle, stirring the stew once more. He removed a gull feather that had floated to the surface. "Magic healed you. Not me." He took out another pouch of herbs, adding several pinches.

Uilleam studied the old man for a few seconds. "What will become of us?" he asked quietly. "Ah've heard you two discussing the full moon."

"You're changelings," said Gobswistle simply.

"*Gobswistle!*" said Etain.

"There's no conceivable point," said Gobswistle, "of sugaring the medicine!"

"How 'bout basic consideration for human feelings?" said Etain angrily. She looked over at Uilleam. "Captain..."

"He's right, milady," said the captain. "Truth can be ugly, but at least it can be dealt with honestly. So...what happens then? On...on the full moon?" Though he was obviously trying to sound brave, to sound like a captain, there was an almost unnoticeable tremor in his voice.

"Stew's nearly ready," said Gobswistle. "Disgusting, but it'll fill a hole. You really want to know?"

Uilleam squared his jaw. "Aye. Tell me straight now."

"You will change into some form of animalistic demon. A dog, a cat, a bear, a bore, anything really. You will go into the *Rage*. You will attack and kill anything living within your reach." He looked over at the rest of the army. "Should we tell them to come eat?"

"Gobswistle!" Etain was aghast. "His brain's addled, old fool he is..."

Uilleam's face was pale. "So he lies?"

"No..." conceded Etain, "no he don't. But he's not told you everything, either."

Now the fear did show in the captain's face. "There...there is more?"

Etain nodded, and placed a hand on his shoulder. "Yes, but it's *good*, captain. Gobswistle was able to limit the magic..."

"Wasn't me," said Gobswistle. "Bowls! We don't have bowls? What we going to serve this vile stuff in?"

"He limited the magic," continued Etain with a silencing glance at the old man. "The demonsouls that would have possessed you, they've been destroyed. The first night of the moon, yeah, you'll change, and you'll have no control over what you do. But after that, you'll be able to control your form, change at will and still be *you*, or never change again

---

74

if you don't want!"

"Forgive me if Ah take little reassurance from that," said Uilleam, smiling wryly. He looked out across the faces of his men. "Full moon, we'll attack whoever's nearest, right?"

Etain nodded.

"Even each other?"

After a hesitation, Etain nodded again. "Do you...do you want to tell them?"

Uilleam shook his head. "Nay. They know magic was done, they think themselves saved. Let them keep thinking that." He looked at both Gobswistle and Etain. "That's why you wanted to know if the horses were near people, isn't it?"

"We want to keep as many people as safe as possible," said Etain.

"Including my men?"

"If we can," said Etain, "yes."

"You were coming to warn us, you said. How did you know what lay within?"

"We'be been here before. Days ago." Etain looked behind her. Kylie lay curled up in the dirt, fragments of cloth draped over her as she slept. "The child is a changeling too," she said sadly.

Uilleam looked at the girl, nodding slowly in understanding. Then he looked at Gobswistle. "But that doesnae explain how you knew about us. That we were headed there."

"I am a Seer of amazing power," replied Gobswistle before Etain could answer. "Unfortunately, as my good friend Etain will only too happily tell you, I am also totally senile." He grinned broadly. "And occasionally, more than a little barking."

Uilleam turned wide eyes to Etain.

She smiled. "Truth is ugly," she said.

Uilleam was staring at the old man. "...Indeed." He took a deep breath. "Well then. Food's ready is it? Ah'll go gather the men, see what we c'n rummage for yeh tae serve in."

Etain watched him go, then as soon as he was out of earshot, span on the old man. "Have you no feelings?!"

"He's a soldier!"

"He's a human being!" snapped Etain. "Who's just found out he's probably gonna start eating his friends four nights from now!"

"Not if they eat him first," said Gobswistle, sprinkling yet more herbs into the stew.

"Ah swear Ah'll shove you in there in a second!" shouted Etain. Gobswistle flinched, gesturing for her to lower her voice. "Will you leave that stew alone?!" she hissed. "How can you be so...so flaming hard-hearted?"

"Oh for goodness sake, woman," said Gobswistle testily. "What do you think I'm making here? Think I'd be throwing so many herbs into a pot simply to make it taste nice?"

Etain stopped. She blinked. "Old man," she said quietly, "what are you making?"

Gobswistle grinned his *oh well that's alright then* grin. "A tonic to sooth the savage beast. Used to make it for Attilla the Pizza. The Hutt. The Hun? Something. Such a temper. Well...more for his wives really. Kept him awake and alert, but made him peaceful. For a few days. Didn't end well. Lots of swords."

"Ethelbert..." a slow grin was appearing on Etain's face.

"Went down fantastically well in San Francisco in the sixties though. Flowerpower and all that." He winked at her. "I'm having one of my less senile days."

"Thought you were hungry," said Fionnlagh a short while later, as they marched at the back of the phalanx away from the ruins.

Cathal, sweaty and pale, snorted derisively. "Stank like pondwater! Ah dunno how ye cuid even stomach it!"

"T'weren't that bad," said Fionnlagh. "Just took a while tae get the taste."

"Yeh went back fer seconds."

Fionnlagh smiled, but said nothing. It was such a beautiful afternoon! The rolling landscape glowed with the brightest of green grass, and the snowdrops shone like diamonds in the vivid afternoon sun. The cries of the gulls that circled overhead sang in his ears like the sweetest of music. He smiled more broadly. "It's a grand afternoon," he murmered. Ahead of him one of the others turned, hearing his comment, and smiled beatifically.

"Yer soft in th'heed," growled Cathal. He rubbed at his shoulder. "Ah wasn't the only one couldnae stomach it. The girrul had none neither."

"Oh hush yer whinging," grinned Fionnlagh. Nothing was going to dent his mood. He tilted his face into the sun, letting it wash over his face for a few seconds. He turned to his friend, who was still massaging his shoulder. "You done summat tae yer shoulder?"

"Must've," affirmed Cathal. "Dunno what. Me arm's been hurtin' all morn, now it's gone intae mah shoulder. Bluidy 'urts!"

"Go see that Gobswistle then," smiled Fionnlagh. "He'll hae yeh mended right soon enough."

"He's daft as a coot!" said Cathal angrily. "Like Ah'd let him wi'in ten leagues o' me."

Fionnlagh shrugged. "Suit yerself."

Cathal rubbed his shoulder. "Ah'm hungry."

There was no moon that night; grey clouds had begun spreading across the sky shortly before nightfall, obliterating everything and plunging the army into an early darkness. They had no torches, and now Etain led them, an ironfire in each hand, Uilleam by her side, his directions guiding them through the darkness. Thunder rumbled in the distance, and the air was still and close.

Kylie and Gobswistle walked hand in hand behind Etain and the captain. Kylie hadn't eaten – the smell of the stew had almost made her sick – yet strangely she felt no hunger. The night, so dark to all her companions, was clear and bright for her, as though the light of the moon somehow seeped through the clouds just for her, illuminating everything around her. Looking back at the soldiers, she'd expected a repeat of the previous night, that the men would have magical green fire rippling over their bodies. Yet the figures behind just looked like men.

"Granddad?"

"Hmm?" Gobswistle looked down at his granddaughter.

"The men, they're not..." she was still looking back at them, "last night, they had this fire dancing over them. They don't, now."

Gobswistle nodded, smiling.

"Well, why?"

By reply, Gobswistle placed a finger on his lips, smiling a very self satisfied smile.

"Last night," persisted Kylie, "they had this green fire. I didn't though. I thought I was a changeling like them?"

"You are," said Gobswistle. "But Athdara's magic, it was different from mine."

"How?"

"She had just one of you to deal with," replied Gobswistle. "I had quite a few more." He frowned. "Sort of me."

"What happened to me in there?" She thought back to the cavern. She remembered diving down the hole – she should have been killed – and something invisible, numerous, fearsome yet gentle, lowering her into the centre of the cavern. She remembered, shivering, the avaricious stroking of invisible hands, wanting her, desiring her. She shivered from the memory. She never, *ever*, wanted to feel like that again. She'd shredded most of her clothes, but couldn't remember doing it. Now she was left in a red tee-shirt and jeans cut off at the knee.

"The demonsouls, the Unseelie court, they sought to possess you. Athdara's magic prevented them."

"I – I started to change, didn't I?"

"Yes. I think so. Look, Kylie, I have to be honest, I don't remember all of it, it wasn't really me, you know..."

"Yeah, I remember, it was Germaine." She scowled at his memory. "I didn't like him."

"No, not one of my...more pleasant...personifications," agreed

Gobswistle.

"But you...*he*...stopped the change?"

Gobswistle nodded. Thunder rumbled again, nearer this time.

"Athdara killed the Unseelie court spirit that wanted to possess me, didn't she?"

Gobswistle inclined his head. "She is a powerful selkie. I was impressed, I have to admit!"

"Did Germaine kill the ones after the army?"

"I..." the old man hesitated. "I think so, yes. Yes, of course, he must've done."

Kylie didn't feel reassured. Something was eating at her mind, gnawing at it like a dog at a meaty bone.

"Hold them! *HOLD THEM!*"

Uilleam's bellowed orders were futile; the horses bolted into the darkness, trailing the branches that they had been tethered behind them, so great was their fear to get away. The soldiers darted in front of them, but the horses jumped them with ease, vanishing into the night.

Cursing, Uilleam marched up to Gobswistle. "It's *us,*" he demanded, "isn't it?"

"They...they sense the wrongness in you," said Gobswistle.

The sound of horses' hooves faded into the distance, to be replaced by the explosive boom of thunder, directly overhead. Lightning flooded the woodland clearing, and large droplets of rain began to fall.

Uilleam grimaced. "Wrongness, aye, that's one word fer it." He looked around the clearing as more lightning flashed. "At least the chariots're still here. We have tents."

"I'll help you," said Etain. "Gobswistle, you look after Kylie..." Etain looked around. "Kylie? Where is she?"

Gobswistle held up the hand she had been holding, seemingly astonished to find it empty. "She...well she *was* here..."

Kylie was darting between the men. "Cathal? Have you seen Cathal?" None of the men had, and she ran on.

She knew now. The feeling of kinship for Cathal, for someone she had only just met, yet he felt like family. That had been strange.

Then she remembered the splinter in his hand, when he'd called them over to look at the tunnel into the gemstone chamber. Then the ache in his arm.

Only moments earlier she'd been holding her Grandfather's hand. Then a memory, half dreamlike, had leapt into her mind, of seeing Cathal and Fionnlagh standing before her in the cavern. They'd been many feet away from her. Outside the circle. Cathal had been scratching at his palm.

She grabbed another man. "Have you seen Cathal?"

He shouted to make himself heard over the almost constant thunder. "O'er yonder!" he gestured behind him. "He's wi' the other bairn."

Whimpering now, the fear riding high in her chest, Kylie ran on.

Fionnlagh huddled under the partial cover of the tree, cold water running down the back of his neck. The fond happiness he'd felt earlier in the day was in danger of being washed away. "Cathal!"

There was no reply.

"Cathal! What yui doin' back there?" There was the sound of rustling through the trees, but no reply.

Fionnlagh was beginning to get worried about his friend. Just before dusk Cathal had started rubbing at his chest. He'd become even paler, and his skin had looked surreally grey in colour. Fionnlagh was worried he'd taken ill, or had an infected wound. In his concern, he'd made to get the old man, but Cathal had stopped him, swearing and cursing he didn't want the old man near him.

So Fionnlagh had backed down.

But he was still worried. Cathal was usually so jolly, so cheerful. To see him that angry, that defensive, it was just *not* his friend.

"You alright?" he called.

"...Fionnlagh..."

The voice was gruff, almost guttural, but still discernibly Cathal. Fionnlagh was on his feet in an instant. "Cathal! Where are you? You alright?"

"...Fionnlagh...help me..."

In the darkness between the trees, Fionnlagh saw two sparks of red light, head height and moving. Though worried about his friend, the young soldier hesitated. "Cathal...?"

Behind him he suddenly heard the young girl's voice through the rain and thunder, calling Cathal's name, her voice filled with terror.

"Cathal, the girrul's looking fer you," said Fionnlagh nervously, "Ah'll go get her, bring her here..."

"No...help me...."

Fionnlagh peered into the darkness. The two red points of light had vanished. "Okay..." he replied hesitantly. "Where...where are you? What's happened?"

"...hurting....I'm hurting..."

"Ah'm coming!" said Fionnlagh, finally mustering the courage to enter the trees. He could see no more than a couple of feet all around him. "Keep shoutin', Cathal, lead me tae ya!"

He'd hardly gone more than two metres into the trees when it happened. Lightning flashed; fork lightning dancing across the clouds, illuminating the whole wooded area.

Illuminating the creature that towered above him, its eyes burning with red fire, its distorted lupine features snarling down at him, ropes of saliva drooling down to the ground from its obscene mouth.

He didn't have time to scream. Something grabbed him by an arm, something *strong*, lifting him high in the air. He felt a ripping sensation, and a gush of warm fluid drenched his left side as he flew through the air back into the clearing. He was vaguely aware of landing in front of the little girl, and her screams seemed somehow so muffled, so distant.

Then came peace, and with it, darkness.

Chapter Ten

The cottage of their banishment was on the outer limits of the village. Squat, small and ugly, it sat in the middle of naked branches of dog rose and bramble.

Myrrdin, his arms filled with bundles of his belongings, stared at it. "So this is my new home?"

Eigyr pulled her hooded cloak tight around her. "Glamorous. My father in law's taste never fails to impress." She sighed, stooping to pick up her belongings. "Come on. Maybe it'll be better on the inside." She shivered as a particularly strong gust of wind buffeted her. "It'll certainly be warmer."

It wasn't. If anything, it seemed even colder inside. It was less a cottage and more just one small room, with two long abandoned beds either side of a small fireplace, and a rickety table underneath the single shuttered window. Myrrdin dumped his bundles onto the table surface; one leg gave way, throwing everything to the floor apart from the wrapped casket that Myrrdin lunged to catch.

Eigyr went over to one of the beds, gently placing her belongings next to it. A few prods confirmed its sturdiness (while raising a cloud of white dust and sending innumerable spiders scuttling up the wall), and she lowered herself onto it.

"This time last month," she said, stretching her aching back, "I was lounging in a monastery, Constans on my knee, eating a rather splendid game pie."

Myrrdin was collecting his belongings off the floor. "I thought you hated it there."

Eigyr looked around her. "Hate seems such a *definitive* word," she said. "If I'd've known my Da would bring me to *this...*"

Myrrdin pushed the leg back under the table. There were no nails – just a carved hole into which the leg was inserted. He leaned on the table gingerly. It creaked, but this time did not give way. "Darrach was only doing your bidding." He turned to her. "Does the company not make up for the accommodation?" he said gently.

"The *company,*" glowered Eigyr, "suggested I get imprisoned in a monastery."

"You were there as a guest," said Myrrdin, unwrapping one bundle. It was Ambrosius' notes. "You could have left at any time. It was only for your safety!"

"Hah!" said Eigyr. She scowled slightly as one of the babies kicked. "And leave I did! I was not going to spend Alban Eiler in some – some..."

"Safe haven?" said Myrrdin, grinning. An ancient pillow flew at him, and an explosion of feathers filled the room. "Thanks for that."

"You *always* enjoyed putting me down!"

"Because you make it so easy!" grinned Myrrdin. "Eigyr, *why* did you come up here?" He placed the casket on the table, his hand resting on it a moment. "What did you hope to achieve?"

"I told you," said Eigyr. "I was being held prisoner. What, you don't believe me?" She pouted.

"I believe you *felt* like a prisoner..."

"Don't *patronise* me!"

"But somehow I cannot visualise Archbishop Guithelin as a key bearing bullying captor."

"He had his moments," said Eigyr, stretching out on the bed. "You try mentioning getting some candles in for Alban Eiler. *Pagan blasphemy! False godheads! The devil is at your elbow!*" A spider scuttled across her forehead and with a little yelp she sent it flying. "I'm going to be eaten alive in here!"

"You haven't changed," said Myrrdin, picking up a surprisingly intact broom. "You still cleverly avoid subjects you don't want to talk about."

Eigyr had stood up, brushing angrily at her dress. "What can I say? I was taught by the expert." She curtsied towards the Druid, graceful despite her advanced pregnancy. "I came up here looking for *you.* Alright? *Happy?* I knew nothing about these damned viking invaders!"

"You know nothing can happen between us," said Myrrdin. He didn't look at her as he said this.

"You think I don't know that?" She lifted her skirt as another spider ran past. One dainty shoed foot descended on it. "I had daddy dearest telling me this for years. We had our chance, druid. We *both* threw it away."

"How did you get Darrach to travel down south? He was always a homebody."

Eigyr snorted. "Hah! Like he'd ever travel for *me*. No, I'd er... been summoned to the borders by dearly beloved Constantine. Conjugal rights perhaps. The soldiers sent to get me were easily persuaded by a little gold. You going to sweep with that broom or stand holding it like little boy lost?"

"Bribery. I shouldn't be surprised. You were never averse to causing trouble if it got you what you wanted." He started sweeping the floor. "And what pray do you intend doing to help? Or is it below your dignity?"

"I shall strip the bedding, and restuff the mattresses." She reached round her back, unlacing her bodice. She caught Myrrdin staring at her. "You expect me to clean and scrub in finest court clothes? Don't worry. I'm quite decent underneath."

*

Darrach strolled down the cobbled pathway, dry walls either side of him broken by the occasional gate towards someone's home. Ropes of purple light lit the path in front of him, branching at every side path like giant veins, pulsing and throbbing. Smoke hung in the air, unmoving, the few people he passed frozen like statues. He looked neither left nor right, knowing exactly which home he was headed for. It was the one right at the back of the row, set back from the others, its land unkempt and overgrown.

The king had made an announcement that morning. The Druid was being placed in the outer rim of Kilneuair, the better to protect the womenfolk and children there.

Darrach knew better. The druid had been banished. As had the devil bedamned Eigyr, ungrateful wench that she was. Messenger birds had already been sent out to the borders, alerting the king's son of Eigyr's presence. No doubt the prince would send out more soldiers to collect her.

No matter.

He doubted they'd beat the vikings.

He found the home he was looking for, and walked up the path. He paused, his wrinkled face tightening in concentration, and the purple light faded from the ground beneath his feet. Voices carried out of the building to him, happy voices that laughed and talked with jolly animation. Puffs of dust wafted out of the open door, and smoke already billowed from the chimney. Ancient blankets hung over the brambles, drying in the cold breeze. The old man's face settled into an angry mask.

He poked his head round the corner. "An' what may Ah ask is the cause o' such jollity?"

Myrrdin ceased his sweeping and Eigyr, who was stuffing a mattress, paused, a handful of reeds in her hand.

"Darrach!" beamed Myrrdin, lying down his brush. "Come in, come in! Make yourself at home!"

"Some home," muttered the woman beside him, shoving another handful of reeds into the mattress.

"S'bigger than th'home yui started off in," said Darrach amiably enough. He watched her working. "An' despite yer pretentions, ye still knaa what yeh aboot." She stuck her tongue out at him, and he laughed, though there was no mirth in the sound. He laid his staff against the wall. In his other hand was a large sack which he tossed onto the table. Regardless of the druid's sudden flinch, the table remained resolutely upright. "Fuid. Didn't think t'king'd given ye's enough time tae get some."

"You'll stay, of course?" asked Myrrdin, opening the sack. He ignored Eigyr's sudden fearsome gaze.

"Nay, laddie, nay," said Darrach, but he seated himself on the bed opposite them. "Things tae do, ye ken."

"I'm hardly a lad," said Myrrdin. "I'm older than you!" He smiled. "I should be calling you 'laddie!'. How old are you now?"

"Older'n Ah look," said the old man, "younger'n Ah feel." He looked over at his daughter, who was wearing a plain white dress, stained now with dust and mould. "Silly question, but why're you in yer undergarments?" His eyes flicked between Eigyr and the druid.

"Get your mind out of the gutter, Da," said Eigyr. "I'm decently dressed, and more to the point I'm about to drop two bairns. I'm like this for cleaning."

"Ah ken ye, Ah ken yeh." Darrach nodded agreeably, then turned to the druid. "So why're *you* here?"

Myrrdin snorted, then started sweeping some of the larger cobwebs down from the reed roof. "In case you couldn't read between the lines, Cináed has banished me from his sight."

"Aye, an' Ah worked that out easy enough. Ah meant – why're you *in here?* This house? Why aren't yeh helpin' preparations?"

Myrrdin stopped his sweeping. "My services are no longer required."

"Required?" said Darrach, laughing gently. "They've niver been *more* required, mon! T'mangonels are ready; the men set oot wi'em this eve. Yeh ken? Eight o' them, bein' towed by horse 'n' cattle, out intae the darkness."

"It's not my concern. Cináed made that perfectly clear. I am an *impotent druid.* I keep things from him, apparently."

"So yeh'll turn ye back on the rest of the folk?" He looked around the tiny room. "So...am Ah tae take it this is yer new forest tae hide in?" He snorted. "Farm out yonder, he has pigs. Yeh want me bring some for company like?"

"HE NO LONGER LISTENS!" shouted Myrrdin, throwing down the broom. Eigyr jumped, but said nothing, picking up the broom and putting it into one corner.

"Him an' him only," retorted the old man, not the slightest bit fazed. "Omnust, he'll listen. Me, Ah'm listenin' now. An' Aiken, *he'll* listen. He's more'n just a nursemaid to your granddaughter."

"She's not-!"

"Yeh cannae hide from yuir responsibilities!"

"My responsibilities are to Jason and your daughter. I've done what I can here." He opened the door for Darrach, his face scarlet. "You said you had things to do?"

Darrach did not move. "The vikings come in three days. Yuir no even gonnae fight?"

"How?" said Myrrdin. He slammed the door. "With what? The Seelie Court took my magic. All I had was the King's ear, and he'll no longer hear what he needs to know!"

Darrach leaned forward, his eyes narrowing. "An' *what* does he need to know?" His voice was gentle but intractable.

Myrrdin leaned on the table, looking out of the window, saying nothing.

Eigyr moved to his side. "Myrrdin?" she said quietly. "What *does* he need to know? Is it the writing Jason left?"

"I don't even know that it *is* Jason's," said Myrrdin after a pause.

"Best yeh tell us what it says then," said Darrach. He leaned over and picked up his staff, leaning on it as he sat expectantly on the bed, his eyes fixed on the druid.

"*Please,* Myrrdin," said Eigyr as Myrrdin hesitated. "Please don't give up. You're no coward."

"Very well." He walked up to the other bed. "It's light. Grab the other side." Between them, they lifted the bed closer to the other ones. Eigyr quashed the urge to shriek in disgust at the number of ancient and mummified rodents underneath where it had been. Myrrdin collected the bundle of writing, and the three of them sat on one bed while he spread the sheets of material out on the other.

Darrach leant forward, reading the uppermost sheet. "Well now..." he breathed. "Ambrosius..."

Myrrdin was instantly alert. Darrach's tone had been one of recognition. "You've heard of him?"

"Aye, Ah have, aye," said Darrach. "And if ye'd no spent so long in t'forests, so would you."

"Tell me."

"No much tae tell. He's appeared tae various courts. Sometimes a wee bairn, sometimes a man, much as yerself, sometimes as an old man, leaning on a stick. Allus with news. Well..." Darrach scratched a bushy eyebrow. "Predictions, more like. Prophecies."

"I've heard of him too," said Eigyr, much to Myrrdin's surprise. "When I was in Wales. Don't look at me like that! I never connected it - I thought it was just fairy stories!"

"Fairy stories play more than a small part in what we face," said Myrrdin. Eigyr flushed, turning away. "This Ambrosius, who was he? Was he Sidhe? Was he *good?*"

"Neither guid ner bad," said Darrach. "As tae bein' Sidhe, well he were somethin' more'n ordinary. He told the truth, is all. Not ev'ry one wanted tae hear it."

"I know that feeling well," said Myrrdin. "But...but surely, if you know the legends, then Cináed would too?"

"Doubtful," said Darrach. "His story is regional, outside o' Cináed's lands. Ah only know 'em as Ah've travelled."

"So..." Myrrdin looked at the pages on the bed. "You trust his word?"

"A Seer's prophecies. Would be foolish not tae listen."

Myrrdin sighed. He'd read and re-read the pages so often, but to hear Darrach's words filled him with hope. "If they are accurate..."

"What do they say?" asked Eigyr.

"The vikings don't attack in three days. They attack in two. The night of the day after tomorrow."

"What?" hissed Eigyr, but Darrach seemed unsurprised.

"And ye'd keep this information tae yersen?"

"I tried to tell Cináed!" said Myrrdin, his voice echoing his frustration of the previous night's confrontation. "He said they were the tricks of Jason's kidnappers, trying to twist victory from our hands! He wouldn't listen!"

"So tell *me,*" said Darrach. "Ah'm all ears."

So Myrrdin began talking. As he spoke, it seemed his fears began to lift. To share the information with someone else seemed a relief, though the events he spoke of were dark, and filled with blood.

The mangonels would be captured, the men sent to guard and use them, to light the warning fires when the vikings headed inland, were already expected. They would be killed. The vikings would send in their Berserkers the night before Alban Eiler, while people slept, not expecting attack until the next day. They would enter Kilneuair from the northeast, via Loch Awe rather than the direct route from the west, as Jason's original visions had foretold. As the vikings attacked, they would use the mangonels against them, targeting the barracks, burning them with the army still inside. The male survivors would be thrown into the firepits they'd dug in the west to protect Kilneuair. All their preparations, all their defences, would come to nothing. Betrayed by the witchwoman Gaira, and her obsidian mirror.

Eigyr paled as she listened. The sky was darkening by the time he finished speaking, and the fire in the hearth had nearly burnt out. She looked at the man she had loved so long. "How...how could you even begin to think of keeping this to yourself?" she said.

Myrrdin said nothing.

"You sentence these people to death by your silence!" She stood, unsure of whether to strike him or hug him. "Cináed may be king, but he's also human! He makes mistakes! If he won't listen, find someone who will!"

"Peace, daughter," said Darrach soothingly. "He already has." He smiled as Myrrdin looked at him.

"Your audience is appreciated more than you know," said Myrrdin, "but it still does not suggest a course of action against a king who will not listen."

"Ah ken ye, Ah Ken ye," said Darrach, "but dinnae underestimate the man. He'll listen soon enough. When the time is right. And dinnae forget Omnust."

"I don't–?"

"It was at his request Ah come, ye ken," smiled Darrach. "He thinks the king is overstretched. He thinks he's holding on to Jason's visions like a drowning man clutches at a branch. He wants *your* wisdom. An' what Captain Ossian listens tae, his men will too."

"If Cináed finds out..."

"The king is old. Not long now until Constantine is king, yon wench, Queen."

"Thank*you,*" glowered Eigyr.

Darrach ignored her. "If he finds out, he finds out. By then, your words will hae been heard. Which rests heavier on your shoulders? Your friendship with Cináed, or the lives of the people of Kilneuair?"

Myrrdin stared at him, then broke into a sad smile. "I do not remember you being such a persuasive speaker," he said.

"Last you saw me, Ah was a bairn," replied Darrach. "Been a lifetime's worth o' livin' done since then, so ter speak."

"I still wish Jason were here though," said Myrrdin sadly.

"You feel a bairn's wisdom is greater than your own?" said Eigyr. "He ran away!"

"It's his voice the king would listen to," replied Myrrdin. "I still do not believe he ran away through fear. If he *did* run away, he must have seen something in the future that made him think it necessary." He sighed. "It's the one thing I fear the king may be right about, him and Omnust. And *you.* I fear he may have been taken."

"Ah've met him only briefly," said Darrach, "but he seems older than his years. Mebbies he's stronger than ye think."

"He has magic, certainly," said Myrrdin. "How strong it makes him I don't know. He has a knife, given to him by the Gwyllion. Its blade is a Seer's Mirror. It's how he made his prophecies."

"He was staring into the blade last I saw him..." breathed Eigyr. "Do you think...?"

"I...don't know. It seems likely."

Darrach was re-reading the top page. "What agreement is he on about?"

"What?" said Myrrdin, momentarily distracted.

"The agreement that yuir no to ferget. Says Jason's on his quest."

"It was with Cináed. If Jason helped us protect the village against the vikings, Cináed would help him with his quest."

Darrach looked up from the sheet. "Quest now?"

"A long story," smiled Myrrdin. "His family were under attack by the Medb. The Gwyllion told him that to defeat her, he would need the Three Books of Huddour."

It was the first time that afternoon that the old man was without words, his self assuredness visibly shaken. His jaw dropped, and his weathered face paled.

"You've heard of him, then?"

"More than heard o' him," murmured Darrach. "Ah stuid by the side of Bec mac Dè the night he was imprisoned..."

"Da?" Eigyr stared at her father. She'd known, of course, that her father was older than most men. But to have known Bec mac De made him, made *Myrrdin,* so much older than she'd ever guessed at.

"Old man," said Myrrdin, "I think it's your turn to talk."

Chapter Eleven

Darrach did not start speaking immediately. They shared some ale first, and a little of the bread Morven had kindly provided them with. As the sun slowly moved upwards in the sky and Myrrdin and Eigyr had done enough cleaning to remove most of their more unwelcome visitors, Darrach finally leant back on one of the beds, a mug of ale in one hand. Myrrdin and Eigyr sat on the opposite bed, a willing and eager audience.

It was more years ago than the old man cared to remember, he said. He'd been a young man, maybe at most in his early twenties. He'd just laid his father to rest. He'd heard, finally, the story of Lailoken and the battle in Strathclyde. With all the idealism of youth, he'd set out to be a soldier himself. His mother had protested of course, but women didn't know the way of men's hearts (*if Darrach noticed the anger that flared in his daughter's face at this point, he chose to ignore it*).

He'd travelled north, enlisting in an army of a laird who now no longer existed, who's lands were now the properties of others. The training had been hard, sometimes brutal, but no more than he expected, and he had money to send home to his mother.

His first posting, during a wild and bitter spring, had been to Mull, to the Columban monastery there. They were to escort Bec Mac Dè, the oldest of the druids, to the monastery. No tithes had been received from the monks since before Samhain, but only that spring had the routes cleared enough for them to travel to it. So fifty three men had set out.

Bec Mac Dè was ancient and frail, leaning heavily on his elder staff, his withered shoulders covered by a cape of raven feathers. But he was also powerful and learned in the old ways, and suspected something amiss with the massive monastery he and Columbus had constructed.

He had been right to be worried. After a treacherous crossing of the waters, and battling through weather fit to strip the warmth from the flesh and the flesh from the bones, they had found the ruins of the monastery. A couple of soldiers were sent to search the ruins by Bec Mac Dè, given a secret task to complete while they were in there. Two days and two nights Bec Mac Dè waited, not allowing any other man in. The two soldiers never returned.

On the morning of the third day, the old man had entered the ruins alone. Darrach himself had been charged with not allowing any other man into the ruins, not even his captain. He'd feared for his life the few hours the druid was gone; his captain was as fearsome as he was broad, and did not take kindly to a lowly soldier barring his way. He'd breathed an inward sigh of relief when the old man emerged, unharmed.

Bec Mac Dè seemed even older when he'd emerged. He'd taken Darrach to one side; it seemed even ancient and powerful druids occasionally needed someone to talk to. Columbus had been given three books of power, he said, by a sorcerer who went by the name Koaladan. They'd been stolen from the cruellest of wizards, a man black in clothing and soul, Lord Huddour. The books were to be hidden, kept safe. They held the secrets of all magic, nearly rivalling that of the Tuatha Dè Dannon themselves.

Knowing his own magic to be young, and only in the infancy of its power, Columbus had turned to Bec Mac Dè. So the Monastery had been built, imbued with the magic of both the infant Christianity and the deeper, more subtle sorcery of the Druids. The books should never have been found.

It was a measure of the integrity of the Druid that he admitted he had under-estimated the power Huddour commanded. The monks had paid for his misjudgement. This, then, would be his last task in this realm – to retrieve the books once more, or to prevent the sorcerer from ever using them again.

Now Darrach was young, but he was not stupid. He did not want to be caught up in the battle between two such powerful sorcerers. But he couldn't just leave. He had his mother to think of, and his own reputation. With a heavy heart, he had followed the small army back across to the mainland and north across the hills and mountains to Loch Linnhe, the reputed settlement of the Britannic lord.

They found the loch on the night of Alban Eiler. Huge black storm clouds circled the loch, lightning illuminating segments of it in flashes of the richest green. Beneath the centre of this revolving darkness sat Castle Stalcaire.

Darrach paused in his narration, and looked at Myrrdin. "Ye ken Alban Eiler?"

"Any man does," replied Myrrdin.

"So tell me." He grinned. "Humour an awd man."

Myrrdin sighed. "It's a time of rebirth. A celebration. When the first crops are planted, when the..."

"No, no, no, yeh dinnae ken," grumbled Darrach. "The connection with the Fair Folk, druid. You of all people, you shuid knah that."

"You mean the Wild Hunt, don't you?" said Myrrdin after a pause. "It has relevance to this tale?"

"It's the bluidy Daionhe Sidhe, o' course it has relevance! It's tae do wi' magic!"

"Your temper hasn't improved over the years," said Myrrdin.

"And I had to grow up with it," muttered Eigyr.

"Hushtae, both o' ye," said Darrach. "Ne'er mind. Ah'll tell ye."

The Seelie Court and the Unseelie Court ride out at the Sabbats. From their world within worlds to this fair land. They change their places of residence, or rather their *doorways* to their place of residence, when they travel.

The Scottish folk bar their westward windows at the Sabbats. The Unseelie Court, you see, collect the souls of the Dead not yet shriven, to swell their numbers. Unlike the Seelie Court, they cannot bear their own offspring. And the Unseelie Court rides from the west. The *Wild Hunt.*

So Bec Mac Dè and his army stood before Castle Stalcaire, thunder and lightning rumbling above their heads. Huddour was aware of them. He'd seen their coming from many leagues hence. He'd had time to read his books, to plan.

From the clouds above their heads a huge flock of crows had descended on them, talons raking and beaks stabbing. Many men lost their eyes. Bec Mac Dè had cast his cloak to the winds; it became a raven as big as any dragon, snapping up the crows like a swallow chasing flies.

A pack of ghastly black dogs, their jaws slavering and their red eyes glowing, pounded across the causeway from the castle to the army, ripping and savaging. The blinded men fell first, followed by many of their brethren.

Bec Mac Dè rammed his staff of ancient elder into the ground. Giant Cait Sidhes appeared from the nearby forest, chasing the hounds as cats might chase mice.

The howling storm descended from the skies, screaming with the tortured souls of the lost soldiers. Many more men were gathered up by the wind and dashed against the walls of the castle. Only Darrach remained alive of the soldiers, cowering by the side of Bec Mac Dè. The Druid held tight to his staff, which sprouted mighty branches, its base spreading roots deep into the earth; soon a giant elder tree stood strong against the storm, the two men sheltered beneath its bows.

Bec Mac Dè was old. He knew his life, his strength, would not last much longer. As Darrach cowered beneath the waving branches, the old man walked out into the storm, chanting in words Darrach could neither understand or even hear. He faced the four corners of the world, his hands up in supplication. Finally he faced west, and began another chant.

From the west appeared another cloud, riding low on the horizon, its ebony depths formed from the bodies of unspeakable monsters, monsters than no man should have to look on.

The cloud twisted round the castle, widdershins to the storm's dreosil, soaking it up, stilling it. Soon the full moon gazed down at them, the starry night clear once more, silent and still. A wall of cloud danced around the castle and the two remaining men, nightmarish forms dancing and singing in its depths.

From within the cloud rode a man on horseback. Beautiful he was, in gleaming gold and white, but terrible to behold. He was the Wild Huntsman, the leader of the Unseelie Court. His voice, when he spoke, was like the rumble of distant thunder, or the crash of waves upon the shore. He demanded to know why the eldest of the Druids had used Words of Command to summon him from his night of hunting on this Sabbat night.

Bec Mac Dè knew he was dying. Maybe that's what made him do what he did, he who had spent his whole life celebrating the value of life itself. He asked the Unseelie Court to bring down Lord Huddour. He knew the Court could not harm him – protected as he was by the ancient magic of the Books, only magic from these same books could cause him harm.

The Huntsman had laughed. Huddour was nothing to him. What cared he what magic Huddour had? He should strike the druid down for defying the hunt. He needed souls; he needed to increase his number.

Bec Mac Dè *had* souls. He had the souls of the army that lay scattered around. He'd bound them with a spell – the Huntsman could not claim them, unless the druid himself allowed him to. And if he was killed, they would follow him to the Summerlands, beyond the Huntsman's reach.

The Huntsman was infuriated. Time and again he tried to claim the souls, time and again the Druid's magic held them fast. The night was fading and he had collected no souls, but neither would he bow to a mortal creature.

He would, he said, seal Huddour within his castle, unable to ever travel more than ten leagues from its walls. Huddour would be alone – he would not be able to summon anyone to his castle by magic. They would have to come of their own free will. The souls of forty nine soldiers would not be enough however. He wanted the soul of Bec Mac Dè himself.

The old man agreed. The tree shrank once more into a staff, which he thrust into the cowering Darrach's hands.

"You who tremble and cower," he had said, "you will go on. There will be a time this staff is needed again. Beware the treachery of the Huntsman."

The Huntsman, hearing, had laughed. A blade of brightest silver pierced the Druid, and he fell to the ground, dead.

The Huntsman looked down at Darrach. "Here then is the bargain your master has struck. Fifty Souls on the night of Alban Eiler to imprison yon merchant of death. But be warned, should he ever gain fifty unshriven souls to trade for his freedom in Alban Eilers yet to come, I shall take them, and gladly. I will not be used without a price!"

The sun sat high in its noontime position, yellow white light filling the sky. On the bed, Darrach turned the staff slowly in his hands. It was old and well handled, a worn and polished ball of root knots formed its handle.

"So this is what the old Druid gave me," he said. "This is why Ah go on."

"Did he say what you were to use it for?" asked Myrrdin.

"What he said tae me, Ah've said tae ye's," replied the old man. "Ah'm tae do sumthin' wi' this thing." He shrugged. "Dinnae knah what. Many times o'er the years Ah've tried tae use it, magic like. But it's just wood." He looked up at Myrrdin. "An' this is who the boy has gone after?"

Myrrdin nodded.

"He's canny brave," said Darrach. "But foolish. He'd o' been better facing the vikings."

"Which is something we *have* to do," said Myrrdin. He sighed, rubbing his forehead. "I...I trust Ambrosius' words."

"So then ye'll talk tae Omnust?"

Myrrdin nodded. "Yes." By his side, Eigyr let out an audible sigh of relief. "But discreetly. Cináed has set his battle plans now. To disrupt them would be treason. We cannot afford to be fighting amongst ourselves when the vikings attack."

"Ah ken yeh, Ah ken yeh," said Darrah, "but yuir talkin' aboot the night *before* what Cináed thinks. He needn't know unless he needs..."

"Then if nothing happens," said Myrrdin, nodding, "he need never know."

"And ye'll keep yer promise to wee Jason aboot helpin' him?" Darrach eased himself up off the bed, groaning.

"Providing we can stop the vikings killing us all!" His smile was cold.

"The' won't kill us all," said Darrach, not very reassuringly. "Just menfolk. Women 'n' children'll go fer trade."

"Oh!" Eygier was suddenly on her feet, both hands over her mouth.

Myrrdin was instantly at her side. "What is it? Are the babies coming?"

Darrach snorted.

Eigyr shook her head. "No, it's what Da said..." her face was pale.

"Oh?" said Darrach as he headed to the door. "Ye finally listened tae sumthin' Ah said?"

"You said the vikings would trade the women and children!"

"Aye, ye ken. They're traders as much as raiders."

"To whom?" said Eigyr, grabbing her father's arm.

"Well, their tribes, Ah suppose," said Darrach. "Or anyone wi' gold, or some such."

Myrrdin stared at Eigyr. "Eigyr, what..?"

Wide eyes turned to look at Myrrdin. "Loch Linnhe's less than two days hard ride from here, and it's on a sea route. Does Huddour have gold?"

*

Stupid sodding boy was still bleedin' asleep. Sun was high in the sky, couldn't he see? Okay, maybe he'd hit him harder than he should the night before, but the boy wouldn't, just wouldn't, shut up! He'd been dragging him since early morning now, and his feet *ached.*

He hooked the back of the boy's leather top over a broken stump of a branch, holding him upright against the tree as Blashie scurried round it like a manic oversized spider, binding him to the tree with the rope. The boy groaned a little, but didn't wake. One eye was swollen and black.

Well if he didn't wake up by the afternoon, Blashie would bind the top of his legs and eat them off. Make him easier to carry, it would. And fill that cavernous ache that rolled and gnawed in his stomach.

"Oy." He slapped the boy's face. "Yew 'ear me?" he slapped the other side. The boy's brow knotted, but his eyes didn't open. "Ah'm goin' huntin' now, coz Ah'm bloody 'ungry, awright?" There was no response. "So no tryin' anythin' til Ah get back, okay?" He grasped Jason's hair, making him nod. *"'Yes sir, Mister Blashie, Ah'll be good Ah promise!'"* Blashie giggled to himself. "Well there yer go, yer see?

Coz don't fink Ah won't eat yer feet if you try anyfink!" He chomped on one of the boy's feet, drool streaming over the leather, but the boy never moved. Blashie scowled. It was no fun if they weren't awake. He prodded Jason in the chest. Jason groaned, but didn't stir more than that. "Useless little bugger," muttered Blashie, and scurried up the tree, launching himself from its branches and into the next one.

Lathgertha slowed her pace. The tracks in the mud were fresh, hardly even starting to dry. Something small, dragging something large. And no more than a mile ahead. She looked around her. For something so small, the damned little creature had made good time. From her vantage point on the cliff edge (for some reason Blashie never ventured far from the sea), she could see Mull, and Huddour himself was less than a day's travel. She needed to catch him quickly.

The trees around her, mainly pine, offered little cover with their narrow trunks, and she crouched low to the ground. This *Blashie* was tiny, small as a child not yet two summers old, and could hide in the smallest of bushes, the scarcest of cover. His tiny stature belied his strength, and she did not want the cowardly little trowe leaping out at her.

Slowly she made her way between the leaves, slowly lifting her feet, studying the ground before placing them down, careful to avoid any dry sticks that could snap under foot. The air was calm and still, and the first breath of true spring warmed the air.

She heard him before she saw him.

"Ooo lovely little deer forlorn, hunt you stick you eat you all..." the creature was singing to itself, halfway down the trunk of a tree two hundred yards in front of her. It was watching a young faun, curled in a bed of nettles, only its ears twitching as it tried to locate the singing.

Where was the boy?

Lathgertha ducked behind a tree, her sword gently hissing from its scabbard. Peering around the trunk of the tree, she could see no sign of the boy. With a scowl, she ducked back behind the tree. So she couldn't just *kill* this noisome little creature. She had no doubts that she could overpower the creature – she'd brought down giants of men, warriors who thought themselves invincible. She'd brought down groups of warriors before they even knew she was among them!

But Blashie, she needed alive. To tell her where the Yellowblade was.

The singing had stopped.

She peered round the tree again. She gave the slightest of gasps as she realised the little trowe had vanished. Had he heard her? But she'd been so quiet! Even the little faun, its ears gyrating as it tried to locate the source of the singing, hadn't noticed her.

She crouched so low to the ground that she could no longer see the faun; just the bed of nettles it lay in. Something scuttled up a tree near to her, and a shower of pine needles rained down, barely masking a suppressed giggle.

So the huntress had become the hunted. She replaced the sword into its scabbard, and from the underneath of one arm guard she drew a small dagger. Her heart rate remained steady; she was not scared.

Something landed almost silently in the tree above her head. Two pine needles landed gently on her face. She smiled, tracking the sound with her ears, not needing to look round. He was good, this creature! Anyone else would not have heard him, so silent were his movements. He must have seen her knife by now – he'd be sure to attack, if only to preserve his own skin. It would never occur to the little trowe simply to run away!

She slowly moved through the grass, her eyes on the last place she had seen him, feigning the act of looking for him. She knew where he was. She could *hear* him. His slow movement down the trunk behind her, his almost silent giggling to himself. She concentrated on keeping her eyes front, as though looking up and down the tree where Blashie had last been. It was no effort not to look round for him as she slowly moved toward the nettle patch. Not only could she hear his concealed breathing, surely no louder than a mouse with asthma, but she could now smell him. He was on the ground now, slowly edging towards her.

Then everything went silent. Lathgertha tensed, and a grin spread over her face. This was it. The Trowe was preparing to pounce.

Which, with an explosion of movement, he did.

"'Ullo, lunch!"

Which operating room? Hurry!

Blood type AB neg, have we got any in? Clear the route! Which surgeon's on call? Have you reached them? Hold that lift!

With a yelp, Jason came awake, blinking furiously as the afternoon sun streamed into his eyes. He tried to lift a hand to shield his eyes, but found both bound to his sides. A stump of a branch stuck painfully into the back of his neck as he looked around.

Through his one good eye he could see he was in a wooded area by the cliff edge. Pine trees towered over him, waving gently in the almost imperceptible breeze. Far out to sea, he could see the Isle of Mull. His stomach leapt a bit. Gobswistle was out there, he was sure of it. He remembered the green missile that had arched through the air the previous night. Was his sister with Gobswistle? Was Etain? Had it, in fact, been Etain flying through the air last night, the Glass Apple clutched in her tiny plastic hands?

If only he could get over there. Oh, to see his sister again! And the fairy, and his grandfather. He twisted against the ropes.

"Ow! That...was foolish!" Jason grimaced as all the lumps, bumps and bruises of the previous days' battering suddenly came to life, complaining in loud pulses about being disturbed.

"Blashie?" he called. There was no reply. Had Blashie run off? Left him tied to a tree to die? What if all Huddour wanted was his knife?

His knife.

He should have stayed awake last night. He could have summoned it while the little demon slept, made good his escape, maybe even killed the thing if he had to.

Except...he couldn't *imagine* himself killing anything. Especially not while it slept.

"Comfortable there, are you?"

Jason jumped at the voice, twisting to see its source. It was a woman's voice, young and gentle, and it came from behind him, out of his view. "Where are you? Who...who are you?"

Something was sawing at the rope that bound him. "Lathgertha's my name. And I'm cutting your ropes. That is, unless you don't want me to."

"You can't stay here!" yelped Jason. "You have to get away!"

The sawing stopped. "Oh? Why's that?"

"There's a-a thing, a creature," stammered Jason, "he's small, but he's dangerous, please..."

The voice behind him laughed, and the sawing continued. "If he's so dangerous, surely you want freeing first?"

As the topmost ropes began to fall away, Jason began twisting and struggling. "I'm fine! You've freed enough, please just run! You have no idea what he's capable of..." The final ropes gave way, and Jason fell to the ground, all his body complaining bitterly. He lay in the short grass, moaning as blood returned to his extremities.

The owner of the voice came into his vision, and he was aware of staring.

She was so beautiful!

Long silken hair fell in gentle waves over her shoulders, and wide blue eyes gazed down at him with obvious amusement, the cupid bow lips quirking up on one side. She stood with one hand on a perfectly formed hip, her other hand holding her sword as she rested its blade on her shoulder. She was small, an inch or so smaller than him, but she was obviously older than him. And as Jason studied her, taking in her chainmail shirt, her round shield across her back, he realised with horror another thing that was obvious.

"You-you're a viking?"

She inclined her head. "And you would be...Yellowblade?"

Jason remained silent, looking around the clearing.

"Looking for your little friend?" asked the viking woman, still smiling.

Actually he'd been looking for Blashie's bundle, hoping against hope he'd left it behind, that he could summon Carnwennan, but he wasn't about to admit that to the enemy. He nodded silently in answer to the question.

The viking named Lathgertha began to grin broadly. "You're so shy! You really don't need to be. I don't bite. Unlike your little friend. Speaking of which..." She lifted her blade off her shoulder, and Jason suddenly saw the bundle that hung from half way down the blade's shaft. It writhed and wriggled, slowly turning as Lathgertha held it mid air. Two furious yellow eyes came into view, filled with wild anger, the only thing visible of Blashie as he sat helpless in his own backback, every other part of his body bound tightly with leather strapping. Of Carnwennan there was no sign.

"Your toothsome little friend thought I'd make a good lunch," said the woman, dropping the impotently growling bundle onto the ground. She picked up a large branch, holding it in front of the immobile trowe. She broke it in half. "Thought we might reciprocate."

Blashie's eyes widened.

Chapter Twelve

Though Jason was no longer bound, he knew he was as much a prisoner with the dainty viking as he had been with the devilish Blashie. He carried the securely bound latter at the end of a long pole over his shoulder; A prehistoric Dick Wittington off to find his fortune. The little bundle growled ferociously, and yellow eyes stared without blinking at the back of Jason's head, but apart from a few killer farts, the creature was unable to do anything.

Lathgertha walked a few feet ahead, the top of her head level with Jason's nose, humming happily to herself as they made their way down to the shoreline. Jason watched her, his young mind not entirely focussed on the peril he was in as he took in her lithe form. She was beautiful! The way the chainmail hung from her, the way her hips moved under coarse linen...

"I can feel your eyes on me, boy," said Lathgertha, not looking round, her tone amused.

Jason blushed, looking away. "I-I was wondering where we're going," he said.

"Hmm, yes..." said Lathgertha dryly. "Of course. We're going to summon the *Fraener*." She continued humming her happy tune.

"What's a Fraener?" asked Jason.

"My ship," came her terse reply.

"What are you going to do to me?"

Lathgertha paused, turning on the sandy track. "To you? If you mean, do I plan on *killing* you, no. Not unless you force my hand." She adjusted the shield on her back. "If you behave yourself, you will leave my company alive and in one piece."

"Then what..?"

"I *know* why you're here, young Yellowblade," said Lathgertha, and she turned down the track once more. "You're here to steal the the magic books from Lord Huddour, and you've seen the future of the viking attack on your village, and oh-so-brave you're going to get the books and save the village *all by yourself.*"

For all his legs were slightly longer, Jason had to trot to mach her pace, Blashie bouncing and grumbling against his back, little explosions of sulphur ripping into the air. "So? I know Gaira told..."

"Oh yes, the little fat witchwoman. Such a friend to the people around her. Mind you," and she grinned, "we did well out of it."

They were at the top of a sandy hill that led down into a little bay. A little track ran through the scrub grass and patchy heather down to the beach, and Lathgertha daintily began making her way down.

"We traded with Huddour," she said as she walked. "But he tricked us. He gave our payment to that rancid little creature you carry." She paused, turning to look up at him. "My husband wants you as a bargaining tool, to negotiate the return of our payment." She smiled as she saw the look on Jason's face. "You *must* know that Huddour has heard of you? You know he sent Blashie after you?"

Jason nodded silently.

"So he wants you, I *have* you. And his favourite pet." She jogged the last few feet to the beach. "Once he has you though, I wouldn't count on seeing Alban Eiler. Not alive, anyway."

Yet again, he found himself collecting firewood. At least the woman worked along with him. Unlike Blashie, there was no sense of danger in her – she'd meant what she said; so long as he behaved, he was in no immediate danger.

But where was Carnwennan?

He'd taken an opportunity earlier, when Lathgertha had vanished into shrubbery to relieve herself, to search the bundle that contained Blashie. It had been the last place that he had seen the knife. But in spite of a detailed search (that almost included him losing a finger to the snapping jaws of Blashie), he'd found nothing.

Lathgertha herself carried no bundles, and wore only the light clothing she'd come ashore with. There appeared to be nowhere she could have hidden the large kitchen knife without Jason being able to see it. A wrenching gut feeling suggested she had not known its worth, and had discarded it miles back.

So he marched up the beach with armfuls of driftwood, helping the viking to build a pyre to summon her ship. Green soggy seaweed had been layered through the fire to create smoke, and a black acrid smog rolled into the late afternoon sky.

As the night drew in and the fire burned low, the viking's mood darkened. She circled the fire angrily. "Where is he?" she muttered.

"Maybe they didn't see the fire," said Jason.

"And wouldn't that just suit you down to the ground," said Lathgertha. "I hope you don't think this is the end of it. What, you think you can run home to your village? That I won't take you to Huddour by foot if I have to?"

"I *want* to see him," replied Jason.

Lathgertha stared at him. "You actually *mean* that, don't you? How old are you?"

"Twelve. Thirteen soon."

"And what do you think, at twelve years of age, *thirteen soon*, you can do against a man of Huddour's prowess?"

Jason shrugged, not looking at her. "Dunno. But I have to try."

"Why? Because of the legends about you?" She laughed. "A bunch of fairytales don't make you a warrior, manboy." She peered out into the night. "Where is he..?"

"I can handle a knife!" said Jason defiantly. The woman snorted. "And I've had bow training!" Even as he spoke he could hear how hollow it sounded, and under the silently mocking gaze of Lathgertha he fell quiet, blushing.

What *did* he think he was going to do when he reached Huddour? He had no magic of his own, he was by himself, and his blade, his namesake, was missing, probably thrown into some river or stream.

"Excuse me..."

The unexpected female voice, soft and scared, made him look up. A young woman, ragged and dirty, stood behind them, a young baby held close to her chest. By her side was a man, by his looks possibly her brother, lean and gangly.

Jason looked over at where Lathgertha had been, but the warrior woman had vanished into the night. He quickly looked back at the couple. "Where..?"

"We – we saw yuir fire fro' o'er the hills," said the girl timidly. "Please – we've been walking all day – the bairn's so cold..."

"We don't want fuid," said the man, and he too was obviously fearful. "Ah c'n hunt – Ah c'n catch a bore for ye's, or fish, but we..." he took a deep ragged breath, "the vikings, they attacked...we've been runnin' so long..."

Where was Lathgertha? Jason span his head round in all directions, desperately seeking the viking. "You can't stay," he hissed, an eerie echo of a conversation earlier in the day, "please, look, just go!"

"Please, young Sire," pleaded the man, as ragged as his companion. With a start, Jason realised his fighting leathers marked him as a warrior, young but dangerous. "Please, we won't stay long, but we're – we're just so cold..."

The man's face didn't change expression, a look of fear and hope etched upon it, as his knees buckled by the side of his sister. At first, Jason thought he was about to kneel in supplication. His eyes wide with horror, Jason watched as the man fell to his knees, still staring at Jason, then fell sideways. Jason and the girl stared at him in confusion, unsure what had happened, whether the man had fainted, but then Lathgertha stepped into the firelight, replacing the little dagger into her wristguard.

The girl's mouth opened, ready to scream, but an elbow caught her on the jaw, and she slumped to the ground unconscious, lying across her dead brother. It was Jason's lunge that prevented the now squalling baby from ending up in the fire.

Lathgertha's face was impassive. "Well caught," she said.

"*You didn't need to do that!*" shouted Jason, cold with shock.

"Didn't I now?"

"*They just wanted to get warm!*"

Lathgertha stooped, rolling the girl off the man. "And so she shall. Her and the babe, *they* have value. There's good trade in mother/child slaves in warmer lands." She grabbed the heels of the man, and with surprising strength began dragging him off. "Don't look so horrified. There's no value in full grown men." She vanished into darkness once more. "Bind her," came her voice. "If she's gone when I return, I will hunt her down and kill her."

The fire roared and crackled under the dusky sky, built high once more by the viking. A different sort of seaweed had been added, and now white smoke climbed upward. The young girl, her arms bound behind her back by Jason, sat in front of the fire, tears streaming down her face, rocking gently back and forth.

Jason held her baby in his lap. He couldn't tell whether it was a boy or girl, but it was now sound asleep, warm and secure. Guilt washed over Jason as he watched the girl rock, her face a mask of grief. He wanted to say something, but his voice caught in his throat, and he looked away. Lathgertha lay a few feet from them, seemingly asleep.

"What-what are you going tae do wi' me?" asked the girl.

Jason stared at her. Did she think *he* was her captor? "I-I..." he struggled for words.

"Are ye gonnae kill me?" She didn't look at him, and her rocking grew faster. "Please, *please* dinnae hurt mah babby..."

"No, no, I ..." Jason shook his head. "I'm a prisoner too, I won't hurt you, I promise..."

The girl looked at him. "But yuir no tied up?"

"No." Jason shook his head, looking over at the recumbent viking. Was she really asleep?

"Yuir no fro' round here," said the girl. "You viking?"

"No!" the denial was louder than Jason intended, and he watched for any stirring of Lathgertha. She remained still, her breathing soft. Reassured, Jason turned back to the girl. "No, I'm from Yorkshire."

The girl looked away, staring into the flames. "Did the' get yuir village too?" she asked after a while.

"No." Jason thought of Aiken and Myrrdin, of Cináed and Omnust. "Not yet. They plan to."

"They killed all the men," said the girl. "Why did they do that? They'd won. They didnae need tae do that!"

Jason looked at the viking. "Her, she said that...that grown men have no value."

"Is that why she killed Ronan? Mah Brother?"

Jason nodded. "I'm so sorry..."

The girl rocked back and forth. "We only wanted tae get warm..." She breathed. "We're people, good honest people..."

Jason remained silent, at a loss for what to say. The baby stirred in its sleep, and by Jason's side, hungry yellow eyes stared at it from the depths of the leather prison.

"What's yuir name?" asked the girl eventually. "Ah'm Ilisa."

Jason smiled. "Jason. 'Cept round here, everyone calls me *Yellowblade.*"

The girl's eyes widened. "*Crowhanhawk* Yellowblade?"

"Folktales and fairytales," came a voice from their side. "Sleep. I'll hunt for food in a while. If the Fraener doesn't make harbour, you've both a long walk tomorrow."

What time was it? Wondered Jason. A mist was rolling in off the sea, slowly making its way up the beach to where they huddled around the fire, and in the darkening sky stars were starting to twinkle. Six? Maybe seven? He'd lost nearly all sense of time since ending up here. It was morning, or lunchtime, or evening. Actual *hours* now seemed superfluous. He'd unbound Ilisa so that she could tend to her baby, and so she could eat the fish Lathgertha had caught earlier. Lathgertha had stared at him, but had said nothing, turning in the sand to stare out to sea, her head resting on her shield. Waves of anger rolled from the diminutive viking; there was still no sign of her ship.

It was too early to sleep. And even if it were late at night, Jason doubted he would have slept. He was on the final descent in a rollercoaster ride, and the finish line was a huge granite wall. That was how it felt. Forty eight hours, give or take, and the vikings would be attacking Kilneuair. Had Aiken and Eigyr delivered his new visions to the druid? He *hoped* so.

He sighed, and stood, brushing the sand from his leathers.

"Where do you think you're going?" said Lathgertha instantly, not even looking round.

"I need a pee," replied Jason. "Unless you want me to do it here."

"Don't leave the beach."

"I won't," muttered Jason, and headed down the beach, passing the prone viking. As he passed her, there was a gentle *clunk,* and he paused, turning his head to look at her.

She'd raised herself up, resting her head in one hand, the other hand slowly tapping her small knife on her shield.

"I said I won't," said Jason. "You don't need threaten me."

"Oh I'm not," replied Lathgertha. "I'm threatening *them.*" The knife blade flicked over to a shocked looking Ilisa. "Little Blashie must be hungry by now."

"I won't run away," said Jason, but he was speaking directly to Ilisa, trying to make his tone reassuring. She gave a tiny nod.

The moon shone down on the rising mist as he walked down the beach, giving the night an eerie haunted look, the mist almost seeming to glow. He quickly did what he needed to, but didn't hasten back to Lathgertha and Ilisa. He needed to think. He needed to *plan.*

So Huddour wanted him. That wasn't really any news. He'd suspected something of the sort when he'd seen Gaira's betrayal. The arrival of first Blashie, and then Lathgertha, had only confirmed his suspicions. So any hope of surprising the ancient warlock was gone out of the window.

What would Myrrdin do? Or Omnust? He snorted. They'd probably not have let themselves be caught in the first place! But both were seasoned soldiers, strong and robust. He was a boy, even if tall for his age, green and inexperienced. And his one strength, his knife, was gone.

Could he reason with the viking woman? The way she spoke, she had no love of Huddour. He shook his head. Lathgertha may not have any love for the lord, but neither would she have any sympathy for a boy she simply saw as a bargaining tool. He could just run away now. He could only just make out the glow of the campfire through the fog. There was no way that Lathgertha could see him. But that would mean leaving the frightened Ilisa and her baby with the viking. He had to rescue her, free her, if he could. She didn't deserve what the viking woman had planned for her.

"Oy."

The voice made him jump, and he turned to the sound of it. It had been a young boy's voice. "Who's there?"

There was no reply, and there was no-one visible in the moonlit mists before him.

"Show yourself!"

A small wet bundle of cloth flew out from the darkness, striking him in the face. With a splutter Jason grabbed it before it fell into the sand. It was a small square piece of cloth, soaked in water and scrunched into a ball. It was the same material he'd found in the village, two days previous, left by the mysterious Ambrosius. Suddenly nervous fingers unwrapped the bundle.

Carpe diem. You'll know when.
Heads up.
And throw this away now!

Jason dropped the note as though an electric shock had gone through him, then after a second's hesitation, ground it into the sand. Carpe Diem? *Seize the Day.* He knew the phrase. But what did it mean?

"J-Jason?" It was Ilisa, walking through the mist toward him.

Guiltily Jason looked down; the note was hidden by damp sand. "Ilisa? Where's the baby?"

"The viking has her. She-she kept her to make sure we both returned."

"I take it I'm taking too long?"

Ilisa nodded silently. She hesitated, twisting her hands, looking back towards the glow of the fire.

"What?" asked Jason quietly.

"Can't you *do* something?" hissed Ilisa urgently. "Help us? Please, you – you're a legend! You must be able to..."

Jason held up a stilling hand as her voice became loud with panic. "Ilisa, I..." *can't do anything* was on the tip of his tongue. Terrified blue eyes beseeched him silently. "I'll do what I can," he said finally. "Stay close to me. Something's going to happen soon."

She took a tentative step towards him. "What?"

I don't know. "you'll know when. Just promise me you'll stay close."

She nodded rapidly. "Thankyou, Yellowblade, oh thankyou...*OH!*" Wide eyes shot over his shoulder and she fell back in the sand.

Jason span, expecting to see Lathgertha standing behind them, knife or sword in hand, that quirky yet terrifying smile on her face.

A huge wooden head was looming out of the mist; the head of a painted green dragon, snarling and menacing, its eyes made of ruby red glass, the moonlight above causing them to flash. It was easily seven or eight feet above Jason's head as he backed away, nearly falling in the sand next to the girl, and was as tall as he was. The sound of creaking wood filled the air, interspersed with the sound of gruff male voices.

Lathgertha quickly lashed the boy and the girl together at the wrists, Jason's left to Ilisa's right. The grumbling Blashie was lashed to Jason's back. *Finally.* They were supposed to be keeping an eye out for her signal. They should have been here hours ago.

"Move." She shoved the twosome in front of her, and the three made their way down the beach to where the vast ship was anchored in the deep fall-away from the beach. Ragnar had better have a decent explanation for this tardiness. They attacked in three days; any delays could mean disaster. She'd have his blood if he caused un-needed bloodshed of their men because of this.

As they headed down the beach and she saw the draconic figurehead, she slowed, her face reddening in fury. This was *not* the Fraener. "You two," she hissed. "Kneel." When they didn't respond quickly enough, she kicked Ilisa in the back of her legs, felling her. "Kneel, I said! Neither of you move!"

She moved to stand under the figurehead, dwarfed by its sheer size. "Where is my husband?" she shouted. How dare he, how *dare* he, send a lesser ship for her! Was it his intention to belittle her? "Where is my husband! Answer, damn you!"

Someone thudded into the soft sand on the other side of the figurehead. "Peace, Lathgertha," came a gruff voice, and a broad and towering figure walked out of the mists, his mousy blond hair held in a long ponytail down his back. He smiled down at her, like a father to a child. "Your master sends his greetings, and asks you to hold your temper..."

The rounded hilt of her dagger hit him squarely between the eyes, and he fell backwards into the waves as they broke against the shore, his eyes rolled back in his head.

"Send another!" bellowed Lathgertha as she retrieved her knife and dragged the hulking figure out of the water. "And choose carefully this time! If any of you speak down to me again, I shall spill your guts!" She smiled grimly as she heard a heated discussion above her head. It seemed some, at least, knew of her reputation.

There was another thud in the sand. A young boy walked nervously through the mist, hardly older than the Yellowblade who knelt in the sand behind. He was unscarred and wiry. Probably the son of some slave. She'd taken down their strongest without effort. Now they sent someone infinitely more replaceable.

"Well?"

"M-milady..." stammered the boy.

"Speak," snapped Lathgertha, "while you still have tongue to speak with!"

"Ragnar is harboured further south, he plans to attack the night after tomorrow, he sent us to tell you to go with us to – to Huddour and negotiate with him yourself..." the words were blurted out at triple speed, one word merging with the other in the boy's obvious distress.

Lathgertha's face, red only moments ago, now turned white. With two lightning quick moves, she had felled the youth and was holding his head under the water, her face void of anything but the coldest wrath.

"Lathgertha!" called the boy from behind her. She ignored him.

"Lathgertha, no!" Beneath her hands, the boy's struggles were becoming weaker. A second later, she released him, and he exploded from the water, coughing and retching. He was worthless. His death would mean nothing to the men above. She needed better.

"Send down the ladder!"

*

The crew of the drekar ship roared with laughter as Jason finally fell over the side of the ship, the girl and her baby landing on top of him. He clambered angrily to his feet, ignoring the ominous growling of Blashie, and helped Ilisa to her feet, all the while watching the men around him.

They towered over him and the two women, their chainmail and helmets glinting in the moonlight. Some of them still held the oars that had brought the ship right up to the beach. Each had swords hanging from their sides, and most of them were scarred, sporting missing fingers and broken noses.

Jason turned to Ilisa. "you alright?"

She nodded silently, hugging her screaming baby to her chest.

Lathgertha stood in the middle of all the men, totally unintimidated by their height. Jason stared at her. The sight was almost comical, this little girl figure squaring off to these formidable vikings, but as she glared silently at the men they began to fall silent, all regarding her with something akin to respect.

She singled out one viking, marching up to him, her head only reaching his chest. "When was this decision made?" she asked quietly. The soldier looked over at another of the men, as though looking for support. "Do not look away from me." Lathgertha's voice was quiet and controlled. "I'm addressing you, I expect the answer to come from you. When was this decision made?"

"Three days ago, milady." His voice was equally calm, but Jason could see the fear in his eyes, controlled as it was.

"How long after I set sail?"

The man remained silent.

"How long?"

"Ragnar decided it prudent to bring forward the attack date," replied the viking. "He took the decision once he'd met with the other ships."

"How LONG!" shouted Lathgertha. The man returned her gaze, but did not reply. "He'd made the decision before I left, hadn't he?" she said. "He had not the courage to tell me face to face! Send me on a fool's mission to collect his gold while *he* claims the glory for himself!" She turned from the man, and jumped daintily onto a nearby barrel, looking impassively at the men before her. "How many crew?" she asked quietly.

"Two hundred, milady," replied another man.

"Berserkers?"

"Forty."

"And who is the captain of this vessel?" her eyes scanned the men, her face unreadable, her voice calm.

The man she had knocked unconscious stepped forward, a large red welt already swelling between his eyes. "I am. *Milady.*" Despite his easy defeat, his tone was still mocking.

Though there was no discernable movement of Lathgertha, maybe the twitch of one hand but nothing more, the hilt of a small dagger almost magically appeared in the centre of the captain's chest. He looked down at it, frowning, then gently fell sideways.

"So," said Lathgertha, as the men stared at the stricken figure, "once again. Who is the captain of this vessel?"

The man nearest to her silently inclined his head towards her. Slowly this gesture spread around the crew of the ship, until all men had bowed their head towards their new captain.

"Raise the anchor," she said, jumping down from the barrel. "Set course for Ragnar. Bedamned if I'm ferrying little boys to warlocks while my husband goes to battle. Throw that over the side," she said, gesturing at the dead captain. She looked at Jason and Ilisa. "And put them below."

"You." Jason glared at the little round figure that lay bound in the far corner of the hold. Gaira sat in amongst bags and barrels of grains, food and liquid, her clothes even grubbier and her head, now uncovered, a shock of wiry red hair.

"Yeah, me," growled Gaira, "what of it, ye's no surprised, now?" She twisted in her ropes.

"Where's Anna?"

"Wi' Aiken, Ah'm sure. Who's yuir friend?"

Ilisa stepped forward. "Ilisa, ma'am..."

"She's no friend," snapped Jason, already working at the rope that bound his wrist to the girl's. "She sold out all the villages around us to the vikings."

"Bite me, ye sanctimonious brat," growled Gaira. "An' yuir doin' sae well? Tell me...where's yuir blade then?" She started as something growled in the semi darkness. "What's that?"

"That would be Blashie," replied Jason. "Want to meet him? You two are made for each other."

"Sounds like a trowe."

Jason finally loosened the bonds, and he and Ilisa stood rubbing their wrists. He began untying the knots that held Blashie in place, and the wrapped creature fell to the ground like an oversized football, his muffled raging punctuated by loud ripping expulsions of wind.

Gaira curled her nose. "T'is a trowe. How'd you catch one? Should've eaten ye's."

"I didn't. Lathgertha did. You know, the one you traded lives with."

Gaira laughed. "Go on, spit yer bile at me. Payin' the price now, ain't Ah?"

Ilisa was staring at the little woman. "You...you told the vikings to attack?"

"Yui'd hae done the same, wee lassie," said Gaira. "Kept me fam'ly safe, yui'd dae no more yerself."

"My...my brother's *dead* because of you, my father, my-my husband..." she gently lay her baby onto a nearby sack, making sure it was secure before turning back to the bound woman. She took a step forward. "My sisters, my mother, they've been taken..."

"You want me tae apologise?" said Gaira, staring defiantly up at Ilisa. "Fine! Ah'm sorry yer folk're gone. But *it kept my folk safe!* Yui'd dae the same!"

Neither Jason nor Gaira were prepared for what Ilisa did next. From within her simple robes she produced a sliver of flint, its edge razor sharp. Picked up from the beach perhaps. Maybe she'd hoped to attack Lathgertha while she slept. Now she swooped up the bound Blashie, slashing at the leather pouch.

Jason leapt at her, trying to pull her hands away. "No! He'll kill us all! I told you, wait!"

"We're all dead anyway!" shouted Ilisa. "At least I can avenge my family!" Though Jason was stronger than her, adrenaline enabled her to throw his hands off long enough to sever the final bond. Blashie exploded out of the pouch.

"Danger, danger, stabbetty sticky vikings, nononononono..." if Ilisa had intended Blashie to attack the cringing Gaira, she was disappointed. The trowe shot upwards, scrambling along the underside of the decking to the hatchway. "Bite, bite, eat, no kill me, kill you first, kill you all!" The hatchway was shredded within seconds, and the creature vanished onto the deck. The screams began almost instantly as Blashie found his first target. "Strip yer flesh from your sodding bones!"

One viking fell in through the hatch, a mortal wound on his throat, and sightless eyes stared at Jason as he stood there in shock, one of Ilisa's hands still held in his. Ilisa screamed.

Lathgertha leapt down into the hold, her sword in one hand. "What have you done?" she shouted, her other hand trying to haul her shield from its fastenings on her back. "You fool! You idiot! You think releasing him will keep you safe?" She began advancing on Jason, one hand freeing the shield from her back. "Bedamned with trading you for gold! That's my men dying up there! I'll kill you here and now!"

As her shield came up over her shoulder, there was a flash of yellow from its underside. Carnwennan sat there, wedged between the shield's handle, its blade gleaming brightly. Jason's heart lurched.

Carpe Diem.

Jason held out one hand.

"*Return.*"

Chapter Thirteen

Etain jogged up to the side of the chariot. "How's he doin'?"

Kylie knelt by the side of Fionnlagh, holding his remaining hand. With her other hand she shielded his unblinking eyes from the rain. "He's still unconscious. I-I think the bleeding's stopped though." She looked at the soldier's shoulder, swathed in bandages torn from bedding. The bandages were a dark brownish-red, and the deck of the chariot swam in blood, diluted by the heavy rain.

"That's good," said Etain, running gently to keep up. "You stay with him, look after him."

"I don't know what to do!" wailed the little girl, her confusion almost palpable.

"You're doin' fine, Kylie," said Etain. "Just fine. You keep on doin' what you're doin'." She stopped in the mud, watching the two soldiers pull the chariot, then turned to spy out Gobswistle. He was a few paces behind, Uilleam by his side. She ran up to him, not waiting for them to catch up.

"She says he's stopped bleeding," she said. "That's good, right?"

"Mebbies he has no more blood to lose," said the captain grimly. "Ah've never seen a wound like that, seen a man live from it."

"You didn't have me," said Gobswistle, his hands deep in his coat pockets. "I'm a healer. One of the best, man. I've given him a potion to sedate him, ease the pain." He looked at Etain. "Oh, stop glaring, woman. I'm still *me*, I'm not some dandy from the eighteenth century."

"Ah'm not glarin', Ah'm grateful," said Etain. "This is the longest you've been lucid." She looked around. "Any sign of the spriggan?"

Uilleam shook his head. "All the man are alerted tae him. They've reported nothin' since the first attack."

"Doesn't mean we're safe though," said Etain. "How'd we miss him, Gobswsitle? How'd we miss Cathal?"

"Dear lady, if I knew that..." the old man sighed. "I wasn't myself. That's not an excuse, but I wasn't. But even Germaine should have known the signs..."

"The old goat was too busy showin' off," said Etain. "Kylie knew."

"Only when it was too late."

"She was the only one of us tried to save Fionnlagh. Stop Cathal."

"Brow beating won't protect us now," said Uilleam. "There's nae time fer self pity. He's a spriggan. Somethin' out o' old grandam's tales by t'fire. We need tae know how tae fight him." He squinted into the distance through the darkness and rain. "We'll make Seilchcladach by daybreak. There's only one direction he can attack from then. It'll be easier tae defend. Until then..."

He was cut off by an unearthly scream, high pitched and prolonged, drowning out the thunder and rain as it reverberated around and through them.

A huge shape lunged through the darkness, skimming their heads, the backdraft of leathery wings throwing them into the mud. There was a scream from a man behind them, suddenly cut off, then there was silence.

Uilleam and Etain stared at each other, then both were on their feet, swords in hand. Voices began filling the night air, angry voices, scared voices. They helped Gobswistle to his feet.

"What the hell was that?" shouted Etain, rubbing the mud from her face. "What was that?"

"Something winged," muttered Gobswistle. His brow was furrowed, as though deep in thought.

"But-but the girrul, she said it was some sort of dog, or wolf she saw!" said Uilleam. As they reached the men behind, the captain grabbed the nearest man. "What did yui see?"

The man didn't look at him, wide eyes scanning the storm clouds above. "Like-like a giant bat..." he stammered, "but wi' a beak, a toothed beak, and flamin' red eyes, like hell itself..."

"Keep moving!" said Uilleam, urging the man forward, then turning to the rest of the men. "Pick yuir speed up! Fore and rear, draw your weapons!" As the men headed past them, Uilleam turned to Gobswistle. "Can you keep the pace up?"

"He's gonna go with Kylie on the chariot," said Etain before the old man could reply. "Me 'n' you, we'll take point either side."

"I'm not feeble," snapped Gobswistle.

"Naw, but you *are* old," said Etain. "You cain't keep up with us for long, and no arguments. C'mon." She grabbed his hand, urging him into a quick trot. "You'll be able to keep an eye on Fion while you're there."

"Fine, whatever," said Gobswistle, "I need to talk...." whatever else he was going to say was cut off abruptly. A huge suckered tentacle shot out from the darkness of the shrubs at the side of the path, wrapping around the old man's face and neck, lifting him high into the air.

"No!" Etain swung her ironfire, slashing at the thick, leathery meat of the tentacle. From the darkness beyond, something growled, a low base sound that vibrated in the very chest. Pieces of meat fell from the tentacle, transforming into glowing coals as they fell, but the tentacle, thick as a tree trunk, held fast to Gobswistle.

Uilleam had sheathed his sword, grabbing a halberd from the back of another soldier, swinging the axe repeatedly at the writhing mass. The growling in the darkness became a roar, but Gobswistle was still held fast, beating against the tentacle ineffectively, his cries muffled.

A number of men ran off into the darkness, seeking the beast beyond.

"No!" shouted Etain, still raining blows with her sword. "Stay on the road!" If the men heard her, there was no response. Yet more men joined her and their captain, halberds and swords hacking away. Pieces of black meat fell to the ground under the blow of their mortal blades. In the darkness, men screamed. "Stay on the road!" screamed Etain.

Dark viscous liquid erupted from the deeper wounds of the snakelike limb, drenching the men as they attacked. Suddenly Gobswistle was released, plummeting into the mud and water, his hands at his throat as he gasped for air.

"Get your men back!" bellowed Etain at Uilleam.

"Get back here! Damn you!" shouted Uilleam, staring into the darkness, his halberd raised. "Fall in! NOW!"

One figure staggered out of the darkness, bleeding from a wound to his forehead. There was no other response.

"Three of them!" shouted Etain as she jogged by the side of the chariot, one hand on its side. "How? How are there three?"

"Ye said all o' the monks were spriggans," said Uilleam from the other side. "Mebbies they survived?"

"They didn't survive," snapped Gobswistle, dabbing at his throat with a rag. "They all perished when it exploded. They were *meant* to!"

"Then how? Ah thought Cathal was the only..."

"He *is* the only changeling!" bellowed Gobswistle.

"We've been attacked by *three* demons, old man," said Uilleam. "Three! Explain that, if there's only one changeling!"

"Did we miss any?" said Etain. "Ah mean...it was dark, we were stressed, we were trying to save Kylie as much as the men..."

"I have no recollection!" said Gobswistle. "I have no explanation! Only..." and his voice became quieter, "only...only an idea." He turned to Kylie, who still sat next to the wounded Fionnlagh, holding his hand as she looked between them all, her black hair plastered around her face and shoulders. "Dear child...earlier on...you were asking me if I – if *Germaine* – had killed the Unseelie Court spirits. Why?"

"I-I don't know," said Kylie, looking away. "I just...I think I saw something..." She looked at Etain almost pleadingly. "I didn't know what I was seeing!"

"What was it?" said Etain. "Child, we're not angry with you – we need to know!"

"You saw all the spirits go into Cathal," said Gobswistle. "Didn't you?"

"I didn't know what it meant!" said Kylie.

"What does it mean?" said Uilleam. "These spirits, they were supposed tae possess the men of Dun Ghallain."

"Yes," breathed Gobswistle, his face ashen as he finally realised what had happened. "One soul, one *shape*, per person. Cathal got them *all.*"

"But – but *we're* still gonnae change, you said!"

"Change you will, so don't sound so cut up about it!" Before the captain could respond, Gobswistle held up a hand. "Sorry, okay? Sorry. It's just...this magic is old, powerful. He holds the magic of two hundred demonsouls. He's...the *ultimate* changeling. A shapechifter."

"What d'you mean?" asked Kylie. By her side, Fionnlagh moaned, and she immediately turned back to him, but he showed no other sign of waking.

"There's no name for it in your language," said Gobswistle. "The American Indians, they'd call it a Limikkin, or a Yeenaeldooshi. A Skin-Walker."

"I don't..." began the captain.

"When you change, you'll change into one thing!" barked the old man. "A Cait Sith, or a Black Dog, whatever, but that's *all* you'll be! All the things that you, your men will change into, so will he! But they'll only be one thing – he can be all! He has two hundred shapes to change into! You all enter the Rage for one night! He's in it now, he'll always be in it!"

Uilleam looked away, staring resolutely at the road ahead. "He's a'ready claimed eleven o' mah men. How do we stop it?"

"If all your men had Etain's ironfire blade, I still don't know if it'd be enough." Gobswistle looked at the wounded soldier, not able to meet the captain's incredulous stare. "I'm sorry."

Uilleam's jaw worked silently, his breathing laboured from their slow run. "Well," he said eventually, "if we c'n defend until full moon, at least that's something."

Gobswistle looked at him. "I don't understand."

"Ye say we enter this *Rage* at full moon. At least he'll gi' us a target other than each other."

Gobswistle caught Etain's suddenly worried glance, but perhaps wisely this time he said nothing.

They reached Seilchcladach earlier than the captain had predicted, the night old but not yet fading as they wearily wandered down the beach. Aching booted feet crunched through the pebbles, shattering frozen strands of dry grass and seaweed. They stopped a metre above the tideline, forming one long line of bodies, their figures vanishing into the darkness either side of the vast crescent bay. Blankets were spread out, and soldiers gratefully sank onto them. On Uilleam's orders, every third man sat upright, a watch while the rest slept.

Gobswistle and Etain hand clambered onto the chariot. There was just enough room for the foor of them to lie flat in it.

Etain looked at the old man. He looked older than she had ever seen him, not just old in body, but in spirit as well. His face seemed leached of emotion as he stared up at the darkness. The rain had finally stopped, and the clouds were beginning to thin. Here and there, a star peeped shyly through.

"You okay?" she asked quietly.

"No," came the terse reply.

"It's not your fault," she said, resting her hand on his chest. "All this, you couldn't have predicted any of it."

"Really?" said Gobswistle. "Because it was *me* who gave them that damned potion, to stop them changing. *At least they'll have a target, other than each other.* His words, Etain." He sighed heavily. "Everything, *everything* I've tried to do to help these men, it's gone wrong. Maybe I should just have listened to Cernunnos. Don't you think? Just kept my nose out."

"Personally?" said Etain, smiling gently. "Think it was the best decision you ever made, not listening to that horned freak. You cain't save everyone, old man. But you've saved so many of these men!"

"Only for a Skin-Walker to undo that!"

"You don't know that!" said Etain. "Stop beatin' yourself up about it! Look," and she levered herself up on one elbow, "this is the most *together* you've been since we landed in this damned place. You're remembering more of what you can do each hour that passes. Get some sleep. You'll come up with somethin' tomorrow."

"You've more faith in me than I do," grumbled Gobswistle.

"'Cos Ah c'n honestly say," grinned Etain, "that Ah've known you longer." She lay down. "Go to sleep."

Gobswistle rubbed at his neck. "I swear that thing's given me a hicky."

"Be hushed."

"My memory's no better than it was."

"You were quoting American Indian names earlier."

"My wife was Indian." He smiled to himself, remembering. "White Crow."

Etain slowly turned her head to him. She knew of his wife, or at least that he'd been married, but she knew so little of her. She'd tried, some time ago, to get him to open up, but he'd become quiet, almost upset. She'd not pursued it. "Ah never met her," said Etain quietly. "What was she like?"

Gobswistle stared at a star that had appeared overhead. "She was...she was the light of my darkness. So full of joy! I was ...*old*... when we finally...when we got together. Didn't look much different to now. It was after Germaine. Grey Hawk, she called me. Because of my nose, I think. It's been broken so many times! Oh, Etain, if you'd only heard her laugh!" He fell silent. "I wish she were here now."

"Where is she now?" asked Etain. "Is she...is she still alive?"

The old man gave a gentle laugh; a private joke. "Second star to the right, straight on 'til morning."

Kylie awoke to the sound of Fionnlagh moaning. She sat up, looking over at Etain and Gobswistle. They were deep in sleep, the old man sucking comically at his moustache. She got to her knees. "Fion?"

Bloodshot eyes opened, blinking against the morning light. "Where..?"

"We're in Seilchcladach," replied Kylie. "How do you feel?"

"How did we get here?" the young man tried sitting up, and she caught him as he fell back, groaning.

"Don't try and move," she said. "You've been injured."

"Cathal..." breathed Fionnlagh, screwing his eyes shut.

"He...he attacked you last night," said Kylie. "I'm sorry, he got your arm..."

Fionnlagh opened his eyes, staring at the stump on his left shoulder. "Praise Bridhe it's no' me swordarm," he said after a few seconds.

"Lie still," said Kylie. "I'll check the bandages." As he stoically lay there, she parted some of the bandages to look at the wound beneath. Her eyes widened. Though she knew nothing of wounds, she knew this was unusual.

Fionnlagh saw the look on her face. "What? Is it infected?"

"No, it's..." Kylie stared. "Well it's...nearly healed. It's just, it's just pink. Granddad gave you a potion. How-how are you feeling?"

"Like Ah've had one too many skins of ale," said Fionnlagh. "Mah head's poundin'. Help me up."

She caught his shoulder, easing him into a sitting position as he tried to find leverage with his one good arm. "You in pain?"

He shook his head. "No. Just a poundin' head. Dunno whether tae be grateful or afeared like." He looked at his stump. "Devil's work. Ah shuid be dead." He looked down the beach, then frowned. "There's faces missin'."

Cathal, he..." Kylie shuddered at the memory. "He attacked last night. He got eleven of us."

Gobswistle stirred, roused by their voices. As he saw the young soldier sitting up, he sat upright himself. "Fionnlagh! My dear man, you're alive!"

Fionnlagh smiled ruefully. "Mah head'd disagree with you, sir. Ah hear yuir tae thank fer healing me?"

"Least I could do, young fella, my but it's good to see you awake!" He looked at Kylie. "My granddaughter taking care of you?"

"She'd make a guid healer herself," replied Fionnlagh, smiling at her. "Gentle hands."

"Has she...has she told you what happened?"

"I told him about Cathal," said Kylie. "The other men."

Gobswistle looked at the soldier. "I'm sorry. I know he was your friend."

Fionnlagh nodded silently. He looked down the beach, at the other men. "Mah friend is dead, sir. A demon resides in him now."

"I'm sorry."

"Demon hurt me, sir. But Ah c'n still wield a blade. Ah just need a target."

"Don't mind me," came a voice from under Gobswistle's elbow. "Ah'm just tryin' to sleep here."

Kylie smiled. "Morning, Etain."

"What's good about it?" groaned the ebony sidhe. "Three hours ain't enough for no-one. Move, old man."

Grinning, Gobswistle slid down the little chariot, allowing Etain to sit next to him. "You always were a morning person."

"Yeah wotever," said Etain, one hand scratching her head. "Fionnlagh. You're awake?"

"Last Ah checked!"

Kylie was looking down the beach. "The captain's coming. He'll want to know what to do, won't he?"

Gobswistle followed her gaze, the smile fading from his face. "Yes, yes I fear he will."

"Do you know how to stop Cathal?" asked Fionnlagh.

Gobswistle shook his head. "No. No, but the day's not over. Never say die! Something may come up!"

"That's no much o' a plan," said Fionnlagh. "Surely...surely if we c'n hold him at bay till full moon..."

"you'll all go into the Rage and defeat him yourselves," finished Gobswistle. "Well. Not *you.* You're still very much human. It won't work."

"Why not?"

"Because I, like a damn fool, gave you all a potion in your food to stop the rage! You all ate it!"

Fionnlagh leaned back against the chariot, momentarily silenced.

Kylie watched the captain draw closer. "I didn't," she said quietly.

Gobswistle stared at her. "Didn't what?"

"I didn't eat the potion."

Chapter Fourteen

Uilleam almost hesitated as he approached the chariot. The sound of raised angry voices reached his ears, and he could see the dark skinned woman's face blazing with anger, her finger pointing wildly in front of the old man's face. The little girl had her arms folded, a look of almost grim determination on her face as she watched the two adults fighting.

"She's ten years old!" Etain's voice reached him as he drew close. "Ten! Even Uilleam wouldn't have her fighting in her army!"

"She has the power!" retorted the old man. "Why not? She volunteered!"

"Because she's *ten!*"

Maybe it would be best to interrupt. "Good morning," said the captain, clearing his throat. "Is it yuir intention tae call yon spriggan down here then?"

"Captain. Morning. Sorry," said Etain. "Didn't mean to get loud."

"It's your defining characteristic, wench," grumbled Gobswistle. "'*Old fool! Old goat! She can't do this, he can't do that, she's only ten...*'"

"Now just you look here!"

"Peace, people, peace," said Uilleam, looking up the beach, his eyes scanning for movement. "Ah'm serious. Dinnae be callin' th' demon down here."

Gobswistle harrumphed, but said no more.

"Fionnlagh. The arm?" Uilleam stared at his soldier. Last night the man had been nearly dead!

"It – it's healing, Sir," said the soldier nervously. "The awd man, he give me somethin'..."

Uilleam quickly walked round the side of the chariot, leaning over to examine the wound beneath the bandages. "This is..." he looked at the old man. "This is a miracle...!"

Gobswistle shrugged. "I'm a herbalist, an alchemist and I used to be a druid." He gave the briefest of grins, dazzling but vanished in a second. "I get some things right." A quick angry glance was flashed over to the sidhe warrior opposite. She ignored him.

Uilleam stared at him. "Well...thankyou, sir. Thankyou."

"Don't be thankin' him," growled Etain. "He'll be shovin' a sword into Fion's hand and sending him to his death, just like his granddaughter."

"I *want* to help!" said Kylie, her arms still folded. "What's the point of being the only one who'll change if I can't defend the rest of us?"

"Kylie!" snapped Gobswistle, looking at her guiltily.

Uilleam stared at the small group. All but Kylie had a guilty expression on their face. He turned to Etain; she seemed the most level headed of them all. "What does she *mean*," he said slowly, "she's the only one tae change? Thought we *all* changed."

Etain glared at the captain for a few seconds, obviously deciding on her response. "*HE,*" she said, pointing at Gobswistle, "gave you and your army a potion to stop you going into the Rage. Fine and dandy, it stops you killin' each other, but the potion can't be reversed."

"We're...*not* gonnae change?" A wave of relief washed over him, quickly followed by an equally strong wave of dismay. "This time yesterday, that would ha' been the grandest of news, but..." he looked up the beach. "This spriggan, the *Skin Walker* you called it, he'll attack again. Ah'd hoped, Ah'd...*reckoned...* on us bein' changelin's tae turn the battle."

"I'm still going to change!" said Kylie. She scurried forward on her knees. "Please, captain, I can help! I'm supposed to help! I didn't eat the potion!"

"Kylie, there is no way," said Etain before Uilleam could respond, "that Ah'm letting a ten year old go into battle with that thing! He'll rip you to pieces!"

"I have to try!"

"Sir," said Uilleam, turning to the old man, "we're no goin' intae the Rage?"

"No."

"Will we still be able tae change form? Become these...these demon things?"

"Yes." The old man looked across at Etain. He looked almost guilty. "I think."

"When? How?"

"When the potion wears off. *Next* full moon."

Etain snorted, leaning back against the wooden side of the chariot.

Uilleam looked at the remorseful expression on the old man's face, then at the look of utter contempt on Etain's face. Finally he understood. "This potion...it only stops the Rage this once, doesn't it? It's no' a cure.The next full moon, we'll transform. Enter the Rage. Am I right?"

"Yes." Gobswistle gave a single nod.

Uilleam looked at Etain. "Ah dinnae ken yuir temper, Ma'am. This would hae been good fer us! If Cathal hadnae changed, we coulda...Ah dunno...we coulda made arrangements! Found cells, locked ourselves away, Etain, this would have been good!"

"You think Ah don't know that?" Etain thumped the side of the cart, then stood, launching herself over the side to land in the gravel below. "It's his solution to Cathal Ah have the problem with!"

"It's not his solution!" said Kylie, jumping down and running up to Etain. "It's mine! Please, Etain, just let me try?" she grabbed Etain's hands in her own. "Please? I can *do* this!"

Uilleam placed a hand on the girl's shoulder, stilling her. "Yuir a changeling too, aren't you?" She nodded. "And you didnae have the potion?"

"N-no sir."

Uilleam looked up at Etain. "Then she's a weapon."

"Are *all* men mad?!" whooped Etain. "She's ten! What part of 'ten' aren't you understanding? She's a child – she's not even had any training!"

"As Ah understand it, if she goes intae the Rage, she'll no need trainin'." He looked over at Gobswsitle, who nodded. "An' she's willin' tae try."

"No," said Etain. One hand was by her pouch.

"Yuir dressed as a warrior," observed Uilleam. "An' Ah've seen ye swing yuir blade. Ye've faced war. You know, you *know*, sometimes a sacrifice has tae be made to win the battle."

"Not on my watch. Not a little girl." She grabbed hold of Kylie's wrist. "You, come with me."

"Shan't!" She hung back, running to stand behind the captain. "Etain, I'll be alright!"

"You don't know that!" Etain tried to grab her, but the captain grabbed her arms.

"I do know that!" said Kylie. "I do!"

"How?" Etain glared at Uilleam. "Ah'd Let go o' me. Seriously!"

"Germaine told me so!"

"*What?* What the hell're you..."

"He said I was younger than he remembered me! How can I get any older if I die here?"

The child. Power there. Power to defeat. Or be defeated. Change her.

Change her now! Red fiery eyes stared at the little group; tiny eyes, barely breaking the surface of the sand. They narrowed, and sank below the surface. Only the smallest amount of sand moved.

Gobswistle and Etain walked down the beach, the shingle noisy in the otherwise still air. The captain of the men of Dun Ghallain had dismissed them, and despite her misgivings, Etain had backed down. For now. She didn't fancy her chances against his men, ironfire or no ironfire.

Etain looked at Gobswistle. "So you remember seeing her any older than that?" she demanded.

"I scarcely remember my last bowel movement," said Gobswistle testily. "How d'you expect me to remember things like that?"

"Oh, Ah dunno, maybe because she's yer granddaughter?" said Etain. "She's important to you? The grandchild of White Crow and Grey Hawk?"

The old man stopped, looking back to where Kylie stood with the captain, the little girl animatedly talking, her arms spinning like windmills. "She looks like her, you know. Her grandmother. Beautiful."

"You remember anything?" insisted Etain. "Anything at all?"

"I wish I did," murmured Gobswistle. "I really... I just... I think *now*, what I am, who I am... I think that's all you're gonna get."

"The lights're on, but nobody's home?"

"The lights are indeed on, but only one person's home. And, my dear friend, there's been so many more than just *one* of me."

"You think she's right?" said Etain. "Think she can pull this off? Ah remember that old letch tellin' her she looked younger than he remembered. That means something, it's gotta." Her tone was pleading.

"I don't know. There's an infinite number of possibilities. Of worlds. Timelines. Who's to say she's in the timeline she survives?"

"So reassuring." Etain glared at him. "Ah hate it when you get all mystical on me."

We tried. We tried in the Cave, she was too strong. No! The old man, **he** *was too strong. The childling, we nearly had her. The fire, it still burns. Can't you* **feel** *it?*

"What if he attacks before full moon?" said Uilleam, looking down at the little girl. "Yuir no gonnae change. He'll kill ye, sure as a fox on a pidgeon."

"I don't know," said Kylie. "I don't. Yes, ok, I won't change, I don't think. But you remember in that Crystal chamber? That green fire that surrounded you all?"

"Tae do wi' the swellin' moon, t'old man said."

"So what did it mean?"

"Doesnae matter," said Uilleam. "Gobswistle, he gave us that potion. Grand idea, mind, but it's made us easy prey." He saw Kylie's look of utter desolation. "Oh, hey, lassie, it's no as bad as that. We're soldiers, ye ken. We c'n fight, we can wield swords and halberds, an' we have bows and iron tipped arrers."

"I don't know what to do," said Kylie. She kept thinking back to the cave, to the green fire. When she'd been...*possessed*...she'd burnt. The demons, they'd stroked her, goaded the magic within her. She'd almost changed then. She could still feel the magic there, simmering below the surface of her skin.

She looked back down Seilchcladach, at the soldiers who stood in little groups, the ones who sat plying games with little sticks and round stones. "But...but I have to try." If she could somehow call that fire, maybe change under her own will...

"Yuir young tae be takin' so much on yuir shoulders," said the captain gently. "Be careful, wee Kylie. The weight may break you."

"Jason would try. My brother."

"Yellowblade?"

"That's what the Guillion called him."

"What's he like? This brother of yours?"

"Stubborn! He likes to argue. He won't back down if he thinks he's right." She smiled. "It's what I hate about him, but I love him for it too. He'd be doing everything he could in my place to help. He's like that."

"You miss him." It wasn't a question; Uilleam could hear the affection in her voice.

"Yeah. And Anna. My little sister. They're down south somewhere." She sighed. "I hope they're okay."

"Why haven't you gone after them? If ye ken where they are?"

"I got told not to." She frowned slightly, remembering that dreamlike land, the strange figure who had called her there.

"By who?" Uilleam looked over to where the old man and the warrior walked along the beach.

Kylie followed his gaze. "No, not them. I – I don't know if you'd've heard of him. Cernunnos."

Uilleam stifled a laugh. "Ah've heard stories of him sure enough. Fairy stories. He's no real, wee lassie. He's a creature o' fantasy."

Kylie looked at him. "Like spriggans?" she said pointedly. "Changelings?"

This time Uilleam did laugh. "Okay, alright, fair point and well taken. What did this *Cernunnos* say tae ye's?"

"He...he said if I went looking for Jason, I'd bring only death. I think he meant the Rage. He said death is my gift."

"Cheerful talk for one as young as yerself." He laid a gentle hand on her shoulder. "Shouldnae be thinkin' o' death at yuir age."

"I've seen a lot," replied Kylie. "You wouldn't believe me if I told you."

"After all I've seen these past few days, Ah think there's sair few things Ah wouldnae believe." He sighed. "We'd best get organised. Men're vulnerable, spread out like that, and the' need somethin' tae occupy their minds. Best get 'em sharpenin' their blades." He started walking down the beach towards the nearest group of men. "You comin'?"

Kylie was looking behind her, through the boulders and scant vegetation.

"Kylie?" something about her stance sent his hand to his sword hilt. "What is it?"

Kylie looked back at him, her face worried. "I thought I heard something." She looked back behind her. "I thought I heard..."

Uilleam quickly walked back to her side. "What? What did yeh hear, lassie?"

"My name," replied Kylie. "Someone called my name."

Uilleam bellowed at the nearest group of men. "You four! Here! Now! Weapons drawn!"

The group of men pelted up the beach, drawing their swords and halberds as they ran.

"You two, go left. You two, right." He looked at Kylie. "Where did the voice come from? Which direction?"

Silently Kylie pointed to the left. Uilleam nodded, following the men a few feet in front. "Stay quiet now," he hissed. "If it's the Skin Walker, dinnae engage unless yuir forced." He looked back at Kylie. "Go join yuir Grandfer." Kylie hesitated. "*Now,* child!"

She turned and ran.

The Horned One. The Bright One. He seeks to interfere! Now! Do it now! While she's away from the ancient one! Let her join the hunt, let her revel in the slaughter!

"It's too quiet, Ethelbert," muttered Etain as she and Gobswistle walked along the shoreline. "He's attacked three times in as many hours, now half a day's gone by."

"Pessimist. Maybe it's given up."

"He's a demon. Give him whatever name you want, but let's face it, he's into one thing. Killing."

"So why hasn't he attacked?"

"Ah dunno..." breathed Etain. "Ah think mebbies he's stalking us. Reconnoitring. Judging our number."

"Think he has the brains for that?" said Gobswistle. "You just said yourself, *demon.*"

"He's also a soldier, however inexperienced. Plus he's possessed by the souls of two hundred Unseelie Court creatures. Who knows what they were before they were turned?"

"Where's Kylie?" said Gobswsitle suddenly. "KYLIE!"

"Ethelbert, what...?"

"Didn't you *hear* that?" He was walking back the way he came, shielding his eyes against the noon sun. "*Kylie!*"

"Hear what?" said Etain, quickening her pace to join him. She had one hand in her pouch of nails. "Old man, what did you hear?"

"I heard the wind on deep waters," said Gobswistle. His whole demeanour had changed from one of relaxed alertness to one of fear. "I heard the threatening noise of the sea..."

"What? Gobswistle, tell me you ain't gone...!"

"I heard Cernunnos, woman!" Gobswistle quickened his pace. In the distance, he could see his granddaughter sprinting down the down the beach towards them. "Herne! Calling Kylie's name!"

Etain took a nail from her pouch; her sword appeared, fiery light challenging the brightness of the sun above. Without another word, she was running down the beach herself, her powerful legs leaving Gobswistle behind as stones flew up from under her feet.

She had got within twenty feet of the little girl when it happened. Even as Kylie ran, her eyes rolled back in her head and her body went limp, her arms falling and her knees buckling, her momentum sending her skidding several feet through the shingle before she came to a halt.

"Kylie, no..." breathed Etain, turning Kylie over. The girl's eyes showed only the whites, and her eyelids fluttered. She placed her hand on Kylie's forehead as Gobswistle fell to her knees beside her. "Gobswistle, there's magic here..."

Gobswistle took a small hand in his own. "It's that damned Sidhe! He's interfering *again!*" He looked desperately around him, as though trying to spy the offending Cernunnos. "Leave her alone! Do you hear me? She's been through enough! Damn you!"

This is not of my doing.

The voice, felt rather than heard, seemed little more than a whisper, coming from nowhere and everywhere.

Etain was on her feet, ironfire blazing. "Show yourself! Coward! She's a little girl!"

Blue fire exploded around the little girl, its shockwave bowling Gobswistle backward and casting Etain to the ground. Without thinking, Etain lunged at the old man, pulling him away from the flames as he struggled to reach his daughter.

"Kylie!" Gobswistle fought against Etain, trying to pull his granddaughter from the depths of the sapphire flames. "Kylie! No! It's too soon!"

Etain held fast, pulling the old man away as the fire rapidly grew in size. As she struggled against the old man, his strength in his desperation surprising her, she was aware of soldiers running up the beach. "Ethelbert, stay back! She's changing! She's going into..."

She fell silent, staring. The men halted too, exclamations of horror exploding from them.

The fire was gone. Where Kylie had been, only seconds before, now there stood a huge cat, sleek and charcoal grey, its stump of a tail flicking angrily. It towered a good three foot above the tallest of the soldiers, its muscles bunching and flexing. On its breast was the smallest fleck of white. Yellow eyes looking at the group of people cowering around it.

The Cait Sith was *hungry.*

Chapter Fifteen

Etain stared up at the vast creature. "Aw jeez...!" She began slowly moving backward. "What do we do now?"

Gobswistle staggered slightly in the gravel as he was pulled backwards by her. "It's too soon," he muttered, his face ashen, "it's too soon, she shouldn't change for another three nights, oh my dear child..."

Further down the beach the men were grouping together, the foremost ones drawing their weapons, their square shields held in front. They slowly began advancing on the huge feline.

A base rumble filled the air as the Cait Sith looked down at the men and their weapons, its lips curling to show huge white teeth.

"No!" Shouted Etain. "No, no, don't antagonise her!" This was *Kylie!* Maybe if she could reach Kylie, find the soul of the little girl within?

The soldiers paused in their advance, looking up at the warrior woman. Her breath coming in short gasps, feeling more fearful than she had in centuries, Etain slowly approached the beast.

Where was she? Everything was black. There were no land marks, no sound, no smell. She existed in a state of nothingness. A wind, felt but not heard, pulled her long black hair around her, swirling it up around her head.

Lightning filled the void, high above her head. Forked, silent and brilliantly blue, it flashed for the briefest of seconds, illuminating nothing.

She felt oddly calm. Not happy, certainly, but unafraid.

She felt him then, stood next to her, a warming presence in the darkness, reassuring and familiar.

"Cernunnos?"

"Welcome, Ravenhair Crowanhawk."

Kylie stretched her hand out into the darkness, feeling for him, but her hand met only empty air. Gently she withdrew her hand. "Where...where am I?" She struggled to remember where she'd been only moments before. Running down a gravelled beach, running towards Etain and her grandfather, and then a ripping sensation, of being pulled from her body, yet leaving part, some...essential yet terrifying part of her behind. "Am I – am I dead?"

A soft laugh echoed in the blankness. "No, child. You are neither alive nor dead. You are between."

"Between what?"

"Your lands and the Summerlands."

Lightning flashed again, and this time Kylie could see him. He glistened momentarily; a figure cast of the most transparent glass, his body refracting the light like some beautifully carved prism.

"It feels..." Kylie struggled to find the words. "It feels like... am I dreaming?"

"Perhaps you are, after an effect. A dream is after all only a different facet of reality." replied the horned figure. "See, Ravenhair, see where you are."

The air began to ripple in front of her, like the darkest of waters stirred by an ill wind. After a moment the image brightened, cleared, and Kylie found herself looking at the beach she had been running down. Etain stood there, ironfire sword burning brightly, as she stared at the giant catlike creature in front of her. She could feel the creature growl as it bared its lethal smile, teeth glinting in the sunlight.

"Is that me?"

"It is a part of you. Your anger, your rage, all that you left behind in that realm. Can you not feel the connection that binds you across the chasm? That cord of spirit that vibrates in such strong resonation in the darkness?"

"Kill it!" shouted the nearest man as the Cait Sith slowly paced down the beach toward Etain, its eyes never leaving hers. "Strike it now!"

"No!" yelled Etain. " Wait! Just wait, damn you! Keep your distance!" As the Cait Sith reached her, its head towering above her, she lowered her sword, her heart pounding wildly. "Kylie? Kylie, can you hear me?"

"I hear you," breathed Kylie. She raised one hand, reaching out for the warrior woman. "I hear you!" As her fingers touched the image, it rippled like pond water. She turned to the glass like figure next to her. "I can't be here!" she cried. "I have to stop it, I have to protect them!

Send me back!"

A smile played over the ancient being's features. "Ah, sweet child, but that is precisely why you must be here, where your judgement, your clarity, your love, is unimpaired by the Rage that burns in your breast."

"I don't understand!" sobbed Kylie. "That's me, there, I'm gonna kill my friend!"

"The cord that binds sings a discordant song."

Kylie gave a little scream as the creature lowered its head towards the flinching Etain. "Help me!"

"I am, little one. Ignore the fear, do not let it own you. You are of magic now. You simply have to feel it. Let the song fill your heart, then make it sing to your own rythm." A hand held hers in the darkness. "Close your eyes. And open your heart. And let it sing!"

The vast yellow orbs held Etain in their impassive gaze, the teeth like ivory daggers glinting in the mouth below.

Etain took a step backwards. "Kylie, it's Etain. You remember me, sweetheart. Etain! Little brown fat fairy from Cookiecrumb!"

The beast showed no sign of recognition. A bass rumble filled its chest, and it took a step towards Etain, powerful muscles rippling under its charcoal pelt.

"Etain," called Gobswistle, his voice filled with fear. "Etain, what are you – no, save her, no, don't..."

"How in hell am Ah supposed to..." began Etain, her voice low as she tried to keep the distance between her and the creature, then she saw what scared the old man. Twenty or so soldiers had fallen to their knees, their bows drawn, taking aim at the giant beast. "Ah said no!" she hissed. "Lower yer weapons!"

"She's in the Rage," shouted back one of the soldiers. "It's the girrul or us! Ye said so yersen! Move away!"

"She hasn't attacked yet!" Etain turned back to Kylie. With a deep breath, unsure if what she was doing was the right thing, she lowered her ironfire completely, allowing it to revert back into a nail which she replaced in her pouch. She held her hands up. "See? No weapon. Kylie, *please*, please try and hear me. Your grandfather, let him help! His magic, it's coming back to him..."

An arrow thumped into the gravel only scant inches from the creature's foot. Yellow eyes looked down at it briefly, then returned to Etain. A fearsome guttural growl rumbled through the air.

"Hold your fire!" shouted Etain. "Goddammit, Ah said wait!"

"Move away, woman." The soldier notched another arrow. He looked to his men. "On my command."

"Your moment is now," said Curnunnos, his voice as gentle as a

feather on her cheek. "*Feel the vibration of the cord, hear its music...*"

Kylie tore her eyes away from the rippling image in front. As the silent lightning filled the darkness once more, she closed her eyes. She felt it then; the slightest thrill of the Rage that burned in the beast that was her earthly body.

Such anger.

Such hunger.

Kylie wimpered slightly. No. This was not right. She could see now, see through the Cait Sith's eyes. How could she feel such anger towards the wonderful woman before her? Towards the woman who had made her laugh, who had made her feel safe, who felt like a part of a family long since lost?

The anger was cruel. It wanted to take all that was important from her. She would not let *it!*

She could see the strand that connected her to the creature in her mind's eye now. Pustule yellow, infected and vile, it pulsed with relentless energy, infecting her with its hate.

Images of biting jaws, ripping teeth flowed along it, polluting her mind with visions of Etain lying in the gravel, bleeding. Of Gobswistle, his hair plastered to his face with his own blood, his eyes staring sightlessly...

No. She would not *see them like this.*

She thought instead of Christmas, the Christmas they would have when they all got home; her, Jason, Anna, Etain and Gobswistle. She thought of Christmas presents, as yet unopened, still waiting for them under the Christmas tree, and of the joy Anna would have as she ripped the wrapping clear to the delights hidden beneath.

"*You're doing it...*" *breathed Cernunnos.*

She thought of summer; summer in an open field, a river bank on one side, a forest of oak and pine on the other. Of a checkered red picnic cloth, covered with plates of sandwiches, bottles of drink, pies and salad. She thought of the sound of laughter as she and Jason and Anna chased each other round the field, simply for the fun of it. She thought of Gobswistle, lying in the grass, his hair brilliant white and wild, his eyes dancing happily as he watched them. She thought of Etain, dressed in checked shirt and plain jeans, slicing the pies and plating the food.

And slowly the anger burned away. The strand of her mind's eye began to hum with a wonderful harmony, its colour now a brilliant blue, banishing the infection, sterilising the anger.

The Cait Sith stopped. The rows of gleaming teeth vanished behind velvet lips as the snarling maw relaxed. Etain stared at the creature. Where before the beast had regarded her impassively, no emotion visible other than anger, now there seemed...Etain almost didn't dare to hope...but there seemed an element of recognition.

"Kylie?" She raised her hand, tentatively at first, then with more confidence as the Cait Sith lowered its head. Slowly, almost unbelievingly, Etain placed her hand on the creature's velvet soft nose. The Cait Sith closed its eyes, unmoving as Etain, wide eyed, gently stroked it.

"Fire!"

Arrows hissed through the air, heading straight at Etain and the charcoal creature.

"NO!" Etain whipped out a handful of nails, casting them into the air almost without thinking, each one becoming for a second a miniature version of her ironfire, seeking out each arrow, burning them from the sky even as the magic faded.

But one arrow made it through.

It caught the Cait Sith high in its shoulder, biting deep into the flesh. It threw itself sideways, screeching in surprise and pain.

Etain stood in front of it, facing the men, her face filled with fury. "She wasn't attacking!"

"Move out of the way!"

"Lower your bows!" Etain grabbed another handful of nails in each hand, and each fist became a prickly ball of yellow-white fire.

The Sidhe warrior and the men of Dun Ghallain faced each other, neither willing to back down.

The Cait Sith limped down the beach, wary eyes on the soldiers as it reached Etain. It growled, but did not bare its teeth. Slowly, watching the men all the time, it sank to the ground, its head now level with Etain's, its shoulder at her chest height.

The man who had been directing the archers stared as the woman turned to the creature, strong hands closing around the shaft of the arrow. The creature growled in pain, and the archers either side of him drew back the bows. He held up a stilling hand. "Wait."

"They hurt me..."

"Men will always attack that which is beyond their understanding. You did well; you control the Rage. But it is a primal force. You cannot banish it. Only...direct it."

"But...but...Direct it at what?"

"Those that brought the change in you so early. Already they prepare themselves. They sense your injury. See through your other's eyes. But hurry, child. The cord that connects you begins to unravel. You will not be able to direct it once the connection breaks, nor can you return until the Rage is spent. Watch, Ravenhair. And listen!"

"Amazing..." breathed the soldier as he slowly walked towards Etain, his eyes fixed on the beast. "Ah'd ne'er hae believed it..."

Etain cast the arrow into the pebbles. By her side the beast growled as the soldier drew near, a constant monotone of distrust. "Ah told you to bloody wait!" snapped Etain. "You didn't need to do that!"

Gobswistle ran up, and without hesitation began probing the wound. The cat yelped, and remonstrative eyes turned to glare at him.

"Be hushed, child," said the old man. "I'm not a midnight snack." Without looking up from the wound he raised a hand, pushing the head away from him. He peered myopically through the silky grey fur.

The soldier looked from the beast to Etain. "Yui said she'd attack," he said defensively. "Both o' ye's!" He slung his arrow over his back. "We did what we thought we had to." He turned to the beast, then after a slight hesitation, gave a quick bow. "My apologies....Kylie."

"It's deep," said Gobswistle, wiping his hands distractedly on the creature's hide, "but no major damage. If she were herself, as it were, I could probably reduce it to a scar by this time tomorrow." He sniffed at his fingers and grimaced. "Can't do anything while she's an oversized housecat. Call her Tiddles, maybe." He shrugged. "She'll live, though." He glared at the soldier. "No thanks to you."

"But..." said the soldier, "Ah dinnae understand....the Rage?"

Gobswistle turned to look at the creature as it lay sphinx like on the shingle. "Not a bad point actually. She should be shredding us by now. Etain, is this you? What did you do?"

"Ah don't think this was me, Ethelbert," replied Etain. She was staring at the Cait Sith. Something had distracted it. Massive ears gyrated on its head, and yellow eyes that had been focussed on them now stared off into the distance. It growled, and this time its lips revealed a glimmer of teeth. "Think it was your old friend, Herne." She stepped back as the creature sat up, the growl becoming louder as it bared its teeth.

"He's not my..." began Gobswistle, then took a step back himself as the Cait Sith now stood, every muscle in its body tensed. The growl became a roar of challenge as it looked down the beach. "Cathal..." gasped the old man.

"To arms!" shouted the soldier at the men further down the beach. He began running down the beach, heading toward the distant spot the creature had been staring at so intently. He ducked as a giant shadow passed overhead; the Cait Sith pounded down the beach, its injury forgotten.

As he stood once more, Etain caught up with him. "No! Don't follow! Get your men up here, this ain't our fight!"

"Ah'm no' a coward!"

Any reply Etain made was drowned out.

A high pitched shriek filled the air, discordant and shrill. It was not the Cait Sith. As the soldiers headed up the beach to where Uilleam and his men had vanished moments earlier something was hurled through the sky, scattering the men as it scattered a trail of viscous red liquid in its wake. It landed with a sickening thud; the ravaged remains of a soldier.

A huge winged creature launched itself into the air, giant leathery wings beating rapidly. In each giant claw it held a soldier, screaming and hacking impotently at their fleshy prison.

Uilleam appeared below the Skin Walker, a large gash on his brow. He had his halberd in one hand, and with the precision of years of training, he hurled it at the creature as it climbed high in the sky, embedding it in one heel. With a scream it released the soldier, but the creature was too high in the air. As the doomed man plummeted to the ground, the captain looked away, not wanting to see the impact or the resulting carnage.

The Cait Sith reached the area. With a bound and a leap it launched itself upwards, huge claws unsheathed, and it landed a blow on the skinwalker's wing, ripping a giant wound through the thin flesh. The second man was released, and he fell screaming to his doom.

The two creatures fell earthwards, clawing and gouging at each other as they fell. The winged beast's flesh began to ripple and change. Tentacles encircled the Cait Sith, binding its limbs to its sides, the tips of the tentacles burrowing against the wound to its shoulder. Both crashed to the ground, plumes of shingle thrown high into the air.

One tentacle arched through the air toward the soldiers, changing as it hissed through the air, thinning and lengthening, a row of razor sharp ridges, yellow and scabrous, down one side. Whiplike, it caught them across their chests. Many men fell, bleeding.

"Fall back!" yelled Uilleam. "Fall back to the waterline!"

"This is not a fight to be won by strength."

Kylie stared at the scene before her. She could see it twice somehow; as Kylie, calm and serene in this strange betweenworld, and through the eyes of the Cait Sith, her fury now directed at the Skin Walker, adrenaline and anger driving her strength.

She looked at the glimmering man beside her. "I have to win. Cathal's hurt so many, he'll hurt more if I can't."

"Evenly matched, you two are. Night and Day, summer and winter, father sun and mother moon. Neither will win on that plane." He took her hand. "Behold. The cord breaks." The image before her rippled and darkened. That glowing cord that bound her to her earthbound form shattered, and the images of battle, so clear in her mind's eye,

vanished. Once again everything became black. Cernunnos tugged gently at her hand and she allowed herself to be led across ground with no surface, no texture.

Etain stared in horror as the two creatures battled. The Skin Walker changed form constantly; first the winged beast, then the tentacled horror, now a giant bear, its jaws locked on the Cait Sith's wounded shoulder even as the feline tore at its back.

Below them the wounded soldiers cowered, their chests and limbs crimson, staining the beach with long tracks of blood as they awaited their fate.

"Gobswistle," she shouted over the screams and roars, "we have to help them!"

The old man nodded silently, not trying to make himself heard. He pointed at the wounded men, then over at a collection of boulders several feet away. Other soldiers already waited there, watching the behemoths as they tore at each other, awaiting command from Uilleam.

Uilleam saw the old man's gesture, and nodded, understanding. He drew his sword. "You get them there!" he shouted to Etain. "I'll block them if Ah can!"

"Here then, is your place of battle. Look well upon it."
Kylie stared.
The Columban Monastery stood before them in the darkness, whole and intact, a construct of glowing, writhing green candlesmoke. Silent wind pulled at the smoke, and ribbons of jade smoke trailed off into the darkness. It stood in silence, vast and imposing, its vast doorway opening to ebony shadows within.

"We have to go in, don't we?" said Kylie slowly, staring into the darkness beyond the doors.

"No."

Kylie turned to look up at Cernunnos. "What?" fear pricked at her. "But – but what are we doing here?"

"I cannot join you in your quest. You must go on alone."

"No, you can't! I don't know what to do!"

"You will, little one. You will."

Even as he spoke, the paved courtyard appeared, whole and uncratered, a rippling sea of green stone, ending inches from Kylie's feet.

"Please," she said, "please don't leave me."

The figure of Cernunnos was no longer visible. His voice echoed all around her. "You are strong, little one. I cannot see the outcome of the battle. But I have faith in you. Now, you must have faith in yourself. Farewell."

Two Cait Siths now circled one another, growling ferociously. Uilleam stood before them, dwarfed by their size. He risked a look over his shoulder. Etain was running towards the boulders, a soldier carried over one shoulder. Around her, other soldiers, uninjured or bearing only small wounds, were helping their wounded comrades to the scant safety of the rocks. But there were so many unmoving forms lying amongst the shingles, trails of blood edging toward the sea from their still figures.

The creatures launched themselves at each other, claws raking large clouds of fur into the air.

Uilleam grasped his sword in both hands.

Kylie hesitated in the vast doorway. Beyond was only blackness, somehow darker and more threatening than the blankness of the betweenworld around her. What was in there? What was she supposed to do? Feeling alone, and incredibly small, Kylie stepped over the threshold into the ghostly monastery.

Behind her, the paved courtyard rippled out of existence.

It was strange, walking through the corridors. So familiar, yet now so utterly alien. She walked past the cells of the monks, heading towards the vast chamber in the centre of the construction. Somehow she knew something awaited her there.

As she walked down the corridor she became aware that the cells were no longer empty. Voices whispered to her, persuasive, almost silent, and movement twitched in the corner of her eye. She ignored them. They were not what she sought.

Finally she reached the vast chamber, the place she had almost died. The place she had been reborn.

There, in the centre of the chamber, glowing as brightly as the Glass Apple, was the ghostly form of Cathal, stood upright, unwavering, his eyes closed. Around him stood innumerable hooded figures, their faces lost in the shadows of their hooded robes. All were silent, all stood facing Cathal. A filament of light spread from their chests to touch the soldier, and to touch each other; an ethereal spider's web.

Waves of anger, of hatred, washed out from the hooded figures as they stood in silence, beating against Kylie, trying to push her back through the archway into the corridor behind.

She held firm. She would not be scared!

"How many?" shouted Etain. "How many down?"

Gobswistle stared over the boulders. "At-at least twenty," he stammered. He stared out at the bodies. How? How had this happened? He'd fought so long, so hard, to prevent it, so many lives, needlessly lost....

"Where's Captain Uilleam?"

"I don't see him...no wait! There he is!"

The Cait Sith tore and savaged the huge wolf that now was the Skin Walker, rolling through the stones as it fought back ferociously, evenly matched, neither gaining ground on the other. Uilleam was only feet away from them, one hand clutching his sword as he desperately checked the bodies of the men of Dun Ghallain, hoping for any sign of life.

Etain appeared by his side. "Uilleam! Get over here! There's no point – they're dead! Save yourself, man!" Uilleam didn't hear her over the roaring beasts. Etain turned to the old man, her face frantic. "Dammit Gobswistle, *do* somethin'! Use that damned anguinum can't you?"

The Anguinum! Why hadn't he brought it out sooner? Cursing himself, he almost ripped his pocket bringing it into the light, his shaking hands holding it high in the air. "Help him!" he bellowed, a heartfelt plea.

The glass apple pulsed once.

"Cathal?" Kylie stood in front of the young man, one hand reaching out to him. She noticed that she too was smokelike, an emerald ghost amongst a host of glowing figures. "Cathal, wake up."

The soldier's eyes opened. Terror shone from his eyes, and they darted around madly, the only part of him moving, before his gaze fell upon the little girl.

"K-Kylie?"

She smiled. "Hello."

His eyes flew from her to the silent hooded figures, dancing from one to the other. "They hold me, Kylie, the' bind me in this nightmare, Ah cannae get free, Ah-Ah think Ah'm dead but they won't let go..."

"you're not dead," said Kylie. "You're...Between, Cernunnos said. What can you see?"

"Monks, terrible monks, binding me, hurtin' me, oh Kylie, Ah'm so scared..."

"It's okay," said Kylie, "I'm here now, you're safe." She took one of his hands in her own. It felt cold, lifeless. "Can you see the real world? Seilchcladach? Try!"

By her side, a cowled figure slowly turned its head towards her.

Uilleam turned from the prone figure back to the beasts, fury and grief burning to the furthest corner of his being. All these men dead, and for what? Killed by a demon who was one of his men, betrayed by his own!

A scorpion, black and terrible, circled the Cait Sith, its daggered tail lashing out. The cat easily avoided the strike.

Something flashed to the captain's right; glancing over he saw Etain and Gobswistle, the old man staring at something in his hands with something akin to horror. Etain gestured frantically for him. He looked once more at the men.

"Ah'm sorry," he muttered, tears flowing freely. He turned to run towards the rocks. He saw Etain's eyes widen in horror, and he saw the old man raising something skyward, something that flashed green in the sunlight.

But he was unaware of the Skin Walker's attack until its sting pierced his back.

"Captain, no, no, they made me do it," sobbed Cathal, his body as motionless as a statue, "Ah've struck him down, lord preserve me, Bridhe forgive me..."

"You can stop this," said Kylie. "You can! I did!"

"Ah dinnae know how, he's falling, no Ah didnae mean tae!" His eyes locked on Kylie, tears streaming down his face. "They see you now."

Kylie looked around. Slowly, one by one, two hundred hooded figures turned their gaze to her. A whimper of fear escaped from her and angrily she swallowed it down. "I'm not afraid of you!" she shouted. "You're just ghosts! You used to be monks! Men of God! It's not your fault you're like this!"

She looked back at Cathal. "You can stop this! These cords, you can hear them! I know, I know because I could!"

"There's so many, they pull at me, they scream at me!"

"So scream back! Scream about anything! About – about your parents, how much you loved them, or your friends, or your favourite time of the year!"

The nearest monk raised a sketetal hand, reaching for Kylie across the webs of light, its icy touch passing through her, insubstantial yet draining. She bit back a scream, looking directly into Cathal's eyes. "Think of your friend Fionnlagh! He lives, Cathal, you didn't kill him; these creatures didn't make you kill your friend, try as they might!"

Another monk drew close, and another icy grasp passed through her body, sapping her strength. A sob escaped her. "Cathal, please..."

The soldier closed his eyes.

"Get him behind the rocks!" bellowed Gobswistle. Etain and the archer hauled the captain bodily across the beach, dragging him behind the barrier of rocks. Gobswistle knelt by his side, gently rolling him onto his front, delicate fingers examining the wound.

"How bad is it?" asked Etain.

The old man looked up at her, his eyes sorrowful, and silently shook his head.

"Can't you do something?" said the archer.

"I can't fight this," said Gobswistle. "I can't, even if I had all the herbs in the world. The poison is magic." His voice was bitter. "I'm sorry. I wish I could do more."

Etain was staring at the creatures. "Something's going on," she called. "Look! The Skin Walker – it's stopped moving!"

More and more monks left the web, their skeletal hands raking at Kylie, draining her strength, weakening her. She looked frantically at Cathal. "Cathal, help me!"

"Ah remember," said Cathal softly, "playin' in the snow wi' me cousins."

One of the strands vanished; with a pitiful cry, so did one of the monks.

"Ah remember," said Cathal, turning his head to look at Kylie, "mah first Alban Eiler. All the candles, and me ma looking sae grand an' happy."

Three strands vanished, and Kylie found herself free on one side. "An' Ah remember mah first time on a ship, feeling sair ill, and so full o' life!"   Several strands vanished, and the cries of the damned filled the hall. Kylie found herself free, her strength returning.

"You're doing it!" she shouted delightedly. "You're doing it! Keep going!"

"Ah remember mah Da's pride when Ah joined at Dun Ghallain, and you made me kill mah captain!"

The web vanished. The hall fell silent. Cathal raised his hands, his eyes wide. "Ah can move...!"

Kylie hugged him. "You did it!" she shouted. "I told you you could do it! That was brilliant!"

A gentle moan broke their embrace, and both turned to the source.

One of the monks had reappeared, a green light blossoming in its chest. Slowly, inch by inch, a tendril of light grew towards Cathal.

"No..." gasped Kylie. " no it's not fair..."

Another appeared, then another and another. All around them the hooded figures reappeared, filaments of light slowly reaching out toward Cathal.

Cathal pushed Kylie away. "They're claimin' me back." He was breathing heavily, his hands clenching and unclenching. Even as she watched, their movement became slower. "No," growled Cathal through gritted teeth as the tendrils of light grew closer. "No. Ah won't let ye's. Damn you tae hell, there's one more thing Ah c'n do."

"It's shrinking!" said Etain. "Old man, look!"

The scorpion was indeed shrinking, blue fire dancing around it as it shrank. The Cait Sith circled it warily, limping slightly, unwilling to attack until it knew what new beast it would be fighting.

"Oh my," gasped Gobswistle. "Oh my oh my oh my, it's Cathal! *Cathal*! How, what-?"

Cathal looked around him. It was good then, that his final breaths should be taken in *this* world. He wasn't scared here. He knew this place. He understood its rules. If there was any sadness, it was that he wouldn't see his family again. Would they be proud? He hoped so. Somehow, he thought they might.

He looked up at the Cait Sith as it towered over him. "Do it now, Kylie," he whispered, bowing his head. "Mekk it quick, afore the' claim me again."

The Cait Sith lunged.

Chapter Sixteen

Lathgertha raised herself from the boards, grabbing up the shield that had been ripped from her hands, staring at the young boy in front of her. "What now?" she said. "Are you going to bare your teeth at me?" She swung her sword in her hand before pointing it directly at Jason. "So the legends are true. The knife is magic." She stared at the blade as it wavered in Jason's trembling hands. "But has it tasted blood yet, I wonder?"

"Get behind me," hissed Jason to Ilisa. She did so immediately, hugging her child to her. Behind them, Gaira struggled ferociously against her binding.

"Noble hero, protecting the damsel in distress," said Lathgertha, slowly approaching, sword and shield raised. "But I think, I *think*, you don't know what you're doing?" she smiled. "I saw the target up on the hill, boy. Hitting straw is vastly different from cutting flesh. And I think... I think you haven't get it in you to kill, have you?"

She was right. Jason's heart was pounding in his chest, and he blinked away the sweat that ran down his face. His mind kept flashing back to the bodies he'd placed on the pyre, to the wounds on them. He couldn't do that to a person. And the viking knew it. He risked a look at Ilisa. "Can you swim?" he whispered.

"What..? Yes, but..." she stared at him in confusion.

"Untie Gaira."

"No! She betrayed us! She..."

"She'll answer to the king! She'll face her justice!"

In front of them Lathgertha laughed, still slowly approaching. "Oh how noble! Save the traitor only to kill her later! Maybe you *do* have it in you to kill!"

Jason backed up a couple of steps, one hand reaching for obstacles behind. "Stay back!"

"Or what? Think you can take me on? Your training must be formidable indeed!" She swung at him, her blade swinging at his neck; he only just brought Carnwennan up in time to deflect the blow. Blue sparks jumped at the blades' point of contact. Lathgertha took a step back, but only one. "good reflexes. An advantage of your age perhaps?" She swung her blade at him twice, both times he managed to deflect the blows.

His arms stung from the impact, and his shoulder joints felt as though she'd tried to rip his arms from his body. He clutched the knife in both hands, trying to keep the point steady.

Lathgertha took a few steps back, studying him appraisingly as she grinned. "Well indeed, young warrior! More fight in you than I thought!" She briefly looked up as something large fell against the decking above. The screams on the deck continued, and Blashie could be heard, shouting and screeching in his terror and fury. She looked back at Jason, her grin gone. "First you. Then the trowe."

Jason threw his knife at her, as hard as he could, but she dodged it easily, her eyes never leaving him. "Throw away your weapon? Are you so ready to...?"

But Carnwennan turned mid air, as Jason intended, returning even faster than he'd thrown, catching her shield from behind, ripping it from her hands and shattering it into splinters as it returned to Jason's waiting hand. He threw it again, and again it flew past her, but this time she watched its flight, turning in place to keep track of it. As it flew towards her she swung her sword at it with a yell, her face no longer calm, but filled with anger, and more than a little surprised fear.

She never touched it. Carnwennan swooped under her sword, already turning in mid air, flying again at the viking as her swing carried her off-balance. Carnwennan skimmed across the top of her wrists, biting deep, and blood splattered the decks as with a yell, she dropped her weapon.

Jason caught Carnwennan, not even looking at Lathgertha now, and threw the blade again, this time at the decks beneath his feet. Carnwennan ploughed with ease through the hull of the ship, and water fountained into the confined area between Jason and the wounded viking. He heard her cursing loudly, but couldn't see her through the water. He held his hand up to his right. His knife returned through the hull to his right, and more water gushed in through a new hole. The knife vanished through the hull to his left, returning through wood and water behind him.

"You'll die for this!" bellowed Lathgertha. "I'll hunt you down, boy!

You and yours! There'll be no safe haven for you, ever!" He could just make out her form clambering through the hatch.

The boat began filling rapidly, the pressure of the seawater already widening the holes. Behind him Ilisa was screaming, clutching her baby to her chest. She hadn't made a move to untie Gaira, and the little woman was spluttering against the influx of water.

Jason grabbed Ilisa. "Get up on deck!" Ilisa stared blankly at him, still wimpering. In her arms, the baby squalled loudly. "Ilisa! Go!"

"The-the vikings..."

"They're dealing with Blashie! Jump overboard! We're still near the shore!" Finally she went, wading through the already knee deep waters.

Gaira was struggling to keep her head above the waters. "Jason!"

Jason waded through the waters towards her, his blade clutched in one hand. He stared at her silently. The ship gently began to tilt.

"Jason, please," gasped the little woman, "cut me free! Please, ye c'n tekk me afore Cináed, Myrrdin, whatever, but..." she spluttered as water washed over her head. "Cut the ropes, boy!"

"You never saw what they did to the villages, did you?" shouted Jason over the roar of the water.

"Jason," spluttered Gaira, "Yellowblade, *please...*"

"I saw it, Gaira. I saw the bodies. What they did to them. And Ilisa, losing her husband, her brother." Jason's breath came in ragged gasps. "And you didn't care!"

"Jason, Ah beg yeh..." frantic eyes stared at him as the water level went over her mouth.

Jason stooped; a few deft slashes and Gaira bobbed up, her orange hair mattered and plastered all around her. He grabbed the front of her clothing, drawing her eyes level with his. "I'm going after Huddour. You're coming with me."

Lathgertha was nowhere in sight as Jason clambered up on deck. Bodies lay scattered across the deck, and injured vikings staggered and ran across the ship, swinging swords and axes at a swift moving shadow that danced and screamed through the rigging. It was a nightmare scene. Jason looked up at the rigging, trying to follow Blashie's movement, and in the darkness of the night something else caught his eye. Blue flashes were lighting up the vast sails, light that came from below. Cautiously Jason made his way to the side of the ship, doing his best to remain out of sight.

He reached an oar hole, the oar now missing, and peered down into the sea below. Vikings swam in the waters, heading out towards the beaches they had only just set sail from. Jason started back as a shape shot up from the depths, burning with a blue fire, engulfing a warrior instantly and dragging him into the depths before Jason could even clearly make out who or what the attacker was. He stared in astonishment. There was more than just Blashie after the vikings tonight.

"Boy! *Boy!*" Gaira's head was sticking up out of the hatch, stubby hands and arms trying ineffectually to hall her up. "If ye's want me tae come wi'ye, gi'us a bluidy hand!"

Jason scuttled through the shadows towards her, one eye constantly on the deck side battle. The screeching form of Blashie seemed everywhere at once, leaping onto backs, onto heads, gouging and biting, then leaping away before he could be touched himself. So far he hadn't seen Jason, but Jason held no hopes of going undetected for long.

He grasped Gaira by the back of her frayed collar, hauling her unceremoniously out of the darkness below. "Shut *up!*" he hissed, still looking around him.

"Dinnae worry about wee trowe, boy..."

"Jason."

"What?"

"It's Jason. *Not* boy." He watched as Blashie launched himself at another viking, then flinched and looked away. "If he sees us, we'll stand no chance."

Gaira was delving into the depths of her clothing, one hand deep between her cleavage. "Hushtae. *Jason.* Ah've dealt with his like before." Several tiny leather pouches were dumped on the deck, and Gaira crouched, rummaging quickly through them.

Jason glared at her, then out at the decking. Only a handful of men remained standing, swords and battle axes in their hands, unwilling to run from such a tiny creature, deadly though he obviously was. "Gaira, we have to go..!"

"Bide a wee!" she snapped back. "Ah dinnae want tae be swimmin' to shore wi' him chasin' after us. Do you?" She was quickly mixing the herbs in the cupped palm of one hand. "Still dry," she muttered, sounding relieved.

Jason crouched back down. "What are you doing?"

"Magic. Proper magic." She closed her eyes, muttering to herself as she closed her fingers over the herbs. She looked at him. "*Old* magic." She stood, no higher than Jason was as he crouched by her side. "TROWE!" she bellowed. "Yer da was a stupid Fachen Pech!"

"Gaira, no!" yelped Jason, trying to pull her down. "You'll get us killed!"

"Boy, trust me!" said the tiny woman, irate eyes staring up at him. "Ah'll no get us killed!" She sighed angrily, staring at his hands. "Ye saved me, Yellowblade. Ah owe ye. *Trust* me!" She looked up at him, then pointedly at his hands once more.

Tentatively, all his instincts screaming at him not to do so, Jason released her.

"Boy! *Rotten sticketty tricky sodding git!*"

Blashie was flying through the air straight at Jason's head, his lank hair streaming behind him, his teeth gleaming brightly. Jason didn't have time to reach for his knife.

"No you don't!" Gaira leapt up; no mean feat considering her stature, and a cloud of herbs was launched into the air, catching the trowe in his gaping mouth.

He fell to the deck like a bumblebee swatted down by a cat's paw. Glaring at Gaira in utter bewilderment, he clacked his mouth open and shut. *Like a dog with peanut butter* thought Jason wildly as he slowly stood, staring at the trowe as it raised a tentative claw to its mouth.

Blashie sneezed. He sneezed again. He looked from Gaira to Jason. "Oh sod *yew*," he wimpered. Then sneezed again. Then again and again, his whole body spasming. He tried to stand; a sneeze floored him. He tried to jump into the rigging; a sneeze brought him to the deck in front of a bleeding viking.

The viking grabbed him by the hair, and Blashie, totally incapacitated with the bodily sneezes, clawed futilely at the hand.

Jason and Gaira watched the little trowe getting carried off from their hiding place. Jason turned to Gaira. "What was that?!"

"Just salt. Pepper. A little horehound."

"Wait, what," stammered Jason, "salt and pep- you *seasoned him to death?!*"

"He'll no die frae that," said Gaira, "won't last more'n a few breaths, best we go!"

Jason quickly scanned the deck. Bodies littered it, some one on top of the other, but the few remaining uninjured vikings were oblivious to Jason and Gaira, gathering around the viking that held Blashie, their swords and knives drawn. *"He even got the Berserkers,"* growled one of them.

"Quickly," hissed Jason, grasping Gaira by the shoulder. "Over the side!"

Gaira scrabbled at the rail; it came only to Jason's chest, but she couldn't reach the top of it. "Damn me! Yui'll have tae help!"

Jason unceremoniously grabbed her under the arms, throwing her up and over the railings into the darkness below. With a final look behind him, he clambered up, one leg either side of the railing as he prepared to jump.

Something blue flashed in the misty water below, silhouetting the rotund form of Gaira as she flailed in the bitter sea. Then another flash lit the waters, and another, then another. Jason crouched low on the railing, trying to make out the shapes these blue flashes delineated. Some sort of seal? But as soon as he identified a shape it seemed to change, becoming that of a woman, or a shoal of children, illuminated from within by blue fire.

"Get yer hands offa me, stinking hairy slaughtery gits!"

Jason looked quickly over at the vikings. Blashie was free, screaming his hatred at the top of his lungs, savaging and biting, his own body now showing wounds as the vikings had taken their opportunity while he was vulnerable. The wounds only served to make him more angry, his attacks more ferocious, and blindingly quick.

Two of the vikings were running towards Jason, heading for the rails as their comrades fought hopelessly against the little creature. Jason didn't wait for them to spot him; taking a deep breath and closing his eyes, he threw himself over the side.

He fell for what seemed forever, before the icy waters finally grabbed him down, the cold burning air from his lungs in a gasp of surprise. Either side of him there were two more splashes, and the vikings began swimming for the shore only metres away, powerful arms quickly widening the distance between them and Jason as he looked up at them, still to surface himself.

Something blue shot from the darkness; the shape of a seal outlined in fire. Almost quicker than Jason could follow, it grasped one of the vikings by the ankle, and seal and man vanished into the darkness. The remaining viking froze in the water, peddling his hands and feet as he slowly turned in place, seeking out his vanished friend. Two smaller seals appeared, grabbing an ankle each, and suddenly the viking was gone.

His lungs burning, Jason stared around him, eyes wide and shocked. Lifeless forms of vikings hung in the murky waters, illuminated by the moon above and the blue fire of the creatures that danced magically around them. As he watched, some of the fiery seals charged the bodies, turning them in the waters, plying with them like toys.

He needed to surface. His heart was racing and his lungs were burning, yet he couldn't move, held in place by both fear and fascination.

A woman shot up from the darkness, her face only inches from him, and Jason screamed, a mass of bubbles blocking his view as he furiously backpedalled in the water, waiting in terror for something to grab him by the ankle and drag him off.

A gentle hand took his own, and suddenly the fear vanished. A strange calmness washed over him as the woman gently pulled him back towards her. Even the burning in his lungs vanished, and he drew a deep breath, the waters around him as warm and fragrant as the breeze through a spring meadow.

The woman was beautiful. Long hair danced around her face, streaked with silver, and at her neck a green gemstone burned brightly on a silver torque. Black eyes studied him, and she bent her head to one side, smiling. Her mouth opened, and lips silently formed a word: *Jason.*

"Grab 'im under the arms!"
What...?
Gentle hands grabbed him by the wrists, pulling him through the darkness, round stones dragging down his back.
Where...?
"Turn 'im on 'is front! We need tae get watter oot!" Heavy round buttocks landed on his lower back, and small hands began pushing at his ribcage. He tried to raise himself up, to protest, but his muscles seemed to have no strength. He tried to take a breath, but gagged on water. As the hands pushed at his ribs, water gushed from his mouth, flooding the stones below. The weight vanished from his back, and he drew himself up onto his knees, retching loudly. Finally the air seemed willing to enter his lungs and he sucked in several deep ragged breaths.

Bloodshot eyes looked around him, and found Gaira and Ilisa. "What...what happened?" He coughed explosively, and dragged a shaking hand over his mouth.

"Selkies," said Gaira. "The' saved us, can ye believe?" By her side a fire burned brightly; the same one Jason and Ilisa had been at less than an hour previously. She poked at it with a charred stick, and sparks danced into the sky. "Pushed us tae shore."

"The vikings..."

"The' took 'em. An' the ship. See?" She pointed into the misty darkness. "No sign of it. Nor that wee damned trowe."

Jason coughed several times, gasping for breath. "There was a woman..."

"Ah saw her," said Ilisa. "She pulled me tae shore, she-she saved mah bairn..."

Jason pulled himself to his feet, staggering slightly. Gaira caught his elbow, steadying him.

"Careful, b...Jason."

"We have to get moving," wheezed Jason.

"Yui havetae recover a while," said the Wisewoman. "Sit. Get warm."

"I'm not cold."

"Okay, so yiur no cold. I am. The girrul, her bairn, they are. Sit."

Jason looked over at Ilisa. The girl was drenched, her blonde hair plastered around her face, and her eyes were wide with shock. She stared back at Jason, trembling, obviously waiting for him to say something.

"Right, fine," he muttered. "We'll stay 'til sunrise." He looked at the fire. It was burning low. "We'll need more wood."

"Yui get t'wood," said Gaira. "Ah'll go see what food Ah c'n find." She smiled grimly as Jason's eyes narrowed. "Ah'm no gonnae run away, boy. Where'd Ah go?" She snorted. "Home?"

*

The dawn broke the next day calm and still, the sky overcast and dull. Jason was awake before either of the two women, his mind too full of thoughts to let him sleep too long. He walked south along the shoreline, his feet crunching through the pebbles.

Tomorrow night.

The vikings attacked tomorrow night.

Every time he thought about it, his stomach lurched. Anna was there. Would she be safe? Would Aiken be able to protect her? He was unsure how far north he'd travelled, but he knew he could never make it back to Kilneuair before the battle.

He could only hope Myrrdin and Cináed took notice of the bundle he'd given them. Or rather Ambrosius. Whoever the strange boy was.

Lost in thought he headed down the beach, his eyes scanning the ground in front of him but not really seeing anything. As such, he'd almost walked over the tracks before he noticed them. Something had dragged itself out of the sea, some of the stones covered in drying blood. He crouched, frowning, studying the marks. This person had stood, heading up the beach into the scant woodland beyond. The gravel was too coarse to hold a footprint, but the indentations in the sand were small. Not one of the viking men then. Only four people had feet small enough to leave such tracks; two were by the fire and one was studying the tracks. That only left one person.

"Lathgertha..."

He quickly looked over to where their makeshift camp was. It was out of sight behind a small rise in the beach, and the fire had died out sometime during the night, so no smoke rose into the sky. Scant reassurance, for Jason didn't know how old these tracks were.

Keeping low to the ground he hurried back to the others. He knelt by Gaira, shaking her roughly by the shoulder. "Gaira! Wake up!"

"What-who..." she spluttered, frowning slightly against the dim morning light. "Jason, what..?"

"Lathgertha escaped!" he whispered. "She came up on shore only just over there!"

"what, how d'you..."

"I saw her tracks! We have to go!" He scuttled over to Ilisa, rousing her more gently. "Ilisa, Ilisa, it's time to wake up."

Ilisa stirred, then suddenly shot up, looking around her in alarm. "The vikings?"

"Lathgertha," replied Jason. "She's nearby somewhere."

Ilisa's baby stirred by her side, roused by her mother's movement, wimpering slightly.

"Everything teks time, boy," grunted Gaira. "Bairn needs cleansing 'n' feeding."

"Like you care," said Ilisa, wide blue eyes flashing with accusation. "Mah village, mah folk, all gone through your evilness."

"Mebbies Ah care enough tae stop mah kith an' kin bein' in danger." She returned Ilisa's glare without rancour. "Yui didnae care what happened tae yon bairn when ye's tried tae set bluidy trowe on me."

Jason saw the young woman tense, ready to launch herself at the little woman. "You've never even told us her name," he said, leaning forward between the two women, blocking their view of each other. "What's she called?"

Ilisa stared at him, then slowly looked down at her baby. She eased its bedding from around its face. "Critheanach," she said softly. "Her name's Critheanach."

Gaira stood. "Right then. Yui stay and tend tae wee Critheanach," she said, brushing down her clothing. "Jason, yui show me these tracks."

Ilisa stared at her, then looked questioningly at Jason. He nodded. "We won't be long."

"Ah can't be near her," whispered Ilisa, looking back at Gaira.

"Ilisa..."

"Ah cannae, sir. She's responsible for the loss of all Ah hold dear..." she looked at him pleadingly. "Please sir, kill her, kill her now..." She grabbed one of his hands, pushing it against the hilt of Carnwennan. "Yuir a guid soul, ye knaa she did evil!"

"There's been enough killing," said Jason brusquely, his face burning, freeing his hand.

"She cannae go unpunished!"

Jason looked over at the Wisewoman, who had been silently listening. He met her gaze squarely. "She'll face her punishment." He looked back at Ilisa. "But it won't be at my hands."

Jason and Gaira walked side by side down to the tracks.

"Thankye," said Gaira quietly.

Jason didn't look at her. "For what."

"Not killin' me."

"I meant what I said. You'll have to answer for what you did."

They walked in silence for a few moments. "Ah did what Ah had tae," she said eventually.

"No. No you didn't," said Jason, turning on her. "You did what you *wanted* to, out of pure selfishness!"

"Ah did it tae keep Aiken safe!" She pulled the remnants of her shawl around her. "Ah had nae choice!"

"You had a choice," snapped Jason. "Don't you get it? Everyone has a choice! Did it never occur to you to let these other villages know? Get them to band together? Form an army? You could have helped so many people!"

"Aiken..."

"Will know by now what you did! Think he'll be grateful?"

Gaira made no reply. Jason knew his words had bit deeply.

"The vikings attack tomorrow night. *Not* the night after. And Aiken will be fighting, so will Cináed, so will Omnust, and Myrrdin. Because despite your betrayal, I still managed to let them know. Your best efforts came to nothing. And my little sister will be in the middle of it all!" He could feel his eyes beginning to fill with angry tears, and he blinked them away. "I wanted to be there, to be part of it, but I saw what would happen if I stayed! So I'm going to find Huddour, and you're coming with me, and if you try to betray me, or-or run away, if you even *try,* I promise you you'll regret it!"

"Ah'm no a bad person," said Gaira quietly. "Don't matter what ye's think o' me."

"No," said Jason. "you're not. You're a selfish coward. And that's worse."

"Little boy so full o' words," muttered Gaira, "an' so empty o' understandin'."

According to the Wisewoman's more experienced eyes, the tracks were several hours old, maybe even before the four of them had returned to the beach. The tracks led south, heading away from them. Somehow Jason didn't find this reassuring. Could she reach the other vikings before they attacked? Warn them that Kilneuair was prepared for them? They returned to Ilisa in silence, neither prepared to speak to the other.

Ilisa was waiting for their return, standing by the mound of pebbles and sand that marked her brother's grave. She pulled Jason to one side.

"Ah'm no comin' with ye's," she said quietly.

"What? But..."

"Yui'll no do the right thing," she said, looking at Gaira. "Yui cannae trust her!"

"Don't worry," said Jason, "There's no way I trust her after what she did. But I can't act as judge and jury by myself. There's too many others involved! So...so where will you go?"

"Kilneuair," she said. "Ah dinnae think Ah c'n mekk it there afore the vikings, but mebbies Ah c'n help after, like?" She smiled; it was a warm smile, and the first time he'd seen her smile. It struck him how pretty she was. "It'd be nice tae do *some* good, ye ken? Besides, Ah know some farms near here; the' have ponies, mebbies Ah c'n borrow one."

"Be careful," said Jason. "Lathgertha, she's heading that way too."

"Ah'll be careful," said Ilisa. "You too, sir." She smiled, and after a second's hesitation, she quickly leant down, kissing him lightly on his cheek. She blushed slightly; so did Jason. "Yuir a good man," she said.

"Hardly a man!" mumbled Jason, grinning lobsidedly. "Look, there's erm.." he cleared his throat, suddenly feeling very self conscious. "there's maybe some mangonel thingies maybe gonna be not far from here – Cináed's sending out a few to guard the coast – maybe keep an eye out for them? The men may be able to help you. Tell them Yellowblade sent you!" How many times could he say *maybe* in one sentence?

She smiled. "Thankye. Ah will. Is there...are there any messages you want sendin'?"

"Yes." Jason thought of his sister. "Look out for a boggart. Ugly as sin, heart of gold. Brass nose. He's called Aiken. He's looking after my little sister, Anna. Tell her I'm coming for her."

Ilisa shot a glance at the Wisewoman, who was pottering around the fire. "He's the one..."

"He knew *nothing* of what she was doing," insisted Jason. "He'll be devastated when he finds out. He's the kindest person you could ever meet. He'll need a friend?"

She hesitated, then nodded. "Ah'll search him out then, sir. Just promise me you willnae trust *her*?"

"Not a chance," he said. He noticed Gaira pause; she'd heard. He didn't care. "So...so we'd best set off?"

"Aye." She nodded, then turned to look at her brother's grave. She knelt, placing one hand gently on it, before standing again. "Well then. Good luck, Yellowblade Crowhanhawk. Blessed be!" smiling, she headed away up the beach, her daughter clutched to her chest.

Gaira came up to his side. "We'd best be off too."

Jason ignored her. As Ilisa reached the top of the beach, she turned to wave. Jason waved back, blushing at his own enthusiasm. He turned to the Wisewoman, pointedly ignoring her raised eyebrow. "You know the way to Castle Stalcaire?"

"Aye." She looked up at him. "That is, if yui trust me?"

Jason glowered at her. "Now listen..." he paused. He stared at the cliff wall that rose from the beach far to the north. Something was moving up the cliff face. Something small and incredibly swift.

Gaira followed his gaze. "What is it?"

"Bloody *hell*!" hissed Jason. "Blashie! He got away!"

"He'll be gannin' home tae his master," said Gaira, trying to see what Jason was seeing. "Ye've the Sight a'right, tae see him fro' here."

"We need to go," muttered Jason.

Chapter Seventeen

The mid day sun was surprisingly warm, and as they walked through the heathers and bracken, Gaira's brow beaded with sweat, and she removed her shawl, carrying it under one dumpy arm. She glared at the young boy as he marched resolutely ahead. Both of them were soaked; small ponds had become large lakes, or fast flowing rivers, and Jason was not prepared to find a way round.

"Why're ye so fashed o'er the wee trowe?" she demanded.

Jason didn't look round. "I wanted to get to the castle before Huddour knew we were coming."

"And?"

"Blashie'll tell him we're coming!" snapped Jason. "He'll be waiting for us! You've seen how fast he is!"

"Way Ah sees it, we're goin' tae our deaths either way," grumbled the little woman. "Will ye slow down! Mah legs are no' as lanky as yuirs!"

"Fine!" Jason stopped, turning to face her. "Whatever! I just want to beat Blashie!"

"An' do what when we get there? Even if we beat Blashie?" puffed Gaira, catching up to him. Jason began walking once more, but at a slower pace. "Whit ye gonnae do? Knock at the door? Demand an audience? Share a meal? What?"

"I don't know, okay?!" said Jason. "Find a way in without being seen. It's a castle – he must have supplies delivered – sneak in on one of the carts maybe."

"Ooo good plan. Feel safer now."

"If you have any better ideas," growled Jason, "please feel free to tell me."

"Oh Ah dunno," said Gaira, lifting her ragged dress as the ground cover grew denser, "yuir a Seer. Yes? So look in that bedamned blade o' yours!"

Jason made no reply. He hadn't even thought of that! He'd seen so much in the blade, of the oncoming battle in Kilneuair, of Gaira's betrayal, but it had never occurred to him to try using it to see what happened with Huddour. He looked sheepishly across at Gaira.

She grinned, not particularly amiably. "Yuir welcome."

There were numerable low mounds of earth, covered with thick moss, interspersed among the heathers and grass, and Jason lowered himself onto one, slowly withdrawing his knife. Though the yellow handle was as chipped and worn as usual, the blade itself was immaculate, as though newly cast and polished, despite its use in the destruction of the drekar ship.

Gaira flopped down next to him. "Well?"

"Give me chance," said Jason. He frowned at her. "Do you have to sit so close?"

The little woman glared at him, then shuffled along the little mound. "So *sorry*, little master, is that better fer ye?"

"Fine," said Jason, turning his attention to his blade. "And don't speak." Out of the corner of his eye he saw Gaira's face redden. "Please," he added. Gaira folded her arms, glaring at him furiously, but said nothing.

He studied his own reflection. How had he done it before? In the maze, he'd been fighting off the Medb. His mind had been anywhere but on the reflection in his blade. He hadn't even known about its powers then. When he'd first seen the viking attacks, he'd been wondering why he was even here, and about his mother. There'd been no real intention to see anything in his blade. When he'd seen the betrayal of Gaira, of the changed plans of the vikings, he'd been thinking about Omnust and Darrach, and again he'd just been turning the blade in his hands. Not looking for anything.

"Well ?" demanded Gaira.

"Give me chance!" snapped Jason. "If you think you could do better..!"

"Believe me, if Ah thought it'd work for me, Ah'd tekk it from you!"

"Like I'd let you!"

"It's *yuir* blade, boy. Yuir magic. *Yui* mekk it work. Nae other can."

"I'm trying, alright?!" snapped Jason. "I only got it to work by chance last time, and you're not helping!"

Gaira dug deep into her clothing, pulling out her clay pipe and tobacco pouch. "Fine. Ah'll no say another wirrud."

"And how come you're smoking? I did history last year, tobacco didn't even reach here until the sixteenth century!"

"Oh, an' now yui c'n tell the distant future too!" Gaira deftly lit the white pipe with the spark from two flints. "Ah trade, boy. Fer herbs, fer tobbaccy."

"With the vikings."

"Amongst others." She closed her eyes, a long river of smoke curling from her nostrils. "Aye."

"It'll give you cancer." Jason turned his blade in his hands.

"Aye, and stunt me growth, no doubt." She puffed contentedly away. "look ye tae yer blade now."

Jason stared at his face in the reflection. Hazel eyes under a thatch of black hair stared back. There was nothing more; no glimmer of magic, no visions of the future.

Jason sighed, bringing the blade closer, studying his features. His face was bruised and filthy, covered with ash, soot and dried blood, and Jason brought up a finger to rub at a particularly dense spot of blackness. He frowned as he only succeeded in spreading the blackness, his finger in the reflection coming away as black as the patch on his face.

He looked down at his finger, about to wipe it through the grass. It was *clean.* A ripple of excitement ran down his spine, and he moved the knife away from him, so that the reflection showed more of his body.

Where there had been daylight around his head, now there was brickwork. Fiery torches burned yellow in sockets on the walls. Jason hung from chains, his fighting leathers ripped and torn. His scabbard was empty. As Jason, ashen faced, reached the limit of his reach, the image didn't halt, but rather kept on pulling back, revealing more and more of the scene. Flames blurred the scene, as though the structure he was held in was on fire, or the area filled with firepits, and the vision rippled in the heat haze. At the opposite end of the chamber (*dungeon? Pit?*) a black figure stood, his face rippling in the heat, indistinguishable. In his hand was what looked like a white hilted dagger. The dagger flew from his hands, turning and spinning, fast and lethal, heading directly for Jason's chest...

With a yell, Jason threw Carnwennan to the ground, not wanting to see his own death.

By his side, Gaira seemed totally unsurprised. "So... we get caught then."

"How far?" The sun was well past midday now, and Jason's shadow grew long. The distant mountains seemed visibly closer. "Are we nearly there yet?"

Behind him Gaira stumbled and grumbled over the uneven ground. "Ah still think we should hae turned back. Yuir gonnae die, ye saw it yerself..."

"I get shown things so I can change them," said Jason. "...I think. How far?"

"Till oor deaths?" She snorted. "No far now. See that glinting on the horizon? Way o'er yon? T'is Loch Linnhe."

"I only saw my death," said Jason, looking far into the distance. "Didn't say I saw you die, did I?" He squinted. The *glinting* that Gaira spoke of was, to Jason, a vast maw of water, stretching as far as he could see, a small island sat at it's opening. "I don't see the castle."

"If ye's can see more'n sun on th'watter, Ah'm impressed."

"I can see a small island, where the loch opens up."

"That'll be Lismore." She half jogged to keep up with the boy's quick stride. "Hell boy, whit d'yer need mer fer?!"

"I *don't* need you, okay?!" snapped Jason. "You – you did wrong! If I let you go, then you get away with it!"

"I did what..."

"Just don't! Okay? Just..." Jason breathed heavily. "Just don't." He slowed down a little bit, allowing the short woman to catch up with him. "Don't you care? About *any* of those people?"

Gaira glared at him. "Whit yer wantin' me ter say? Repent o' mah sins? Ah cannae change what happened!"

She stumbled over a clump of heather, and she fell to one knee. "Get yer hands offa me," she growled as Jason took her under one arm. "Ah c'n manage. An' Ah'll answer fer whit Ah've done."

"I'll make sure of that," muttered Jason, turning away from her and striding off once more.

"Boy, if Ah'd wanted tae run away, Ah'd be gone long afore now."

"I'd stop you."

"How?" She jogged slightly to keep up, her eyes scanning the ground for more hidden traps. "Really, boy, how? Would yeh kill me now? Do as Ilisa asked then? A knife in mah back as Ah ran? Tie me up? With what?"

Jason stared into the mountainous distance. He had no answer.

"Aye." Gaira snorted. "Like or no', Ah'm here o' mah own free will."

The village they entered was, to Jason, totally bizarre. It was mid afternoon when they'd discovered a granite path down the side of a cliff, narrow at first, wide enough for a cart, or for two or three people to walk side by side. Gaira had suggested going down it, to see if it could lead to a shortcut across the vast bay that now faced them.

As they descended the path, granite walls rising steadily on their right, the path had broadened. By the time it levelled out, only metres above sea level, it was as wide as two fields.

On this plateau sat the village. Squat ugly buildings, the same bleak stone as the plateau itself, grew like stumpy mushrooms across the granite, clinging limpet-like to the unforgiving surface. There were no plants, no greenery, just the group of buildings, acrid smoke rising from their roofs from the peat fires that burnt within. Even the sky was empty of the usually constant circles of birds.

"Where are we?" muttered Jason.

"Aneithcraig," replied Gaira glumly.

"You know it? What is it?" It baffled Jason; how could anyone *live* here? What happened in bad weather? How were the houses not washed away?

"Heard of it awny," muttered Gaira. "Fishing village. See?" She pointed into the distance. Just beyond the village, the plateau came to an abrupt end, a wall of granite towering into the sky.

Stacked like oversized buckets in the right angle it formed with the cliff face were innumerable strange round boats, and next to them, piles of netting and oars, battered and well worn.

Jason looked at the little woman. Her surly demeanour was gone, replaced by something new. She looked almost scared. "What?"

"We should turn back," she said, not meeting his eye.

"Why?" Jason looked out across the sea to their left. To his eyes, Loch Linnhe was so close he could almost reach out and touch it. "Maybe we could hire a boat, take us to Loch Linnhe...?"

"You got coinage?" asked Gaira. "Ah havenae. No, we should turn back..."

"We could at least try!"

"Ah cannae *be* here!" Her voice was scared, almost pleading.

"Gaira..."

Whatever Jason had been about to say was interrupted by a bellow from in front. A Large burly man was marching up towards them from the nearest building, a long knife in his hand. "Hey! Away now! Yuir no welcome!" His voice sounded more fearful than fearsome, and the dull blade wavered in his hand.

Gaira tugged at his arm. "See now, we're not wanted, so let's be gone!"

Jason pulled his arm back, then hold both hands up. "Hi! Hello, we're here from Kilneuair..."

"Go back where ye came then!" bellowed the man as he approached. Even with the distance between them, Jason could see the fear in his face, hear the bluster in his voice. "Whitwey yer here fer?"

"We-we..." Jason watched the man warily. Scared as he was, for no obvious reason Jason could see, he was potentially as dangerous as the vikings they had so recently escaped. "Please, we mean no harm, we'll go if you want – we were just looking for transport to Loch Linnhe..."

"Is it no' enough yuir wi'in t'boundries, bairn?" growled the man. "Bringin' yon pech with ye! Ye wantin' tae draw his eye like?" He stared at Gaira, his eyes wide. To Jason's astonishment, Gaira moved behind him, like a little child hiding behind its parent.

"You mean Huddour, don't you?" said Jason quietly.

"Be hushed!" yelped the man. "Devil's spawn!"

"Look, don't be afraid, no please, put the knife down!" The man had reached them, his face pale, the knife wavering in front of him. "Look, we've been sent by King Cináed and Myrrdin, we're here to...we've been sent to stop Huddour!" He flushed slightly, at this mixing of lies and the truth.

But it worked. The man's knife lowered slightly. "But...but yuir a bairn!" his tone was not derisive, but more questioning. "The king sent ye? Wi' a *pech?*"

Jason had no idea what a *pech* was. He nodded silently.

The man stared at Jason and Gaira. "The *king* sent yer wi' a pech? A boy? How...how can Ah trust ye's? Yui could be th'work o' Stalcaire's master!" The knife came back up. "Prove it, boy!"

Prove it? Jason's heart was racing. How could he prove a *lie?* He could feel his mouth drying out, his tongue cleaving to the roof of his mouth. "Er.."

"Yuir *name*," hissed Gaira from behind. "Tell 'im yuir name!"

"My name? My name!" He felt a flood of relief flooding through him. Maybe there were some uses to being legendary after all. "My name is Yellowblade Crowanhawk. I was named by the Gwyllion..."

"Aye, an' Ah'm Herne th' bluidy hunter," growled the man. "yui mockin' me now?"

"Oh fer...Yuir *blade!*" hissed Gaira, peering up at the frightened man. "Show him yer blade!"

"Slowly now!" said the man, as Jason eased Carnwennan from its sheath. Jason nodded, and gently lifted the gleaming blade up, its point down, to hold it between them. He slowly released his grip on the hilt; Carnwennan hung in the air, gently rotating, flashes of sunlight illuminating the man's face.

The man stared at the slowly spinning blade, his face unreadable. His knife fell from his fingers, ringing loudly on the stone below, and he started slightly, his gaze torn from Carnwennan.

He looked at the boy and the woman, then looked around him. There was no-one else in sight. "Get ye's inside," he muttered, retrieving his knife from the ground. He walked away from them, not looking back.

Jason looked at his companion, his face questioning. "What..?"

"Oh no," snapped Gaira, "dinnae be looking tae me! This was yuir idea!"

"Fine..." muttered Jason. He squared his shoulders, re-sheathing his blade. "Fine. So we go in." With only the briefest of hesitations, he set off after the man, leaving Gaira by herself on the rocks.

She watched the boy walk away. Now was her chance. There was no-one else in sight. All she had to do was turn round, walk away, just keep on going, see no-one...

The wind tugged gently at her hair, and she pulled her tattered and salt stained clothes tighter around her. No. Running away was for cowards. She'd been many things in her time. A coward had never been one of them.

In the distance, Jason turned to face her. "You coming?" he called.

Resolutely, she set off after him.

The dark windowless room stank of fish. Jason gagged slightly as he ducked under the low door frame, one hand over his nose. As his eyes adjusted to the dark, he saw the glowing embers of what had once been a large fire, stacked in a shallow pit in the middle of the single room. One chair sat by the side of this pit, and it was to this chair the timid man headed.

The man seated himself on the edge of the chair, perched as though ready to flee at any moment as he watched Jason, and then Gaira, enter the room. He rested his long knife over his knee, one hand on the well worn hilt. It wasn't a battle knife; Jason realised that. The timidness of the man suggested he'd never fought in any battles. Would probably have run away in fact. It was maybe some sort of knife for cutting up fish. This didn't make the knife any less dangerous however, and Jason kept a wary eye on it in the soft amber light from the fire as he edged further into the room.

The man stared at them, his eyes wide. "So...the king sent ye's?"

"Yes," said Jason, trying to sound authoritative. "Yes, we were sent by Cináed Mac Ailpin to..."

"Ye's gonnae kill Huddour?" interrupted the man. "Kill him dead like?" His tone was almost pleading.

"Or get killed tryin'," muttered Gaira.

The man glared at her. "Ah wus speakin' tae yon warrior bairn, pech," he said, almost spitting the last word. She ignored him, her feet clearing a circle of floor from soot and ash, before sitting down, leaning in towards the embers, warming her hands.

"Me dah, me grandfer, the' died under his rule, ye ken," said the man. "Ah came here, hopin' Ah were away fro' him, his men, but his reach, oh it's sair long, an-an' strong!" He looked beseechingly up at Jason. "Can ye's really stop him?"

He sounded like a little child in his wide eyed earnestness and fear, realised Jason. "I...I'm gonna try," he said. "I have to."

"The legends then," said the man, "the stories aboot ye's, they're true then?"

Jason stared at him, totally at a loss what to say. He didn't *feel* like the stuff of legends. He took a deep breath. "They're prophecies. I've yet to fulfil them." That sounded like an evasion, even to him. "But Myrrdin, he thinks they're accurate."

"O'course he does," said Gaira. "He's yer grandfer."

"The druid's yer gran'fer?" said the man incredulously.

Jason glared at Gaira. "Yes. Yes he is."

The man looked from the boy to the little woman. "He's a sair powerful druid. And you're his kin?" His lips trembled, as though he were trying to suppress a grin.

Jason nodded silently. The man, with his nervous, almost childish mannerisms, were beginning to unsettle him. "Okay, so you know about us," he said. "Who're you?"

"Me?" said the man. He twisted his hands in front of him. "Bothen. Clan o' Cary. Why?" His eyes narrowed, and he stood. "Why? Yui plannin' on sellin' me oot tae Huddour? There's strength in names. Strength, yes," and he turned away, his hands still twisting away at his chest. "Strength in names, strength in names...."

Jason looked over nervously at Gaira, who was staring wide eyed at the man. As she felt Jason's stare, she turned to him, silently tapping the side of her head. The man obviously wasn't all there.

He turned back to the man who called himself Bothen. "What...what happened here? Where are the rest of the villages? I saw the fires, but you're the only..."

"Gone away, tekken," muttered Bothen, scratching at the few black wisps of hair on his head. "Alban Eiler, come tae take her, fifty or more'll open the door..."

"Sorry," said Jason, frowning, "d'you mean the vikings?"

"Vikings, aye, vikings," said Bothen, "but no' fer them, fer *him* d'ye see." Something clattered through the roof up above, startling both Jason and Gaira, but the man hardly twitched. "Damned gulls, the' smell the death a'ready, and me blood still flows, still pumps, still shows..." He began pacing in the tightest of circles. "Eat me before Ah'm gone, peck and blind, not yet not now..."

Gaira lightly touched Jason's arm. "Best we go?" she whispered.

Jason gave a quick nod. "Erm, Bothen, listen, we've got to go now..."

"Tekk me?" said Bothen instantly.

"What?" said Jason and Gaira together.

"Ah c'n cut!" declared Bothen, retrieving his knife. "Ah c'n fight!" He swung it ineffectually through the air. "See?"

"That-that's very kind of you," said Jason politely, "but we're in a hurry, see? And it'll be dangerous."

"Hurry, yes, but how ye gonnae get there? Walk an' run? Swim? Fly?"

"I..."

"Ah've a boat! Ah c'n sails ye's there! Wind'll be up in a while –

Ah'll get ye tae the castle afore the sun's gontae bed!" He sounded like a child begging to play.

Something clattered over the roof again and the man gave out a wordless yell of anger.

A boat? Jason looked over at his reluctant companion. A boat would halve their journey. She shook her head silently.

"Saw that, Ah did," said Bothen. "Pech! Pish pash posh, builder of ruins!" He turned back to Jason. "Please? Please." He followed Jason's eyes to the knife in his hand. "Ah-Ah'll leave mah blade behind if ye's want, but he's got mah people! Mah daughter, she kept me safe like, kept me whole, please?"

Jason looked down at Gaira. "He could save us time. Something happens on Alban Eiler. I don't know what, but something important."

Gaira didn't look at him. She stared into the embers, one finger scratching her nose. She got to her feet. "Whatever."

The harbour, if it could be called that, was small, gloomy and full of treacherous rocks. The boat they were heading down the rocky steps towards was large and oval, bobbing merrily in the swell, tugging angrily at the rope that tethered it to the harbour wall.

As good as his word, Bothen had left his knife in the dark little building, much to Jason's relief. The man still made him wildly uncomfortable, but he felt a lot safer now the man was unarmed. And it would only be for an hour or so. Once they'd reached land, they'd send him on his way again.

"Quick now," said Bethon, jumping into the dancing boat and holding a hand out to Jason. "In, get in, afore his eyes look o'er here."

"You sure this is safe?" said Jason. The boat looked ancient, its base filled with black ropes and battered oars.

"Seen twenty seasons, warrior child, one afternoon in't gonnae sink it." The man thrust his hand towards Jason. "In!"

Taking Bothen's hand for balance, he gingerly stepped into the boat, almost falling instantly as the boat bucked beneath his feet. He made his way over to the far side, sitting down on the plank there.

Gaira held her hand out for help, but with a distasteful glance, Bothen turned away.

"Fine." Gaira jumped into the boat, remaining on her feet even as the boat danced wildly under this sudden addition of weight. She grinned as Bothen stumbled briefly.

Bothen straightened, his face filled with anger. He advanced through the coils of ropes on Gaira, one hand raised.

"*Bothen!*" Jason was surprised by the authority in his own voice. "We have to *go.*"

Bothen paused, his hand still raised as Gaira stared unflinchingly up at him. Then he turned, sitting on the middle plank with his back to the little woman. "And go we shall, warrior child." He placed an oar into the rungs either side of him, then cast off the tether.

Strong arms quickly pulled them out into the waters, leaving the silent lifeless village behind them. Gaira stared back at the village, her brow furrowed.

Jason stared at Gaira. She was staring into the sky, watching the birds as they circled overhead, her face pale and scared. Bothen sat between them, his face ruddy from exertion as he kept an even rhythm going.

"Gaira?" he called. "What is it? What's wrong?"

She quickly shook her head, pointing first at the sky, then at Bothen. Jason looked up at the gulls, then down at Bothen.

He frowned. "I-I don't get you?"

She frantically placed a finger to her lips, then pointed forcefully up at the sky, then at Bothen again.

"Ah see ye's, pech," said Bothen, amiably enough. "Eyes in th' back o' me head, me." He looked up at the birds. "Aye, the' follow. Smell the death, don't they though?"

Behind him gestured with her hands in exasperation, as though to say *well?*

Bothen lay down his oars. "See now. We're at the mouth of Loch Linnhe. Here'll do." He smiled broadly, then reached down to the coils of black rope. "Wee Jason, can ye's grab yon rope by yer feet?"

"What..what for?" Jason watched as Bothen hauled the rope over the side of the boat. As it fell, Jason noticed its end was knotted to the side of the little craft.

"It's tae speed us up. Only minutes away now, warrior child." He smiled at Jason. "Go on. Go on then."

"But surely they'll slow us down," said Jason. "I thought you send the wind'd be up? Where...where're your sails?"

"Sails?" grinned Bothen. "Who needs sails? I have a far faster method!" He sighed as Jason didn't move, then stood, grabbing the ropes by Jason's feet. "Oh very well, I shall do it."

"Where were the gulls?" demanded Gaira suddenly. "The gulls in the roof? There was nae life in that village! Where were they?"

Bothen leaned over the side of the boat, watching the ropes uncoil, the current pulling them behind the boat. He smiled up at Gaira. "Mirror mirror under bed, which feisty pech will end up dead?" He looked over at the shoreline. "Oh look, here he comes now. The er...*gull.*"

His heart suddenly pounding, Jason followed his gaze. Something had entered the water, something small, with sharp pointed ears, and greasy hair that trailed out behind it as it swam.

Jason leapt to his feet, fear keeping him upright in the rocking boat.

Carnwennan shone brightly in his hand. "Who are you?"

Bothen grinned. "Oh please. How gullible are you really? Ever hear of the vikings leaving one person alive in a village they've raided? And a man at that!" He looked at Jason's glimmering blade. "So this is the legendary Seer's Blade Gaira's told us so much about?"

"Y-You're Huddour," breathed Jason. He should have known. He *should* have!

'Bothen' laughed, clapping his hands delightedly. "You see? It only took you an hour to work it out! Even the pech knew something was wrong before you did! And speaking of which..." he turned in his seat, one finger pointing at the cowering woman. Rope leapt up from the deck, binding her in seconds.

"No!" Shouted Jason. Without thinking, he drew his hand back, throwing Carnwennan forward, feeling the powerful magic flowing through him, directing the blade at the sorcerer's head.

A large hand caught the blade mid air, and Huddour turned the blade in his hands, staring at it intently. He sniffed it, then made a pretence of waving away a smell. "*This* is what the Gwyllion gave you? A kitchen knife?" He smiled. "How very terrifying. If one was a root vegetable I suppose." He held up its handle. "And what a vile hilt!" Holding the blade and hilt in opposing hands, he pulled the knife apart without effort, dropping the yellow handle over the side. "I shall have something much more fitting constructed when we reach home."

Jason lunged to the side of the ship, trying to catch the hilt, watching in horror as it sank into darkness. "No..."

"Awww have I broken your ikkle toy?" laughed Huddour. The smile faded, and suddenly Huddour's face was only an inch from Jason's. "Silly little boy. My powers are beyond your comprehension. You've failed. The Gwyllion failed. And Myrrdin and Cináed, failed and failed." Jason's blade came up, stroking his cheek. "And silly little boys who fail get punished." Huddour gently pulled the blade down Jason's cheek, and Jason whimpered against his will as a thin red line of blood was left behind.

And then Huddour was seated again, the blade of Carnwennan thrust into his belt. Jason fell to the deck. Ropes began to slither over him, binding his arms and legs.

"Ah, young Blashie!" said Huddour as the little trowe, gasping, clambered over the side of the boat.

"Flippin' makin' me swim," wheezed the little creature, "An' Ah hates sodding water, but no, couldn't get in the boat till they couldn't escape, an' water full of wetness too..."

"Oh be still, you sad little trowe," said Huddour. "You can have the pech if that'll keep you happy."

"Ooo..." Blashie clambered over to where Gaira, eyes wide, lay bound.

"'Ullo, lunch!"

"Not now," snapped Huddour, one hand striking the little creature over the back of his head. "Alban Eiler! When we use the boy!"

"Yes Sire, sorry Sire, did good though, didn't I? Bringing you the boy, told you he'd come, didn't I?"

"Yes, yes, you did very well of course," and Huddour ruffled the creatures soggy head, "and you have all that gold waiting for you when you get home! Aren't you lucky?"

The water began to boil and churn around the boat, and Huddour clapped his hands delightedly. "Ah! My pets!"

Shapes constructed of water began rising either side; large horses, white froth for manes, fiery red pits of anger for eyes. They raked at the air with their liquid hooves, biting and fighting with each other as they surrounded the rocking boat.

Huddour smiled happily at Jason. "Didn't I tell you I had far faster methods! You don't get much faster than Kelpies! You see what the ropes are for now? Or do you need more clues?"

Jason closed his eyes. He'd lost. He'd failed in his mission. Anna and Kylie, they'd be trapped here forever. He could only pray Cináed had got his warning.

Chapter Eighteen

Myrrdin looked despondently around at the small gathering of people. Darrach sat on one of the logs, Eigyr by his side, layers of woollen blankets pulled tight round her figure as she stroked her belly, stretching every so often to ease her aching back. Closer to the large fire was Aiken, sitting contentedly with the little girl Anna dozing in his lap.

Omnust paced round the fire, his face alight with expectations as he kept darting glances at the Druid. Around him were eight soldiers, either seated or standing, all waiting expectantly. A few village folk were dotted here and there; old women leaning on sticks, weatherworn men nervously stoking the fire. Behind them the moon shone brightly in the early evening, almost full now, its light dancing across the surface of Loch Awe as they sat on its banks. Far into the distance sat Kilneuair, streamers of smoke reaching lazily up into the still air.

"Less men than yui were expectin', then?" said Darrach quietly.

"Yes. Yes, far less." Myrrdin could not keep the disappointment from his voice.

"Would yui hae me empty th'barracks, mon?" said Darrach, leaning on his staff. "Think yon king might hae noticed that."

"But..."

"Two men fro' each o' the barrack rooms. Th' men left behind knae this meetin's happenin', no worries on that score. They'll hear what you have to say." He looked up at the Druid. "When yui find yer voice, anyway."

"Sorry," said Myrrdin sheepishly. "Sorry. I was just expecting..."

"Wars can be won wi' words as well as wi' weapons. Yui just hae tae find th' right ears tae assail." Darrach smiled. "Look around you. These ears're willin' tae spread what the' hear." He poked Myrrdin with one bony finger. "So make sure it's good."

"I'll do my best," said Myrrdin wryly as he slowly stood, brushing flakes of bark and ash from his robes. "I just hope it's good enough."

The nervous muttering of the small group quickly faded. Those standing quickly found themselves an area of ground to sit on as Myrrdin moved to the side of the fire, and Myrrdin felt the sudden weight of numerous eyes on him.

"Thank you all for coming," he said slowly. "Are there any here who don't know why Omnust and Darrach bid you come?"

No-one replied. A few people shifted their position, getting more comfortable, looking up patiently at Myrrdin.

"Good. So you know of the new visions of Jason." He breathed a sigh of relief inwardly. He'd almost expected a replay of his meeting with Cináed, of the anger and disbelief he'd encountered. "So you know...you know that the vikings attack tomorrow night. The King does not believe this to be the case; he believes the writings brought to me by Lady Ivory to be fake, written by his captors."

"Ye think him killed then?" said one old woman. The old man by her side shoved her, frowning.

"I...no, no I don't," said Myrrdin. "I think he's been captured, but I do not believe his life has been taken. I remember the prophesy just as our king does, though my interpretation may be slightly different. *Even predictions prove costly, And the young shall fail through adversity.* Yes, I believe for the moment Jason may have failed. But not us; I ... feel ... the failure is personal to him only. I also remember the rest, and one part in particular. *Two Birds become four, The curse a gift, The gift, a curse.* We will see Jason again.

"Our story lies within the prophecy too. *Follow the steel of the two birds in flight. Fight in the innocent's shadow.* Jason's shadow hangs over us now; an offer to take heed of his final prophecy, to follow his lead. To draw blood in the name of the young.

"If we do not do this, if we do not make our plans tonight, in this final shadow before tomorrow, we will be lost. And we must be quick, for time is no longer our friend, and we have a king who, convinced in his own mind he knows the true way of things, may work against us should he discover this ... *mutiny*. For that is what this is. We go against our own king, who has shed blood for us, brought soldiers for us, who has only our survival at the core of his soul. He may, and probably *will*, see this as the ultimate betrayal. Our watchword then has to be, must be, *secrecy*." He looked around the small group of people. "There may be some of you, those with children, or grandchildren, who will not want to walk this path. If you wish to leave, do so now. There is no shame in it. All we ask is you keep your silence."

The people looked at one another, looking to see if anyone would stand. No-one moved. By his side, Darrach poked him gently with his staff, nodding sagely. Myrrdin felt the first stirrings of hope in his breast.

"It's time then," he said, removing a bundle of cloth from his robes, "for you to hear the final prophecy of Crowanhawk Yellowblade." He looked over at Aiken, who was rocking Anna back and forth. "Not all of you will hear things that will rest easy on your heart."

Morven stood at the vast table in the deserted kitchen, hacking at the vast haunch of meat before her, taking her temper out on the lifeless flesh.

How could she have been so foolish? Getting drunk, and at *her* age, with the Captain? What had she expected to happen?

Certainly not what *had* happened. The rumour mongering, the gossip, the panic that had spread through the little parish like a withering blight. Oh she'd berated her girls, that was for sure. Those that had gossiped. More than half she'd reduced to tears, and they'd gone around her these last few days like sheep hiding from the wolf.

But the person she'd chastised most was herself. Practically throwing herself at Omnust. At least that was how it felt now. She'd made a point of avoiding the captain, ducking out of the mess hall as he'd entered, sending a girl to serve him if he'd asked for her. Which, over the first two days, he's done several times. He'd stopped now.

A handful of mutton was thrown into the pot, and she began sawing off more meat. Something flickered in the corner of her eye and she paused, looking over at the shuttered window. Moonlight streamed in through the slats, but for a second it seemed that something had skittered in front of it, briefly blocking the moonlight. She stared at the shutter for a few moments, unsure.

"Stupid awd biddy, eyes playin' tricks..." she turned back to the meat.

Before her knife had chance to reach the meat, something banged against the kitchen wall, and a baby's cry filled the air.

"Who's there?" shouted Morven, walking over to the window. "What's going on?" She quickly unshuttered the window, leaning out into the night. "Show yoursen'! Dinnae be thinkin' Ah'm afeared now!"

A few feet to the left of the window, a small figure lay curled up on the ground. A child perhaps, a babe in its arms, clutched to its chest. The baby bawled loudly, but the figure didn't move. Morven could just make out blonde hair. "Hey! You alright down there?"

When the figure made no response, Morven began to worry. Had the vikings arrived already? This person, had they been attacked? She quickly grabbed her shawl off the peg, and headed for the main door.

Outside, on the road in front of the barracks, a horse stood, its breathing laboured and its coat frothed and steaming. A quick glance at its bridle told Morven the horse was from their own stables. But most of the horses had been sent out with the mangonels. Its flanks were bleeding, as though whoever had ridden it had driven it hard.

She hurried round the side of the building, following the sound of the crying baby, to where the kitchen window was. "Hoy! You alright? Whit're ye doin' out here?"

The figure moaned, and Morven quickly knelt next to it. It was a young woman, her blonde hair matted around her face. In her arms, the baby screamed.

"Hey, come on now," said Morven, gently lifting the woman's head, "come on, sit up now..." she eased her into a sitting position. "Yuir safe now, child," she said, smoothing the woman's hair back. "Let's get ye's inside, get some fuid down yer bairn's neck."

Gaira stirred the milk in the pot, waiting for the fire's heat to warm it. "What's yuir name, lassie?"

The girl looked up at her, oval eyes wide and scared. She sat on a chair next to the fire, swathed in all the shawls Morven could quickly lay her hands on. "Ah'm...Ah'm Ilisa, ma'am." In her arms, the baby wimpered, and she began rocking it. She looked nervously around her, pulling the sleeves of her dress down over her hands.

"It's Morven," corrected Morven. "Ah'm no *ma'am*. Bairn's hungry. When were she fed last?"

"Ah've nae milk left," mumbled the girl, giving the baby a finger to suckle on. It screamed even louder. "She's no fed since yesterday..."

"Ah bless the wee bairn, what've ye been through?" smiled Morven to the babe as she brought the milk over. "Can ye's spoonfeed, little one?"

"She c'n try," said Ilisa. "Thankyou."

"Och," smiled Morven, "Nae need fer thanks. Couldnae leave ye's out in this cold, could Ah?" She smiled broadly as the little one sucked hungrily on the offered spoon. "See, she catches on quick." She studied Ilisa as she fed the baby. Her hair was longer than it first appeared, cascading in matted lengths over her shoulders. Her clothing seemed almost too big for her, hanging from her shoulders and almost obscuring her dainty hands.

"Can Ah ask," she said gently, "what were you doin' oot there? That horse yui came in on, it was sent out days ago, with our mangonels."

"Was the vikings, ma'am," said Ilisa. "The' got mah village, mah folk, me and mah brother we scarce escaped, then mah brother..." she took a shuddering breath. "Mah brother were killed, the' captured me again..." she began sobbing, almost silently, yet causing her whole body to spasm with the strength of them.

"Oh sweetheart hush..." said Morven, quickly pulling up a stool, sitting on it so she could rub the girl's back. "Hushtae now, yuir safe here, no-one's gonnae get ye's in here." She waited until the girl got herself under control once more. "How did you get away? Did you escape? Did the' let you go?"

"The boy," said Ilisa, "the boy saved me."

Morven froze. "*Boy?*"

"Yellowblade." She smiled, seemingly remembering. "He was so brave."

*

Cináed stared at the two women; the timid, cowering young woman, clutching the babe, and the kitchen woman, proud and erect, her jaw belligerently denying her nervousness.

"You saw Jason?" His tone was harsh.

"Not me, Sire," said the kitchen woman. "The girl. Ilisa. She says he rescued her."

He turned to the girl. "*Tell me.*"

She didn't look up, her fear palpable. "Sire, Ah..."

With an effort, he stood away from the door, gesturing for the two women to enter. "Forgive my manners. I do not mean to be so fearsome. Please, come in. Seat yourselves at my table."

The kitchen woman, Morven if he remembered correctly, was the first to move, heading over to the round table with only the slightest of hesitations. The girl scuttled after her, terrified of being left near him by herself.

Cináed smiled grimly. If only he could make the vikings as fearful.

He seated himself at the table, looking over the model village that sat there at the young woman. "Please. Tell me what you know. I promise I won't shout."

Wide blue eyes regarded him briefly, then she looked down, gently stroking her baby's forehead. "Ah...dinnae know where tae begin..."

"Where did you meet Jason? Erm, Yellowblade?"

"T'were on the beach. Me an' me brother, we'd fled oor village. Aneithcraig." She shuddered, and Morven took her hand. Bolstered, the girl continued. "Sorry. The vikings, the' wiped us oot. Me an' mine, we only just escaped. Went south. We met up with Yellowblade – he was a prisoner – the viking killed my brother, took me prisoner."

"There was only one? Where was their ship?"

"She'd been sent tae find Yellowblade, she had no ship. It-it came later."

"I knew it," breathed Cináed. "I *knew* he hadn't run away. Continue, young Ilisa."

"He-he had this knife, see, only the viking woman had hidden it. Soon as he found it, he-he must hae used magic, as it flew through the air like a-a bird, an' he sank the ship, an' he help me escape, an' there was this woman, he said her name was Gaira, small, like a pech, he helped her escape too..." She paused, her eyes shut, as though the memories pained her. By her side, the kitchen woman's face paled at the sound of Gaira's name. "We parted this morn. He said...he said Ah were to look out fer mangonels, the men wi' 'em might help me."

"One ship down. Praise be, but that is good news! And Yellowblade?" said Cineád intently. "Where is he now?"

"North, he said. Said he'd left here so as not tae bring danger tae ye's." She blotted her nose with the palm of one hand. As she brought her hand up her sleeve fell back, revealing a bandaged wrist. She followed the king's gaze. "One o' the men did that. Where the vikings bound me."

"Did he say anything about..." Cináed thought for the words, "did he have any...visions? Dreams?"

She looked up at him, her cupid bow lips trembling. "Ah...Ah don't understand?"

"Did he say anything about the viking attacks, woman!" He cursed himself as the woman flinched.

"He...he said somethin' about Alban Eiler bein' important," she stammered. "That's all, that's all I remember, Sire."

Cináed leaned back in his chair. "So. The night *after* tomorrow..." he took a deep breath. "The Druid was wrong."

"Sire?"

"Nothing, child. Just a...confirmation of what I already knew." He sat back, a bizarre feeling of relief and disappointment wash through him. It was the news he'd been wanting, yet it also meant that his friend, his councillor, his battle companion of so many years was, after all, fallible. "But Aneithcraig is two days' ride from here..."

"We were south of it, Sire," said Ilisa. "An' the first mangonel, the' gave me a horse, directing me ontae the next one. An' the' gave me a fresh horse an'..."

"And so you made good time," nodded the king in understanding. "So the mangonels, were they..." he gestured to the model of the village on the table. "Were they arranged as you see here?"

Ilisa studied the model, and the tiny representations of the mangonels in the areas beyond the village. "Ah think so."

"Good." Cináed stood. "Good. Perhaps we yet stand a chance. You," and he looked at Morven. "It's Morven, is it not?"

"Aye Sire."

"Go and find Captain Ossian, bring him here. I shall go and summon Myrrdin personally. There are a few rumours that must be put to rest." He looked at Ilisa. "Remain here, if you will, and warm yourself. I would have you speak to my captain."

The girl waited until she could no longer hear their footsteps before standing and stretching, the baby clutched under one arm. She walked over to the bed, gently lying the baby, stirring now, onto it, tucking its swaddling around it.

"Hush little one," she whispered gently, kneeling on the floor. "No point in crying, little precious girl. Sleep."

She stroked its forehead until the child's eyes began to flicker shut. The girl sat back on her heels, smiling to herself. Then she slowly lay out along the floor, one hand slowly creeping under the bed, searching almost silently until it found its prey.

She stood, returning to the table, and placed the obsidian shard of mirror on the table. She stroked its surface lovingly. "Hello husband."

Morven stood outside the door to Omnust's barracks, the corridor around her deserted. Did the king know she had been with Omnust when the rumours had started? Did he know she was his drinking companion? She could feel the blush on her face. The king was no fool, and there had been many soldiers in there, any one of whom could have told him.

Maybe that was why she felt as though she was being punished by being sent for the captain. To have to tell him, face to face, that the king had summoned him. At least she hadn't been banished. Like Myrrdin. From what little Morven could glean from the king's comments, the meeting would not be pleasant.

Before her fear and shame could get the better of her, she pounded loudly on the door. "Captain Ossian? Ah've a message for yui fro' the king!"

The door was opened far faster than she would have expected for a room full of sleeping men. She grimaced as the smell of the confined quarters assailed her. "Is..is Capt..."

The young soldier who'd opened the door grabbed her wrist, pulling her inside. With a quick look up and down the corridor, he eased the door shut, making sure it didn't slam.

"Now what the devil..." began Morven, her fists already clenched.

"Be still!" hissed the soldier, listening at the door.

Morven looked around her. All the soldiers were awake, most of them dressed in their battle leathers. They all looked more than a little nervous. "What's going on?" she whispered.

"No-one's coming." The soldier at the door turned to Morven. "What message for Omnust?"

"Ah don't really think that's fer..."

"The message, Morven! What is it?" There was obvious fear in the young man's voice.

"The king, he's erm... he's summoned Captain Omnust tae his

chambers."

"What?" As well as the young man's yelp of surprise, there was a general fearful muttering around the room.

"There's a young girl," said Morven, looking curiously around at the men, "a survivor of a viking attack, in th' king's chambers. Says she's seen Jason. Th' king wants Omnust tae talk wi' her. Look, just what is goin' on here?"

"Omnust's no' here," said another man.

"Where is he?"

"There's a meetin'. Out by th' loch. The Druid's there, some people frae the village, some o' us too. The Druid, he says the vikings attack tomorrow. Says he has proof."

Morven felt the blood drain from her face. "Oh no..."

"What? What is it, woman?"

"The king," said Morven. "He's gone aftae Myrrdin hisself. What's gonnae happen when he finds him gone?"

"They must be warned!" The soldier who'd pulled her in opened the door. He looked back at the other men. "Warn the other men, let them know."

"Ah'm comin' with you!" said Morven immediately.

"Woman, yui'll slow me down," replied the soldier. "Stay."

"What is it wi' men an' names?" snapped Morven. "Ye dinnae need slow yer pace, boy. But Ah'm coming with, so either set off or stand aside."

A shadow moved in the depths of the mirror.

"Surprised to see me?" Lathgertha grinned. "Did you enjoy my performance? And look! We have a daughter now. Her mother was so talkative in her final moments!" The shadow in the mirror writhed and twisted. "Temper, husband, you know I can't hear you. The mangonels await your collection. The men were so willing to help a stricken maid it was almost too easy." She tipped her head to one side. "Speaking of *easy,* perhaps you have an unfair advantage. After all, they *still* think you attack the day after tomorrow, they *still* think they know where you'll attack... I think this mirror's outlived its purpose, don't you?"

One dainty hand lifted it from the table. "You tried to rob me of the hunt. Who knows what I may let slip between now and tomorrow?" She gently tossed the mirror onto the crackling log fire. "See you soon, Ragnar."

Within seconds, the heat of the fire shattered the glass. At the sound, the baby awoke. And screamed.

Chapter Nineteen

"We havetae send men!" said Omnust, staring at Myrrdin. "Wiseman, the' call ye's, but yiur sentencing' those men tae death wi'out a trial!"

"The mangonels are lost already, Captain," said Myrrdin wearily. "Were you not listening?"

"We havetae *try!*"

"No," said Myrrdin, raising his voice above the mumbling of voices that supported their captain. "Listen to me. Our best defence of this town are the visions of Yellowblade. But this defence comes at a price. We know the vikings capture the catapults, use them against us. We even know *where*. But suppose they find those siege engines gone? Our best defence is our fore-knowledge. They consider theirs to be surprise."

"But..."

"If they see anything that makes them think we're alerted to them, their plans change; everything is changed. Our one chance of victory is snatched from us forever!"

"We could bring th'men back," said Omnust. "Leave th'mangonels."

Darrach snorted from his seat on the log. "Aye, an' if ye's were plannin' a raid on an enemy, found a horde o' their weapons, nae guard around, would yui think '*oh how kind 'n' generous o' them*', or would ye's suspect a trap?" He prodded at a nearby stone. "Yuir a captain, mon. Nair had tae make a sacrifice afore?"

"It's a pointless discussion," said Eigyr, interrupting the captain as he rounded, red faced, on her father. "The sacrifice is already made. According to Jason, or Ambrosius, *whoever,* the men are already dead." She looked up at Myrrdin. "The question is, what *do* we do?"

Morven tightened her grip around the soldier's waist as the horse plummeted through the darkness. Kilneuair already faded into the distance, and Loch Awe shone brightly in the moonlight. The king would have discovered the absence of Myrrdin by now, possibly even Omnust. She kept looking back over her shoulder, expecting an any moment to see horses riding out after them, torches flaming, swords drawn.

The young man obviously had the same thoughts. "Are we pursued?"

Morven shook her head. "No, there's no-one."

"We won't have long," said the soldier. "There's men still who think the druid a forest madman."

"Oh, lord," breathed Morven, "this is bad."

"Aye, Morven," replied the soldier. "Bad indeed." He spurred the horse on.

"We relocate," said Myrrdin without hesitation.

"The town?" said Omnust, his face incredulous. "But..but there's no time, the people..."

"not the town," replied Myrrdin. He crouched low in the dirt, and brushed an area clear of twigs and leaves. "See." He quickly sketched the streets of Kilneuair. "We originally thought the Berserkers would enter *here,* so we've dug oil pits, filled trees with arrows and lances, hidden small mangonels in false wooden houses with collapsible walls. We now know they enter *here,*" and he pointed to the other end of the dirt sketch, "and that they have mangonels with them. We know they're after the barracks, thinking the army sleep within. We cannot dig new pits, nor relocate the mangonels. We don't have the time, and if we're to do this discreetly the work would be too noticeable."

Omnust and the soldiers crouched by him. If the captain had anything else to say about the men he'd thought to save, he kept his tongue. "So we leave the pits, the mangonels. We relocate half the weapon hordes." He looked up at his men. "See? If they enter from the northeast, they have to enter through this wooded area. There's pines, vast oaks. The branches could hide any number of our men. If we arm them with pitch-arrows, we cuid mebbies tekk out th' mangonels afore they even enter the town."

"Wood will burn, yes," agreed Myrrdin, "but the Berserkers will not be stopped so easily."

"Captain," said one soldier, leaning in, "if I may? We can block these roads with carts, barrels, leaving only *this* road clear. If we can lure them towards the pits we've dug?"

Omnust nodded. "Aye. Aye, that'd work." He smiled at the man. "Fine idea."

The soldier reigned in the horse, turning it to face back through the woodland. "What is it?"

Morven sat gasping on the back of the horse, straining her eyes to see in the moonlight. "Four...no five horses."

"The king?"

"They bear no torches, I cannae see..." she slid down from the horse. "Yui were right. Ah'm slowin' the horse. You go on!"

"Morven, are ye..."

"Yes!" wheezed Morven. "Go on now! No, wait!"

He paused, the panting horse turning as he held it back. "Ma'am?"

"Yuir name," she said. "Ye've no told me yuir name."

He smiled briefly. He looked no more than sixteen. So *young*. "Bedevere."

"Godspeed then, Bedevere," smiled Morven. "And Danu light yuir path." She made a shooing gesture. "Go!"

"Hide yuirself, Morven," he half shouted as he spurred the horse. "They're no expectin' yui here - head back!" With that, he was gone.

Morven looked around her. Brave heart, foolish choice. What was she to do now? Even as Bedevere's hoof beats faded into the distance, the sound of other horses drew closer. She had scant moments to hide.

The bank down to the loch was steep, the waters many feet below where she stood now. But it offered the best cover. "Oh...Danu, cast yuir gaze wide," she muttered, lowering herself over the edge, "yuir watchin' o'er more than one damn fool tonight..." She began sliding down the icy bank, its frozen soil biting into her rump as she descended, with more than a few well chosen curses, down its incline.

Voices above froze her movement, and she pressed herself back against the bank, her heart pounding so loudly she felt sure it would betray her.

"There's hoof prints, Sire!" She recognised the voice. It was the soldier who had challenged her, that night in the mess hall. She scowled. She'd *known* he was trouble. "It reigned in here. Someone dismounted too. There's footprints."

"A man's?" With those two words, Morven recognised the king's voice, and the anger contained in it. *Oh please don't look over the side, don't look over the side...*she closed her eyes, fearing discovery at any moment. Her breath came in fearful little gasps as she tried to press her body even further back.

"No, Sire. Too small." There was a pause, and she could hear him slowly approaching the side of the bank. "A child, perhaps. Or a woman." His voice was louder, almost overhead, and a trickle of soil fell down onto Morven's head. She squashed a hand to her mouth, muffling her wimper. "They go down over the bank, Sire."

"I have no desire to track women or children, Vortigern," snapped Cináed. "There's more tracks here. The horse rode on. Did it still bear a rider?"

The sound of the arrogant soldier's footsteps moved away, and Morven let out an almost silent sigh of relief, opening her eyes once more.

"Aye, Sire. The tracks are of a horse that's driven, no' set loose."

"Then remount! By all that's sacred, I will quash this foolishness!" There was a hiss of steel, followed quickly by the king's angry shout. "Stay your blade, man! These are our people! Would you spill their blood before the vikings even land? We quash, Vortigern, *not* kill."

There was a muffled apology from the soldier, and Morven felt a fierce gratitude to the king. Angry he may be, but he had not lost sight of his purpose. Her heart beat a little less fearfully for the people he hunted.

She waited until the pounding of the horses had faded before slowly trying to turn, to make her way back up the bank. One foot pushed against a large rock as she sought leverage. The rock, loose already, gave way, sending her rolling down the bank. She drew her legs and arms in tightly, expecting the harsh ground beneath to break her fall, and perhaps her body.

Strong arms caught her, breaking the fall, and she found herself being set gently onto her feet. She stared at her rescuer; at the gaping hole of a nose, the overlong arms, the bizarre blue beard, the colour accentuated by the light of the moon. He was a creature of nightmares.

He was also crying.

"you're – you're..." Morven stammered, trying not to let her fear control her, "you're the boggart, aren't you?"

He nodded silently, his eyes streaming with tears, his brow creased in grief. One long arm reached out behind him, and a little girl came running out of the darkness, hugging his arm with both of hers.

"An' wee Anna," said Morven, bending down to her. "You're Gaira's little helper, aren't ye's?"

The boggart stifled a sob. "She's gone tae me..." the voice was a raw wound.

"What?" Morven's mind, already full of questions for this creature, stumbled over his words. "No, Ah mean Ah heard she'd been took, but no, there's a girl, Ilisa, she's seen Jason, he's got Gaira with him! But where's the others? Omnust, Myrrdyn?"

"Why hasn't he come back?" asked Anna. She peered round the boggart's arm at her, her eyes shaded with green stains. "I want him back!"

"He'll come back soon, Ah'm sure," said Morven, "an' he'll bring Gaira with him!"

"No!" The anger in his voice made Morven step back in fear. By his side, the little girl hugged his arm even more fiercely, the look on her face too angry for one so young.

Morven looked at them in confusion. "But she's your friend..."

"She's not who she thinks!" shouted Anna. "I hate her, I want Jason!"

Morven looked in confusion at the boggart, who was breathing heavily, the tears soaking his beard.

"All o' those people," breathed the creature angrily, "all o' those villagers, dead, tekken, all because o' me!"

"What...what d'yui mean?" She grabbed an arm, making him look at her. "Because of you? Which people? Which villages? Boggart, where is Omnust?"

"He's called Aiken!" shouted the little girl. "It's not his fault!" She looked up pleadingly at her sobbing friend. "It wasn't your fault! It was her, she did it, she's all dark and twisty, I saw her..."

Morven looked from one to the other. "What did she do?" she asked quietly.

Aiken gave a barking sob. "She sold them! She sold them tae the vikings! Tae keep *me* safe!"

"Where's Aiken?" asked Myrrdin, looking around the clearing as the small group of people threw handfuls of dirt onto the smouldering embers.

Eigyr ran a hand over her swollen belly. "He's gone," she said. "When you read out that section about Gaira."

"Cannae blame him," muttered Omnust. "The've been friends since she were a bairn, he told me. He doted on her."

"Seems she felt the same way," said Eigyr. She frowned slightly. "Babes are creating tonight." She leant back, trying to straighten her back.

"No," said Myrrdin grimly. "No, her feelings went far beyond friendship. And people have paid the cost. We should go after him."

"We've no time," said Omnust. "The work, we havetae get started tonight." He sighed. "The boggart'll return when he's ready. He knows we need his arms."

"I pray he does nothing foolish," said Myrrdin. "But you're right. We must return. We..."

"Hushtae!" Darrach was on his feet, amazingly agile for one so old. "Listen ye!"

Myrrdin followed the old man's gaze into the darkness beyond, Omnust by his side. For a few moments he heard nothing, then in the distance he heard it. "Horses..."

"One only," said Omnust. "But one is too many. Hide yerselves! Do it now!"

There were few places to hide. They were outside of the woodland, and only a few trees dotted the landscape. People went running in all directions.

"Stay close!" shouted Myrrdin. "Try not to get separated!" He turned to Eigyr, holding a hand out to her.

She slapped it away. "Go hide yourself," she snapped. "I can stand." She eased herself up as quickly as she could, grimacing slightly.

The hoof beats were closing quickly. After a moment's hesitation, Myrrdin turn, following Darrach to the nearest tree.

Eigyr took a step towards another tree, then faltered, doubling slightly, one hand clutched to her belly. "Oh you have *got* to be kidding..."

"Eigyr!" hissed Myrrdin's voice from his hiding place.

Eigyr sank back down onto the log, her brow beading with sweat. "God, you have the *worst* damn timing..."

The rider entered the clearing, and Myrrdin, who had been stepping out from behind the tree, ducked back behind it. Only Eigyr was visible as the rider drew up to her.

"Milady..."

"Oh what do *you* want?" snapped Eigyr testily. "If the king sent you..."

"Morven sent me, milady," said the rider, breathing heavily. "The king, he knows you've gone, he seeks Myrrdin, and the captain. Where are they?"

"Morven sent you?" It was Omnust's voice; he emerged from behind a tree. "What's happened? Is she alright?"

"I have little time," said Bedevere. "The king, he rides out with men, he's not happy..."

The rest of the people were emerging, whispering worriedly amongst themselves at the discovery of this secret meeting. Myrrdin approached.

"How did he discover..."

"A girl, a survivor from Aneithcraig," said Bedevere, "she's seen Jason, he helped her escape, but the king wanted you and Omnust to talk to her..."

He was interrupted by a sharp yelp from Eigyr.

Myrrdin turned to her, his eyes widening in comprehension. "Eigyr, the babies? But...it's too soon!"

"Try telling them that!" snapped Eigyr. "Ohhh..! Where's that damn boggart! He promised me he'd be here!"

"Milord," insisted Bedevere, "you must go! They'll be here any moment!"

Myrrdin thought wildly. The babies were important, more important than even Eigyr herself realised. More important than Kilneuair? He reached a decision, and prayed it was the right one. "Then come they must. We are out of time. A forced march by an angry king may kill the babes. Take her, Bedevere, get her out of sight."

"Myrrdin, damn you!" snapped Eigyr, trying to rise. "I'm not leaving you to..."

"You'll do as I say!" said Myrrdin, almost shouting. "Bedevere, take her now!" Even as they spoke, the rumble of horses could be heard in the distance.

Unsure, the young soldier looked over at Omnust, who nodded grimly. "Do it, boy."

The soldier grabbed Eigyr's wrist, pulling her up behind him. She suppressed a scream, glaring wildly at Myrrdin.

"Don't you dare send me away!" she shouted. "I've had babies before!"

Myrrdin quickly walked up to her, taking one hand. "Eigyr..." He looked up at her. "If there is one thing I can save tonight, I'm glad that it is you."

"This isn't goodbye!"

"I pray not. I wish I had been a braver man." He pressed her hand against his lips. "Perhaps it is best I wasn't. Your children, so eager to join the fray, have a whole history to live through. I cannot risk changing that."

"Don't you get all mystical on me," said Eigyr. "You know I hate that." She cupped his cheek with her hand. "And never have I met a braver man." She leant down, hanging onto the soldier with one hand, planting a firm kiss on Myrrdin's lips. "A promise for the future. Who knows what it holds!" She drew quickly away, her eyes gleaming, not looking at him. "Ride on, man. Do it quickly."

Bedevere spurred the horse on, and the small group drew together to watch as it thundered away.

Myrrdin stared after them. "Who indeed, milady. Who indeed."

Eigyr's voice carried back to them. "And if you're wondering what *that* was, O chivalrous Knight, my waters just broke!"

Myrrdin laughed; his smile was quickly supplanted by a frown.

Darrach walked up to him. "Hope yui ken whit yuir doin'," he said easily.

"So do I," breathed Myrrdin, turning to the sound of the approaching horses. "Time will tell."

Five horses entered the clearing, the king at the fore. He reigned in his horse, his face pale and thunderous as he dismounted. His armour glinted icily as he walked silently up to Myrrdin, his gloved fist clenching.

Myrrdin knew the blow was coming, but did not try to avoid it. The metal on the glove ploughed across his cheek, tearing skin, but he did not fall. He returned the king's stare as he felt the blood begin to flow down his cheek.

Cináed turned to the rest of the group. "People of Kilneuair, this...*druid* fills you with false messages. The proof has presented itself to me this very evening. Return to your homes. Do not speak of this night, do not repeat the lies of the druid. I have no anger toward you; there will be no repercussions you need live in fear of. But..." He looked silently from face to face for several breaths. "*Leave. Now.*"

The last two words were said with such venom that the nearer folk whimpered. The older ones holding onto each other for support, they quickly began to leave the clearing.

Myrrdin watched them go. "Cináed..."

The king span. "You are entirely too *familiar*, Druid." His face was contorted with contempt. "Madman of the Forest." Behind him, a couple of the men on horseback stifled a laugh. "What did you hope to accomplish? Hmm? Tell me, I'm fascinated."

"I had only the defence of our people in mind, sire," said Myrrdin quietly. The blood dripped down onto his shoulder.

"Did you?" said Cináed. "Did you now? By having the army sitting out tomorrow night, an all night vigil for an attack that won't happen?"

"Sire, the prophesies, they're *real...*"

Cináed continued as though Myrrdin had not spoken. "Keeping them awake, weakening them, *tiring* them, for when the true invasion happens? Are you in the pay of the vikings, I wonder?"

"Please," begged Myrrdin, "I beg of you listen. You used to! The attack, it's been brought forward, the direction of attack has changed, if I can just show you..." he looked down at the map he'd drawn in the dirt.

The king followed his gaze, and dragged his foot through the rough diagram. "Enough."

"Cináed, please..."

"I said *enough!*" He stared at the druid, his anger an almost palpable force. "You embarrass yourself, Druid." He looked over at his men. "Vortigern. Escort your men back to the barracks. The ironsmiths will have the doors ready to bar. Make sure that Omnust and his men cannot leave. Make sure they know they are to rest. That I have no anger toward anyone." He looked back at Myrrdin. "No. That is not true. I have anger. I have anger, Myrrdin. I have anger for a man who cannot admit his mistakes even when their resulting screams deafen those around him." He returned to his horse, remounting. He looked over at Omnust. "And he has found an echo for his voice in you, Omnust Ossian, repeating his words like a trained raven.

"I strip you of command, Omnust Ossian. You are captain no longer. Captain Vortigern, you now command this army. Secure the men, and then..." he turned his dark circled eyes to Myrrdin, "bring the Druid to my chambers. I have someone I wish you to meet. *Old friend.*"

Chapter Twenty

"Pull up," said Eigyr, wincing as a powerful contraction rippled across her belly. "Pull up, damn you!"

Bedevere slowed the horse to a trot. "Milady?"

"Just stop!" She sagged against his back, gasping for breath. Reluctantly, the young soldier brought his horse to a stop, and Eigyr gratefully slid to the ground.

"Milady," said Bedevere, looking around him, "we cannot stop here."

"Unless you think it's humanly possible to burp up two brats," said Eigyr, lowering herself to the ground, "we are stopping."

Bedevere dismounted, crouching by her side. "Are – are you alright?"

"Are you blind?!" shouted Eigyr. "No, you damn fool, I'm *not* alright!" She let out a low growl as the contraction gained strength. "These babies are coming, and they're coming now, oh *god* where's that boggart?" She took a slow deep breath, followed by more shallow breaths. "It's fading. Help me up." She looked up at the red faced soldier. "Help me up! I'm not infectious!"

"Sorry, milady," stammered Bedevere. He grasped her hand. "Ah've never, sorry, Ah've not seen a woman...you know..."

"Tell me something I hadn't guessed." She got to her feet, brushing her already stained dress down. "I can't ride. But I'll walk. As far as these little squealers let me, anyway."

"Where..."

"Kilneuair, man, where did you think?" She set off across the mossy ground. "There is no way, you hear me, that I am giving birth in a damn...*wilderness!*"

"Milady..."

"What now?!"

"It er..." he pointed sheepishly. "It's the other way."

Morven crouched down by the side of Aiken, watching as the king and his entourage rode by. She resisted the urge to stand, to call out, when she saw Omnust. His face was haggard, almost bereft. The rear of the group was brought up by Vortigern. If Omnust looked despondent, the soldier on horseback by contrast looked triumphant. Withering looks fell from the soldier's eye to the cowed Omnust.

She broke her stare, counting the other horses, looking at their riders' faces. She gave a slight sigh of relief. "They didnae get Bedevere," she whispered.

"Who?" said Aiken. He'd dried his eyes now, though he kept heaving soulful sighs that were rapidly beginning to fray Morven's nerves. The boggart unnerved her. A creature from the tales of the Peaceful Ones, living and breathing.

"The young soldier who brought me here," replied Morven. She looked after the men as they faded into the night. "Ah hope he's no hurt them."

The boggart took a deep breath, and Morven almost turned to berate him, until she realised he was smelling the air. He looked at her. "There's little bluid been spilt," he muttered. "They're afear'd though." His large ears twitched. "The king's shown his temper."

"There's little blood spilt?" she stood up, trying to see where the figures had gone. "Who's blood?"

"Myrrdin."

She turned back to him. "Is he alright?"

"The smell's no strong." Aiken shrugged. "He's fine."

The tone of his voice worried her. It was blank, without any feeling. "Are...forgive me, are *you* alright?"

He shrugged again; an almost random movement. "Ah'm breathin', aren't Ah?" He looked down as Anna took his hand, and smiled. "Ah'm fine, an' wee Anna's keeping her eyes on me."

Morven nodded silently. "We'll give them a while," she said, "then we'll head back ourselves."

"What fer?" asked Aiken quietly. "Jason's gone. The king'll nae listen tae sense. An' when the people find out what Gaira did...they'll no welcome me. The'll drive me oot, like all the other places."

"You dinnae *know* that," said Morven nervously. "Ye's judgin' them wi'out..."

"Ah've lived through it afore, ma'am," said Aiken softly. "Ah'm used tae it, Awd Aiken, allus looking fer work..."

Morven paused, giving herself a moment to think. She'd seen this strange creature training in the field behind the barracks, seen him pick huge rocks and throw them as though they were loaves of bread. She knew that her town needed him. She'd also seen the affection with which he was held, though she'd had little enough to do with him herself.

"This is yuir home, mon," she said. "Those people, they're yuir people. Whit, yui think so little o' them, you think they'll spurn ye's because of Gaira?"

"She sold out all o' those people..."

"*She* did, Aiken," said Morven. "Not *you*." She reached up, and after only a second's hesitation, grasped his arm in what she hoped would be a friendly manner. It felt like normal flesh. "All o' those people, sat round the fire when Myrrdin told them, what did they say?"

"Dunno. Didnae stay, did Ah?"

Morven dropped her hand. "Then think of the wee girrul. She wants her brother back. Suppose he returns to Kilneuair, only tae find her gone. Think he'll be happy? Tae find not only his friend, but his sister gone?"

Aiken was staring off into space. The ragged flesh around the holes of his nostrils twitched as he inhaled..

"Aiken?" Morven was not used to being ignored. Even by a boggart. "Are you *listening* to..."

He held up a hand. More of a claw, really. "Hushtae."

"Now look..."

"Someone's a'comin'," hissed Aiken, hoisting Anna up into his arms.

"Who?"

Aiken sighed. "Someone who wants a promise keepin'." He bent down to Anna. "Anna, stay with Melvin..."

"Morven."

"Until Ah come back."

"No!" yelped Anna. "No, I wanna stay with you! Don't you leave me too!"

"It's only for a few moments, little one," said Aiken softly. "'Til Ah brings 'em to us."

"It's alright Anna, we won't move until he returns," promised Morven. She lifted Anna up, cradling the trembling girl to her chest.

"Ah won't be long," said Aiken, turning to walk away. "There's work for Awd Aiken yet."

"Milady..." Bedevere hesistated as the woman bent double again. "Yui should rest."

"Oh will you *stop* being so damn formal!" panted Eigyr. "There's just you and me. It's Eigyr." She leaned one hand against the nearest tree, the other hand stroking her stomach. "I'll rest when there's a roof over my head and a bed under my back. Not before."

"Yes Eigyr," said Bedevere meekly.

Eigyr grunted. "That's better." She slowly straightened. "There. It's fading." She wiped her forehead with a grubby sleeve. "Onwards."

"They're getting closer together," said Bedevere, as he lead his horse after her. "Aren't they?"

"You're a real one for stating the obvious," said Eigyr. He was right. The babies were close now. She swallowed down the fear that began to bud in her stomach. "How...how far now?"

"On horseback, minutes only." He peered through the trees into the distance. "On foot, longer."

"Great," muttered Eigyr. "Great, just typical, only weeks ago I was in the lap of flaming luxury, but oh no," and she hiked her skirts up, "not good enough for me, I have to go in search of damn druids, and now I'm wandering through hideous wastelands, two devil begotten sprogs threatening to plop out between my legs..." she paused as another contraction tightened across her belly. "Oh blessed Bridhe..." She doubled up, and started to fall.

Two strong arms caught her before Bedevere even had chance to step forward. "Lady Ivory," said Aiken, "ye's cannae be having the bairns oot here..."

Despite the pain, Eigyr felt relief flood through her. "Have...have you been taking lessons from yon soldier?" she gasped. "Stating the obvious? *Oh!*" Her fingernails bit into Aiken's arms as the contraction gained strength.

Aiken scooped her up into his arms as though she weighed nothing, then looked over at Bedevere. "We'll tekk her tae..." his hesitation was obvious, "we'll tekk her tae Gaira's. There's herbs there. Medicines. We'll hae the place to ourselves."

Bedevere mounted his steed. "Can you carry her that distance?"

Aiken nodded grimly. "That 'n' further, an' at good speed."

The soldier nodded. "I'll keep to your pace. Lead on."

"Can yuir hoss manage two more on its back? Ah've friends need collecting."

*

Lathgertha had moved one of the chairs from the table to by the fire. She sat in it down, gently rocking the sleeping baby back and forth. She could become accustomed to this. If only her husband would settle somewhere long enough for her to. It was relaxing, somehow.

She'd started to nod when the door was kicked open, soothed by the dying fire, and the gentle breathing of the baby. At the sound she shot up, the baby falling to the floor. She'd withdrawn most of the dagger from her sleeve before she remembered her pretence, and quickly hid the knife, making a show of picking up the screaming child as the king swept into the room.

Cináed stared at her. Maybe he noticed the brief flash of anger on her face. She hoped not. "Ilisa. Sorry if I startled you." He turned to the open door. "Bring him."

Two soldiers entered the room, a man in filthy white robes held between them. Lathgertha stared at him. His cheek was encrusted in dried blood, his black hair and beard tousled and muddy. Yet he had an air of quiet dignity that was at odds with his appearance. *Myrrdin,* guessed Lathgertha as she rocked the sobbing baby.

"Ilisa, may I introduce Myrrdin, druid, councillor and court jester." He smiled, though there was no warmth in his eyes. "Myrrdin, may I introduce Ilisa of Aneithcraig, former prisoner of the vikings, freed by Crowanhawk Yellowblade." He looked at the guards. "Wait outside."

Myrrdin watched as the guards left, then turned to Cináed. "Sire, if we could just talk..."

"Talk?" said Cináed. "Actually yes, we should talk. Please, be seated. Let's keep this dignified shall we?" He gestured to the table, the setting of so many of their previous talks. "You too, young Ilisa. Let's all be seated."

Lathgertha hung back. There was a tone in the king's voice that spoke of barely restrained emotions, utter exhaustion, perhaps even madness. This man was dangerous. She watched as the king, then the druid, seated themselves. The king pushed a chair out with his foot, smiling. She looked over at the druid, who gave a curt nod.

She had her knife. She seated herself.

"Now," said Cináed, stretching out in his chair. "The druid here has been on a little adventure tonight. He's been telling the people of Kilneuair that the vikings have brought forward their attack. That Yellowblade has had some *new* visions. Kilneuair will be raided tomorrow night."

Lathgertha's eyes widened. How? How had the boy got the news to them? She had to warn Ragnar!

The king noticed her shock. "Do not be afraid, young Ilisa, you confirmed for me yourself they are only lies."

"Sire," said the druid, his voice low and calm, "the visions of Jason are true. If you were to only look under your..."

"Ilisa," interrupted the king. "Humour me. Would you be so kind as to tell the druid what Jason said to you?"

She looked from the king to the druid. "I..." she found herself suddenly having to suppress a smile. "He told me Alban Eiler was important to the vikings. Th' full moon. Ah-Ah think he meant they planned tae attack then?"

"Of *course* that's what he meant." He smiled, then looked at Myrrdin, who had closed his eyes. "You see? You see how simple it is to discover the truth? And all that fuss you made, over those whimsical tales of...what did you call him...Ambrosius?"

"NO!"

Lathgertha rocked back in her chair, startled. The king was the one she'd thought would show his temper. But it was the druid who launched himself to his feet with a bellow, catching even the king unawares.

The druid ran to the king's bed even as the chamber doors opened and the guards entered. "You are spied upon!" shouted the druid. "There's a mirror..."

"Seize him!" The king was out of his seat.

"There's a scrying mirror under your bed!" The druid's voice was desperate. He grabbed the frame of the bed, casting it over on its side. "See! See for your..."

He stared at the empty floorboards, his voice lost. The guards grabbed him, forcing his arms behind his back. He never looked away from the floorboards.

"Again, druid," breathed Cináed quietly, "you embarrass yourself. Take him to the cells. No, stay..." the king's eyes narrowed. "There's a pigsty behind the houses opposite. Chain him up with the pigs. It should be a grand reunion."

Lathgertha lifted the whimpering baby, kissing it gently. It was the only way she could hide her smile.

Omnust stared at the doors. Either side of the door frame were two large metal brackets, bolted through the wall. Two large oak beams rested against the wall next to each door.

He looked at Vortigern. "Soldier, think on what yuir doin'. The vikings, they attack less than a day from now."

"Yuir no longer mah captain," said Vortigern slowly. "Yui betrayed the king, plotted behind his back. Ah simply follow his orders."

"Ah plotted only tae save our people!" said Omnust heatedly. Two of the new captain's men moved to his side, each placing a hand on his shoulders. He shrugged them off angrily. From the corner of his eye he saw his own men from the banks of the loch, each of them held by a guard. "Damn it, man, the king is addled!"

"The king has instructed me to make sure yuir rested. Yui'll be confined tae quarters until sundown on Alban Eiler."

"Yui cannae keep us prisoner!"

"If yui cannae follow orders," said Vortigern coolly, "Ah've been granted authority tae shackle you."

Omnust looked behind the swaggering soldier. The ironsmith stood there, his face a picture of woe. By his feet were numerous chains and shackles. He didn't meet Omnust's glare.

"On sundown, yui will be released, and yuir weapons and armour returned." He smiled. "Be sure tae bring yuir halberd an' shield."

Omnust lunged at him, his hands closing around Vortigern's throat. The two men fell to the ground, Omnust's strength far greater than the wiry young man's. The other guards leapt forward, the hilts of their daggers raining blows on the back of his head. Darkness crept around the corners of his vision, and he sagged against Vortigern.

Vortigern angrily pushed him off, rubbing his throat. "Seal them in."

Omnust found himself thrown bodily into his quarters, the two men from the same quarters quickly following suite. The men in the cramped chamber surged forward, helping them to their feet. Behind them the doors were slammed shut, and the sound of the two oak beams being dropped into place could be heard.

"No!" blood flowing down the back of his neck, Omnust launched himself against the door. "Vortigern! Wait! Yui're sentencin' us tae death!" He heard the usurper captain laughing on the other side, and charged the door with his shoulder. The door creaked, but did not break. Again and again he charged it, but the oak beams were too strong.

Omnust turned from the door, taking two steps towards the window. Metal bars now gridded it, blocking any exit.

With a cry he grabbed the nearest cot, hurling it against the window, where it shattered like dry kindling. Another cot was flung against the wall as his men cowered; several more cots were over-turned.

His anger spent, Omnust fell back against the wall, slowly sliding to the floor. "They've got us now," he whispered. "They've got us, flies in a honeypot, Mother Mary, Lord Jesus hae mercy on our souls..." He looked up at his men. "We're gonnae burn."

Chapter Twenty One

The mangonel was obviously strategically placed, overlooking the rocky bay below. Had it been manned, the two viking ships, driven high onto the beach, would have been easy targets. Ragnar smiled grimly. His wife had been as good as her word. The two soldiers lay by the wheels of the large catapult, their throats slit. Nearby was the body of a young woman. Her wounds were more severe. Lathgertha had obviously had some fun with her before despatching her.

He turned his horse, and looked back to where his men were flooding onto the beach; the Berserkers in their furs, calm at the moment, their potions yet to be brewed. Behind them, the rest of his army, some on horseback, all armoured and ready for the march ahead.

He looked again at the mangonel. It still had the harnesses for the horses attached, and in its base were numerous large rocks, wrapped in pitch-soaked cloth.

Had the little witchwoman not been so obliging, these *savages* could have caused untold damage to his men. Oh, they would pay for their arrogance. Hel would welcome many new souls into Niflheim this night. Tyr the One Hand watched over him and his men.

He looked over as some of his mounted riders approached. "Harness them to the mangonel," he said. "The dawn is young, but we must make haste. There are more to collect before we reach our mark."

"Can't anyone wring that damn thing's neck?" gasped Eigyr as the cockerel bellowed its welcome to the rising son for the fifth time.

Morven mopped the woman's ruddy brow. "Ye've more tae think on than the bird, don't ye think?" By response, Eigyr let out a low controlled moan, one hand clasping Morven's free hand tight enough to drain the blood from her fingers. She bit her bottom lip until the grip was loosened, then looked at Aiken, whose head and arms were hidden under Eigyr's robes. "How's she doin'?"

Aiken's head appeared above the cloth. "She's close. Sair close."

"you've been saying that for hours, you vile noseless creature!" roared Eigyr. She lay back on the bed, gasping for breath, as the latest contraction faded. "Oh Lord, I can't do this, please, I'm so tired, I can't..."

"Hushtae, child," said Morven. She soaked her cloth, wringing out before blotting at the woman's head again. "It's just a baby, you've had one before. As soon as it's out, th'pain goes, and yui'll have a wee one tae hold..."

"For your information," grunted Eigyr, "there's two of the little sods." She stared at the ceiling, her breath coming in ragged gasps, her face pale and clammy. "There's something wrong isn't there?" she asked. "It shouldn't be taking this long. I know it shouldn't."

"The'll come when they're ready," said Morven, trying to sound reassuring. "Each one comes at its own pace."

"Be still with your platitudes!" bellowed Eigyr. She raised her head. Her voice was far stronger than her body, and it was a strain to hold her head up. "Aiken?"

Aiken looked at her, then at Morven. "She needs some herbs," he muttered. He dunked his hands into the bucket of water by the bed. "Ah kens where Gaira keeps 'em."

Morven watched him go. There was something in his manner that *scared* her. "Ah need fresh water," she muttered, standing to go.

Eigyr grabbed her hand. "I'm not *stupid*," she said, her voice strong even as she lay back on her pillows. Her eyes held Morven's. "Something's wrong. You know it. I know it. Don't patronise me. If he can tell you anything, I want to know." She looked away. "Go after him then."

Morven caught up with Aiken as he headed into the back store room. Bedevere was already in there, nailing up the craterous hole in the wall with planks of ancient wood. Seemingly simply for something to do.

Morven grabbed Aiken's arm as he went to the shelves of herbs and salves. "What's happening? Is something wrong?"

Aiken didn't stop rummaging amongst the pouches and bottles. "She dies."

"...what?" Morven could feel the blood drain from her face. Behind her, Bedevere gave a small gasp, stilling his hammering.

"She walked tae long, woman," snapped the boggart, "an' tae hard. The babes hae turned in her belly. If it were one, Ah cuid mebbies turn it back, but they're fighting fer space in there..." He picked up a pouch, opening it and sniffing its contents. "She's no strength n'more. Her spirit fights wi' the best o' them, but her body, it's been pushin' tae long. There's nay strength left." He set the pouch down, picking up another one.

"Can't you...can't you do anything?" asked Bedevere, walking up to them.

Aiken turned to him. "Aye. Ah can. Ah c'n save the bairns."

"Well... then that is what you must do, surely?" said Bedevere.

"No," said Morven firmly. She knew what the boggart intended . "*No. There has tae be somethin' else yui c'n do! Gaira, she was a Healer, surely there's somethin' here...*"

"Ah'm lookin', mistress!" The distress in Aiken's voice was obvious. "Ah'm lookin', Ah'm doin' me best, Awd Aiken's trying..." his face crumpled and tears spilled down his cheeks.

Morven looked at the long rows of herbs. "Ah'll help. We'll do it, Aiken. Just tell me what Ah'm lookin' fer."

"Lady?"

Eigyr opened her eyes. "Who's there?"

"You had your babies yet? Can I see them?"

With an effort, Eigyr turned her head to one side. The little girl, Anna, stood by her bed, her curly blonde hair shining in the early sunlight. Eigyr smiled. "Would that they were, little one," she said softly. "They seem somewhat reluctant to join us."

Anna's head quirked to one side. "Does it hurt?"

Hurt? Eigyr laughed quietly. "Not so's you'd noticed." She studied the little girl. Her face was bright, curious, not the slightest afraid. "What's that on your eyes?"

Anna giggled. "Aiken showed me. Lets me see the fairies. You wanna see?" She held up one hand; green liquid seeped through her fingers.

"No, child..." Eigyr could feel her belly beginning to tense once more. "No, maybe later, I'd like it, later."

"Okay..." The little girl sounded doubtful. "Only they want to tell you something."

"...What?"

"The fairies," replied Anna. She sat down on the stool Morven had been seated on with a thump. "They've got something to tell you. Please? It doesn't hurt none."

Eigyr was unable to reply. Pain washed through her body, leaching her strength as her womb tried to expel the babies trapped within. Her eyes screwed shut, and she grabbed handfuls of bedding as she tried, and failed, to draw in breath.

She was dimly aware of the little girl moving by her side, standing on the stool. "You alright, lady?"

She could make no sound.

"Okay...I gotta do it. The stick head man says I've got to. You'll like it, I promise." Moist cool fingers gently stroked each eyelid. "See? Doesn't hurt."

The pain began to fade, and Eigyr was finally able to draw a ragged breath. She opened her eyes, her pale brow etched with lines of pain. As she looked around her, the frown vanished, and a look of astonishment spread across her face. "Oh..."

Anna clapped her hands delightedly. "You can see them! Aren't they pretty?"

"They're...they're beautiful," breathed Eigyr.

"But you gotta listen now," said Anna. "'Cos they can't talk very loud, see. Took me ages to hear them. The stick head man, he says you gotta listen."

They'd found innumerable herbs, Aiken identifying them by scent. Herbs for strength, herbs for bloodloss, herbs and salves for the speeding of healing. But he had little herblore. He'd done what he could, mixing a tisane of various herbs, giving others to Morven to form a poultice from.

It wasn't enough.

He knew that even as he and Morven headed back to the birthing chamber, and from the look on her face, he knew Morven was equally aware.

Bedevere followed, his young face earnest. "Is there anything' Ah c'n do?"

Aiken shook his head, his feelings of futility robbing him of his voice.

It was Morven who spoke. "Go find Darrach. He needs tae be here." Despite his misery, Aiken was glad she was here. She had an air of effortless authority. "An' go tae the girruls' quarters. There's a girrul there, Bridget, she's a bairn not three weeks old. She'll be wi' milk; bring her."

"Yes Morven." He headed towards the passageway out of the warrenlike structure.

"An' if yui c'n find a change o' clothes, change!" she called after him. "Yui don't want seein' as a soldier!"

Myrrdin scratched the back of the little pig, the stiff bristles of its pelt like straw under his fingers. The little Grice grunted contentedly, arching its already curved back under his touch, its curly tail straightening, before falling sideways into the straw. A few of its sisters rummaged around Myrrdin as he sat in the centre, pummelling him with their tiny tusks as they rooted for food.

The stench was *indescribable.*

He rotated the shackles on his wrists and ankles, easing their bite. The chains ran evenly to all four corners of the little sty, keeping him in his central position.

Around him, the little town bustled to life. People were already marching purposefully up and down the little back lane, ostensibly ignoring him, but every so often a bundle of food found itself propelled into the pigsty, accompanied with a little nod from the man or woman who'd thrown it.

The grice pigs, fearsome little creatures, got most of the food. Myrddin did not care. His thoughts were back in the previous night, in the king's chamber.

He had been so sure, so *sure* that the mirror shard would be there. That the king could finally be made to see sense, that preparations would get underway for the raid that was now only hours away.

He no longer doubted the veracity of the visions Eigyr had presented him with. So who had moved the mirror? And why?

"Mekkin' yuirself at home, Ah see."

Myrrdin started, looking up at the figure who stood silhouetted in the early sun. "Darrach. I never heard you approach."

The old man shrugged. "Ah'm quick." He sat on one of the railings. One of the pigs immediately ran up, growling angrily. Darrach poked at it with his staff. "Vicious little beggars. How'd you no' get bit?"

Myrrden shrugged. "I'm quick. How's Eigyr?"

"Dunno." Darrach scratched at the stubble on his chin. "In't seen her."

"She's in labour!"

"So?" Darrach picked a piece of dry grass from his hair, and flicked it over the fence. "Since when's she wanted me tae bother with that?"

"She's your daughter, Darrach." Dread ate at Myrrdin. Those children, they *had* to survive. How could Darrach be so callous to his own flesh and blood?

"She's strong, mon," said Darrach. "She'll be fine. She'll send fer me if she needs me. Mah question is...what do we do next?"

"What's happened since last night? What's Cináed done?"

Darrach scowled. "Wee foolish pup he is. Sealed all a' the soldiers in their quarters, put bars across the doors 'n' winders. Willnae let them oot 'til termorrer."

"He's killed them..." breathed Myrrden. "The damn fool, he's killed them!"

"And no' just that," said Darrach. "All group gatherings havetae have a soldier present. One o' Vortigern's men." He snorted. "Just in case anyone from last night wants tae be repeatin' whit the' heard." He stood. "But nay worries. There's none sae sneaky as them in need. We'd best mekk a move, don't yui think?"

"Erm, I'd love to," replied Myrrdin, "but I'm a bit restricted to go walking around, don't you think?" He rattled his chains.

"So magic them off!" said Darrach. "Mekk 'em explode, burn 'em, whatever. Ah've heard o' yuir fires, whit ye c'n do..."

"I told you," growled Myrrdin, "the Seelie Court robbed me of my powers. I have no magic. Remember?"

"Oh..." the old man's face fell. "Oh, aye...Damn. Sorry." He seated himself again. "What...all of it?"

Myrrdin glared at him. "No. No, not all of it. You want to see what they left me? Allow me to demonstrate!" He closed his eyes.

In front of him, a breeze stirred the straw. A few wisps lifted into the air, spiralling gently, then a few more, until a small whirlwind of straw filled one corner of the sty, the little pigs backing away nervously from it.

Myrrdin opened his eyes and the wind fell. "Useful, don't you think?" He tried to stand; the short length of the chains prevented him and he fell back into the straw. He swore loudly. "Everything is going wrong! Everything I've tried to do, worthless!"

"Och, stop pityin' yersen," said Darrach. "Yuir a Wise Man. A druid. Use yer heed 'n' tell me what needs doin'. Ah'm quick. Ah'm sneaky. But Ah've no got yuir smarts."

Myrrdin sat in silence, staring at the old man. He remembered his thoughts just before Darrach had appeared. "The mirror shard Jason spoke of," he said quietly. "The one Gaira placed. It was gone last night when I tried to show the king."

Darrach frowned. "An' don't Ah know yui were countin' on that tae convince him?" he said quietly. "Who would be moving it?"

"I have something for you to do," said Myrrdin. He thought of the young girl in the king's chambers. He thought of Ambrosius' words. *Look out for the traitors.* "I need you to ask around Kilneuair, as quickly and discreetly as you can. Find anyone, *anyone*, who knows Ilisa of Aneithcraig."

"Go wait outside, Anna," said Morven, lifting the child down from the stool. "Let her rest."

"I wanna stay!" said Anna, hanging on to Morven as she tried to place her on the floor. "I want to hear what the fairies are saying!"

"Morven..." Eigyr's hand waved weakly in the air. "Leave the child. She's been good company."

Anna looked up at Morven. "See? Please, can I?"

Morven looked at Aiken, who was spoon feeding the weak tea to Eigyr. He gave a brief shake of his head.

"You wait outside, child," said Morven, leading Anna by her hand to the door. "We'll no' be long."

Anna pouted. "She said I can stay."

"Lady Ivory's very poorly, Anna," said Morven. "We need to...we need to take care of her and her babies."

"Can I see the babies when they come?"

Morven smiled as warmly as she could. "Of course yui can, little one. We'll bring them out to ye." She opened the door. "Go on now." Anna moaned, stamping her little foot, but she did as Morven asked.

Morven sat next to the ashen woman, lifting the poultice to wipe away the green stains above Eigyr's eyes.

Eigyr caught her hand. "Leave it," she said. A smile played across her blue hued lips. "It's nice."

Morven nodded gently, moving the poultice to Eigyr's brow, looking worriedly at Aiken.

Eigyr shifted slightly in the bed. "The pain's going." She looked over at Aiken. "Thankyou."

"'Tis herbs awny," said Aiken gently. "They's stayed the pain. Fer now."

"I'm dying, aren't I?" Eigyr closed her eyes as she said this.

Aiken looked down at the bowl in his hands, stirring the liquid within. "Aye," he said eventually. "Aye, milady. Ah did whit Ah could...it just wasn't enough. Ah'm sorry."

Eigyr took a deep breath. "It's fine," she said softly. "It's not so bad. The tea's helped. I don't hurt any more. The babes, though. Can you save them?"

Aiken nodded dumbly, but Eigyr could not see.

"Yes, Eigyr," said Morven, taking her hand. "Yes, of course we can. But Lady Ivory, you understand what that entails? What we have to do?"

Eigyr nodded. "I'm...I'm not frightened. My father brought me up to be made of sterner stuff than that."

Aiken lifted the bowl. "Yui'd best finish the tisane."

Morven took the bowl from him, lifting the spoon to Eigyr's lips.

Aiken watched the two women for a moment, tears silently streaming down his cheeks. Then he stood, walking over to the little table on the other side of the room, its surface covered with a single cloth. He removed the cloth, dropping it to the floor. On the table sat a small dagger, an oilstone and a small skin of oil.

He looked back at Morven, feeling her gaze upon him. She simply stared at him for a few moments, then her gaze dropped, falling briefly on the table, before finally looking back to Eigyr.

With a trembling hand he lifted the skin, and removed the stopper, trickling a little oil onto the stone.

Bedevere burst in through the door, the dumpy little Bridget behind him, her son held over her back in a woollen papoose. "Sweet blessed Mary..."
Screaming filled the air, a sound of unutterable agony, coming from the birthing room. Bedevere ran through the corridors, his heart pounding.
Anna sat crouched by the door, her hands over her ears, and the woman quickly moved in front of Bedevere, lifting the pale faced child away, pressing her head to her breast.
As Bedevere reached for the handle, the screaming stopped, as though cut short by some unseen hand. He froze in terror. Was some sort of attack taking place? The Lady Ivory, Morven, the boggart, were they injured?
The door was wrenched open, and Morven came out, slamming the door behind her, sobbing as though her soul was wounded beyond recovery. Her hands were soaked in blood. She stared up at Bedevere, as though for a moment she didn't recognise him.
"We hadtae do it," she sobbed, "we hadtae, we needed tae save the bairns..."
Bedevere stood there, not comprehending what the kitchen woman meant. Bridget moved up to him, her face red but calm.
"Come away now," she said. There was quiet resignation in her voice. *She* understood. She took his hand in her small chubby fingers. "Come away."
Bedevere didn't move. "But..but the babies?"
"They live," sobbed Morven. She moved away to the window, bracing herself against the sill. "Two boys. They live." Seeing the blood on her hands, she wimpered, wiping them savagely on her dress.
The door opened again. Aiken came out, his face a strange mixture of utter bereavement yet also pride. In each arm he held a baby. Large brown eyes looked at the young soldier.
"She's askin' fer yui," he said, his voice so gentle, yet so full of pain. "She knew yui'd return."
Bedevere took a step forward. "She – she lives?"
"She has scarce few breaths left," said Aiken. "Yui'd best go in."

The sun, now fully above the horizon, streamed in through the eastern window. Eigyr lay on the bed, her face and lips drained of any colour, the bedding over her torso piled high. Under the bed, red liquid slowly pooled.
She opened her eyes as Bedevere entered. "You came..."

Bedevere went to her side, taking her hand. "Ah'm here, milady, Ah'm sorry, Ah couldnae find yuir father."

Her other hand was raised briefly into the air, before falling back to the bedding. "No matter. He's where he's needed, I think. As much as we love each other, we have little time for...for family." She smiled, but the smile quickly vanished, a frown filling its place.

Unsure what to do, the soldier stroked her hand. "Ah'm...Ah'm here, Eigyr."

"So you've said." The smile returned. "And you remembered my name! Don't grieve for me, Bedevere. Don't grieve for someone you hardly know. What I ask of you now," and she slowly, painfully turned her head to look at him, "what I have to ask of you, it'll be so hard on you, it will take you to places you cannot imagine, do things your soul screams against..."

He squeezed her hand. "Command me, milady. I shall do your bidding, though my very soul may scream."

And as she began to speak, Bedevere began to realise the depths of his promise.

Chapter Twenty Two

The sun was above the house tops by the time Bedevere had emerged, his face pale and drawn, his eyes haunted by words that the others, try as they may, had not been able to overhear. He'd looked up as Morven half rose from her seat, her face questioning. He'd shaken his head, then rapidly stumbled through the corridors, stopping only when he reached fresh air, breathing deeply.

Morven quickly recovered her composure, stripping her stained clothing and donning other robes from Gaira's store. Her hands were scrubbed, in fact were raw from scrubbing, and her face was washed and clean. She'd hardly known the woman after all. She should not let it affect her so.

The body was prepared now, lain out on a single sheet, the sheet stitched tightly around it. She'd been the only one prepared to do the gruesome task. She had to do it, even with the urgency that hung unspoken in the air. Alban Eiler was tomorrow. At least there were no west-facing windows in the room.

She paused by the door of the room where the others waited. Her damned eyes still leaked liquid, and she angrily scrubbed at her face before opening the door. Aiken and Bedevere stood, their faces questioning. Bridget remained seated, the now cleaned babies asleep in her arms, her own child lying on a pile of clothing by her side, plying with his toes. Anna, the quickest of them to recover her equanimity, sat next to him, grinning, tickling his feet at random intervals.

"It's done," said Morven shortly. "We'll grieve later. The bairns live. It's what she wanted. But now, as Aiken would say, there's work tae do." She pulled up a chair, completing the little circle as Aiken and

Bedevere seated themselves once more. "The vikings attack tonight. Omnust, Myrrdin, the' had a plan. The' shared than plan last night, afore the king came along. Who heard them?"

No one responded. Aiken regarded her sorrowfully. "Oor friend lies still warm next door, ma'am. Surely..."

"Aye, she lies dead, an' a wish tae God and his Host she didn't!" She was astounded by the emotion that resonated through her words. She'd thought herself under control. "And hundreds more'll join her if we cannae dae somethin' tae stop it. Who heard Myrrdin's words last night?"

Aiken looked away. "Ah left, after what he said about...after what he said." He looked over at the tiny babies. "Best Ah did, too. For them, anyways."

"I was too late to hear them," said Bedevere. "I was with the Lady Ivory for the most part."

"Then we need someone who *did* hear them. Or Myrrdin himself." She looked at Bedevere. "Where're the cells?"

"He's no' there," said Darrach.

Morven knocked her chair over as she sprang up. The old man stood behind her, leaning on his staff. "Where'd you come from?" she barked. "Ah-Ah never heard yui..."

Darrach shrugged. "Ah'm quick."

Bedevere also stood. "Sir, your daughter, we tried..." he struggled to find the right words. "Ah'm sorry, we tried, but..."

"Ah saw, wee fella, Ah saw, an' a sat wi' her while Morven stitched." He placed one hand on the top of his staff, then rested his chin on his staff. "Ah've done ma peace wi' her."

Morven stared at him. She'd been alone in the room, she would have sworn it, but something about the man made her stay her tongue. There was something of the Seelie Court in this man, something of the Druids.

Darrach looked over at Bridget; she returned his gaze more than a little nervously. "Those mah gran'children?" he asked.

She looked across at Morven, who nodded. She looked back at Darrach. "Aye, sir, the' are. Would ye like tae..?"

"Naw, naw, dinnae fash yuirself." Darrach looked almost uncomfortable. "Do the' hae names yet?"

It was Bedevere that spoke. "She named them, just before she passed."

Steely eyes turned on him. "An' what she tell *yui* fer?"

"She...she asked for me," replied Bedevere.

"Did she now." Replied Darrach. "Ah ken yeh. So come on then, let's hear the names."

"She said not to use them yet." His tone was apologetic, but something in his expression urged Darrach not to pursue the matter. "Not until Myrrdin has heard them."

"Man interferes wi' everythin'," muttered Darrach, but he didn't sound angry. "Have it yuir way then. He's out in yon pigsty, other side of the road tae the barracks. Chained up, if yui please."

"He's alive?" said Morven, relief colouring her cheeks. "An'...An' Captain Ossian? Is he alright?"

"Depends on yuir point o' view," replied Darrach. He searched around the floor for a seat; seeing none he seated himself crosslegged on the floor, lying his staff across his lap. "He's no' a captain any more. That honour's gone tae Vortigern." He grimaced. "An' foul a cap'n Ah've nair met."

"Aye, Ah know 'im," muttered Morven, shuddering as she remembered. "Tried tae have a go at me, in me own mess hall. Was Omnust that saved me. The men'll never follow him."

Oh some do," said Darrach. "Some do. Nine or ten, but when they're the only ones not locked up, the only ones with weapons 'n' shields, nine or ten's enough."

"But Captain Ossian, the rest of the army," said Bedevere, thinking of his comrades. "What's happened tae them?"

"Yui a soldier, boy?" Darrach squinted at him critically. He'd done as Morven suggested, and now wore loose britches and a battered old shirt.

"Aye Sir," he replied. "Came here wi' Omnust and Myrrdin."

"Funny," said Darrach. "Dinnae look awd enough tae have hairs on yer plums, let alone swing an axe."

Bedevere blushed.

"The king, in his infinite wisdom," said Darrach, addressing Morven once more, "has sealed those men as follow Ossian in their barracks, wi' iron and wood. They'll no' be let out afore tomorrer night." He looked round at the questioning faces. "D'yer no' ken whit that means?"

Morven broke the silence that followed. "No," she said. "No, we don't, man. But we will do, when yui tell us. And ye'd best tell us everythin', and best mekk it quick."

The two soldiers watched as the young girl headed towards them, her arms laden with food and a skin of wine. They grinned. She was comely, and already known to them. As she reached them, the nearest stepped out into the narrow street, blocking her way.

"An' where're yui going wi' that wee armful?" he asked, grinning down at her.

"Ah've nae time fer yuir foolishness," snapped the girl. "Ah've been sent we' food fer the druid." She looked past them, to where the pigsty was visible in the distance.

"Oh, been sent, have ye?" grinned the soldier. "Running errands fer the king, are we?"

"Captain Vortigern sent me," said the girl, adjusting the weight in her arms. "Wannae explain tae him why yuir no' lettin' me do his biddin'?"

The soldier's smile faded a little, and he looked uneasily at his friend. "We've been told nothin' o' that. We were told not tae let anyone near. Said too many people'd been feedin' him this morn, he did."

"Then tekk it up wi' him," said the girl, trying to shoulder her way past. "Ah'm busy."

The soldier stepped in front again. "Yui weren't sae reluctant a few nights ago."

"Look," said the girl, "that was then. This is now. Things've changed." She looked up at the soldier, her red hair dancing in the light midmorning breeze. "Will you let me by, mon?"

"What's it worth?" leered the soldier. By his side, his friend chortled.

"Me not goin' back and tellin' the new captain how childish his men are," said the girl smartly.

"Fair brave voice yui have on ye," said the soldier. "Mebbies yui should do that then. In fact," and he folded his arms, "mebbies Ah shuid come with, mekk sure yui get there safely."

"Will you let me past?!"

"A wee dram, first," grinned the man.

"What?"

"O' the wineskin. Surely ye's don't mean one man tae have all that tae hisself?"

The girl met his gaze, and his smile broadened as he saw the first flicker of fear in her face. "Fine." She unslung the skin from her shoulder, thrusting it at him. "An' Ah hope yuir sick."

The soldier quickly broke the wax seal, and took several deep swallows from the skin, before passing it to his companion. "Now," he said, looking back to the girl. "Tell me again, exactly who sent ye's? Vortigern, ye's say?"

"Honestly now? No," said the girl. "Morven sent me."

"The kitchen woman?" The soldier stared at her. His vision blurred briefly, and he shook his head. The drink was potent! "Why's the kitchen woman sendin' ye's to feed the pig talker?"

"She didn't," said the girl. She grinned. "She sent me wi' a skin o' Gaira's sleepin' potion tae give tae yui fools. Then me and mine're gonnae free the *pig talker.*"

"What?" He shook his head again. "What...what foolishness is this?" Darkness filled his vision. "Girrul, what have ye done?"

The girl watched as he fell to his knees. "Night night."

The soldier pitched forward into the mud, his companion falling across his back.

"That was fun," said the girl to herself, before turning to look back down the street. "Darrach! It's done!"

"Aye," said Darrach from by her side. "Ah saw."

The girl screamed, almost dropping the food. "Yui bluidy eejit!"

"Been called worse," said Darrach amiably. "Here." He thrust a length of rope at her. "Bind them. Give me the fuid. Ah'll tekk it down tae him."

The girl snatched the rope from him. "Thought yui were bringin' the ironsmith," she said angrily.

Darrach nodded. "Ah ken ye's, Ah ken ye's. He's on his way true enough. Ah'm just a wee bit faster, is all."

Myrrdin looked up as Darrach ambled up. "Did you find anyone?"

Darrach seated himself on the railings again. "Knocked on ev'ry door o' the central town. Nae-one seems tae know her." He tore off a piece of bread, proffering it to Myrrdin. "Yui hungry?"

Myrrdin shook his head angrily. "No, I'm not hungry, man! Don't lie to me! How-how have you knocked at every door already? Scarcely an hour's past. And don't tell me you're *fast.*"

"Suit yersen." Darrach tore of a small piece of bread, and began sucking noisily on it. "Ah am though. Fearsome fast." He smiled a toothless smile. "Yuir no' the only one with a bit o' magic, yui ken. Mah Dah, afore he died like, he tought me how tae walk the ley lines. Bec mac Dè teached 'im. The fairy paths, ye ken. Corpse roads."

"You...you know how to walk them?" Myrrdin could not help but smile. "Darrach, you are a man of hidden talents."

Omnust chuckled, still sucking on the bread. He finally swallowed, much to Myrrdin's relief, and looked at the druid. "Ah...Ah'm the bearer of bad news, Ah'm afraid. Mah daughter. Ah remember how yui two were."

Myrrdin went cold. "...no..."

Darrach nodded. "Yeh ken. Ah sat wi' her, whilst Ah was on the paths. She couldnae see me."

Memories of years past flooded Myrrdin's mind; days spent by the river, laughing and chasing each other; nights in front of the hearth, the leaping flames the only light as they lay together, loving one another.

Gone. All gone.

"Dinnae fret so," said Darrach, easing himself down from the wooden bar. "The bairns, the' survived. Feisty wee boys an' all. The' hadtae cut them free though..."

"Be still!" Myrrdin lunged at the old man, his chains rattling loudly. "She was your daughter!"

Darrach said nothing, studying the druid intently. Finally he looked away. "Here's the ironsmith. We'll have ye's free soon enough. Ah'll be off then. Got people tae round up. There's a lassie further down, tying up yuir guards. She'll tekk ye's tae the others."

"No, *wait...*"

But Darrach was gone. Myrrdin sank back into the straw, the pigs grunting around him. Eigyr. Gone. It didn't seem real. How could she be? Only hours before, her voice had filled the night, her lips had burned against his. A promise for the future? That promise meant only death.

"M-Myrrdin, sir?"

He opened his eyes. A massive bear of a man stood before him, a chisel and hammer clutched in his hands. The man looked fearful. No, not fearful; he looked guilty, like a child about to be caught out for something he'd done wrong.

"Sir, Ah'm here tae free yui."

Myrrdin closed his eyes once more.

Everything was happening so *quickly.* Aiken looked around him. Morven had left for her girls' quarters less than an hour ago, laden down with numerous skins of a sleeping concoction she'd found in the stores. She'd returned half an hour since. Now, people were swarming up the path into Gaira's home, quickly filling it. The various sacks of grain and dried meats had become seats for the older ones, and the room hummed with muted conversation. He looked over at Morven as he recognised faces.

"These're all the' folk from last night," he whispered.

"They are indeed," nodded Morven. She smiled a greeting as more people entered. "And those they've told as well. An' those *they've* told. And all mah lasses fro' the barracks." There was more than a hint of pride in her voice.

"But-but..." Aiken looked at the younger women as they bustled around, helping the old folk to their makeshift seats, welcoming others as they entered. "Surely...won't the' be missed?"

Morven shook her head, her face grim. "The king has barricaded himself in, the' say. Him and that lass, and that damned Vortigern. No one in, no one out."

"He's lost," said Aiken. "And he'll tekk guid men wi' him."

"He's a guid man," said Morven defensively. "He's just been stretched too far." She sighed wearily. "But yes, he'll be the cause o' the loss o' many more guid men. Unless we stop him."

"Oh aye, like as we c'n dae that," said Aiken. "We've no army."

"According to Omnust, we do," said Morven, watching her girls. "*My* army. Soldiers of brooms 'n' brushes." She saw something outside, something that made her stand, a savage grin on her face. "An' we're sair dangerous when crossed!"

Aiken stood, following her gaze through the window. "Oh mah sainted mother..."

More girls were walking up the path, eight or nine at least, giggling amongst themselves. Behind them they dragged seven staggering soldiers, encased in rope and iron, stumbling over their feet as though drunk.

Morven nudged the boggart. "A guid start, don't yui think?"

*

Cináed awoke from dreams filled with fire and blood, with flashing swords and the flight of arrows. He lay gasping on his bed, staring at the ceiling. He looked to his window. What time was it? He climbed out of bed, shivering as his feet touched the stone floor, then walked briskly over to the window, pulling back the vast curtains. Sunlight flooded the room, making the king squint against the light. It was almost noon. Had he needed sleep so strongly?

It was so *cold.* Where was his guard? Surely he knew to keep the fire banked; the ashes in the grate threw out no heat, the fire having died many hours ago.

Cináed drew a breath, ready to shout for the man, before his memory returned. The guard was locked in his barracks, along with the rest of the army.

The king's face reddened with shame. Foolish, *foolish* pride, to lock his entire army up. With the clarity brought from the first night's sleep in a number of days, he thought back on the events of previous nights.

It was Myrrdin, the druid, who had worked against him, so sure was he in the visions of Ambrosius. And who had brought the forest man here but he himself? It was no surprise then that his men had listened so intently. For so had he, and for many years before these events.

He should not blame his men.

He would summon Vortigern, have the barricades lifted. The men would need food, weapons, they would need to finalise their plans...

He shivered.

But first he needed warmth. He pulled a blanket from the bed, wrapping it over his shoulders as he went to the fire. There was wood piled there, and a small bucket of wood shavings for kindling, two flints sitting on the hearth by its side.

He knelt down, reaching for the poker and shovel, riddling the ashes through the fire grate to clear a bed for the kindling.

Something glinted in the sunlight.

Cináed leaned in, frowning, his fingers questing through the warm ashes. With a stifled yell he snatched his hand back as something sharp bit into his fingers. He sucked at his fingers, tasting blood. More carefully, he reached back into the ashes, and withdrew the tiny piece of glass.

He held it up. It was *black*.

Horror washed over him as Myrrdin's words returned to him from the night before, mocking him. Mindless now of cutting his fingers, he thrust both hands into the ashes, retrieving piece after piece of shattered glass, lying them out on the floor in front.

Trembling hands rearranged the pieces, creating their former shape; that of a piece of obsidian mirror. Even as he stared at the glass, something shadowy formed within its depths; the shape of a viking helmet.

"No!" His hand flashed out, scattering the pieces. He staggered backward, hitting the round table, scattering the model pieces of the village. He turned, staring down at Kilneuair as it lay in ruins before him.

"Myrrdin..." he breathed. How blind had he been, so sure in his own judgement he had ignored his oldest friend? "Myrrdin..." He set off towards his chamber doors, walking, then running, then sprinting. He threw open the doors. "Myrrdin!"

Ilisa stepped round the door frame, a dainty hand pushing against his side. "Hush, your majesty," she smiled, her baby asleep on her shoulder.

Wide eyed, Cináed looked down.

The golden hilt of a dagger protruded from just below his ribs.

Part Four

Chapter Twenty Three

Vortigern ran down the hall. The doors to the king's chambers were open. The shout had come from there. His sword drawn, he entered the room.

The king lay on the ground, a pool of blood by his side, a knife protruding from the blanket that wrapped him.

"Sire, what...?"

"The girl," gasped Cináed. "The girl, she's not who she said..." He looked down at the knife. "She meant to kill me ... the blanket, she couldn't pierce deep enough..." One shaking hand reached up and grasped the hilt of the knife. He closed his eyes as he pulled out the knife, stifling a yell. "Help me up."

"Sire, yuir hurt, ye shouldnae be moving." He knelt by his king.

"Damn it man," gasped the king, "I've had worse and still held my sword. Help me up!"

Vortigern offered his arm, and Cináed grabbed, hauling himself to his feet. His legs almost immediately buckled, and Vortigern caught him round his waist. He helped the king over to his bed, and lowered him down. Blood drenched the left side of the king's night robes.

"Thankyou," said Cináed, his breathing shallow. "Thankyou. The bitch bit deeper than I thought." He parted the tear where the knife had pierced his clothing, looking at the wound beneath. He quickly closed it, panting. "Listen. Listen to me. The druid, he was...he was right, captain. The vikings, they come today. I was wrong. You understand me? I was wrong! Go to their barracks, remove the barricades."

"Sire, yui need a healer," replied Vortigern, the concern in his voice obvious. "Ah'll go get..."

"Gaira is gone!" snapped the king. "There are no others. I can treat myself! Go!"

He watched the captain run out of the door, then clutched his side, grimacing. Blood oozed between his fingers.

No. He would *not* succumb.

He gingerly stripped off the night shirt, wincing as the lips of his wounds parted. He felt fresh warmth run down his side. He stood, steadying himself momentarily against the bed frame, then staggered over to the fire. He reached into the grate, grabbing a handful of ash. He hesitated momentarily, mentally preparing himself, then pushed the dry ashes against the wound. His yell echoed around the room, and he fell to one knee. After a moment, he grabbed another handful, repeating the procedure. With a moan, he fell sideways. Painful though it was, it should stay the bleeding. Now he needed binding. He looked over to his bed. The sheets would suffice.

Unable to stand unaided, he began dragging himself along the ground.

*

"Now...*push!*" Omnust leaned on the wooden slat, recovered from a broken cot. It was shoved between the metal bars over the window, and he and two of his men pressed down with all of their might.

The slat splintered, casting the men to the ground, the bars unmoved.

Omnust was on his feet instantly. "Another," he growled. "Bring another."

Another slat was pushed between the bars, and Omnust and his men prepared to assault the impervious bars once more.

Someone pounded on the door, staying their work. *"Omnust!"*

Omnust recognised the voice. *Vortigern.*

"Yui come tae gloat?" he shouted.

"Ah come bearing news. Fro' th'king."

Omnust walked up to the door, looking back at his men and seeing their faces as wary as his own. "What? Has he come tae his senses at last?"

Outside the door, Vortigern leant against the wall, smiling. "Seems so. Seems the young maiden wasnae all she seemed. Seems she stabbed him."

A ripple of consternation rippled through the barracks, and Omnust heard his men shouting from the other rooms. "He's dead?"

"Och no," said Vortigern. "Not yet. Sair hurt though. Told me tae lift the barricades."

"What're yui waitin' fer?" bellowed Omnust. "Release us, Vortigern!" He pounded the door.

On the other side of the door, Vortigern's smile became a grin. He removed a roll of parment from his belt. "Th'king made it official, ye ken. That Ah'm captain."

"Vortigern!"

"E'en has his seal on it. A fair reference for a man seekin' his fortune."

"Vortigern!" Omnust's voice echoed through the corridor. "Damn it man!"

"A present fro' a dead king tae present tae the king's son." His smile faded, and he replaced the roll in his belt. "Ah'm goin' places, yui ken. Ah'm no' stayin' here tae be stuck like a pig. Ah cannae release yui. Ah'm headin' south for Constantine. Cannae afford yui stoppin' me." There was silence from the other side of the door. "Omnust? Yui understand, don't ye's? Captain tae captain?"

"You're no captain!"

"True enough," said Vortigern, "if Ah let yui oot. But Ah've papers say otherwise. An' th' new king needs a strong arm by his side. In case..." he smiled again. "In case he shuid meet wi' an accident." He stood back from the door. "Ah'm sorry, Omnust. Ah really am, but mebbies Ah'll see yui again."

"When hell freezes over!"

"Aye," said Vortigern. "Most likely." He headed off down the corridor, the shouts of the men following his as he left.

"Is it...is it done?" said Cináed from his bed.

Vortigern smiled down at him. "Aye Sire. But the main doors, they're still locked. They wait in the armoury, for ye's tae release them."

Cináed frowned. Of course. He remembered last night, blinded by anger, going from door to window throughout the large building, locking every exit that led to the town outside. He looked over to his left, to where a small table sat. "The keys...they're in the drawer there."

Vortigern opened the drawer, withdrawing the large loop of keys. "Thank you, Sire."

"Are they...are they angry?"

Vortigern nodded. "Aye, Sire. Shoutin', the' were."

Cináed nodded. "And well they should. I was a fool, captain. A blind fool who would not listen."

Vortigern nodded silently.

"Water," breathed the king. "I need water. My mouth is parched."

"Yui need rest, sire," said the captain gently. "Yuir *weak*. Sleep some. Ah'll send men wi' water, fuid as well."

His side burning with pain, the king gratefully closed his eyes.

Shattered jars lay across the floor of the vast kitchen, their contents of dried fruit and brined meats a random splash of colour across the grey slate floor. Lathgertha ate hungrily, drinking from the flagon of ale she'd found in one of the widowless pantries. The child, Critheanach, lay slumbering in a wicker basket of warm ashes on the hearth of the cavernous fireplace, warm and content. She'd fed the baby as soon as she'd awoken. Not from any compassion; simply to silence its cries.

It would have been quicker to kill it. She did not know why she hadn't.

But now she needed to escape the confines of the barracks. She'd been to every door, every window she could find. But all the doors were locked, all the widows shuttered and secured. She was trapped.

She had no fear of discovery. The king was dead, and the soldiers imprisoned in their chambers. She had the whole of the place to herself.

She was robbed of this notion by the jingle of metal from the corridor beyond.

Silently she eased herself out of her seat, removing her knife from her wristguard. She'd discarded the dead woman's robes, leaving her in her chainmail and britches, freeing her movement. She crept on silent feet to the door, peering round the corner.

A soldier stood at the door to the armoury, smiling as he stared at the vast collection of swords, armour, bows and innumerable other weapons. As she watched, he pulled the double doors closed, locking the doors top, middle and bottom. She ducked back a little as he walked across the corridor to the mess hall, where he pulled the doors closed once more.

What was he doing?

Silently and cautiously, she moved out into the corridor, her knife ready.

"You." She held her knife out, poised to strike. "What are you doing?"

The soldier turned slowly, one hand on the hilt of his sword. He looked at Lathgertha, his eyes narrowed, his eyes flashing toward the king's chambers. "The lady Ilisa."

She'd caught his quick glance. "You know I'm no such thing." She looked at the bundle of keys in his hand. "Those keys. Can they get me out of here?"

He gave the briefest of nods, the rest of his body immobile. "Aye. The' c'n get us *both* out of here."

"And why would I take you with me?"

The soldier didn't move. "Ah'm no common villager fer yui to intimidate," he said. "Ah'm a captain o' the king."

"The king's *dead.*"

"Not yet," said the soldier. "But soon, Ah grant yui. If not by yuir sting, then by the blades of yuir brethren."

"Give me the keys and I'll let you live." She slowly walked across the corridor, circling him.

He turned on the spot, his sword still undrawn. "Try tae take the keys, Ah'll kill *yui.*"

He seemed totally fearless. With good reason. Lathgertha had lost the element of surprise. Her skill was in the unseen attack, the throw of the blade. The man was more than a head taller, and twice her weight. And trained in combat.

"Gaira is no' the only one who knows th'value o' trade," he said.

Lathgertha blinked. "What?"

The soldier smiled. "We c'n fight. If that's what pleases yui. Debatable which will lie dead at the end. But yui and yuirs, ye's want land here. A foothold. *Ah* want power."

"What are talking about, *power?"* said Lathgertha. "You, you're a common soldier. What power?"

"A common soldier wi' the king's seal," replied the dark haired man. "A common soldier who heads tae the ranks o' Constantine as a trusted captain. A common soldier who can create trade routes fer yui 'n' yuirs."

"A common soldier with delusions of power," said Lathgertha. She didn't lower her blade. "How do you intend...?"

The man looked down at the king's chambers again. "As yui dealt wi' one," he said, looking back at her, "so Ah'll deal wi' the other."

She smiled. "You're ambitious."

He returned the smile. "And yuir not?"

"What's your name?"

"Captain Vortigern. Milady." He made a slight bow, his eyes never leaving her face.

She lowered her blade. "Let me out of here, Captain Vortigern," she said. "Then we'll talk."

The afternoon sun shone brightly down as Morven studied the collection of carts before her, and at the gathering of people and cattle. "How many carts?"

"Fifteen, Morven," said an old man, stroking the nose of the ox harnessed to his cart. "An' we hae five sets of hands fer each cart."

"You know which trees contain the weapons?"

"Aye."

"Right, be off. We need them back here within the hour. We head tae the forest wi' 'em."

One of her girls came out through the door. "We're ready, Morven," she said. "What d'yui need?"

"Are all the soldiers secured?"

The girl smiled. "Aye, Morven. Tied like wee piggies. Squealin' like 'em too."

Morven stared at her. "Yui've no' hurt 'em, Ah hope."

"No more'n they deserved," replied the girl.

"So long as the' c'n still swing a blade," muttered Morven. "We'll need them tonight, Ah fear."

"Ma'am, yuir no gonnae set them free?" said the girl, abashed.

"Yui think the'll still think the druid wrong when the vikings attack? Stupid girl! The'll fight wi' us same as anyone!"

"...Yes ma'am."

"And don't *yes ma'am* me so meakly, girrul!" snapped Morven. "Don't Ah know how troublesome the've been tae us? Who kept yui safe fro' them, eh?"

"You, ma'am." The girl shuffled her feet nervously.

"Aye, me, Ma'am, and don't ye's ferget it!" She sighed, swallowing down her ire. "Get the girls. Go round the houses. We need knives, any sort o' knives. Anythin' we can use as weapons. And mekk sure they're sharp!" She looked around her. "And where's the druid?"

"He...he's wi' Eigyr, ma'am."

Morven gently opened the door, peering round it.

Sunlight shone through the shingled roof, long fingers of light filling the air, dust motes dancing brightly within then. The druid, no more than a dark silhouette in the light, stood at the head of the wrapped figure, one hand placed gently on its brow.

She knocked lightly on the door. "Sir? We're ready. It's time."

The shadowy figure did not move. "Do you know what it's like," he said quietly, "looking through time yet to come, knowing that at each time, in each place, your history is already written?"

"Sir?" He did not seem to be addressing her.

"There is a child out there," said Myrrdin, unmoving, "sitting with your people. She sees me as her grandfather. She loved me, but I could not return that love. She fears me now, and that fear is deserved. She is the child of a child yet to be sired, born of a woman I've never met." His hand stroked the cloth beneath his fingers. "My heart has been stilled in this room. Its blood lies cold, thickened with anger, with hatred, and with the surety of *death.*"

Morven remained silent, unsure what to say. There was such emotion in the druid's voice, a pain and agony she'd not heard from anyone.

"My story would end now," said the druid. It was as though he was unaware of Morven's presence; he was speaking his feelings aloud. "If it were my choice, I would lie next to you, drape my face with linen, and follow where ever you flew. How can I love again?

"Why did you seek me out? Why did you choose me over safety, when my very presence summons death in all her crimson finery?" He bent, touching his forehead against hers. "Death I brought to Gwenddolau, my closest of kin. Did I not learn to close my heart? How many more must follow my carrion trail?" His voice broke with emotions, and he grasped Eigyr's cloth covered hands with his own. "My feet leave bloody prints through every land I cross!"

Morven quietly retreated.

Ragnar stood on the hillside, looking out across the landscape before him. Gentle waves lapped the shore far below him as it sat on his right, stretching out into the distance like a becalmed sea.

Another viking rode up the hill to his side. "You called me?"

"I see a figure," said Ragnar, squinting against the light. "On horseback, a soldier I think. He's left the village, rides through the forest.

"Does he head our way?"

"No. I think not. At least, not deliberately." He smiled. "I do not think he's spied us. Our presence is not expected, after all. If he comes within range, kill him, otherwise, save your arrows." He looked back down the hill. "Are the mangonels ready?"

"They are loaded, the gears tightened. We simply need to light the pitch when ready."

"Good." He urged his mount down the hill. "We wait until the moon is risen." As he rode down the hill, he could feel the excitement building within him. As always before a raid, his blood pulsed through his body, carrying strength to every corner of his being. He burnt with energy.

He reined in by the group of Berserkers, dismounting to watch. The closest of the men looked up at him, giving him a single nod, which he returned. They sat bare chested, dressed only in fur britches, seemingly impervious to the cold. For a group so battle scarred and dangerous, they sat surprisingly still. In each hand they held a small wooden bowl of water. A large pouch was passed from man to man, and each man took a handful of dried mushrooms and leaves from it before passing it to the next.

Once the bag had travelled all round the group, one man began to chant wordlessly, his words a rhythm that all the men began to sway to. Ragnar watched intently, enjoying the spectacle. As one, the men dropped the plant matter in the bowls, their hands crushing the mushrooms and leaves into the water, still following the rhythm of the chant, releasing the powerful hallucinogenics into the water.

This ritual would go on for an hour or more, Ragnar knew, building in intensity until as one they would all consume their potions. Two hours after that, they would be *deadly.*

"Give me a reason not to slit your throat."

A cold knife edge pressed against his throat, a dainty yet strong hand grasping the hilt of his sword as he reached for it. "Hello, wife."

A thin leg wrapped round his shins, throwing him face first into the dirt. Around him, his men who had been watching the Berserkers, turned at this new spectacle, laughing.

"You sent me away!" She grabbed a handful of his hair, pulling his head back and pressing her knife against his throat. "You cost us a ship!"

It took only a quick twist of a shoulder, the sudden thrust of one hand, to throw his wife off. Then he was on top, her knife in his hand, its blade pressed against her throat as he knelt on her arms. Her knees ineffectually pummelled his back. Around them, the men roared.

"Where's the boy, my love?" he smiled.

"Gone!" snapped Lathgertha. "He's gone! Him and that damned witchwoman, escaped!"

"You let a *boy* beat you?!" his tone was mocking.

"He had a magic knife, you dog!" shouted Lathgertha, writhing beneath him. "It *flew!*" Around her, the men roared with laughter. "Shut up! We lost a *ship!* All hands!"

Ragnar leant back, his hands on his hips. "We have more than four hundred men. Eighty Berserkers. I think that'll be ample."

She managed to wrench an arm free, and a fist found its mark between his legs. He rolled off her, groaning, dropping the knife. More laughter.

Lathgertha stood, angrily brushing her hair out of her eyes. "Don't you care about your men?" she demanded.

Ragnar glared at her, and slowly stood. "Of course I care. You think I don't? We're not here to raid anymore, woman. We're here to destroy. You see any cages? Any wagons for the transportation of slaves?" He picked up the knife, and threw it hilt first towards his wife. "The boy has friends down there. Family. Remember? We kill *everyone.* Not even the finest army could stop us."

Lathgertha looked at him, a slow smile spreading across her lips. "The army won't be a problem."

"What do you mean?"

"The king had them barricaded in their barracks. For mutiny. Before I killed him."

Ragnar's smile mirrored her own. "Well then. I guess we have a target for their mangonels."

Chapter Twenty Four

Morven clambered out of the back of the cart, her arms laden with various bags. She waddled up to Bedevere, who was stood beneath the trees, directing the various men and women who milled about, their arms laden with quivers of arrows and sealed leather bags of pitch soaked rags.

"Where're mah girruls?" she panted.

"That tree o'er there, the loch side o' the path," replied Bedevere. Pointing, not looking in her direction. "No!" He shouted to one of the men. "Not that tree! It's too high tae jump doon from, man! The next one along!" He looked at Morven. "They're willin'," he said, "but the've nae idea. Think a high vantage point'll keep 'em safe. Dinnae think the vikings might torch the trees."

Morven bit her lip. She hadn't thought of that either. "How's it going?"

"Look," said Bedevere, pointing. "See fer yuirsen. Fust five trees've men already waitin' in them. The've got hundreds of arrers, plus the trees're low enough for them tae mekk a quick escape." He pointed between the trees. "Ah've got women, hacking doon the brambles, fillin' the space between the trees." He sighed, obviously feeling the stress. "It willnae stop the Berserkers. But it may slow 'em down long enough fer the men tae escape." He looked down the path to Kilneuair. "More're comin', an' the remaining women 'n' bairns're positioning the carts in the streets, fillin' them with pitched rags. When the vikings enter, the'll be torched. There's only one road left clear."

"The one tae the firepits 'n' mangonels."

"Aye." He looked over at another gaggle of men as the clambered up an ancient pine. "Whit did Ah just say? Damn fools! Yui jump down frae there, yui'll bust yuir legs! Come down now!"

Morven nodded approvingly. "Yuir bossy fer a young un."

"Aye, well," said Bedevere, angrily watching the men, "fear mekks men of us all. Look, Ah need tae pitch in, will you be alright?"

"Go, mon, go," said Morven. "Ah c'n see mah lasses." As the young soldier headed off, still shouting, she waddled over to where a group of four women stood. "Blessed Bridhe, what're ye's doin'?"

The girls had a burnt out torch held between then, and they were running their fingers through the greasy material, smearing their faces with the black substance. One of them, Bridget, turned to face Morven. "T'was Bedevere's idea, ma'am," she said. "Tae hide our faces in the dark. All the men're doin' it."

"Where's the bairns?" demanded Morven. She'd left Bridget at Gaira's place, with instructions not to leave unless she found herself in danger.

"Wi' Aiken," replied Bridget, with no hint of apology.

"Ah told you *not* to leave them," said Morven heatedly.

"That's mah man up there," said Bridget, pointing across to another tree. "Think Ah'm gonnae sit 'n' hide while he fights fer me?"

"So where's Aiken?" Morven understood the girl's position entirely, but she had to think of the bairns.

"Headed tae the church, wi' the little girl." She dipped her finger into the greasy soot, smearing more of the muck down her cheeks and neck. "Mah bairns are there already. All o' the small uns are."

Morven nodded. At least the little parish church was on the boundaries of the town. Hopefully well away from the battle. "The church, eh? Father Donald won't like that."

"He's comin' back," said Bridget. "He's leavin' them there, then he's joining Darrach at the firepit." She held the torch out to Morven. "Yui want some?"

Morven stared in repulsion at the charred greasy mass, then shrugged, dropping the numerous cloth sacks. Little puffs of white powder billowed into the still air. "Give us it here then."

Aiken kicked on the church doors, his arms laden with the two babies, who seemed to be doing their best to rouse the occupants all by themselves. "Open the door!" He looked down at Anna, who was clinging to his leg, silent tears running down her face. "It's only for a wee while, lassie," he said, raising his voice over the babies' cries. "Ah'll come back fuir ye's, we'll go find Jason t'gether."

Anna clung tighter to his leg. "*Please* don't leave me, *please!*"

The small gridded window in the door shot open, and two fear filled eyes stared out. "Get away! Get away from God's house, yui-yui blue bearded heathen *devil!*"

Aiken glowered at him. "Ah dinnae have the time tae argue, sir," he said. "Ah've bairns, bairns that need safety. Open th'door or Ah'll kick the bluidy thing down!" He jostled the babies, trying to raise them for the priest to see.

The window slammed shut.

"See?" said Anna. "They don't want us, please take me with you, please don't leave me here!"

The door opened, and the priest edged his way out, his golden fish pendant held out in front of him. Behind him, the aisles swarmed with little children, some plying, some screaming. "Are they *yours?*"

"This is Anna, sir," said Aiken, "yui've seen her afore. She's Yellowblade's sister."

The priest grasped Anna's wrist, pulling her from Aiken's leg and across the threshold of the church. Anna screamed in protest.

"No! I won't go! Aiken, please, I'll be good, I won't run away, please!" She tried to push back past the priest, but he pulled the door further closed, his body blocking her path. Tiny hands reached out for Aiken as she screamed.

"And those?" he said, gesturing at the babies.

"They're...they're Lady Ivory's," said Aiken, his voice shaking as Anna's screams tore at him. "Th' king's grand children."

The priest hesitated, clearly torn between being in such close contact with the demon he perceived Aiken to be, and taking the grand children of his beloved king. He finally dropped the golden fish, and reached for the babies.

Anna pushed past as he took the babies, wrapping herself around Aiken. "No, Aiken, no," she sobbed, "please, everyone's left me, please don't leave me, please, I'll be good..."

"Oh, wee Anna," said Aiken, his own voice breaking now, "Ah havetae, don't you understand? It's only for a wee while, Ah'll be back, Ah promise on mah life..."

"You *won't!*" shouted Anna, "you won't, you'll leave me, just like Jason, and Granddad, and Kylie, Aiken please, *please!*" her powerful sobs shook her whole body.

The priest had lain the babies on the floor inside the door, and reached out, forcibly dragging Anna off Aiken, pulling her screaming and kicking into the church. Angry eyes regarded Aiken. "Be off with you."

The door slammed shut.

Aiken stared at the door, tears streaming down his face as he listened to Anna's screams fade.

He felt as though his heart had been cleft in two.

Cináed stirred, opening his eyes, momentarily disorientated. Where was he? Memories of half recalled dreams filled his mind; hammering at the main doors, then at the windows, as though someone tried to gain entry. He raised himself from the bed, immediately falling back as his wound opened.

"Vortigern?" his voice came in a dry croak, a deathly whisper with no strength.

The room was deserted. He turned his head to the window, and whimpered. The sky beyond was orange, the moon already peeping over the tops of the houses. He looked at the little table by his bed. Its drawer sat open, empty, its surface bare of any food or water that had been promised.

He eased himself up onto his elbows, wincing at the pain, but willing himself to ignore it. He looked down at his makeshift dressing. A small patch of dampness darkened its centre, made almost black from the ash beneath.

Was it good, he wondered, that he'd bled so little? He could make out his pool of blood on the floor. How much blood had he lost?

He tried clearing his throat. "Vortigern!" Again the dry rasp.

He was so *thirsty*.

The kitchen was just down the corridor. They'd have water there. He tried to move his legs. They twitched, but did not lift. He lay back on the bed, breathing rapidly. Where was Vortigern? His dreams of hammering, were they just dreams, or had someone broken in? Someone dangerous?

He pushed himself up, grabbing the bedding to pull himself fully up, crying out at the pain. With his hands he swung first one, then the other leg over the side of the bed. He propelled himself upwards, trying to stand. His legs, weaker than a baby's, collapsed beneath him, and he fell with a cry to the floor.

So be it. If he could not walk, he would crawl.

Inch by inch, he pulled himself across the floor, each movement twisting at his wound. He hadn't the strength to go round the congealed pool of blood; instead he dragged himself through it, his bare flesh sticking to it.

He finally reached the door, pulling himself out into the long corridor.

A moan escaped from his lips. The kitchen doors, which he knew should have been open, were closed. As were the doors to the mess hall. And the armoury.

He closed his eyes. There had been more than one traitor locked in the barracks with him. "Oh Myrrdin forgive me," he breathed. So many choices gone wrong. The best of advice had fallen on the deafest of ears, because *he* was the king, and kings were *not* fallible.

He would burn in hell for his choices. He closed his eyes, waiting for his breath to finally fail, for his heart to cease its erratic pounding. He would face his judgement before God.

Movement above him. The sound of feet, of something crashing. Omnust's voice shouting *'Again!'*

Cináed opened his eyes. His men. They were still trapped upstairs.

God had other plans than to take him then. There was still some good he could do here. Slowly, painfully, he dragged himself towards the stairway, fifty yards and a hundred leagues away down the corridor.

"It's sair close," muttered Darrach, staring at the pit.

"I know," replied Myrrdin.

The pit was well hidden in the muddy road. A layer of mud lay across the thin reeds above the various pots and skins, matching perfectly with the dirt track either side. The slight delve in the road was only noticeable to those who knew what to look for.

"If the' get th' mangonels this far..." continued Darrach, but Myrrdin cut him off.

"I said I know," he said. The firepit was only a street from the barracks. Easy striking range for the powerful catapults. "We'll just have to pray they *don't.*" He looked down the street. Two wooden huts sat either side of the road, lights burning in their windows. Only a trained eye would see the twine that bound the walls together, or the reed roof that was only one reed thick. "But we have our own. Are the men in there?"

Darrach nodded. "Hae been fer three hours. Ev'ry one's ready, druid. Ev'ry one waits."

Myrrdin looked up at the sky. "They won't have to wait long," he muttered. "The night is almost upon us." He looked around him, at the darkened windows that faced into the street from all sides. He frowned. "We're missing something."

"What?"

Myrrdin turned on the spot. "We're missing something!" He stared at the buildings around him, panic building in his throat.

"We've missed *nuthin,'*" insisted the old man, leaning on his staff. "The old 'uns hide along the banks, the bairns in yon church. The trees are laden, doon here an' in the forest, the menfolk an' the womenfolk are all armed. Ah'm tellin' ye's, we're *ready.*"

"The houses," breathed Myrrdin. "How could we have missed it?"

"The...?"

"The houses, Darrach, the *houses!*" He pointed frantically. "We've been so busy - there's been no fires lit, no candles to light the windows; the whole town looks deserted! You can see the lights of the village from miles away – the vikings, they'll know something's wrong!"

"Oh Blessed Bridhe..." Darrach straightened. "Look, Ah'll sort it. A c'n walk the Paths, it'll take nae time..." he didn't sound confident.

"Yes," said Myrrdin, "yes that may work...take one of the candles from the huts, use that..."

"Doesnae work like that, mon," snapped Darrach. "Ah c'n neither push, pull, carry nor drop on the Path. Ev'rything *stops*. Yeh ken? Might as well try pushin' a mountain." He set off down the lane. "Dinnae fash. Ah'll use what flints there are. Ah'll be quick!" With that, the old man vanished. Within moments, light flared in the window of a house, then another and another.

Myrrdin prayed he would be quick enough.

"Sire?"

The druid turned at the sound of the voice. It was the ironsmith who'd freed him that morning.

"Morven said yui were askin' after me?" said the man.

"Yes," said Myrrdin. "Yes I was. What's your name?"

"Bernard, Sire."

"Bernard. I need you to come with me. We head to the barracks..."

"Sire, Ah've *been* there all day like yui told me," said the man bitterly, "Ah've been tryin' tae break the locks, tried everything, an' the winders too, but my master's master, he made them years ago, Ah cannae break 'em."

"You didn't have me with you," said Myrrdin. "Two pairs of eyes may see a solution where one sees only the problem. Quickly now!"

"Keep the men back," shouted Ragnar breathlessly as he urged his mount on. "The potion is biting."

The Berserkers raced in front of the army, their faces wild, their axes and swords shining in the moonlight. As they ran, they screamed, saliva cascading down their chins and beards. Far out in front, two Berserkers clashed as they ran. They fell to the ground, biting and hacking at each other. One fell still. The other, screaming triumphantly, ran off down the track. The rest ran over the corpse of their fallen comrade, oblivious.

Far into the distance, lights flared in the windows of Kilneuair. Ragnar smiled, donning his helmet with one hand, before drawing his sword. How sweet this would be. How *easy*.

"Let the Sacking of Kilneuair begin!"

A battle cry went up as four hundred men pounded through the dark to the little down.

Chapter Twenty Five

The budding branches should have provided no cover for the people in the trees. It was down to Bedevere's fast thinking, Morven knew, that made them almost invisible as they hugged the tree trunks, or lay out across the sturdier branches. Loose fitting brown clothing hung in rough creases from their forms, blending in with the coarse bark, and their painted faces could not be seen at all in the dark shadows cast by the all but full moon.

The night was still and quiet, filled only with the nervous anticipation of her and the people around her. She sat straddling the large oak branch, three of the many leather bags she'd brought in her lap. She carefully undid it, looking at the several loosely tied cheese cloth bags within. She smiled grimly. If this worked, any vikings with torches would be in for a nasty shock.

She looked behind her. Bridget lay along the length of the branch, another three of the large bags tied tightly against the coarse bark, their tops already open. She gave Bridget a reassuring thumbs up, and Bridget returned it. The girl had to grab onto the branch as the movement tilted her position.

On the other side of the vast trunk, out of sight of Morven, sat another two of her girls, equally armed. None of them had arrows – they'd had no time for, or even expectation of, training, but each held a large knife.

"Morven?"

Morven looked back at Bridget. "What?"

"It's so quiet," whispered the girl. "What if the' dinnae come? What if the've changed their minds?" Wide eyes reflected the moon. "What if the king was right?"

"Then we're in fer a long cold sleep wi' the squirrels," snapped

Morven. "Because we're no gettin' down."

Bridget flinched at the anger in her mistress's voice. "Yes ma'am." She turned away, hugging the branch more tightly.

The gentle call of a wood pigeon echoed down the lane. Morven moaned, her heart pounding. That was Bedevere's signal.

They were coming.

"Mary, Bridhe, Danu protect us," she whispered, her blackened cheek pressed against the oak. Behind her, Bridget's breath speeded up.

They heard them first, the animalistic screaming that filled the night air, sounding more like mad dogs than men. Then they saw them. Four score of bare chested, bearded men, their feet carrying them along at a terrifying pace. Swords and axes shone silver as they were swung through the air.

They reached the first of the trees where the men hid.

"Now!" It was Bedevere's voice, and a volley of arrows flew from the trees, striking the men as they ran. Several men fell dead, killed instantly, their faces furrowing the path as they skidded along it.

The injured men never even slowed, but turned towards the trees the arrows had come from, rough hands tearing the arrows from their bodies. More arrows flew, and more of the men fell, but some reached the trees, climbing at incredible speed.

A man was hauled from a tree, his bow still in his hand, and a Berserker fell on him, his axe coming down on the shadowy form again and again. It took five arrows in his pale back before he finally fell himself.

Uninjured Berserkers turned from the lane, racing for the trees, and more fell as more arrows poured from the darkness. Morven heard muffled thumps from the undergrowth as men and women jumped from the trees, and she sent a silent prayer of thanks in Bedevere's direction for advising them not to climb too high. She clung to the tree. The battle had not reached them yet.

The Berserkers leapt after the fleeing men, leaping through the gaps in the trees. But only the people of Kilneuair knew the paths. Huge piles of brambles awaited the vikings, snaring their skin, their furs, their hair. They waded through the thorns, oblivious to the injuries they sustained, trying to pursue their prey. But the trees off the path were also filled with waiting archers, and slowed as they were by the brambles, their pale forms made easy targets.

Five Berserkers swarmed up the tree diagonal to Morven and her girls, faster than seemed possible, screaming and baying. One of the archers jumped down into the lane in panic. He was immediately set upon by another Berserker. His screams mingled incoherently with the Berserkers'.

By Morven's side, Bridget gave a muffled cry. Morven clung to the tree, her eyes tight shut. It had been Bridget's husband.

Arrows flew from ground level; from the archers who had jumped from the trees. Bodies littered the path, and though they were largely those of the viking warriors, the bodies of the men of Kilneuair were growing in number.

"*Hold yuir arrows!*"

Morven opened her eyes. That had been Bedevere's cry. She looked down, fearful of what she would see.

Bodies covered the lane for a good hundred yards; forty or more Berserkers, their bodies pierced by countless arrows, lay dead in the mud. Still more were visible in the brambles through the trees. There were archers' bodies too; old and young folk alike, hanging from the trees, or lying broken beneath their bows. At least ten of their men and women were dead.

Bedevere was already shouting orders, recalling the men who'd jumped from the trees, sending the fastest of the men to collect as many still useable arrows from the bodies as possible. Many other men and women were arming themselves with the fallen Berserkers' weapons.

The whole attack had taken less than five minutes.

Morven turned on the branch, looking toward Kilneuair. Pale bodies ran through the darkness towards it. A good thirty Berserkers still bore down on her town.

"Morven!" hissed Bedevere from the foot of her tree, startling her. "Yui hurt?"

"N-no," she replied. "No, we're fine."

"Guid," said Bedevere. "Be ready. The main onslaught is moments away only."

"That *wasn't* it?"

"No. They were just tae soften us. Scare us. At least four times that number head our way."

Cináed fought the wave of darkness that threatened to consume him. Where was he? He was doing something, doing something.... He shook his head, trying to clear his mind. He sat halfway up the ancient wooden stairs, holding on to the banister as he struggled for breath, his heartbeat shallow and fast. He was so tired, so *thirsty*.

The barracks were almost in darkness, only a few wall lamps burning, their oil unreplenished.

Why was he sitting on the stairs? He frowned, and tried to stand. Pain flooded through his side, and with it, the remembrance of what he'd been doing.

His men. He had to free his men. He turned on the step, pulling himself up its incline slowly, painfully, one step at a time, holding tightly onto the banister.

He was two thirds of the way up when his missed his grasp on the rail. He fell forward, and his knees gave way. He screamed as he rolled down the steps, a harsh cry ripped from his throat.

He lay crumpled at the base of the steps, his wound re-opened, and this time he did bleed. He could feel it running over his stomach.

He was spent. What strength he had was gone. He closed his eyes, sobbing softly. Darkness threatened once more, and this time he welcomed it.

Cináed Mac Ailpin.

A voice? But he was alone. Who..?

Turn and see.

Slowly, every muscle and bone in his body singing with pain, Cináed rolled over, looking up the staircase. The upper landing was in total darkness, yet he could still make out the figure. It seemed almost as though the figure was made of glass, for Cináed could see through him easily, and he seemed to...to *gleam*. It was a man, yet not a man, insubstantial yet very real. Above his head, shimmering in and out of existence, was a pair of regal antlers.

"You're...you're not real," gasped Cináed.

The figure made no reply. It raised one hand. In this hand was a crystal jug, the finest Cináed had ever seen, faceted and bright. And *so real*. It was filled with water.

"Oh... please..." begged Cináed, reaching up, "please..."

Come for it. The figure slowly backed away from the head of the stairs, vanishing into darkness.

"No..." croaked the king, "no, wait..." There was no reply. "Damn you," breathed Cináed, "damn you, wait..."

Slowly he began to climb.

Ragnar cursed. He saw the faint shine from the bodies of the Berserkers that filled the lane in the distance, the spectacle growing as his horse pounded towards it.

"Hold!"

Lathgertha reined in by his side. "What is it?"

"It's a trap," he growled through clenched teeth. He looked round as the other mounted vikings approached. "I said *hold!*" He turned on his wife. "They know we're coming. What did you tell them?"

"I – I ..nothing, Ragnar, I swear!" She stared at the bodies in the distance.

" '*Who knows what I may let slip!*' Your words, woman!" He looked back at his men. "Men of the Fraener, go wide, avoid the forest! We'll cut across open land to the target." He turned back to Lathgertha. "The rest," he shouted, his eyes never leaving his wife, "follow my wife down the lane!"

He turned his horse, still holding Lathgertha's eyes. "Enjoy." He spurred his horse on, his men following.

Lathgertha watched them go, her face burning. Several colourful curses sprang to her mind to shout after him, but she found no voice in her throat. Yellowblade. Somehow that *brat* had managed to warn them. She should have killed him when she had the chance.

She pulled her horse to one side as the mangonels thundered past her, their giant wheels ripping up the earth as they followed her husband's men. Of course. Only the trusted men of Ragnar would get the siege weapons. The foot soldiers brought up the rear, swords drawn and shields ready.

She looked down the lane to the shadowy forest. So they wanted to play at soldiers, did they? She looked back at the remaining men, still a good ten score. "Light your torches!"

Movement from the corner of her eye made her spin, her sword drawn. There was nothing there. She stared uncertainly. She could have sworn an old man had stood there, leaning on a staff. She stared at the empty ground for a moment, then spurred her horse on.

"What're the' doin'?" whispered Bridget, straining from her position to see down the lane.

"They're stoppin'," said Morven. "The' see the bodies." She stared at the bobbing lights of the torches. Without looking down she drew out one of the cheesecloth pouches, white powder puffing out around her fingers. "Come on...just get wi'in range..."

"You." Lathgertha pointed at one of the mounted men. "That pine. Torch it."

The man nodded, slinging his shield over his back. He removed an arrow from its quiver. A flaccid fresh pig's bladder was tied along its length, a cupful of flammable oil contained within. Its tip was wrapped in pitch soaked cloth. He leaned over to the next man, who held his flaming brand out. The flaming arrow was notched, and the arrow flew through the sky, drawing a line of orange fire behind it.

"See how the vicious little owls like their nest being flamed," smiled Lathgertha.

The arrow struck the tree midway up its trunk, the force of the impact rupturing the bladder. Flames exploded up, and with a yell, the three men jumped to the ground.

"They're in the trees!" shouted Lathgertha triumphantly. "Torch them! Burn them all!"

The mounted vikings rode forward, lighting arrows as they rode.

"Get yuir bags ready!" shouted Morven. "Throw them at anyone carrying a torch!" There was no point in keeping her voice down; the vikings were targeting trees indiscriminately. Fires leapt up all around them as the arrows found their mark. The archers remained in the trees as long as they could, firing volleys of arrows at the advancing army, before the heat forced them out of the trees.

Behind her, Bridget already had two little bags in her hand. A viking looked up, an fiery arrow ready to fire, and seeing the tree full of women, took aim.

"Oh no you bluidy don't," yelped Morven, throwing the little bag. It burst against the man's helmet, and a cloud of white powder temporarily obscured his face. As the cloud reached his arrow, there was a loud *wump!* and a ball of fire exploded around his head. He fell from the pitching horse, beating at his flaming beard.

"Aye, yui didnae know flour's explosive, did ye's!" bellowed Morven. "Keep throwing!" she shouted at her girls. "Any one as carries a torch or arrer!"

It was impossible. Lathgertha dismounted, unable to draw her eyes from the lane. Her men were being *beaten.* Balls of fire filled the path, burning the men, frightening the horses to the extent that they pitched their riders, plummeting off through the trees. The trees burned, but the archers kept firing, never stopping, until it seemed they would be trapped.

"Fall back!" she called, but her voice was lost in the roar of the fires and the screams of both men and horses. "Fall back! Hel take your souls!" It was no use. She turned back to the remaining men, her footsoldiers. "Go down to the loch! Follow the banks!"

It was hard, making their way down the steep bank in the darkness, and many of them stumbled and fell. Lathgertha didn't wait. She squelched through the mud, clambering over the larger rocks. Hel take Ragnar. She didn't want this. She was sick of travelling, sick of the sea, she wanted to be *home.* And now these, these savages, these *slaves,* not only had the audacity to fight back – they were *winning!*

She needed time to calm down. To think. To plan. The bank of the loch rose high above her head as she clambered over a particularly high embankment of rocks and boulders, but the ground beneath it opened out into a wide clearing of sand and rubble, the reed beds of the loch beyond casting long feathery shadows along its length.

There was more than enough room for her men.

Morven clambered gingerly down from the tree, taking the hand proffered to her by Bedevere. He was smiling.

"Flour, Morven?" he said. "*Really?*" He was wounded; blood trickled down his right arm from his shoulder, and his face was black from soot, his hair singed.

"Aye," nodded Morven, "Gaira's hoard. Dry as a bone. Yui werenae here last Lughnassadh for th' harvest. A dropped a bag intae the kitchen fires b'accident. Damn near blew th' windows out!" She looked around. "How many did we get?"

Bedevere's grim smile faded. "Too few. There should be more; it was too easy."

"It's still a victory," said Morven. "An' it's a victory we wouldnae have if it weren't fer yui."

"We lost seventeen, Morven. Seventeen people, an' Ah cuildnae save them. A dozen more wounded." He looked behind him. Bridget was at her husband's side, holding his hand, rocking gently as she sobbed. Down the path were many more people wandering between the bodies. As Morven watched with him, one man came across a viking who still moved. She looked away as the man swung his axe.

"We'll collect our dead," said Bedevere. "The rest can go tae th' wolves."

"Nae time fer that," said a voice by their side. It was Darrach, wheezing as though he'd been running.

"Darrach, what...?"

"Nae time," said Darrach, leaning heavily on his staff. "Th'captain, he goes cross country tae the toon, he's got best part o' ten score wi' him, 'n' our own mangonels. Yuir needed back there, soon as." He took a deep breath, trying to calm his breathing. "Begger this for a lark. Now...There's more doon by th'loch, but the awd folk'll handle them. Wee Jason had a story just fuir them. Ah'll be at oor own mangonels, head there if ye's can."

And he was gone. A small twist of dust span in the air where he'd been standing.

"We ran away," said the warrior, his blond hair stuck to his scalp by sweat, his head steaming in the cold.

"We did not *run away*," said Lathgertha. "Did you not see? We were being slaughtered!"

"We are vikings, woman," said the man. Around him, the other men rumbled their agreement. "We stay, we fight, we live or die. We do *not* run."

"You want to go back up there? Be my guest!" She stared at him, challenging him to reply. "We need to plan, don't you understand? Everything we thought we could do, everything we've done in the past, has always been based on surprise! The attacks in the dawn, the fires, they've only worked because we met with the least resistance! These people know we are coming. They're prepared!"

"We are v..."

"We are vikings, we fight, we live or die, yes I know," said Lathgertha heatedly. "I do not like defeat. Not at the hands of people fit only to be slaves!"

"What would you have us do, Lathgertha?"

"Return to Gokstad," replied Lathgertha immediately. "Raise more men. More weapons. More ships! You think me a coward for that?"

The man said nothing. Nor did he look away.

"Think, you idiot. We've just lost a third of our men. We're not even *in* that damn town yet!"

There was a loud splash behind her, and she span, sword in hand. Ripples spread outwards from the reed beds a few yards from the shore. A fish? She turned back to the warrior. "You tell me then, okay? You tell me what *you* would do."

The soldier was no longer looking at her. An arrow protruded from his throat, and as he opened his mouth, dark liquid flowed over his chin. He fell lifeless into the sand.

Two more loud splashes, and again Lathgertha span, numerous men running to her side as they looked out across the loch. Apart from the ripples from the reeds, there was nothing to be seen. Two more men fell dead.

Lathgertha backed away from the shoreline. "How..?"

A figure popped up from the waters, a long reed strapped to its head, the bow in its hands already notched with an arrow. The arrow was loosed, the figure gone back below the waters before the arrow found its mark.

"They're in the reeds!" bellowed one of the men, drawing his own bow.

"No, don't waste your..." Lathgertha held up a hand, but it was too late. The arrow plunged into the reed bed. A second later it bobbed up to the surface, its target missed. She grabbed his bow, pulling it down. "They're too deep, idiot! You'll just waste your arrows!"

"Then we go after them." He lay down his bow, drawing his sword. Beside him, numerous other warriors drew their blades, and they waded into the waters. With a yell, the leading man vanished under the waters, pulled feet first. He didn't emerge again. Beside him, another, then another vanished. The remaining men retreated to the bank. More people popped up; more arrows flew. This time one of Lathgertha's men was quicker; one of the water folk fell sideways, an arrow in her chest.

"Head for the high ground!" shouted Lathgertha, running down the shoreline. There was another pile of boulders in front of her. As she approached it, a figure appeared right at the top. It was an old woman, her grey hair hanging limply around her. In her hands she held a rope.

"Go back," she snapped. "Yuir no' welcome round here."

"Old hag," growled Lathgertha, "you're begging for death." Behind her, the men shouted their challenges as more archers popped up and down from the waters.

The old woman shrugged. "Aye, it'll come soon enough." She grinned. "Won't be now, like." She jumped out of sight, and the rope pulled taught.

The vast pile of boulders collapsed, rumbling down the embankment into the waters, blocking Lathgertha's path. She swore loudly, turning back to her men. "Stop wasting your arrows!" she shouted. "Back the way we came!" she shouted. "Damn Ragnar and all his bravado, we return home! We take the Fraener."

Chapter Twenty Six

"Ah told yui," said Bernard as the druid sagged against the doors. "The locks're too strong."
Myrrdin stepped back from the barrack doors, throwing the hammer and chisel to the ground. "Have you no larger chisels? Heavier hammers?"

"Aye Sir," said Bernard. "In there. In the forge."

"Then we waste no more time on brute force." Myrrdin walked into the middle of the street. "Stand by me. Look for something we've overlooked."

"Sir," said Bernard nervously, "surely we shuid be mannin' the mangonels..."

"There's men at both." This was a lie; *he* was meant to be at one. But he could not leave the army trapped; easy targets for the mangonels he knew thundered their way.

"Or in the trees," continued Bernard nervously, "with the archers..."

"There's five to a tree already."

"Or at the firepits..."

"Darrach mans the eastern one. Aiken the west." Myyrdin's tone was becoming impatient.

"Or..."

"Dammit man!" bellowed Myrrdin, rounding on the ironsmith. "There's a whole *army* locked in there! Who would be infinitely more beneficial, to us, if they were out here! Now stand by me, and *look*!"

Bernard moved next to the druid, dwarfing him, then turned to follow Myrrdin's gaze. "What...what d'we seek?"

"Something that would allow us access," muttered Myrrdin, studying the walls and windows. "Some weakness, some...some *entrance* that has no lock, something we haven't thought of..." He ran his fingers through his hair distractedly.

Bernard's eyes scanned the roof. Then stopped. "Would a chimney do?"

Myrrdin followed his gaze. And smiled.

Darrach burst in through the doors of Gaira's home, marching without preamble up to the small group of men who lay tied in pairs in the middle of the floor.

The nearest soldier glared up at him. "Come tae finish us off?" he demanded.

"Oh be hushed, ye damned fool," said Darrach, removing his knife from his belt. "Berserkers're on their way."

"The king has already *told* us," snapped the soldier, "those are lies. The attack happens tomorrow, like Yellowblade says!"

"The attack happens *now,*" said Darrach, lying his staff on the floor and sawing at the ropes that bound them, "*like Yellowblade says*. We need yuir strength!"

As the ropes fell away, the soldiers began clambering to their feet. Another turned to Darrach. "Where're our weapons?"

"Next chamber," replied Darrach, ignoring the belligerent tone, moving over to the next soldiers. "Hidden in amongst the sacks."

"Yui'll pay fer this," growled the first soldier. "Yui 'n' yours. Those damn women! This is ... this is sedition!" He directed another man after their weapons. "Yui'll be arrested, put tae trial! Ah'll see tae that!"

Darrach scowled at him, retrieving his staff. "Ah'll be gone, ye daft beggar," he replied.

"Darrach Drummond," began the soldier angrily, "Ah'm arrested yui fer..."

But the old man, as good as his word, had vanished, leaving the soldier addressing empty air.

They headed out into the night, strapping their swords to their belts, replacing their daggers in their sheaths. The town seemed unutterably quiet. There was no movement in the streets, and no voices could be heard from the first houses they past, though candle light burned in most of the windows.

"Where is ev'ryone?" whispered one soldier.

"Be hushed!" snapped another. "Somethin's not right..."

The first side street, on their right, was blocked with a huge cart, stacked high with empty barrels. Barrels blocked the street either side of the cart. As they wandered nervously through the town, every side street was blocked in a similar fashion.

"Do ye's...do ye's think t'awd man were tellin' the truth?" The soldier's nervous voice, though quiet, seemed to fill the forsaken street.

Before he could reply, a scream filled the air. Bass and Animalistic, it echoed through the buildings, its source indiscernible. As one, the small group of soldiers drew their swords, forming a circle, all areas of the street covered.

Another scream filled the air, then a cacophony of voices joined it, and the sound of running feet could be heard from the northern end of the street.

"Berserkers...!" The soldier Darrach had freed first stared up the street. There was no question now. He'd seen them attack before, far on the eastern coast. There was no time for recrimination, no blame to be issued toward either his king or the druid. It did not matter who was right or wrong.

They were under attack.

"Behind the fences," he hissed, already moving himself. "Let them get in front. Blindside them."

The men scattered, diving over walls, fences and hedges. Within moments the street was empty. Hidden eyes watched the road, waiting for the arrival of the invading force.

Pale forms shone in the distance, and the screaming reached feverpitch. Three times or more in number than the hidden soldiers, they pounded down the street, wild bloodshot eyes hunting for a foe, any foe, their beards and hair streaming around them.

They were fast; it took only a few heartbeats for them to pass the soldiers, racing down the street towards the barracks and the firepits. Silently, their weapons raised, the soldiers of Kilneuair emerged, their faces cold and set, any feelings of fear for the moment suppressed. soundless feet carried them up behind the Berserkers, deadly fast, and blades flashed down.

The battle was joined.

"The' fight," gasped Darrach, arriving by the ironmonger's side, gasping for breath. "Knew the' would. Where's the druid?"

Bernard pointed silently to the roof of the barracks. A tall lean silhouette could be seen against the silvery moon, gingerly making its way along the central beam to the large chimneys.

"Whit the blitherin' hell's he doin'?" whooped Darrach.

"He's gannin' in through the chimneys," replied Bernard. "Gonnae try freein' the army."

Darrach cursed loudly. "We've no time! The Berserkers're awny two streets away!" He turned away. "Ach, the stupid...you, you'll havetae do. You ken how tae work a mangonel?"

"Aye, sir. Constructed them, didn't Ah?"

"Right, an' sore proud ye must be of the ones t'vikings're poundin' towards us wi'." Darrach's tone was scornful. "Git. That house over there. Git gone now!" With one final contemptuous look at the figure on the roof, Darrach vanished.

The chimney was large. Myrrdin peered down into the darkness, his heard pounding, his sweat beading on his brow. He'd be able to brace himself against the walls, but it would be a slow climb down. Already he could hear the clash of steel upon steel in the streets beyond. The Berserkers had reached the town.

He had to try.

Without any further hesitation, he climbed up over the chimney stack, and began his slow descent into darkness.

*

The north-western road was silent. Ragnar reigned in his horse at the brow of the slight hill, looking down into the town. There were no trees here, no place for hidden archers. The road led into town along a dirt track at the base of the hill, turning into a wide road as it reached the first of the ramshackle buildings. The buildings themselves had few windows, few vantage points for lookouts or archers. Candlelight shone through the shuttered window, and smoke curled from chimneys and reed roofs into the velvet sky.

Good. No defences. They were not expecting attack from this route. They would pay for his losses. For every man he had lost, they would lose ten. No prisoners. No mercy.

He looked back at his army. "Send the mounted ones first!" he shouted. "Mangonels, bring up the rear!"

He led the attack, racing ahead of his men, down the side of the hill and onto the track. As he suspected, no-one leapt out to confront him. No arrows flew from windows. He smiled grimly, driving his horse on.

At the first turn in the road, he pulled up sharply, and behind him he heard the other men rein in their horses, shouting loudly.

A thick pile of bramble lay from one end of the road to the other, at least as high as a man. Had they been on foot, this would have been a major problem. Ragnar smiled. They were not on foot. He had twenty riders, each with horses that could easily jump this flimsy barricade, their leather wrapped legs ample protection against the thorns. And they had the mangonels.

"Ride it down!" he shouted. "Bring the mangonels forward; they follow us through! We'll clear a path to the heathens and *burn them with their town!*"

He urged his horse forward, flanked either side by his men as they pounded toward this insignificant obstacle. Oh how they would pay, these arrogant country folk, daring to kill his men, thinking they had even the slightest chance of turning his attack!

They reached the barricade; ten horses, side by side, jumped at once.

"NOW!"

A rope pulled taught, hidden figures either side of the road heaving at it. Long pikes, their wooden tips sharpened, leapt out from the earth they were hidden in, pointing directly at the chests of the horses as they leapt. The screaming of wounded animals filled the air. Ragnar fell into the centre of the brambles, thorns tearing at his flesh as he thrashed around, only just avoiding the plunge of his dying horse.

People began pouring from the houses and shadowed streets; old folk and young, men and women, boys and girls. *Scores* of them, easily the number of his army.

And all were armed.

Cináed lay gasping at the top of the staircase, one hand clutched to his side. In the darkness beyond, the pounding of Omnust and his men on the doors seemed distant, unimportant. The pain, and its frantic companion thirst, had become the defining focus of every breath. He closed his eyes. Darkness without, and now darkness within.

He wanted to *sleep*.

Only for a few minutes. A few minutes without pain, without the eternal dryness.

His breath began to slow, becoming shallower, and the haggard face began to relax as consciousness gratefully released its grip. His hand slid gently from his side, his knuckles rapping gently on the floorboards.

Water cascaded over his head, bitingly cold, soaking his robes. With a gasp, the king came to, staring around him, shaking his head to try and clear it. "Wh-who's there?" he demanded, his voice little more than a rasp. There was no-one visible in the darkness.

"Again!" Omnust's roar, so far away only moments ago, now filled Cináed with renewed urgency. Trembling hands smoothed his soaking hair, guiding the tiny rivulets to his waiting mouth, moistening the blighted dryness of his tongue. As the pounding on the doors began once more, he tried to stand, using the balustrade of the staircase to pull himself up. His legs gave way almost immediately.

He didn't cry out.

So be it.

He began to crawl, like the weakest of babes, towards the doors of his imprisoned army.

The man was *powerful*. The blade in his hand was no weapon; it was a scythe, and the most it had cut before now was grass and barley. But the strength behind his blows was driving Ragnar back, driven as he was by an almost blind fury.

All around him, his warriors were engaged in hand to hand combat, kitchen knives, scythes and blunt steels rebounding off sharpened axes and swords, splintering shields. Arrows flew through the air from both sides, but the townsfolk had the advantage of rooftop positions, of narrow windows that baffled the flight of most arrows. His horses were either dead, injured or riderless. Only one mangonel had made it through the barricades. The others now burnt behind him, their pitch soaked boulders, once intended for use against the town, now burnt fiercely in their cages beneath the giant catapults, targeted by flaming arrows from hidden archers.

They were *losing*.

Anger consumed the warrior viking. This could not be! He braced his feet in the dirt, his round shield blocking the blows of the raging man. He ignored the screams and cries around him, focussing only on his opponent. He'd fought the armies of kings before. One heathen should be easy.

With each blocked blow of his opponent, Ragnar was given a clear, if brief, point of attack. His sword found the man's side, but the man jumped back too quickly for him to bite deeply. He was reassured to see a small trickle of blood through the man's shirt; the first look of fear on the man's face. Ragnar began driving his attack home. With fear came doubt. With doubt, *weakness*. His blade found its mark again in the townsman's side, then in his leg, then, as the man stumbled, he struck home the fatal blow. Glorious vindication filled him as he withdrew his sword from the body. He would *not* be beaten by savages!

An arrow flew from a rooftop, its tip a burning star. Ragnar sidestepped it, and with a lightning snatch, grabbed it from the air. A woman ran at him, a large knife raised above her head. He stabbed out with the arrow, striking at her before she realised her danger, and he buried the arrow in one eye. He'd dragged the arrow out, bloodied but still aflame, before she'd started to fall.

The mangonel sat in the middle of the crossroad, still harnessed to its horses, ignored by both sides. Its vast bowl was pulled back, the tension already at its fullest. Careless now of any attack, Ragnar ran up to it. Clenching the arrow between his teeth, he stooped, retrieving one of the cloth wrapped boulders. He gasped at its weight, but held on, grimly lifting it up into the bowl. With ferocious joy he plunged the arrow into the cloth, and the boulder burst into fiery life.

The mangonel wasn't aimed. But it would strike *somewhere* in the town. He pulled the lever.

Aiken hopped from foot to foot, the lantern in his hand flickering angrily at the movement. He could hear the battle that raged a few streets away, and every fibre of his body urged him to join in.

But no. Myrrdin had given him a job. To man the pit, to cast his lantern into it when the vikings reached him. According to Myrrdin, Jason had specifically instructed him to be at *this* pit, to guard it himself, no matter what. He wouldn't disobey Jason. If Jason wanted him to be here, there *must* be good reason. He trusted the young boy, more than he'd allowed himself to trust anyone for a long time.

Apart from Gaira.

It hurt to think of her, of the little woman he'd known since she was a child, found on the western shores, the friend he'd had for most people's lifetime. It hurt to think of the things she had done in that lifetime.

A distant sound caught his ears, distracting him from his thoughts. It was a different sound to the battle raging in the streets beyond. A heavy thud, followed by a whooshing sound, like flames fanned by a wind. As he turned to look toward the source, a giant fireball rose into the air, inscribing an orange arc against the starry sky. Aiken's eyes widened as he followed its trajectory. It was heading towards...towards...

"The church!" yelped Aiken, dropping the lantern. "Anna!" He tore off down the street, sprinting at first, then as he got faster, bounding ten feet at a time, clearing the barrels scattered on the road, then skimming the top of the cart that blocked the road, his heel clipping one edge. He fell tumbling along the road, but recovered almost instantly, his short but powerful legs carrying him on. "Anna! Father Donald!"

He cleared a startled cow as it stood chewing its cud in someone's yard, and a battalion of chickens flew screaming into the air as he shattered their little hut. The missile was gaining ground on him, in front of him now despite his speed, roaring its way towards the church.

"No...!"

He redoubled his speed, his leaps becoming even longer. He could see the church in the distance now, oblivious to the peril that burned through the heavens towards them.

The missile began its downward descent, the church its only target, and its light illuminated the ground and buildings beneath as it eagerly raced towards destruction.

Maybe it was desperation that gave Aiken his strength, but to Aiken it felt as though some hidden energy flooded through him as he ran, and yet again his speed increased, bizarre images of peaceful woodland next to gentle rivers momentarily filling his mind, and a plan focussed in his mind as though scripted by another's hand.

He leapt onto the roof of a stone building to his right, then from this vantage point, he launched himself through the air, turning as he did so, facing the flaming boulder as both he and it plunged through the air. His long arms encircled the boulder, hugging it to him, his trajectory pulling the boulder away from its target. He felt the flames eating through his simple luman, and he could feel the heat licking around his arms as the viscous pitch stuck to his skin.

The hay cart could almost have been placed there deliberately, directly under the path of the missile, and both boggart and boulder exploded into it, scattering flaming strands of dry hay high into the air.

For a moment, nothing moved in the fiery mound. Then the flames heaved a little, then heaved again. Finally, Aiken emerged from the burning debris, the pitch still clinging to his now naked body, still burning brightly.

He was grinning from ear to ear. He'd done it! He'd saved wee Anna! So he was burning a little; so what? Hadn't he once held glowing metal while Bernard hammered away? Heat and cold, what were they to him!

Staggering a little, giggling almost sheepishly, he staggered towards the door of the church. "Father Donald! Anna? Did ye see that?" He pounded on the door, leaving small splashes of flaming pitch on the wood. "Father Donald! Open the door!"

The small window opened in the door, and Aiken's fire illuminated the angry features of the father. "Get away now! Devil! You burn with the fires of hell! Let the truth be seen!"

"Now hang on, did ye no see..."

The window slammed shut.

Cowed, still burning brightly, Aiken turned away. Perhaps it was best. What did he expect after all? Gratitude? And what would have happened if they *had* thanked him? Vanished, he would have, reappearing God knew where.

He paused. No. He wasn't going to just walk away! He'd just saved everyone in there! He walked back up to the door, braced himself, then slammed one massive slab of a foot into the door. It exploded from both hinges, far easier that Aiken had expected, and he stumbled, bracing himself self with one hand against the door frame, burning a blackened handprint into the sandstone. He glared at the cowering priest as he stood defensively in front of the children.

"Ha' ye no at least some trousers fer me, yui ungrateful bugger?"

Chapter Twenty Seven

Omnust stared as the flaming boulder streaked through the sky, momentarily silenced as he watched Aiken hurtling through the street in pursuit of it.

He turned to his men. "They're in the damn town!" he roared. "Again! Try again!" All the of the beds around him lay in shattered pieces, some scattered under the barred window, others around the door as the men had tried in vain to break through both door and window. "You," and he pointed to one soldier, "clear th' door frame. We'll keep tryin'!" His hands were bloodied and splintered from his attempts to break the door, and many of his men bore the same marks.

Quickly the soldier began pushing the fragments of wood to one side, his injured hands wrapped in pieces of torn sheets. He paused, frowning, then looked up at Omnust. "Captain?"

"What is it?" Omnust was jamming another piece of wood between the bars of the window, and didn't even look round.

"Quiet!" shouted the soldier, and Omnust span, his face thunderous. But the soldier was not addressing him; from the room next to them, and from across the hall, came the sounds of crashing wood and loud curses. "Quiet, all of you!" bellowed the soldier. "Captain, sir, ye'd best come here!"

Omnust lay down the beam of wood, quickly picking his way through the detritus of the quarters to the door. "What is it?" he said cautiously. "Vortigern? Come tae gloat again?"

The soldier shook his head. "N-no, sir. It..." he looked up, his eyes wide. "It sounded like the king, sir. Callin' yuir name."

"What?" Omnust pressed his ear to the door, but all he could hear were the sounds of labour from the neighbouring rooms. "Damn it, *BE STILL!*" Quickly the noise abated as the army recognised the captain's bass voice. He pressed his ear to the door once more. "Who's there?"

Cináed opened his eyes. Who'd called out? Bewildered, he looked around. He was leaning against a doorframe, in a corridor lit by a single moonlit window, but had no recollection of how he'd got there. Moist hair clung to his face and brow.

"Who's there?" came the voice once more. "Name yourself!"

"Captain...Captain Ossian?" The familiarity of the voice began to dispel some of the king's confusion.

"Sire!" There was so much relief in that one word that Cináed almost flinched from it. "Sire, the vikings are in the town, yui need tae open these doors!"

"I..." Cináed leaned back against the door, his breathing ragged. "I do not know that I can, Captain." He looked down at his wound; in the dim moonlight of the one window, it appeared his whole side was soaked in blackness. "I...I am injured, twice betrayed. Ilisa, the girl, Vortigern..."

Something banged against the door above his head; Omnust's fist. "Sire, yui havetae try! Please!"

"I am dying, Captain." Cináed leant back against the door, closing his eyes. "That viking bitch..."

"Sire, ye'd leave us here tae die?" Omnust's tone was accusatory.

"I tried," wheezed Cináed, "I tried to save you, to save you all...yet I chose not to listen to the one man who told the truth..."

"Myrrdin found others tae listen!" came Omnust's voice, angry now. "Us! All of Kilneuair, it prepared fer tonight!"

"And I repay you by locking you away..." said Cináed. "I'm sorry, Captain. Death shall be my atonement."

"You called my name!"

"I called no-one, Omnust." He smiled thinly. "If you heard my voice, it was used by someone far older than myself."

There was a silence for a few minutes. "Then Vortigern will have his way," said the captain quietly. "He heads to Constantine e'en as we speak, with yuir seal o' captaincy in his belt."

"I do not...?"

"He left you tae die, Sire; think he heads to yuir son wi' anything other than murder in his heart? He knew the viking girl had injured you, yet Ah saw him outside, talkin' tae her, we *all* did! Think he were talkin' peace?"

"Constantine...will not listen..."

"He carries your seal! He plans on becoming yuir son's captain, then Constantine *meeting with an accident!* His words, Sire!" There was desperation in the captain's voice now. "He seeks power, he aided the viking girl's escape, he heads south tae kill yuir son!"

The words finally stirred something in the king's chest. "He...he would not dare..." He opened his eyes.

"He left yui tae die, Sire! Left us locked in here, cursed all the townsfolk tae death, he thought!" A fist pounded on the door once more. "Sire! Dinnae let him kill yuir family! Yuir people! Sire, in the name of God, *on yuir feet!*"

Myrrdin gingerly inched down the ever narrowing chimney, his feet groping in the darkness for purchase. Filtering through the darkness were the sounds of metal on metal, of frantic screaming and bellowed orders.

"Damn me..."

It had seemed a good idea in the heat of the moment, but now in the blackness, with the sounds of protracted fighting echoing dully around him, the idea felt cowardly, foolish. As though he were hiding. Or that, once again, he had made the wrong choice.

Another voice, closer than the others, filled the enclosed plase. Myrrdin could make out the last words; *on yuir feet!,* and recognised the voice as Omnust's.

"Omnust?" he called. "Captain Ossian!" There was no reply. Were the barracks already under siege? Was he too late? Cursing, he tried to hasten his pace, hands and feet scrabbling blindly. As he placed his weight on his left foot, the brick on which he balanced gave way. With a yell he plunged down the chimney, his left leg bent, slowing only when the chimney itself narrowed to a point that, with his leg bent behind him, it held him firmly. He grabbed at the bricks, trying to pull himself upwards, but his foot jammed against the brickwork. He looked down; dim light was coming through his legs from below. The vast kitchen fireplace sat there, less than five feet below, lamplight from the room beyond gently illuminating it.

Myrrdin was trapped.

In the streets, the battle raged. Bodies of both heathens and vikings lay scattered on the street, equal in number. Ragnar blocked the attack of the man who charged him, the large scythe sparking as it struck his blade. Another man, having dispatched a warrior, ran to his friend's aid, and Ragnar began falling back before their onslaught, their rage matching those of his Berserkers.

Where were his Berserkers? Where was Lathgertha, the other contingent of men?

Many of the houses that contained archers were now burning, others had their doors broken down as the warriors hunted the unseen attackers, but the archers always seemed one step ahead, an escape route used, then blocked in seconds by flame or bramble, and other houses became the source of hidden warfare. Though the bodies in the street were equal in foe and allies, the hidden forces meant Ragnar's men, that Ragnar himself, faced defeat.

Again and again the two men attacked, one with a scythe, the other a stolen viking sword. Ragnar focussed on the attack. He'd handled greater numbers, and of trained foes. These heathens would not bring him down! As the scythe swung round, he angled his sword to catch it, wrenching it from the man's hands and casting it down the street. The man fell back, panting heavily, casting around for another weapon, leaving Ragnar with one opponent.

This man was older, slower in his responses, and he was unused to the weight of the weapon. Ragnar could use that to his advantage. As the man swung, the weight of the blade carried him round, and Ragnar was easily able to avoid the swing, dancing back as he swung his own blade, striking the man in one arm. Not a lethal blow, but the man's arm fell to his side, useless now.

Ragnar grinned, slowly swinging his sword. The man hung back, his blood colouring the dirt road, his one good arm not strong enough to wield the heavy sword. "Now you die," said Ragnar softly.

The man stiffened, his eyes wide. The blade fell from his grasp as he gently sagged sideways.

Lathgertha smiled at her husband, her blade dripping with blood. "Miss me?" she said breathlessly

"He was mine!"

Lathgertha shrugged. "He was anybody's."

"Where're the rest?"

"They wait at the Fraener." She looked round at the raging battle, her face pale. "We cannot win this."

"You *ran away*?"

"I protected our men!" shouted back Lathgertha angrily. "We scarcely have enough men to man the oars! We need to..."

"I'll be damned if I'll..." He didn't complete his sentence. Lathgertha had knocked him to the ground as an arrow, aimed for his head, whistled through the air above them.

"They're organised!" said Lathgertha heatedly. "They *planned* this! Yellowblade, somehow, somehow the boy warned them!"

"So where's the army!? Why do we battle only peasants!"

"*Only?* Look around you! We're being massacred by *only peasants!* You see our Berserkers? No? Because they're all *dead!* Why do they need the army? They're still locked in the barracks!"

Ragnar was already on his feet, looking around. "We stick to the plan. We still have one mangonel. That horse, over there. Bring it."

"Rangar..."

"They'll burn tonight, woman. They'll pay for their resistance. Now bring that horse!"

Morven reigned in the cart by Gaira's home, and the people in the back quickly vacated it, the uninjured helping the injured inside. "Where's t'other carts?" she bellowed. The carts bore the injured and their kin; the rest had headed toward the sound of battle, toward the mangonels.

"They're comin'," replied one of her girls, bowed by the weight of the injured man she bore. "They're just behind ..."

Morven jumped down. "Get them inside, quickly now!" She took the man's other arm, shouldering the burden with the young girl. "Tekk 'em through tae the back."

"Ma'am ..."

"The big room, right at the back, where Gaira kept her potions! There's bandages, lotions." She let another couple in before her before heading into the darkness.

"We need a healer," she said quietly as she looked around. The makeshift repair Bedevere had made on the back wall was full of gaps and holes; moonlight streamed into the room. Two dozen people lay on blankets scattered around the room, their kin doing their best to make them comfortable, to bind their wounds. Outside she could hear the clatter of hooves. More wounded were arriving.

Bridget appeared by her side, her blackened face streaked by her now dry tears, her clothes patch worked by stains of dirt and blood. "We have none," she replied, though Morven's words had been spoken to no-one in particular. "Gaira, she's gone. Druid's vanished." She began unwrapping the bundle of candles in her hands. "There's just *us.*" Her voice was bitter.

Morven scrubbed at her face with a fragment of rag, removing what she could of the pitch black. "Then we'll havetae do," she said matter-of-factly. "You know herbs?"

Bridget was throwing candles out across the room to the waiting hands of the carers. "Basics only, ma'am. Nettles, agrimony, shepherd's purse ..."

Morven nodded. "Yui ken enough tae be useful. Go look through those jars." Then she caught the woman's arm as she moved off. "Bridget ..."

"Ma'am?"

"Ah'm sorry about yuir man."

Bridget stared at her, her eyes bright with fresh tears, then she nodded, heading over to the shelves.

"Morven!"

Morven looked up, the reigns to the cart in her hands. "Bedevere!" She was astonished at the depth of emotion she felt to see the boy still alive. "Where're t'others?"

Bedevere jogged up to the side of the cart. "They head tae the barracks, where the fightin' is. Where're yui goin'?"

"There's wounded out there. Ah'm bringing them back."

"By yuirself?"

Morven snorted. "And who else is there tae help? Why aren't yui wi' yuir men?" Even as she spoke, she became aware of movement in the darkness behind the youth. A number of soldiers lumbered into the clearing; the soldiers who had been tied by her and her girls only hours previously. Her stomach lurched in fear.

Bedevere must have recognised the look on her face. He smiled mirthlessly. "There's no recriminations, Morven. Ah found 'em wi' the Berserkers. Or what was left o' them."

"We beat them," gasped the nearest soldier as he drew close. "We beat the buggers."

Morven was staring at the men, counting them. "Where're the rest?" she asked gently.

The soldier just looked at her, his face grim, giving her all the answer she needed. Behind him, the four other men drew close, and Morven could see their wounds.

"Get them inside," she instructed. "See Bridget." She raised her reigns.

"Hold, woman," snapped Bedevere. "We're coming with."

"Ach, man, they're wounded – they need healin'!"

"Healing can wait," growled another soldier. "We were wrong. The Druid were right. We can still bear arms."

Morven did not argue. The set of his jaw, of all their jaws, told her the strength of feeling they bore. "Then what're ye's doin' here?"

"We heard the carts," replied Bedevere, already clambering into the back. "We wanted the horses. Quicker than foot."

"Then climb aboard," said Morven. "An' hold on tae yuir booties!"

Crying?

Myrrdin tried to turn in the chimney, peering downwards. It was a baby's cry, loud and shrill. Immediately his mind flashed back to the young woman, Ilisa. Or whoever she'd really been. She had a child with her. Was she below?

"Hello?" there was no reply. "Ilisa!" Nothing. Only the increasing volume of the baby's cry. He swore quietly to himself. No mother would leave their bairn unattended, especially if their home was under attack. So he'd been right to be suspicious.

Why had Jason had no visions for him? Had this Ambrosius

deliberately omitted them? Or had Jason simply not seen anything that had relevance to him? He cursed his own stupidity, and twisted angrily, and futilely, in the darkness. What use was he, stuck in the chimney like a cork?

And in the kitchen below, the baby screamed.

*

Ragnar sat astride the horse, mercilessly pummelling its flanks with his heels. Behind him, Lathgertha stood in the bows of the mangonel, bracing herself between the vast structure.

Behind them, the barricades of the town were working against the townsfolk. The remaining vikings held fast at the head of the road, barring the way through for the townsfolk. The brambles had been set aflame, and the flames were spreading to the nearby houses. The flames would not last long, but it would be enough.

Ragnar smiled savagely, urging his terrified mount on. Behind him, the sounds of battle began to fade.

He would have his revenge.

Cináed found his feet at last. The corridor swam around him, all angles and inclines, and he braced himself against the doorframe, beads of perspiration running down his face. His wound flamed ruthlessly in his side, engulfing him in darkness, and he took several deep breaths, waiting for the darkness to diminish. He could hear voices coming from the barred doors all around him, but he could make no sense of the words.

But he knew what he had to do now.

Shaking hands grabbed one of the beams that blocked the door, and weakened muscles pushed at it. It rose an inch, then another, before the king, gasping, let it fall.

No. He would *not* give up. One hand crept down to his wound. Cináed took a deep breath, bracing himself, then thrust his fingers into the wound.

Pain flared up, washing through him, and a scream was forced from his lips. The voices around him grew louder, almost panic stricken, but he ignored them. The corridor washed back into focus as his pulse rate quickened.

He crouched, putting his shoulder under the beam, then pushed upwards, focussing only on the task in hand, ignoring the pain in his side, the thirst, and the tiredness.

The beam fell to the floor.

There was a cheer from the other side of the door, shouts of encouragement. But Cináed was unaware of them.

He was staring at the eldritch figure before him, at the antlers that glimmered with blue fire.

Cináed smiled weakly, nodding as though in answer to an unvoiced question, then closed his eyes, grasping the next beam.

Omnust heard the last beam fall to the ground. "He's done it..." he breathed, taking a step back from the foor. "He's bluidy done it!" His foot collided with the door, shattering the lock, and the door flew open.

The king lay in the middle of the corridor, unmoving. The lamplight from the opened room flooded his still features.

Omnust knelt by his side, feeling at his neck for a pulse. "Open the others!" he bellowed as his men spilled out. He breathed a sigh of relief as his fingers found a faint flutter. "He's alive! God preserve us..." he scooped up the king, registering a moment's shock at the lightness of the man; at the frailty. Thuds filled the air as the final beams were thrown down. His men spilled into the corridor.

"The armoury," said Omnust. "Get to the armoury."

In his arms, the king stirred. " ... Omnust?"

"Ye did it, Sire," smiled Omnust as he walked quickly to the stairs. "Ye did it. We're free."

The king smiled.

And his eyes slowly closed.

Chapter Twenty Eight

Aiken's exposed skin was a patchwork of black and pink, large globules of the pitch having set onto his skin as it cooled. He'd wiped off as much as he could while it was still warm and liquid; now he picked furtively at the blackened crust, wincing as it nipped at his skin.

His eyes kept being drawn to the eastern houses. Moments ago, the sky had blossomed with a ball of fire, rising above the roofline of the houses. Someone had lit the eastern firepit, blocking either entrance or exit from the road Aiken stood on.

Yet he heard no approaching sounds of battle; the clash of metal on metal still came from the north, from the same direction the fearsome fireball had been launched.

"Aiken!"

Aiken yelped, jumping backwards as Darrach appeared seemingly from nowhere, the straw and dust on the ground swirling around him. He was red faced and sweating, and looked tired and drawn. He leaned heavily on his staff, staring at Aiken as he quickly composed himself.

"What is it?" asked Aiken. "The vikings, are the' comin' ..?"

"Two of them, aye," gasped Darrach. "The *main* two. Go hide now. Wait ..." he looked at Aiken's empty hands. "Where's yuir lantern?"

"Sir, Ah dropped it," said Aiken apologetically, pointing at the lantern on the ground, its glass shattered and the oil staining the dirt beneath. "Dropped it when Ah wuz chasin' bluidy fiery rock..."

"Is ev'ryone ignorin' their instructions now?!" snapped the old man, fumbling in his robes. "Here. Mah flints. Go grab the lantern an' pray there's enough oil in its wick tae burn. Moments, boggart, moments're all we need!"

"We're losing?" said Aiken dismally. He stared at the orange sky in the east.

"Losing? Naw!" Darrach barked. Had his lips twitched, it could have been mistaken for a bray of laughter. "We neither lose ner win. Same as them cussed vikings. But we have a chance ..." he looked northwards as the sound of hooves and yelling suddenly started getting louder, his eyes widening. "They're coming, boggart! Light that lamp and pray!"

"Ah don't understand..."

"Jason *did!* Light the lamp and hide, fire the pit when they pass!"

"But..."

Dust and straw spiralled into the air. Darrach was gone.

Aiken watched the dust in bewilderment as it slowly descended, then grabbed up the shattered remains of the lantern. The sound of hoof beats were getting louder, and Aiken could discern the sound of wheels turning.

A mangonel was heading his way.

Without further hesitation, he sprinted round the side of the nearest house.

The vast doors to the armoury were locked. Ancient mechanism sent thick metal rods up into the door frame and down into the foundations. Without the keys, it was impenetrable. Leaving his soldiers in front of the doors, Omnust grimly jogged down the corridor, the king as limp as a rag doll in his arms.

He paused for a second at the entrance to the king's chambers, his face pale as he stared at the gold hilted dagger on the floor, at the pool of dried blood, at the bloody drag marks along the floor.

That the king still breathed was nothing short of a miracle.

He gently lay the king on the bed. "Sire?"

The king's eyelids fluttered.

"Sire?" Omnust resisted the urge to shake the old king. "Sire, the keys..."

Cináed shook his head slightly, frowning. "Vortigern..."

He did not need to say more. It answered the captain's suspicions. God curse that man! God burn him!

"Water..." breathed the king. "I need water..."

"Stay here," said Omnust, then silently cursed himself. Where else would the king go? "Ah'll see what Ah c'n find."

On the way out, he retrieved the dagger.

"Ragnar, *watch out!*"

Lathgertha's warning was not needed. The viking had seen the slight dip in the road in front, the trackless yard of surface, out of place against the deeply rutted road either side. With a loud curse, he wrenched the reins of the horse, forcing them into the grass down the side of the road.

He was too late; one wheel struck the smooth dirt and sank immediately, and with a *crack!* The wheel was splintered, casting Lathgertha out of the mangonel as it listed, riding now on one wheel only.

Ragnar spared her a split-second glance. Already she was on her feet, racing after him, neither asking or expecting him to wait. He urged the horses on.

Aiken struck feverishly at the flints as he steadied the lantern between his knees. "Come on come on come on..." The flints sparked, but the dusty wick would not light. Cursing, Aiken ripped the wick out of its barrel, turning it and shoving the dry end into the oil well. Again he struck the flint, and this time the wick flared into life.

"Yes!"

He peered out around the side of the building. The remains of a wheel still rocked by the side of the firepit, and in the distance he could just make out the receding form of the mangonel, chased by a dainty yet lithesome woman.

Lathgertha lurched to a halt.

A *voice?*

She turned, breathing heavily, looking back down the road. A light flared in the distance, small, almost unnoticeable, but definitely there. As she peered into the darkness, she saw someone creep round the side of a house, heading towards the broken wheel. She reached for her dagger, momentarily forgetting she'd left it in the barracks, cursing when she remembered. She drew her sword, and began making her way down the street, slowly, and keeping to the shadows.

Aiken reached the pit. How was he to light it, buried under the boards and dirt? There was no oil left in the lamp, nothing to burn through the wood to ignite the oil beneath. And the wick guttered already.

He crouched down by the pit, one hand digging through the dirt, trying to find a board of wood to lift.

"*Don't.*"

Aiken looked up. The woman stood on the other side of the pit, her sword held back over her shoulder like a small javelin, aiming straight for him.

"Stand up."

Slowly, raising both hands, the flickering lantern in one, Aiken stood.

"You're the *boggart,* aren't you?"

Aiken said nothing.

"I see now what the little pech saw in you," grinned the woman. "Both ugly as the runts of Gullinbursti, who else could you love?"

Aiken's jaw jutted, but he said nothing. He looked at the path before him. Two steps would take him to the middle. That was all he needed. He took one step forward; the hidden boards creaked under his weight.

"What?" said the woman, bringing her sword round to hold in front of her. She windmilled it a couple of times, its blade hissing through the air. "Are you going to try and take me on? Really? Are you as stupid as the pech?"

"Ah'll no take ye's on," muttered Aiken. He took another step towards her, and the boards visibly bent beneath him. "Ah've nay blade ner halberd. Whit ye think Ah c'n dae?"

"Stay back," said the woman, her smile fading. "I'll stick you where you stand."

"Ah'm as far as Ah needs tae be," replied Aiken evenly. He raised a slab of a foot, then stamped it down onto the ground. Wood splintered loudly.

"No, what're..." the woman stepped back, staring. "Stop!"

Aiken's foot came down again. Oil spilled up, and Aiken sank up to his ankles in the liquid as the boards gave way. Smiling, he raised the lantern.

"Stop, you fool!" yelled the woman, raising her sword javelin like again. "You'll burn too! What good will it do you?"

"It'll trap *you*," snarled Aiken, and all the venom he held for the woman was spilled out in those three words. He slammed the lantern down.

The huge fireball threw Lathgertha from her feet, and her hair smouldered.

Aiken stepped out of the firestorm, a moving pillar of fire. "Haven't ye heard?" he yelled over the roar of the flames. "Boggarts dinnae burn!" He turned, walking away from the viking woman, from the hellish firepit, brushing the burning liquid from his skin like so much water. He felt fierce. He felt, for the first time, like a warrior. He turned back to the wall of flames.

"That's fer wee Jason!" he bellowed, his emotions making his voice raw. "An' fer wee Anna! An' fer the King! An' – an' fer Myrr ..."

The sword flew through the flames, silencing him before he was even aware he was in danger.

As his men pounded against the armoury doors, Omnust stared out of the barred windows either side of the main doors. To the left and to the right, the night sky was lit up by orange fire. He could hear the rumble of hooves, the loud scraping of something being dragged down the road. He cursed. "*Where is the druid?*"

"Omnust!" bellowed Myrrdin for what must have been the tenth time. The pounding on the doors resonated through the chimney, and ash rained down onto the druid, choking him and blinding him. It was no good. The pounding drowned out his voice. Below him, the baby screamed in fear.

"What happened?" demanded Ragnar, staring at his wife. Her long hair was gone; tufts of blackened hair framed her reddened face, and her eyebrows were melted to her skin.

"We're *trapped,* is what happened!" she shouted back. "That damned boggart! He's lit the firepit! Both burn, and the side streets are filled with carts and brambles!"

"No matter," growled the viking. He leapt down from his mount, walking quickly to the damaged mangonel.

"No matter?!" screamed his wife. "No matter! We've *lost!* We're trapped, I *told* you we should have left!"

"Be still!" He lifted her from her feet by her neck with one hand, his eyes blazing. "We are *vikings!* We do not run!" He threw her to the ground, where she lay nursing her neck.

"Look," he shouted, pointing. "There! The barracks! We *have* our targets!"

"We must flee!" retorted Lathgertha, easing herself up off the ground. "Before they come to finish us off!"

She fell silent as the tip of his sword touched the underside of her chin. "If you are not with me," he said slowly, "then you are against me. Which is it?"

She stared at him, registering the anger in his eyes; the blind hatred that could not be reasoned with. One hand pushed the blade away. "With you. *Husband."*

He nodded, but did not sheath his blade. "On your feet. Light the boulder, woman, and help me position this thing."

The pacing of the false walled house was all that was keeping Bernard sane. The sounds of battle filled the air around him, so close he expected vikings to burst into the little chamber at any second. The sky was orange with fire and the screams of men and women.

Why had he followed the king's orders? Hadn't he known they were wrong? Omnust and his men should be out there, fighting the vikings. Now the town's only hope were the townsfolk themselves; poorly trained and scared. There was no way he could see a victory.

"Get the mangonel ready!" gasped Darrach, appearing in a swirl of dust. Bernard did not startle; too many times before had the old man appeared for Bernard to respond so. But the old man's appearance – the ashen face, the sweat, the sheer exhaustion on his face...

"Darrach, are ye..?"

"Ah'm fine, Ah'm fine," said Darrach angrily, lying his staff on the ground. He began fumbling at the leather straps that held the walls together, his ancient fingers struggling with the loops and knots. "Get the roof off now!"

The 'roof' was a single layer of reeds, tied together in a sheet, resting over a frame and tied in place. Bernard quickly undid its strings, hauling the bulky material down. Even as he did so, the front 'wall' of the building fell outwards, and Darrach quickly moved onto the next wall.

With Bernard releasing the straps on the remaining two walls, the small mangonel was quickly free of constraint, the night air cold and bitter around it.

"Now," gasped the old man, retrieving his staff, "light ... light the pitch, then fire, an' ye's keep firing 'til yuir oot o' rocks!" He leaned heavily on his staff, drawing a shaking sleeve across his forehead.

Bernard caught him by the arm as he seemed about to fall. "Darrach..."

"Bluidy leave me be!" the old man angrily shook off his arm. "Do as yuir bid!"

"But..." Bernard looked back at the mangonel. "Where ... Ah mean how ... what'm Ah firin' at?"

"It's bluidy aimed a'ready, yui fool!" The old man sounded almost hysterical. "At where Jason said! But now, man, now!"

Before Bernard could question him more, the old man was gone.

"Right..." muttered the ironsmith, picking up his lantern, "right..."

A pitch soaked boulder was loaded quickly into the waiting cup, and with a few deft movements, the pitch blazed into life. Bernard hesitated as he held the lever to launch the missile. "God watch me, Danu protect me," he muttered, "old man, yui'd best be right."

The boulder shot skyward.

Morven stared at the scene before her.

The vikings were grouped at the entrance to one road, surrounded by fire as the brambles across the road burnt ferociously. They hacked and swung at the villagers, trying to keep them from the road.

Neither group was gaining ground.

All around her, bodies filled the area; men and children, women and vikings, most dead, some still moaning. Bedevere and the soldiers were running from body to body, helping the injured to the cart, dispatching the injured vikings without hesitation or mercy.

She looked away, unable to feel any sort of vengeance or victory as each wounded viking was killed. They were still people, scared and begging for mercy. That they'd shown no mercy for her townsfolk did not, at least at this moment, quell her nausea as each of their screams was abruptly silence by sword or axe.

"...Morven..."

Morven span in the cart, looking down. Darrach hung from the side of the cart, clinging to it like a drowning man. His staff fell to the road with a clatter. She jumped down, catching him under his arms. "Darrach, what..?"

"Get ... get the townsfolk out o' here," he gasped, leaning gratefully on her.

"What're yui sayin' ..? Here now, on the cart with ye's ..."

"It's the final part," gasped the old man, not arguing with her as she led him round the side. "The final part o' Yellowblade's prophecy, but oor people ..." He looked southwards, and Morven followed his gaze. "Oor people must move," gasped the old man. "*Now.*"

Morven's eyes widened as a flaming missile roared through the air, already beginning its descent. She could see where it would land already.

At the junction where the townsfolk and vikings fought.

"Bedevere!" she bellowed, running from the old man, only vaguely aware of him crumpling to the ground. Above the sound of battle, the young soldier didn't hear her as he dispatched yet another viking.

"BEDEVERE!"

This time he heard, so did his men around him. She didn't have time to explain; so one hand pointed.

It was over less than twenty heartbeats later. The townsfolk scattered, running toward houses, hiding behind carts. The vikings never thought to look above them.

"Fall back!" bellowed Omnust. "The king's chambers!" He leapt back from the window as orange light began flooding through it, following his men down the corridor.

The boulder took out the window that only two breaths before Omnust had been peering through, its strength and velocity punching a hole through the door to the kitchen. As it struck the back wall, it rebounded back into the kitchen, scattering burning pitch throughout the kitchen.

Omnust peered down the corridor. The hole left in the wall was more than room enough for a man to fit through.

Or *men.*

"Quickly!" he ordered. "Out into the street! Weapons or no, there's two o' them an' eighty o' us!"

Smoke billowed up the chimney, and Myrrdin, half choked by the falling ash, began coughing violently.

"Om-Omnust?"

His voice cracked, weakened by soot and smoke.

Myrrdin closed his eyes. So this is how it ended. Lives within lives within lives. And this life, this particular life, he was destined to die through his own stupidity. He'd never sire a son in this life. In this reality, there'd never be a Jason. There'd never be an Anna. Maybe that was for the best.

As the smoke below thickened, as the flames became stronger, he settled back against the stone to wait.

Below, the screaming of the baby was growing fainter.

"They're coming!" screamed Lathgertha, pulling on her husband's arm. "You haven't killed them; you've freed them! Come away! Ragnar, *please*, come away! We have to ..." she was thrown backwards by his blow, sent sprawling into the grass. She wiped the blood from her lip, staring at him. "Hel can have you," she hissed. "If I see you again I'll slit your throat!"

Ragnar ignored her as she sprinted away, leaping over barrels and clambering up the side of a house.

Hel *would* have him. Valhalla called now. He was not afraid.

He was a *Viking!*

As the Guard of Cináed Mac Alpain bore down on him, he fired the final missile.

The kitchen below was a furnace. The heat of the fire roared up the chimney, and the druid could feel the soles of his boots start to smoulder. With his magic gone, so had his resistance to the elements. He would *burn*. The screams of the child had faded to a whimper, made nearly inaudible by the roar of the flames.

He wished he could have saved her. At least that would be something.

Maybe this was Fate's revenge, he thought. For all those men he led to their death at Strathclyde. For the loss of his closest of allies, the closest of friends.

Maybe it was his time.

He never heard the approach of the missile. It sped through the hole in the window, and shattered the remains of the already smouldering door, striking the chimney breast with such force that the outer brickwork fell away.

Myrrdin shot out of the bottom of the chimney, coughing and spluttering.

He was *alive?!*

Not, he realised quickly, for long. The oak beams above him crackled and spat, and burning nuggets of wood fell around him. The vast kitchen table, the chairs; all burnt ferociously.

The only thing not burning was the crate by the fireplace, the tiny infant cradled within. As larger chunks of wood plummeted downward, Myrrdin grabbed up the child, and fled.

Part Five

Chapter Twenty Nine

The sky was starting to brighten in the east; an orange glow that echoed the glow that came from Kilneuar.

Omnust stood in front of the still burning barracks. Two of the brick walls had already collapsed, and still the flames showed no sign of abating, their yellow tongues licking hungrily at the bare skeleton of the building.

"If we'd not got out..." he breathed.

"But you did," said Myrrdin, standing by his side. "You got out. All of you. All of *us*."

Omnust turned to face him, only vaguely aware of the others as they approached; the men, the women, his soldiers. "We got lucky."

"Did we?" said Myrrdin, studying the flames. "I do not think so. I don't believe luck played any role in tonight." He smiled, turning to the captain. "I believe Jason played a huge hand in this. Without him..."

"Wi'out him we'd hae been lost," said Omnust. He didn't sound pleased.

"What troubles you, Captain Ossian?" asked the druid gently.

"We should hae *been* out there," replied the captain. "We could hae helped, we'd no' hae lost so many." His voice was bitter.

"We lost far fewer than if we had been unprepared."

"Or if the king had had his way." Angry eyes turned to Myrrdin. "Where is he?"

"With the rest of the injured, at Gaira's house," replied Myrrdin evenly. "He's badly injured, but with care he should survive."

Omnust snorted, but said nothing.

Myrrdin nodded gently. "I understand your anger," he said quietly, "but do not overlook the fact that we won."

"Wi' how many dead?"

"People would have died whether you'd been there or not. Perhaps even you yourself."

"He got away," said Omnust after a pause. "That viking? Leapt clean through the firepit. Eighty of us, we couldn't e'en stop one man."

"Omnust," said Myrrdin, placing a soot stained hand on his shoulder, "do not berate yourself. Captain, *we won!*"

"Wi'out mah help." He stared at the barracks. "Bluidy useless, Ah was." Then he flinched, and a wry chuckle escaped from his throat.

Myrrdin looked at him. "What?"

"Ah sounded like young Yellowblade."

*

Morven mopped the king's brow. He was asleep, finally. A proper sleep, not related to his injury, which was now packed with a herb poultice. He'd eaten, and had drunk half a skin of water, before finally drifting off. He was away from the rest of the wounded, in Gaira's store, surrounded by sacks of grain, flour and dried meat. Not ideal, but at least he had some privacy in here. And, from the murmurs she'd been privy to with some of the wounded, some *safety*.

"How is he?" Bedevere had poked his head nervously round the door.

"He'll recover, in time," said Morven. "He's a tough'un, oor king. Ah've seen bigger men than 'im surrender tae wounds like that." She stood up, brushing down her clothes. "How's it goin' out there?"

"Near ev'ry rooms full," said Bedevere. "Yuir girruls're guid, Morven. The' ken whit tae do."

"Of course." She couldn't keep the pride from her voice, and Bedevere smiled slightly. She studied him. Less than a day ago she would have thought him a gangling pimpled youth. Now she saw a man before her, a captain in the making, maybe more. She cleared her throat, looking away. "How many wounded?"

"Sixty seven," replied the youth. "Bridgit's gone out wi' the cart an' a couple o' soldiers, but she don't expect tae find many more."

She didn't look at him as she asked her next question. "And ... the dead?"

Bedevere hesitated before answering. "A ... a hundred and seven."

Morven shut her eyes, a whimper escaping her.

"It could'a been worse," said Bedevere. "It *should'a* been worse, but

Myrrdin, Yellowblade ..."

"Ah know, Ah know," said Morven. "But it's ... it's so *many*. Has anyone reported people missing?"

"We've been canny lucky there too," said Bedevere. "The only person reported missin' so far is the boggart."

Aiken.

The wound of his loss bit deep; for all her initial reservations about the simple creature, he'd proved himself brave beyond measure. "What about his charge? What's her name, *Anna,* has she been told yet?"

Bedevere shook his head. "We've sent word tae Father Donald when we sent that child Myrrdin saved; he's keepin' the children there the next few hours, feedin' them like. Until we've moved all the bodies."

"Good," said Morven, "Good. Aye, well then. Tae work."

"Morven," said Bedevere, "the King ..."

"What?"

Bedevere shut the door to the room, leaning on it. "The ... the townsfolk ..."

Morven looked at him intently. *"What?"*

"It's just ... they don't ..." he sighed. "Not all the townsfolk would be happy if he survived."

Wide eyed, Morven looked at Cináed, then up at Bedevere. "And yui?"

He returned her gaze. "Ah feel their anger."

"We *won,* Bedevere."

"In spite of him," was his sharp reply, and Morven heard the bite of anger.

"We were all where Jason said we should be," she said firmly. "What makes you think he wasn't where *he* was supposed tae be? Who freed the army, saved 'em from burning?"

Bedevere had no reply, and looked away. She saw the anger in his face, and knew the retort he was biting back: *who put them there?*

"So what dae the *townsfolk* think we should do wi' him?" she asked.

"Ah've posted soldiers," said Bedevere, avoiding her question. "Omnust's men. The'll stay outside these doors."

Morven sat on Gaira's old cot at the front of the building. It was the first moment's peace she'd had for more than a day, and her whole body ached for sleep. But the sun was streaming in through the eastern windows, announcing the start of a new day, new tasks.

But a few minutes sit-down wouldn't hurt.

Her head had nodded halfway to her chest when she heard the squeaking of the cart wheels, the mutter of voices.

She quickly roused herself, pinching at her cheek to awaken herself. No good would come of sleeping with so much work to do!

By the time Omnust, Myrrdin and Bridget entered the room, she had a brush in hand, sweeping up a veritable storm of dust. She had not seen Omnust since before his imprisonment, and the smile that lit her face when she saw him was genuine and warm. She had to resist the urge to throw down the brush and hug him.

Instead, she simply said; "Yuir safe then."

She felt herself blush down to her collarbone as her smile was returned even more warmly. "Ah'm safe," he replied, "and so're muckle others, thanks tae you."

"Me an' mah army o' brooms 'n' brushes," she replied. She realised she was staring at him as she grinned and blushed even more profusely, quickly looked back to her sweeping. Behind Omnust, Bridget was suppressing a knowing grin. "Have ye's eaten owt yet?"

"Actually," said Myrrdin, "We we hoping to speak to Darrach. You know where he is?"

Now her smile did fade. "The man's restin'," she said firmly. "An' poor bugger needs it. Fair near killed him last night, runnin' around, keepin' all tae their tasks."

"Is he alright?"

Morven looked at the druid, frowning. There was more than friendly concern in that question. "Given rest an' no' disturbed, and aye, he will be. Why?"

Before she could answer, Bedevere burst into the room, a bucket of bloodied rags in one hand. "Movern, we need more ..." he fell silent as he saw his captain and the druid.

"It's Bedevere, isn't it?" said Omnust. "The one Yellowblade bashed the shins o'."

"...Yes Captain." Bedevere quickly lay the bucket on the ground, snapping to attention.

"At ease, soldier," smiled Omnust. "Ah'm no' feelin' quite sae terrifyin' t'day."

"Yes captain."

"At *ease,* Bedevere," insisted Omnust. "Bridget here, and the Druid, the' told me 'boot last night."

"Sorry, Captain," stammered Bedevere, suddenly looking like the child he'd once been, "but there were nae one else tae tekk charge, an'..."

"Ah'm proud of yui, mon," said Omnust, clapping him on the shoulder. "*Right* proud."

Bedevere nodded mutely, silenced by his captain's praise.

"As am I," said Myrrdin. "Don't feel any shame in usurping your captain." By his side, Morven noticed Omnust's smile falter. She *felt* his pain. "You stepped up to the mark when a man was needed."

"Thankyou ... sir," said the young man, obviously unsure how to address Myrrdin. Then he looked at the druid. "Sir, Ah ... Ah need tae speak with you."

"Oh?" said Myrrdin. "What about? Can it wait until after we've spoken with Darrach?"

Morven felt her heckles rising. "Myrrdin, captain, Ah'm sorry but ye's cannae ..."

"It's about Eigyr," said Bedevere, cutting her off.

The druid paled. "What ... what about her?"

Morven picked up the bucket of rags. "Bridget, come. We'll tear up some more sheets."

Darrach was sat up in his cot, mashing the larger chunks of his broth with his spoon, when Myrrdin entered the crowded makeshift hospital. He scowled, spooning a mound into his mouth. "Wondered when ye'd come," he muttered.

Myrrdin said nothing, seating himself on the edge of the cot.

"Cat got yuir tongue?" demanded the old man.

"You know why I'm here," said the druid quietly.

The spoon hovered a moment. Darrach looked down at his bowl and continued eating. "Aye."

Both remained silent for a while, listening to the moans of the other injured, and to the quiet conversations between relieved loved ones and their kin.

Darrach broke the silence. "Albain Eiler today, isn't it?"

Myrrdin nodded silently. His face was pale. His youthful features were careworn now, fresh lines circling his eyes and creasing his brow.

"Yui spoke tae Bedevere then?" Darrach could see the pain, the resignation in the druid's face.

Again the silent nod.

"He's told yui the bairns' names?"

"He has. Yes."

"They important?"

"They...." Myrrdin smiled slightly; a private joke. "They're a new chapter, it seems."

"Really now?" said Darrach. "In who's story?"

"*My* story." Weary fingers probed the druid's brow. "But ... you know that's not why I'm here." He looked sadly at Darrach. "You're stalling."

Darrach ate another spoonful, his scowl not fading. "Ah'll no' survive."

"I cannot force you to do this."

"Oh, can ye no' now?" Darrach set the empty bowl on the floor, using the length of his beard to wipe his mouth. "An' how else you goin' tae reach young Yellowblade afore nightfall?"

"You'll do it then?"

"Ah'll honour the agreement," growled the old man. "If Jason helped us, we'd help him. Ah read it, didn't Ah?" He sighed, and lay back in the bed. "Ah'm awd, Lailoken. Awder'n Ah shuid be. Mebbies ..." he closed his eyes. "Mebbies this is why."

Myrrdin shook him by one knee. "You did well out there."

The old man snorted.

"You kept everyone on track, organised."

Darrach blew a raspberry with his tongue.

"You know I'd not ask if ..."

Darrach's eyes flashed angrily, though he didn't raise himself from the bed. "Yuir gonnae kill me. Dinnae expect me tae be grateful, damn yui." He turned on his side, away from the druid, and pulled up the blankets. "Ah'm tired."

"Go?! But – but ..." Morven spluttered in shocked anger. "Yui need *rest!* Food! Why – where..?"

Omnust sat on a sack of grain, pulling the flushed woman down next to him. "We go to help Jason. We made a *promise.*"

"Promise be damned!" yelped Morven. Was the man *mad?* Two days he'd been without sleep, without food. She could *see* the tiredness in him, emanating from every pore! "Jason is ..."

"...Alone," finished Omnust, taking one hand. "And probably scared. If Myrrdin's right, he's held prisoner."

"He ... he has his *knife!*" insisted Morven. "An' even so, even if he's prisoner, surely a day's rest won't hurt!"

"It's Albain Ailer," said Omnust. "This Huddour, he's got oor people, the people from th' villages around, he's goin' tae *sacrifice* them. Sacrifice Jason. *Tonight.*"

Morven couldn't keep the tears from her eyes. "*Ah don't want ye's tae go!*"

Strong hands cupped her face, raising her eyes to his. Gently he thumbed away her tears. "Ah'll come back."

"How do you *know?*" She pushed away his hands, hating her weakness for showing her emotions, furiously embarrassed and utterly terrified.

He raised her hand to his lips, kissing the knuckles with whiskery lips. "Because Ah've got someone tae come back to." He held her chin, turning her once more to face him. "Haven't Ah?"

She stood up, angrily wiping her cheeks, aware of his hurt expression, trying to ignore it, yet feeling it totally. "Go then, if ye's must." She went up to the western window, slamming it shut. "Get yuirself killed. An' whose gonae look after yuir army?"

"You know the answer to that, woman." She heard the growl in his voice, and heard the hurt it hid. "Bedevere. The men hold him in high regard, it seems." His voice was bitter. Almost jealous. He headed to the door. "Ah'll ... bid yui farewell," he muttered. "Ah'm sorry if Ah misunderstood."

As he opened the door, she grasped his forearm, stilling him. "Yui ... yui didnae misunderstand."

He closed the door, almost slammed it, and grabbed her in the fiercest of hugs. They clung to each other, unmoving, for untold moments.

"Yui'd better come back," she whispered.

"Can you manage this?" asked Myrrdin. He, Omnust and Darrach stood side by side on the path outside Gaira's home. The midmorning sun beat down on them.

Darrach shrugged, his forehead knitted. "Dunno." He leaned heavily on his staff.

"Have you ever taken anyone on the Paths with you?"

"Never tried," said Darrach grumpily. "Me Dah, he said as Ah cuid awny move flesh 'n' bluid. Told me Ah shuid practice. Never did. Never had need tae."

"Druid," muttered Omnust, aware of many eyes on their backs, "is this safe?"

"Future history seems to say so," replied the Druid. "At least for me."

"That's no' very reassuring," said Omnust.

"What do we do?" asked Myrrdyn.

"We mekk like little girruls in the meadows," said Darrach.

"What?"

"*We hold hands.*" He grabbed the captain's spade like hand, and Myrrdin placed his hand over the old man's hand where he held onto his staff.

Morven watched from the doorway as the spiral of dust and leaves slowly began to descend once more.

"Goodspeed," she whispered.

Chapter Thirty

"Bothering dingbats, blisters and boils!" Gobswistle sucked his singed fingers, throwing the flints down in frustration. The vast pile of dry twigs and brittle seaweed sat in front of him, stubbornly refusing to light.

"Colourful colloquialisms," said Etain, walking down the shingled beach toward him, her arms laden with wood.

"This – this damn fire thing just ... *won't!*"

"Maybe you're doing it wrong," said Etain, dropping the wood to the ground. "Want me to try?"

"I've been lighting fires for over ..." he paused, frowning. "Well I don't know, but a damn long time." He looked up at her, squinting sourly in the early morning light. "You think you could do better, feel free."

"Snap all you want," grinned Etain, squatting down beside him, "Ah weren't the old fool who forgot to bank it up last night." She reached to the pouch on her belt, pulling out a small rusty nail. She pushed the nail under one corner of the small bonfire, then touched it with one finger. The nail glowed orange, tiny flames licking around it. Within seconds the kindling around it began to flame, and Etain withdrew it, returning it to the pouch.

Gobswistle glowered at her. "Show off."

The warrior shrugged, arranging the twigs and seaweed so that they caught the glowing flames. They sat in silence for a few moments, watching as the flames grew. Etain's face was calm, thoughtful, almost happy. Gobswistle's wrinkled features were frozen in a thunderous glare.

"You were dreamin' last night," said Etain eventually. "Muttering for hours."

"Was I?" The old man didn't look up from the fire. "And?"

"What were you dreamin' about?"

"Dreams don't mean nothing," said the old man sullenly.

"Most don't," said Etain. "Yours *do.*"

Gobswistle looked at her briefly, then looked back to the fire, placing a couple of branches onto it.

He was avoiding the question, realised Etain. Which meant he didn't like the dream he'd had.

She decided to change tactics. "The vikings'll be reaching land soon, won't they?"

"No."

"But Ah thought..."

"They reached it yesterday."

Etain nodded, guessing what the old man had seen. "Your dreams, Ethelbert. What did you see?"

Gobswistle huddled into his coat. "Fire. Lots of fire." He shuddered. "Children, fighting. And a chimney."

"...And Jason?"

"He ... wasn't in my dreams," said the old man. It sounded almost like an admission of guilt. "He wasn't in the village."

"Do you, I mean, I know it's a long time ago, but can you remember anythin'?"

"What is this?" demanded the old man, rounding on her. "The Spanish Inquisition?"

"OK, *woah*, and don't take your temper out on me, old goat!"

Gobswistle stood, his hands deep in his pockets. He paced slowly up and down, obviously deep in thought, before turning back to his friend. "I remember losing someone I loved," he said quietly. "And you know what kills? I don't remember *who.* No face, no name, just the *loss.*" He looked away. "I *hate* being old."

It was not just the loss of an arm that was the problem, realised Fionnlagh as he swung his sword; it was the loss of *balance*. The stump was healed, not even red any more. Thanks to the old man's potions, the wound might have been years old rather than a few days.

But he was used to having two arms. He smiled at the thought, pausing to wipe his sweaty brow. Of *course* he was – wasn't everyone? But he'd lost the counterbalance to the swing of his blade, he'd lost the protection of a shield arm.

So he practiced. He'd been practicing two days now, the battle in the cove now distanced by time.

They'd fought.

They'd won.

Time to move on.

And somehow the constant training with blade and axe, either alone or partnered by one of the surviving soldiers, prevented the memories of the battle, of the loss of Cathal, the captain and so many of his comrades, from taking over his waking hours as they did his slumber.

He raised his blade once more, ready to take on the invisible foe, then paused as he heard someone, or perhaps something, heading down the beach toward him. He turned, looking back at the cliffs.

A large black cat was walking slowly down the beach towards him, its black stumpy tail flicking as amber eyes fixed on him.

He thrust his blade into the shingled ground. "Kylie."

The tail flicked again, possibly in recognition, but the eyes never left him. Large velvety pads carried it closer.

Gently, moving slowly, Fionnlagh picked up a large flint rock.

The Cait Sidhe paused, large eyes flicking from the rock to the young man's face. The tail began flicking angrily, and powerful muscles tensed.

"Ye's really dinnae want tae do this," breathed Fionnlagh.

A bass rumble from the creature's throat gave him his answer.

"Fine," said Fionnlagh. He brought his arm back. "Yuir choice."

The rock hurtled through the air, not at the creature, but far out into the shallows.

With a yowl of delight, the cat launched itself down the beach, plunging into the water. Its head vanished under the water as it waded through the shallow waves; once, twice, then with a triumphant growl it bounded from the waters, padding up the beach with the rock held daintily between its teeth, looking as proud as could be.

It stopped in front of the young man, and sat on its haunches, dropping the stone in front of him. The furry head tilted to one side, and it gave a gentle *chuff.*

Fionnlagh grinned. "yuir no' a puppy, Kylie."

The cat wriggled forward on its rear end, growling expectantly.

"Yui look silly."

The cat looked from the rock to Fionnlagh, and gave a soft moan.

"Fine. Whatever!" Still grinning, Fionnlagh launched the rock once more.

It was fun watching the Cait Sidhe play.

Fionnlagh sat back in the shingles, sword by his side.

She'd grown bored of plying fetch, having been distracted by the fishes the rock had startled. Giant paws slapped at the waters, pinning down whatever moved, giant ears facing attentively forward as she lifted her paw, seemingly astounded as the fish launched itself to freedom. Growls and whimpers of delight filled the morning air as she bounded through the shallows after her prey.

"Yui could'a caught some, lassie," said Fionnlagh as the giant cat lumbered towards him.

With the quickest burst of blue flame, Kylie replaced the cat. "I wasn't hunting, Fion."

"Ah'd've been happy wi' a baked fish."

"I was just plying." She grinned, running her fingers through her salt entangled hair. "You want fish, *you* catch 'em."

Fionnlagh snorted, standing and retrieving his sword. "Some fearsome cat yui are. Bet the beasties live in fear of you."

"If you *must* know," said Kylie, "I had a really good game of tag with some wild boars earlier."

"See now!" said Fionnlagh, fighting to hide his grin as they walked side by side down the beach. "Fresh meat! Roasting on a fire, fine as ye's cuid want, and whit dae we have? Vegetable broth, made by yuir grandfer. *Yum."*

"He's a good cook!" She saw the look he gave her. "...Sorta. Anyway, he's your captain now." She halted, looking at the direction they were taking. "No, not up there."

They'd been moving towards the base of the cliff, not really paying attention. Innumerable stone mounds lined the ground in rows; the cairns of the men they'd lost. Uilleam's was the largest.

There'd been little discussion as to who would replace the captain. The remaining men knew of Gobswistle's fight to save them. Perhaps they could even sense, through his ramblings and odd behaviour, the authority he could command.

Kylie and Fionnlagh headed back down to the shoreline.

"Hey," said Kylie, "did you hear about the cat who swallowed a ball of wool?"

"*What* now?"

"She had mittens!"

Fionnlagh groaned. "Oh that is so..."

"What's it doing when you hear 'woof...splat...meow...splat?'"

Fionnlagh grinned. Her good mood was contagious. "Surprise me."

"Raining cats and dogs!" She laughed at her own joke.

"That is *bad*!"

"Is it bad luck if a black cat follows you?"

"Ah know this!" smiled the young man. "Depends if yuir a man or a mouse?"

"You've *heard* it!" she made a show of groaning.

"KYLIE!"

Both turned at the sound of the voice. It came from the waters by their side; a young boy's voice.

A sandy haired boy was wading through the deeper waters, waving madly at them.

"Dai..." breathed Kylie, walking towards him.

Fionnlagh placed a hand on her shoulder. "No, wait..."

"It's okay!" said Kylie, ducking out from under his hand. "I know him! Daileass!" She ran down the beach, waving herself. "Dai!"

As she reached him she picked him up, hugging him closely. "You're alright! Dai, I was so frightened..!"

"Away, Ah'm fine!" said the boy, wriggling free. "Me Mah came 'n' found me, Kylie yui should see her now, an' – an' Ah've got more family, there's so many of them, an' Ah watched yui playin' an' you're so *big!*"

"You said I would be!" she hugged him again. "You're okay? What're you doing here? Where's Athdara?"

"She sent me tae get you," said Daileass. "She's got a present for you."

"Where is she?"

He pointed down to the curve of the high cliffed cove. "She's comin'. Fam'ly're helpin'. See though! See what she's got!"

As the vast shape rounded the cliffs, Kylie's eyes widened.

"GOBSWISTLE!"

The old man grunted, looking up from the little rock pool. Etain. Of course, it had to be. Only she had a voice that could break boulders. Tough. He was *busy*.

He turned back to the pool, up to his knees in water and seaweed. The crab had been taunting him, mocking him in the midmorning sun as it basked on the rock, the size of a fist and a welcome addition to the pot. And of course, as soon as it had seen him, it had plunged into the icy pool.

He wasn't daunted so easily!

Hands gently parted the carpet of weed, and his eyes lit up as he saw a round shape in the depths. He lunged down.

"Ethlebert! Where are you!"

"Oh..." Gobswistle straightened, a round orange rock in his hands. "...singed dangly bits." He let the rock fall. "What is it, woman?"

"What're you doin'?" Her voice was getting closer. "The men are hungry!"

"What am I, their wet nurse?" called back Gobswistle, parting the seaweed once more. "I'm doing my best!"

"Well hurry up!"

"Bloody woman," muttered Gobswistle, peering myopically into the depths. "Always bossing, and calling me names and..." he fell silent as he saw movement by one foot. "Aha! Thought you could hide from me did you?" He watched as the large crab scuttled through the water. "I have a hot tub you may like, young fellow."

Hands plunged down into the water.

The remaining soldiers had distributed themselves around the cauldron Etain stirred, seated patiently on the ground.

Stirring the gloopy concoction, Etain winced. Not much of a breakfast. Dry grass seeds, various herbs, and some edible sea urchins.

It smelt *rank*.

She looked into the distance, about to call the old man again when a loud yelp filled the air. Instantly many of the soldiers were on their feet, hands to their weapons. Etain jogged a few paces up the beach.

"Gobswistle? You okay?"

"I'm bloody fine, just stay there, vile creature!"

Etain felt the blood rush to her face. "Now look..."

"Not *you*, woman!" His voice sounded pained, and another yelp filled the air. Something small and round flew through the air as though kicked. "Damn! Too hard!"

The soldiers looked nervously at Etain as she started to walk towards the sound of his voice, on the other side of a shingled rise. She held up one hand, stilling them.

"Gobswistle, what's goin' on?" If they were under attack again...

Gobswistle staggered over the brow of the rise, and Etain had to clamp a hand over her mouth to stifle her guffaw.

There was more seaweed than old man visible, and what little of Gobswistle could be seen looked severely annoyed. He limped up to Etain, not pausing as he reached her.

"Not one word," he muttered, heading to the pot. Several of the men had started laughing as he hobbled past them, and he silenced them with an ominous scowl.

Etain trotted by his side. "Can I ask...?"

"I was hunting crabs!" snapped the old man. "Okay?"

"A ... *crab* did this to you?"

"He was big!"

"Ah'm sure." Etain grinned broadly.

"*And* feisty!"

"*Terrifying.*"

"He grabbed my toe!" yelped Gobswistle. "See?!" He held up the offending foot. There was a definite dent in the toe of the sodden silver boot.

"You did well to get away," said Etain as they reached the pot. "What, did ya fight tooth an' ... claw?"

"Be hushed, vindictive woman." He began pulling off large streamers of weed. He looked around, deciding where to throw it, then with a shrug dropped it into the bubbling pot.

"Ethel*bert!*"

"What?" said Gobswistle as he slowly emerged from the greenery. "It's edible!"

Etain peered into the pot. "you're makin' glue."

"I cooked," muttered Gobswistle, stirring the green mass into the depths. "*You'll* eat."

Any response Etain had was cut off by the sound of children's voices.

"Grandad!"

"Etain!"

Turning, they saw the two children pounding up the beach towards them.

"It's Daileass," breathed Etain, all thoughts of food forgotten. "Daileass!" She started running towards them, Gobswistle only a few steps behind. "Kylie, Daileass, what..?"

The boy grabbed her hand, trying to pull her down the beach. "Come see! Come see what me ma's got!"

"It's huge!" cried Kylie delightedly, grabbing Gobswistle hand, hauling him along. "Come see! Athdara's waiting!"

Etain and Gobswistle allowed themselves to be dragged along the beach, the soldiers following in bemusement.

"It's a ship..." breathed Gobswistle, gasping for breath.

"What's left of one," replied Etain.

The vast wreck of a viking ship sat in the waters off the shore, holed and battered, its dragonhead the only thing left unscarred.

"I don't understand," said Gobswistle.

"That thing!" said Etain, remembering. "That thing you were promised would help us! This is it!"

"We can't board *that!*" whooped the old man. "Look at it!"

"Look," said Etain, pointing. "There."

A figure was wading out of the water, silver hair dancing around her head as she approached. It was Athdara, looking calm and regal as she reached them, her depthless black eyes looking from one to the other. At her throat, a gemstone burned.

"You helped me, ancient one, warrior," she smiled. "It seemed only just that I return the favour."

"you ... look well," said Gobswistle, obviously at a loss for words. She simply smiled.

"Where..." said Etain, "where did you get this? What happened to the vikings?"

"The boy Yellowblade did this," said Athdara, turning to look back at the wreckage. "My kind ... we dealt with the humans."

"Jason?" said Gobswistle. "You saw my grandson? He's Alive! Where – where is he, what ...?"

"He is on the mainland," replied Athdara. "Where you need to be. We will carry you to him, for it is Alban Eiler, and his peril strengthens with every moment we pass through."

"But – but that thing's wrecked, how are we going to...?"

Etain laid a hand on his arm, smiling. "Ah think that's my job," she said. "Cookiecrumb it ain't, but you taught me well."

By her side, Daileass clapped his hands delightedly. "I wanna watch!"

"Fine by me," said Etain,drawing a nail from her pouch. Her ironfire, usually so fierce, glowed a gentle pink, a slim line of rippling mist. "Stand back though. It's gonna get foggy."

Chapter Thirty One

The darkness of the deep oubliette was broken only by the flickering light of a few lanterns, casting black rippling shadows in the darkness. The vast round chamber was filled with people, scared and quiet. Some were injured; their moans and cries were the haunting calls of the dead.

Jason watched as the diminutive woman he'd been captured with wandered around the chamber, one lantern clutched in a chubby hand, as she dispensed what aid she could. She knelt by one young woman, who lay on the damp stones, her face ashen and bruised with pain.

Gaira turned to Jason. "Boy. Come here."

Jason pushed himself away from the wall. "What?" He couldn't keep the sullenness from his voice.

"Ah need yuir help," muttered the woman, hearing his tone but ignoring it. "See. Her leg's broke. Ah need tae set it."

"What do you want me to do?"

"Pull on it when Ah tell ye's. But *gently.*" She took the woman's hand. "What's yuir name, girrul?"

"Jean, ma'am," replied the woman, breathing shallowly.

"Ah'm Gaira then. Here," and she rummaged in her robes, pulling out a salt stained pouch. "The herbs'll tekk the edge off the pain." She held out a finger full of the grey foliage. "Sorry, Ah've nae water."

The girl nodded dumbly, and took the herbs from Gaira, chewing on them slowly.

Gaira nodded. "Good girl, good girl." She lifted a corner of the woman's dress, biting at the seam with her teeth. Having loosened the stitches, she tore a long length of material from it. "Ah've no stick tae set it, but Ah c'n bind it in place. It'll hurt, mind."

"Ah'm no afeared o' pain," replied Jean. "Do what yui havetae."
Gaira looked up at Jason. "Ready?"
Jason held the ankle of the misshaped leg. "Yup."
"Right, and ... *pull!*"

Jason mopped the woman's brow with a remnant of cloth. "How's the pain now?"

"Better," said Jean quietly. Jason knew she was lying, but said nothing. There was an emptiness around the woman, as though nothing mattered to her any more.

"How ... how long have you been here?"

Jean gave a quiet laugh. "Oh wee boy ... Ah've nae idea." They'd moved her over to the wall, and now she eased herself up to lean against it, wincing as the bone in her leg grated. "Nae light, no sun nor moon. Days. Weeks. Forever."

"When did ... when were you taken?"

"We were preparin' fer Alban Ailer. Smokin' the meat, dippin' the candles. Six days til it arrived."

"Alban..." said Jason, thinking back to his conversation with the creature, Blashie. "That's full moon isn't it?"

"Aye."

"Then ... I think it's Alban Eiler today."

Jean closed her eyes, leaning her head against the wall. "Some celebration!" She opened her eyes, looking to where Gaira tended yet another injured woman. "She a healer?"

"Yes." *Amongst other things.*

"She's kind." A smile played across the woman's lips.

"She ..." *put you in here*, were the words that almost escaped angrily from Jason's lips. "She's difficult to understand."

"She's yuir friend though?"

Jason didn't want to argue with her; there seemed no point. "We were travelling together."

"She's a pech, isn't she? Thought the' were all dead."

"I've heard ... others call her that, but she's not said so herself." He watched as Gaira dressed an open wound, sprinkling a yellow powder into the exposed flesh. He turned back to Jean. "What *is* a pech?"

"She's no' what Ah expected."

"How d'you mean?"

"well..." Jean thought for a moment, her pale brow furrowed. "They're supposed tae be angry. *Wicked.*"

Jason suppressed his derisive snort. "I can go along with that."

"Couldnae blame them though."

"What," said Jason, "for being wicked?"

"Time was, we were wicked to them." She winced, biting her bottom lip as her bound leg pained her.

"What do..?"

Jean gasped, clutching her leg. "Go tae her, boy. Ah need more o' them herbs."

"She'll sleep now," muttered Gaira, rubbing her hands on her robes. "Mebbies as well." She stood, walking away into the darkness.

Jason helped Jean get more comfortable, then stood, following her. They reached an unoccupied area of the chamber, nearly in total darkness as Gaira had left her lamp with the injured woman. He caught her arm. "What do you mean?"

"Two things," said Gaira, shaking off his hand. "Nae herbs left. At least, that the sea hasnae ruined."

"And the second?"

"We're in Huddour's pit. At Alban Eiler."

"Meaning?" He felt the cold settle in his stomach as he heard the fear in her voice.

"He wants us, boy. Fifty o' us. There were fifty three o'us last night. Three vanished while we slept. Includin' yon Jeannie's bairn. These folk, the' say the vikings that took them, they were countin' them. Thought extra would bring more money."

Including Jeannie's bairn. That explained her emptiness. "But why fifty? What's special about that?"

The little woman shrugged. "We've been tekken by a heart blacker'n mine. Whatever it is, it won't be good."

"Then we have to *do* something!" said Jason desperately. "We can't just give up!"

"If you have yuir way, Ah'm tae be dead sooner or later anyway." She sank to the floor, her back against the damp mossy wall. "Makes nae difference tae me."

Jason crouched beside her. "If you're so sure we're all gonna die, why've you been helping them?" he demanded. "Most of them you put in here! Why help them?"

"Passed the time, dinnit?" She didn't look at him, her hands picking out her filthy fingernails.

"You weren't just *passing the time*, Gaira."

"Ah'm a *healer,* boy. What was I supposed tae do? *They* dinnae knah me history."

Jason looked over to where Jean, finally, slept. "She said you were kind."

Gaira grunted.

"Why *help* them?" insisted Jason.

"Because," said Gaira. Even in the darkness, Jason saw a tear roll down a cheek and in spite of himself, he felt his heart soften a little.

"Because what?"

Gaira finally looked at him. "Because *yuir* here!" The words were almost ripped from her throat.

A myriad of thoughts flooded through Jason's mind. Finally he said "I thought you didn't believe in me."

"Ah didnae. But on the ship, an' then wi' Ilisa ..." She sighed, blotting her eyes. "Ah saw ... Ah saw a man. That Lathgertha thing, *she* believed in you. Huddour, he believes in you. He's afeared o' you, boy. There's *magic* in ye's."

"You've got to be kidding!" Jason was stuck between laughter and anger. "Huddour's got my knife! He took my magic! Remember?"

"Look around, boy."

"What?" Jason's eyes scanned the chamber, taking in the people huddled around on the ground.

"What do you see?"

Jason looked around again. Women and children huddled together, those closest to the lamps warming their hands in the meagre heat. Babies were hugged close to their mother's chest, wrapped as best they could in the shawls and dresses they bore.

"...frightened people," he said eventually. What was she driving at?

"Look again," said Gaira shortly.

"I don't get what ..."

"Frightened *cold* people." The little woman glared at him in silent challenge. "Don't yui ken?"

Jason finally realised.

The people around him shivered in the cold, huddled together for warmth, their breath fogging in the air around them. He sat there bare armed save for his elbow and wrist guards. His leathers, though thick, offered little protection from the biting cold of the oubliette.

Yet he wasn't cold.

He looked at Gaira. "What ... what does it mean?"

"It means, Crowanhawk Yellowblade, blade or no, that there's magic in yuir blood." She leaned closer to him, her voice hardly more than a whisper. "It means, boy, yui need tae *find* it."

The three stone figures almost filled the small windowed chamber. Light streamed across their immobile forms, flooding in to the uppermost pinnacle of the castle. All three were twice the height of a man, their very size imposing as they stood in their never changing semicircle.

One was in the form of a cloaked woman heavy with child, most of her face and hair hidden under a hood. What little could be seen of her face was gaunt and hollow.

The middle figure was a skeleton, its bones disproportionately thick, the skull bearing only one eye socket, directly above the nostrils.

The final figure stood upright like a man, and had the arms of a man, but there the resemblance ended. Its head was that of a goat, horns curling down past its ears, the lips curled angrily back in a frozen snarl revealing doglike teeth. The legs and feet were the feathered legs and talons of an eagle.

Each figure held a red leather-bound book to its chest; The Three Books of Huddour. The Book of Life, the Book of Death, and the Book of Transformation.

All three heads faced forever in the same direction, sightless eyes staring at the single door and the spiral staircase beyond.

The door opened, creaking on its seldom used hinges, and Huddour walked in, walking to stand directly in front of the central statue.

"Greetings my children," he smiled, his eyes gleaming. "Soon." He patted the leg of each figure, as though reassuring a frightened child. "*Soon.*"

He walked over to the western window, glassless, as were the others. The wind ruffled his thin covering of hair as he stared out over the western horizon. "*Finally.* I will be avenged for the humiliation caused by the Trickster. The Huntsman. The *Fool!*" He smile became a grin. "I may even usurp him. He'd make a fabulous slave!" He giggled to himself. "I'd call him Blashie the Second!"

He walked back round to the skeletal statue. "Balor, my friend. It's been too long, has it not?" He reached up, grasping the immobile forearm in greeting. "It's good to see you, you old one eye'd fool!" His smile faded, and he stared at the impassive skull. "I need the knowledge to summon the Wild Hunt. Balor ... give me the book."

Rats! He could hear them, as he scurried along the side of the wall. He was *hungry*. His master had given him that old woman earlier, but she'd been slow. Boring. No joy of the hunt. Rats, now. Small, hardly more than a snack, but they could *run!*

He was in the depths of the castle, scurrying through the dry sewer system, happy to be away from his master. Horrid Huddour was happy, and when he was happy it was best for Blashie to stay out of sight. Huddour *happy* made Huddour *cruel.* The sewer system, utterly black and hardly used, made a safe haven for the little trowe, and provided entertainment. So many rats, scurrying around, never knowing where their danger lay. The darkness meant nothing to him; he could see as well in the darkness as in broad daylight. One of his master's gifts.

His chamber had a fire blazing away, ready to roast any of the little creatures he caught. Eat them raw, fine and good, but *hot* meat, much better, more juicy, more flavoursome.

"Here little ratty ratty baked potatty..." He heard the rats scuttle away from his singing and giggled happily. The hunt had begun! He sang to himself as he scuttled after them.

"Little ratties sleek and fat,
"Blashie hears just where you're at,
"Pulp you, bash you, roast yer brain,
"Blashie's on the hunt again!
"In the castle all alone,
"Huddour sits upon his *throne*,
"He sits and giggles like a lass,
"'Til Blashie bites him on the..."

Blashie stopped. *Voices?* He scuttled slowly along the wall. Why could he hear sodding voices? No-one was supposed to be in the sewers, it was *his* place, no-one else's, who dared to wander his place?

He paused as the voices got louder. Arguing, they were. They were on the other side of the wall. And he could smell *manmeat*. He could smell that sodding stickety thing, that manboy he'd caught. Blashie growled to himself. Sod what Huddour wanted. *He* wasn't down here. Blashie was. And he *owed* the boy.

He scurried up and down the wall, trying to find an entrance to the oubliette. The best he found was a rathole burrowed through the mortar, enlarged over the years by the greasy bodies of the tasty little creatures, wide enough to get his arm through but no more. Growling to himself, Blashie pressed a large ear against the opening and listened.

"Dinnae tekk yuir temper out on *me*, boy!" snapped Gaira as she watched the youth kick the walls in frustration.

"I didn't want to be here in the first place! I was sent! By the Gwyllion!"

"Sing a different song, boy, Ah've listened tae this 'un long enough."

"Oh am I boring you?" snapped Jason. "*So* sorry." Around him, he could hear the grumbling of the other prisoners as their arguing roused them. He leant back against the wall, sliding down it to sit down. "Sorry," he repeated, this time a little more contritely.

"Yeah, well..." Gaira shrugged. "None of us want tae be here. What can yui do?" She closed her eyes. "...Ah hope Aiken's alright."

"Just Aiken?" said Jason, looking at her. "Not anyone else?"

The little woman made no reply.

"Why..." began Jason, "why do you *hate* people so much?"

"Don't hate 'em," replied Gaira. "Don't trust 'em. It's different."

"But why?"

Gaira didn't look up, her fingers twisting gently at a corner of her shawl. She looked up into the darkness. "See this place?" she said eventually.

Jason followed her gaze. Vast curved bricks and mortar surrounded them, ancient and green with moss. "What about it?"

"We built it."

"'*We*'?"

"Mah folk. The pech." She sighed sadly. "That's what we did. We *built*. Or mined. Tales say we came over from the biglands, tae the east. Sair numbers o' us o'er there. Lived in what we built, where we mined."

Something clicked in Jason's mind, and he felt a grin threatening to appear. "you're telling me ... you're *dwarves?*" He saw her stony eyes glint angrily in the semi light. "Sorry." He tried to ignore the Disney song now *hi-ho-ing* loudly in his mind.

"You wannae hear this?"

"Yeah," said Jason, "sorry, please, go on."

"The Lairds, they'd heard o' us. Got us tae build their fortresses. We built 'em *strong*. Vitrified them. Arka–Unskel, Dunideer. Other places. But them Lairds, they got greedy. Wanted our knowhow."

Jason could sense where the tale was leading. "The pech, they wouldn't tell them, would they?"

"Proud buggers," said Gaira, nodding. "Daft buggers." She fell silent, still picking at her shawl.

"So...so what happened?" prompted Jason.

"Them men, they wus allus at war wi' each other. Killin' meant nothin'. Killin' oor chiefs meant less. A way to mekk us do their biddin'. 'Cept it didnae. We went intae hiding. Began oor own war. We build them castles, we cuid bring 'em down. Never thought..." She sighed. "Few of us. Many o' them. Rewards were offered for us. Villages we thought friends sold us out for money. Or attacked us theirselves.

"That place, Aneithcraig?" she looked at Jason, her eyes shining. "Our last home. Most sailed back tae biglands fro' there. No' safe going cross land."

Jason said nothing, his face burning as he understood more than he wanted to.

"They must hae forgot me," said Gaira. "Aiken found me, bairn Ah was, brung me tae his place. Then tae Kilnueair. Townsfolk, they'd grew used tae him. One more oddity were nowt tae them. The' kept me *safe*." She stared at Jason. "How cuid Ah not dae the same?"

Blashie was *bored*. Silly little pech thing, sobbing her story to the boy. Who cared?

A rat scrambled up the wall. The little trowe had been still so long that the rat was unaware of him. It froze briefly as Blashie eased himself away from the hole, looking at the rat in delight, then as Blashie made a frenzied grab for it, it scrambled for the hole, diving into it.

"No you *don't!*" yelped Blashie, thrusting his hand into the hole after it. The rat, having no other recourse, launched itself into the air.

"It doesn't excuse you, you know," said Jason quietly. "All those people you gave to the vikings, the people in here, you could've helped them."

"Help them? *Help* them?" Gaira stood angrily. "Have ye no' be listenin'? They did the same tae me! Ah did what Ah hadtae..." she was cut off as something large and furry landed on her head, small claws raking at her skull as it launched itself off into the darkness. "Bluidy rat!" she yelped.

Jason was on his feet, staring up in the direction the rat had come from. A Bony hand and forearm waved in the air, trying to catch the fleeing rat. "Gaira! Look!" At his shout the arm vanished, and an all too familiar yellow eye peered down at him through the small hole.

"What? What's there?" still scrubbing at her hair, the little woman stared up at where Jason had pointed.

Jason ignored her, feeling at the wall in front of him. The stones were ancient but firm, but the mortar between them had softened with damp and the invading moss. He quickly found a hand hold, then a foot hold.

"Boy! Be careful!" He ignored Gaira's call, torn between fury and immense pity for the woman, and began to climb. Moss and mortar showered down as he climbed towards the hole. Below him he could hear voices rising as more of the prisoners saw what he was doing. Some were urging him to come back down; most cheered him on.

Blashie's eye was gone by the time he reached the hole, though he could still hear the creature as it scurried away. He pressed his eye to the hole. He shouldn't have been able to see anything, but he could make out a round tunnel on the other side of the wall, and in the distance, Blashie was bouncing around the tunnel, yelping as he went. So Jason had scared him. *Good!*

He probed the mortar. It was drier than the walls below him, and less moss had eaten into it. But it still crumbled slightly under his fingernails. The hole showed the thickness of the brick; less than two feet. If he could get the stone out, he could get into the tunnel, then who knew where? He quickly dropped to the ground, landing catlike on his feet.

"I need something sharp," he said, looking at Gaira and the womenfolk around her. "Something I can ..." he looked at the people who were staring at him open mouthed. "...what?"

Gaira looked at him, then back up at the hole.

Jason followed her gaze, then paled as he realized what he had just done.

He'd climbed a vertical wall to a height of twenty feet, two thirds the height of the oubliette, then dropped back down to a stone floor without even thinking about it. His legs should've been shattered by the drop.

"Ah think," said Gaira, thrusting a battered metal spoon into his hand, "yui've just found some o' yuir magic."

Chapter Thirty Two

The vast ship pitched through the waves, ropes from its fore pulled taught in the waters below, held by fiery blue shapes that sped through the waters. The landscapes to the right of them, imperial cliffs and forests, sped by as the drekar ship headed north. On its deck, the men of Dun Ghallain sat on the numerous benches, hanging on to the superfluous oars for dear life. Kylie, Etain and Fionnlagh sat at the aft of the ship. All the occupants were systematically being drenched by waves of water that crashed over the bows.

"Gobswistle!" bellowed Etain, her hands wrapped securely to one of the ropes. "Are you mad?! Come down!"

At the fore of the ship, his arms spread out delightedly, Gobswistle leant out over the waters.

"What *is* he doing?" moaned Etain, feeling her breakfast churning in her stomach. "Gobswistle!!"

"*I'm the king of the world*!" bellowed the old man, his hair streaming behind him.

"Grandad!" shouted Kylie. "You'll fall in!"

"Leave 'im," said an ashen faced Fionnlagh. "If he falls in, Ah'm no goin' after him." He hiccupped, then rapidly hauled himself to his feet, wrapping the rope around his wrist as he leant over the side.

Kylie winced in sympathy at the retching sounds. From the way her stomach was doing summersaults, she'd soon be joining him.

"Ah c'n *ride* like a mayun!" shouted Gobswistle, his arms flailing in the wind. "And Ah c'n *spit* like a mayun!" And, as though to demonstrate this, he hawked deeply from the back of his throat, spitting the resulting mass out into the air.

And fell back spluttering as it was immediately blown back at him. He wiped the mess from his face, his grin still not fading.

This was *fun!*

The selkie were as good as their word, hauling the creaking wooden vessel through the waters at a speed he doubted even the fastest of cruise ships could manage. He turned, looking back across the men, expecting to see his delight mirrored in their faces.

Most of the men had their eyes closed as they hugged the oars, their faces an odd mixture of white and green. Gobswistle was disappointed. Surely he couldn't be the only one enjoying this? Seeing his granddaughter at the aft of the ship, he waved happily. She at least would be finding it fun. This was better than a rollercoaster! His smile faded as she stood, then lurched over the side of the ship, one hand clutching a rope, the other holding her hair back.

Oh.

Oh well.

He turned back, arms stretched out either side, and leant out once more. At least *he* could enjoy it.

"I'm the king of ..." his words were cut short as the ropes suddenly went slack, and the ship, robbed of its speed, lurched.

"Thankyou thankyou thankyou thankyou," muttered Etain, pulling herself to her feet. She looked about her. The ship still moved forward, carried along by the wind, but the violent pitching had finally stopped. "Where are we?"

Fionnlagh stood by her side, wiping at his mouth. "Don't know, don't care, want tae get on land." He belched loudly. "Sorry."

Kylie, wiping her mouth herself, looked to the fore of the ship. "Where's grandad?" She couldn't see the old man anymore.

"Oh he flamin' *hasn't,*" growled Etain, making her way aft to fore. "Gobswistle?" He was nowhere to be seen. "Ethelbert!"

"Down here!"

Etain ran to the fore, to the vast dragonhead. "Where?" she peered over the side. "Oh for ... I *told* you to get down!"

Gobswistle glared up at her, hanging by one hand from the front teeth of the dragon. "Recriminations *later* seems a good idea. How about helping me up?"

Etain grinned.

They stood on the island at the mouth of the loch, many of the men collapsing with thankful moans onto the reassuringly immobile beach.

Athdara had come ashore. As she approached the old man and Etain, her silvery hair danced around her, ribbons of light dancing in the mid day sun.

"This is as far as I can bring you," she said. "The kelpies have this loch; we can afford no quarrel with them."

"How much further is it?" asked Etain.

"With the wind behind you, you'll reach Castle Stalkaire before nightfall." She looked back down the loch. "But beware, Ethlebert. Your grandchild is not the only Cait Sidhe nearby. Nor are they the only army Huddour owns."

"We'll be careful," said Gobswistle. "Thankyou, dear lady, for your help."

Athdara nodded, smiling slightly. "I wish you well, Ethelbert." She turned to go.

Etain noticed something. "Athdara, your stone ...?"

The selkie hesitated, her hand flickering to her now naked throat. She looked at Etain, and smiled. "He is on his way back to us," she said. "My sister carries him."

"Your sister?"

"My family is large," and her smile grew. "Thank you, Etain, you freed me in more ways than you know."

"Hey," said Etain, returning the smile, "anythin' for a sister."

Athdara turned, walking towards the tide line, then paused, looking out to the mainland. "Someone comes," she said, seemingly more to herself. She frowned, looking at the old man. "But ... you're already here?"

"What?" Gobswistle blinked.

Athdara didn't reply, and with one more puzzled look toward the mainland, she walked down into the waves, diving gracefully under the water's surface.

"Who's coming?" shouted Gobswistle after her. "Are they dangerous? Should we hide?"

"Gobswistle!" shouted Etain, pointing to the east.

A vast plume of water shot up from the mainland coast, crossing the waters to the island almost instantly, showering the people collected there with water.

Out of nowhere, three figures appeared. A young dark haired and bearded man, dressed in grubby white robes, an older soldier, broad and scar-faced, and an old man, clutching a staff.

As Gobswistle and Etain stared open-mouthed, the old man collapsed to the ground.

"Don't just stand there!" bellowed Myrrdin, kneeling by the old man. "He needs help!"

"Who is he?" asked Fionnlagh. He stood by Kylie's side, many feet away from where the small group huddled around the stricken old man, half hidden by the shadows of the trees around them. "Is he

Gobswistle's son? Grandson?"

"No, he..." Kylie stared down at the man, her eyes wide. So familiar, yet so totally unfamiliar. "He ... *is* Gobswistle. Only younger."

"...What?"

"Me and Grandad, we're from the future, like Jay and Anna. Grandad is what he will become."

"That's..." Fionnlagh looked at the young and old versions of each other. "That's creepy."

"Yeah," said Kylie softly. "It is."

Myrrdin knelt by Darrach's side, holding his hand. "Darrach?"

Watery eyes opened. "Ah..*told* you yui'd kill me," wheezed the old man.

Myrrdin looked desperately from Gobswistle to Etain. "Can't you do anything?"

Gobswistle simply stared at his younger self, his mouth opening and closing soundlessly.

"He's off on one," said Etain. "*You're the druid. Can't you?*"

Myrrdin shook his head dumbly. "No. I have no magic." He looked back down to his friend. "I'm sorry, Darrach."

The old man pulled his hand away. "Sorry ... for what? Promise had tae be kept. We're here. *You're* here." His hands scrabbled in the sand. "Mah staff..."

By his other side, Omnust pushed the grey wooden staff into his hand. "It's here, Darrach."

Darrach brought the staff up onto his chest, clutching it tightly with both hands. "Bec Mac Dè bequeathed this tae me at his death." He looked up at the druid. "Said it'd be..." he wheezed loudly, gasping for air, "...it'd be needed. So now, Ah do the same tae thee." He raised it, tilting its head of tightly carved roots towards Myrrdin. "Tekk it, Lailoken. Make good wi' it."

Myrrdin closed his hands over Darrach's, not taking the staff. "Darrach, I can't..."

"Aye ye can," said Darrach, "and ye will. Ah'm no' afeared. Mah time, is all. Eigyr waits fer me in the Summerlands."

Myrrdin's eyes closed briefly with the pain of hearing Eigyr's name. By his side, Etain stared at him.

Darrach removed first one, then the other hand from under the druid's, closing the younger man's hands around the staff. "It's yours, mon. Mebbies allus was." He smiled weakly. "Promise me one thing though."

"*Anything,* Darrach."

"Mah daughter's bairns. Keep 'em safe?"

"Always," said Myrrdin. He was aware of Etain standing, pulling the befuddled old man with her, but did not raise his eyes to them.

"Always."

"Ah ken yeh," breathed Darrach. His eyelids flickered, and his head rolled gently back. His hands fell away from the druid's, leaving him holding the staff. As Myrrdin and Omnust watched, the old man's skin faded from pink to grey, then white. The clothes he wore began to sag and, as the wind danced along the shoreline, a stream of dust was carried from the old man's face as he slowly faded to dust.

Within moments, all that was left were empty clothes.

Myrrdin sat alone on the shoreline, staring sightlessly at the hills and mountains surrounding the loch. First Eigyr. Then Aiken. And now Darrach. And the men, women and children of Kilneuair, those who'd died following his orders, based on the scrawl of a child. That they'd repelled the vikings, that they'd won, seemed almost ... *hollow.*

"Myrrdin?"

Myrddin turned, startled by the voice. As Etain approached, he quickly stood up. "Etain."

"Here," she said, holding a bowl out to him. "It's not much, but you look like you could maybe do with something."

He took the bowl. "Thank you." But he made no effort to eat, looking at the woman in front of him. "You look ... different."

"I look older, don't kiss up to me." There was no real reprimand in her voice, and her smile was warm.

"You sound different too," said Myrrdin, a slight smile curling his lips.

"Yeah...well..." Etain shrugged. "Been around as long as me, you'll sound different too. How you holding up?"

Myrrdin said nothing, looking at her for a moment, then sank onto the sand once more, lying his staff across his lap. "Sit with me?"

After a second's hesitation, the warrior seated herself next to him. "Okay. Sure." She looked back to where Gobswistle stood with Kylie. He scowled across at Etain, whether out of jealousy, fear or some other emotion she couldn't tell. "Ethelbert, he said earlier ... he remembered losing someone dear to him."

Myrrdin said nothing.

"Myrrdin, are you okay?"

"Think I'll run off into the forest again?" The sudden bitterness in his voice coloured his cheeks, and he looked away, not wanting to meet the warrior's gaze.

"Ah'm guessin'," said Etain eventually, her voice gentle, "it was this Eigyr."

"Yes." He sighed. "You still read me so well. Yes, it was, we were..." he stirred the food in the bowl. "We married. Briefly. It didn't last." He felt rather than saw Etain's wide eyed gaze, and turned to her. "You'd been gone so many years, I didn't know..."

Etain held up a hand. "Hell, you and I, centuries ago, Ah hardly remember. Just ... surprised me, is all." She looked out across the waters. "Did you love her?"

"With all my heart."

Etain nodded gently. "Good. Ah'm glad." She looked back at him. "Be a shame to waste you. Damn, you're cute." She nudged him gently, grinning.

Myrrdin smiled back. "She's .. she *was* ... outspoken. Volatile. Like you, in many ways."

"Flatterer."

"I ... I miss her, Etain."

"That's good," said Etain. She patted his arm. "That's *real*. Shows you're *human.*"

Myrrdin saw her glance up at the old man as she said that. "What's he like?" he asked. "What am *I* like? You and I, do we ever...?"

"That was a one off," said Etain, more sharply than she intended. She moderated her voice when she continued. "We become ... friends. Good friends. But you have secrets. Lots of them. *Hell*. Didn't even know about Eigyr 'til now."

"Where are you now?" asked Myrrdin. "The you from this time? When do I see *you* again?"

"Now? With Constantine. Down south. Fighting at the borders."

"Does *he* know?" He looked over at Gobswistle. The old man, seeing Myrrdin looking at him, flustered, turning nervously away.

"No," replied Etain. "No need for him to. Ah knew nothin' of what was going on up here with your king. He was just, you know, Constantine's father."

"So you have your own secrets," said Myrrdin. "Does he remember? Being me?"

"No. Well ... not really." She shrugged. "Just flashes. Every now and then. He's an old man now. Half the time he ain't all there even."

"You didn't answer my question," said Myrrdin. He smiled gently. "When do I see *you* again?"

Etain stood, brushing the sand off her leathers. "Eat yer food." She smiled at her own evasion, then headed up the beach to the others. "We'll be setting off soon, so hurry up!"

Smiling, Myrrdin began to eat.

The ship lurched through the waters of the loch, battered and beaten by waves that would have been more at home out on the open sea.

Omnust sat on the oars' bench next to Myrrdin. "Is this ..." he gasped, trying to ignore the twisting of his stomach, "is this Huddour's doing?"

Myrrdin nodded grimly. "I think so. Not an attack against us directly; just any ship that enters Loch Linnhe."

Omnust swallowed deeply. "Ah'm no' reassured." He looked down at the fore of the ship, to where the old man and the Black Celt sat in deep conversation. "So ... he's you?"

"Apparently so."

"Well, man, why ye look so worried? Surely that means we survive this, this invasion or whatever..."

"He does," muttered Myrrdin. "In *his* time line."

"But if he's you ..."

"A *variation* of me."

"He's guid enough fer me," muttered Omnust. "If he, *yui*, mekk it tae that age, means we do alright."

Myrrdin said nothing, turning the staff in his hands.

"You were being very *pally* with him," muttered Gobswistle. "Sitting next to him on the beach."

"Like Ah'm sat next to you now, you mean?" said Etain.

"It looked *more* than that," said the old man. He picked a withered piece of seaweed from his beard, turning it in his fingers. "What, were you trying to rekindle ..."

"If you even finish that sentence Ah'm throwin' you in," snapped Etain. "You're kiddin', right? Ethelbert, he's *you.*"

"Yes, I *know* he's me. A younger, '*cuter*' me." He could feel his cheeks burning, but he didn't care. "I heard you back there."

"And you were listening in because ..?" She sighed. "Anyway, *if* you were listening, you'd've heard me say that we become friends. Nothin' more. Apart from anything else, he's just lost Eigyr." She looked at the old man. "You remember Eigyr?"

"I ..." he fiddled with the seaweed, then flicked it away. "I have the pain he felt. I have the name now for the pain. But no face, no *image*, to marry the two."

"Maybe you should talk to him."

"Why? I don't remember us talking." He looked down the ship at his younger self. "I don't remember leaving Kilneuair, I *certainly* don't remember Onmnust or Darrach..."

"You don't remember Eigyr either," replied Etain. "But you *know* she happened. You feel the loss, and it's lord knows how many centuries ago to you."

Gobswistle stared at her silently for a moment, then looked away. "What would I even *say* to him, for heaven's sake?"

" 'Hi there' would be a good start," said Etain, smiling. "He ain't gonna bite none. He's *you*. Ask him, I dunno, ask him what Eigyr looked like. How you got together, got married, what made you split ..."

"I was *married?*" interrupted Gobswistle. He glared almost accusingly at his younger self.

287

"Go *talk* to him, Ethelbert."

Gobswistle was silent for a while. "No," he said finally. "Best I don't."

"But..."

"No *buts*, dear lady." He smiled sadly. "Too much history. If I ... if Eigyr's memory is brought back, what happens to those of White Crow? My wife? I remember her, I remember our life together ..." he trailed off into silence, then cleared his throat. "If he starts asking about my past, suppose I say something that changes what he experiences in the future? Alters a decision somewhere in the future? Paradoxes, Etain, Paradoxes."

"You cain't *not* talk to him," said Etain, "we're going to war here."

"Then we'd better find Kylie," said the old man, resting his chin on his knees.

Etain looked around, her eyes widening.

Kylie was nowhere to be seen.

Chapter Thirty Three

The slug did not stand a chance. The rat, hungry and agile, snatched it up, holding it between its forepaws as it ate.

Something grated above its head; a fine shower of sand and dust rained down onto the little creature and it paused, looking around. But silence fell in the darkened sewer once more, and the rat turned back to its meal.

This time it was the rat that didn't stand a chance. The brick fell from the wall above with a gentle hiss of loose mortar, landing on the rat with a thud and a startled *squeak*.

Jason wriggled out through the hole, his shoulders only just narrow enough to fit through the gap. With a final twist he plunged into the malodorous slime below. He lay there a moment, oblivious to the stick as the enormity of what he'd just accomplished washed over him.

He'd just *escaped!* He looked at the bent spoon in his hand, giggling slightly. He'd escaped!

A scurrying sound from down the round tunnel brought him back to his senses.

He'd escaped into the sewer, surrounded by rats, with no idea of what to do next.

He quickly stood, shoving the spoon into his belt. He might need it later. He leaned through the hole. "Gaira!"

"Jason! You did it!" He saw the tiny woman waving below. Around her other figures had gathered; his silent audience. They waved at him, their faces lit with renewed hope.

"I'm fine!" called back Jason. "I'm going to..." to what? He had no plan as to what to do next. "I'm going to find a way out, see if I can find the opening to the oubliette." That sounded feasible.

"Get the books is what yui'll do," called back Gaira. "Wi'out them yui'll no' stop Huddour!"

He nodded silently, then with a final wave, he ducked out of the hole. That, he had to admit, was a plan.

Fionnlagh slashed the lower of the thick branches away from his face, spluttering as dry leaves, insects and goodness knows what else showered down upon him. "Kylie, what're we *doing?*"

"We're going to the castle," replied Kylie simply. Unlike Fionnlagh, she was already dry from their impromptu swim across the loch, Fionnlagh borne across on the Cait Sidhe's broad back. His fighting leathers had soaked up the water like sponges, and the afternoon sun carried no warmth into the shadows of the trees.

Fionnlagh shivered. "We shouldn't hae left them."

"They have Myrrdin *and* Gobswistle," replied Kylie. "They have all they need."

"A grown man led by a ten year old," grumbled Fionnlagh. He slashed away more branches. "Dammit, child, there was no reason for us tae leave!"

"You said you trusted me," said Kylie, ducking under leaves and branch. "Don't you?"

"Just ... just tell me what we're doin'!"

Kylie stopped, brushing her long hair back from her face. "The cords that bind," she replied. "They're singing again." She smiled at him, a smile startlingly like her grandfather's, then ducked under the next branch.

"Oh lord..." breathed Fionnlagh, looking out at the ship that bucked in the waters, wishing he was on it, "...that doesn't sound good."

He followed.

It was the same hole in the wall. There was the stone, in the slime underneath the hole, the rat's tail sticking out from under it.

He'd come round in a complete circle. Jason swore quietly to himself, mindful of not letting the people below hear him. They had their hopes pinned upon him. He felt less than heroic as he looked down at the stone, then back down the sewer. He'd followed the direction he'd seen Blashie run off in, sure that it would lead to other passages. And now, here he was, back at the beginning. Who knew how much time had passed?

Maybe he was tackling it badly. He'd walked the length of the sewer and had been brought full circle. But the sewage had to come *from* somewhere, and just as obviously *go* somewhere. From somewhere suggested it came from the castle above, therefore there should be an overhead pipe/tunnel/hole.

He began walking along the sewer again, this time looking up. Dry roots and ancient spider's webs hung down, reaching for his face as he searched the darkness, and rats scuttled around his feet.

He found the in-feed tunnel surprisingly quickly, set roughly at right angles to the sewer below, its mouth almost hidden from view by overgrowth until Jason stood underneath it. The sewer he stood in was roughly eight feet in diameter; if he jumped, he may just be able to grab onto the inner walls.

He crouched in the half dry muck, then launched himself upwards.

His leap carried him several feet up into the interior of the vertical tunnel, catching him totally by surprise, and he scrabbled at the wall to find purchase. He hung there in the darkness, gasping for breath, his eyes wide in surprise. A slow grin spread over his face. This was going to be *easy!*

His hands and feet finding purchase in the smallest of holes, he clambered up the sewer. Light was blossoming above his head; a small circular patch of light that neither helped nor hindered his ability to see in the darkness. As he clambered it grew, and he realised the circle of light was smaller than the diameter of the sewer; a simple hole cut into wood.

It was, he realised with some revulsion, a toilet seat.

"What the hell is this?" hissed Fionnlagh from behind Kylie. A tiny yet firm hand grabbed his wrist, urging him into silence.

Hidden by bramble and gorse, Kylie and the soldier peered into the small clearing.

A group of simply robed figures stood there; young men and women, dotted at random through the short grass, their faces blank and pale. Forty or more figures, frozen in time.

"What're they doing?" whispered Fionnlagh.

"Their feet," whispered Kylie, "look at their feet!"

At first Fionnlagh didn't understand what she meant. They were just feet, after all. Then he saw it. The grass under foot, the dandelions and clover, grew around the feet of the figures, some of the grasses actually growing through the seams of the clothes, emerging through pockets, bursting through holes. The feet of some of the figures were obscured completely by overgrowth.

"They've been here *years,* they must have,*"* said Kylie. "But they're alive! Look; you can see them breathing! What do they do for food? Sleep?"

"They're not soldiers," said Fionnlagh. "They've the look of villagers, or travellers. It's sorcery, child." He looked down at Kylie. "Is them you're hearin'?"

Kylie frowned. "It ... It must be," she said finally. "I wouldn't be able to hear it otherwise." She stood, suddenly decisive. "I'm gonna see if I can stir them."

Before Fionnlagh could catch her, she was marching up to the nearest person.

The door opened silently, and Jason's dark haired head appeared, looking up and down the corridor.

Daylight!

After over a day locked in the oubliette the sunlight streaming through the unshuttered windows was welcome. Jason stood there for a moment, letting the sunlight wash over his skin, before moving up to the sill of the window.

Beyond the window was Loch Linnhe, vast and still, the sun dancing upon its mirror like waters. And around the loch, woodlands, hills and snowpeaked mountains rose into the skies, ancient and regal. In the sky, almost invisible in the afternoon light, the full moon was rising.

What was *that?* Jason squinted. There, far into the distance?

He paled. A viking ship fought its way through the waters, the loch around its bows boiling like the waters of a kettle.

If the vikings were coming, he needed to make a move. If it were Lathgertha, or her husband Ragnar, they would not be coming in peace. He looked indecisively left then right down the stone corridor. On an impulse, he turned left, jogging silently along the stone.

He past window after window, and he paused by a couple, looking down into the courtyard below. A sick looking tree grew in the centre, and Jason, remembering Aiken's tale of his family, felt a pang of both pity and anger at the sight of its blighted branches.

But where were the *people?*

He came to a stop in front of a large oak door, its hinges black with age. Tentatively he turned the handle, pulling the door open. He listened intently, but all he could hear was the gentle moaning of the wind around the castle walls.

He began to climb the spiral staircase, his nerves jangling. Somehow, he thought, he'd have felt less threatened if he did see or hear someone. The utter stillness of the castle was unnerving.

But all thoughts of other people vanished as he passed through the door.

He stared at the three statues, and at the leather bound books they clutched.

His mouth agape, almost tempted to turn tail and flee, Jason slowly walked forward. It couldn't be, it was too easy after all these days, but his eyes would not lie to him.

The Three Books of Huddour.

A giggle escaped his lips and he clapped both hands over his mouth. He reached out with one hand, poking at the statue of the woman, ready to snatch his hand back, to run full speed back down the stairs, but his fingers encountered only solid stone.

Feeling bolder, Jason crept closer, constantly looking back at the doorway, expecting at any moment for either Blashie, Huddour or Lathgertha appear there. They didn't.

He reached up; his fingers brushed the base of the first book, but he wasn't tall enough to reach it. He was about to start to clamber up the statue when he remembered the spoon in his belt. Grasping its bowl, he shoved the handle up at the spine of the book.

The book tumbled to the ground, its cover falling open, its pages turning slowly in the breeze from the windows. Jason stared at it dumbly, not believing his good fortune.

The second book fell just as easily from the skeletal figure's hands.

The third book needed prying free; the goat headed statue clung to it almost avariciously. Jason ripped its cover wresting it from the stony fingers, but within moments he hugged all three books to his chest.

This was it.

The quest was *over*.

He closed his eyes, waiting for the portal in Asenby to summon him, to call Anna and Kylie to him, to reunite him with them, with his grandfather and Etain, a single tear falling from a closed eye as he realised just how much he missed them, how much he *longed* to go home...

"Now what?" said a voice conversationally. "I mean, now that you've got the books. Seriously; what's next in your list of things to do?"

Huddour emerged from behind the statues, Blashie dancing round his legs.

"Oh don't look so surprised, young Crowanhawk," smiled the sorcerer. "Little Blashie here told me about you climbing up the wall after him. So all your magic *hasn't* left you then? We knew, didn't we, that there would only be one place you would come." He placed a fatherly hand on Blashie's head. The little creature crooned with delight.

Jason, white faced, made no reply. Why hadn't the magic worked?

"Not as chatty as the other day then?" said Huddour. "Shame. No matter. Blashie, make sure the books go back to their proper place. Then bring the boy to the courtyard. The day grows old; time to plan our celebrations!" He paused by one of the windows. "Hmm. Seems the vikings are coming too..." he leant out. "No, no, I tell a lie ... it's a black woman, an old man, and what appears to be his son." He saw Jason's eyes widen as he recognised the description, and smiled warmly at him before turning back to the window. "Well, and they've brought changelings with them!" He sighed, moving away from the windows. "Really, I don't have time for this." He made a gesture at the window; an almost random flicking motion. "Blashie, do as I asked."

Fionnlagh wasn't about to let Kylie go into the clearing alone. Two large steps brought him up to her side. "Kylie, Ah don't think this is a good idea..." he said.

Kylie was pale, a frown knitting her brow. "It's not them..."

"What's not them?"

"The Cord. I-I don't understand ... *oh!*" she started as the nearest figure suddenly moved.

The woman pulled her feet free from the turf with a ripping sound, then set off across the clearing towards the shore. If she saw the girl and the soldier, she showed no sign.

Around them, the rest of the figures were stirring. Feet were pulled free from their binding of grass, and one by one, the people began walking towards the shoreline.

"What's goin' on?" asked Fionnlagh, his sword unsheathed and raised.

"I don't know," admitted Kylie. "I thought I heard them ..."

"What do you mean, *heard* them?"

"Like I did with Cathal!" said Kylie, staring at the figures. "When – when I stopped his attack, when he *heard* me ..."

"These folk, then," said Fionnlagh, "they gonnae attack?"

"I don't know," said Kylie. "C'mon; let's follow them."

"They're staring at the ship," said Fionnlagh.

The people stood single file along the shore, staring impassively at the viking ship in the distant waters.

"But why?" said Kylie. "What're they doing? I don't understand what I'm *hearing...*"

"Kylie," said Fionnlagh, suddenly pointing at the ship with his blade, "Kylie, look."

The waters, already rough around the ship, were churning into life. Creatures could be seen in the waves that pounded the hull; horselike creatures, fierce and angry.

"What're they *doing?*" cried Kylie.

"They're drivin' the cursed thing at the shore," said Fionnlagh. "They're gonnae beach it."

"But – but the waters're shallow, that's *good,* Grandad won't let anything ..." she fell silent, staring at the people around her.

"Kylie? What is it?"

"We need to get under cover," whispered Kylie, pointing.

The figure nearest to them had faint blue fire crawling over her body.

"HOLD ON TIGHT!"

Gobswistle's bellowed instructions, hardly audible over the roaring of the waters and the creatures it contain, were not needed.

Every man clung to whatever he could find; the rigging, the benches, the rails of the ship. The ship pitched and rolled in the waters, the creatures pounding at its side pushing it towards the shore. The oars were being systematically ripped from the ship, shattering within seconds of striking the water.

"Cain't you *do* anything?!" shouted Etain over to the old man.

"Like *what?*" Gobswistle was momentarily silenced by a wall of water crashing over him. He grimly clung to the rigging. "These are *kelpies!*"

"*Like* stop them!" Etain began pulling herself along the rails towards the old man. "Use the anguinum!"

"Their magic is stronger," said a voice from her side. She looked down at Myrrdin as he clung to one of the benches. "And they're under the control of Huddour. We must ride this out!"

"We can't!" bellowed the stocky soldier Myrrdin had named as Omnust. He was pointing towards the shoreline. "More devilry!"

Etain looked to where he pointed. Black Hounds lined the shore, red eyes staring at the ship as it drew closer, lips drawn back in a silent snarl.

"I know what I'm hearing," said Kylie quietly. She looked up at Fionnlagh. "It's the men of Dun Ghallain. I *think.*"

"I still don't ken ..."

"When I first changed, when I went into the Rage, Cernunnos, he pulled me out, took me to..." she tried to find the right words. "To where I could *help.* I can't explain it, but I could control the Rage, I could help Cathal control *his..."*

Fionnlagh stared out from their hiding place. The ship was perilously close to the shore, and the men aboard could be seen, the fear and anger obvious even from this distance. On the shore, the Black Hounds paced restlessly, their eyes never leaving the ship.

"Why don't they attack us ...?" said Fionnlagh.

"I don't know, I don't think they're *alive* as such, I think Huddour's got their souls. But, Fion, I can *hear* your army!"

"Can you help them?"

"I think so," said Kylie. "I think Cernunnos showed me how." She closed her eyes.

The ship lurched as it hit the first of the rocks, throwing Etain to the deck. Around her, the men struggled to keep their feet as the selkies pounded the ship, driving it further and further onto the rocks. Below her feet, wood splintered, and water began flooding the lower deck.

Then everything stopped.

The selkie vanished, and around the grounded ship, the waters began pulling back to the loch, leaving the ship on the rocky ground.

Etain lunged to the side, looking down at the creatures below. They were already closing in, their growls now audible, and with a curse, Etain plunged her hand into her pouch. "Arm yourselves!" she yelled as her ironfire appeared in her hand. "The critters're here!"

Gobswistle staggered up to her, his combat jacket soaked and weighing him down. By his side, Myrrdin had his sword drawn, his face grim. Omnust joined them, his own sword ready.

None of the other men moved.

"Didn't you hear her?" shouted Myrrdin. "Ready yourselves! If we're going down, we're going down fi..."

"Save your dramatics, boy," said Gobswistle, lying a hand on his arm. "They're not listening."

The men of Dun Ghallain had frozen in their movements; some had even paused with swords half drawn.

"What the *hell?*" said Etain, running up to the nearest, pulling on his arm. He remained immobile, not looking at her. She looked back in panic at Myrrdin. "Huddour?"

Myrrdin looked at her helplessly. "I – I..."

"Out of my way," said Gobswistle, shoving past him. He marched authoritatively up to the soldier Etain had joined, pulling down his eyelid, peering into their depths. He then made a show of taking the man's pulse, nodding to himself.

Etain glowered at him, then looked over at Myrrdin, who was simply staring at his older self. She turned back to him. "Ethelbert, what *are..?*"

"Look!" snapped the old man. "See for yourself! His eyes, woman, his pupils! They're glowing red! His pulse is at least one – sixty! He's going into the Change, they *all* are!"

Even as he spoke, Etain could see the green fire starting to shimmer over the man's body. "But – but *how - ?*"

"Kylie," replied Gobswistle. "*Kylie's* doing this." He peered across at the woodland beyond. "Somewhere out there..."

As the Black Hounds circled the ship, their growls were answered from the decks above.

Chapter Thirty Four

The forest was silent, its leafy shadows undisturbed by the sound of animal or bird. The air was still, though only yards away the waters of the loch stirred and moaned as they lapped against the shore.

It seemed as though the whole landscape was holding its breath, awaiting some major catastrophe.

A whisper darted through the shadowy depths of leaf and branch, nimble and agile, shaking the leaves, showering the collected droplets of water to the ground below. The whisper grew, its temerity changing to boldness, and a thunderous roar began to fill the shadowed forest.

"Kylie, slow down!" yelped Fionnlagh, hanging on to the cat's muscular neck with his one hand as he rode on her back. "Ah cannae keep hold!"

If Kylie heard him, she paid no heed, her body twisting and leaping as she bounded between the trees, shadowy forms all around her keeping pace with her.

Something swept through the air overhead, something vast and leathery, and the Cait Sidhe roared in greeting.

"They're gaining!" yelled Gobswistle from his vantage point, tied as he was to the neck and shoulders of what had once been one of the soldiers, who now was a vast winged eagle. He pointed desperately down to where Kylie could be seen as she flashed between the trees. Other forms followed her; large apelike creatures carrying Myrrdin and Omnust piggyback as they kept pace with the Cait Sidhe, and behind these were numerous other shapes of dog, feline, and less identifiable creatures. The transformed Men of Dun Ghallain.

Behind this sepulchral army more dark shapes leapt through the trees. Their snarls and howling could be heard even at the height Gobswistle circled at. And they were gaining on his friends.

A hiss of air and a vibrating roar announced Etain's arrival. Like Gobswistle, she was airborne, sitting astride a golden lion with the leathery wings of a bat. Unlike the old man, she wasn't tied on. This was her element.

"Where've you been?" he shouted.

"Scouting ahead! There's a clearing coming up, not half a mile away. They're gainin', Ah see it; we'll make our stand there!"

"We need to let Kylie know!"

No need. Gobswistle started as the voice filled his mind. *Kylie touches us all. She sees what we see, hears what we...*

"Yes, al*right*, I get the picture," said Gobswistle, still not used to the telepathic touch of the soldier he was tied to. "So land in the clearing!"

As you wish.

Gobswistle flung his arms around the eagle's neck as it arrowed towards the ground.

"There's no point in hiding," shouted Myrrdin has he dropped to the ground. "They're dogs; they'll sniff us out."

Omnust ran up to him, his sword drawn. "What do we do?"

"We have an advantage," replied the druid, turning in greeting as Etain ran to join them. Behind her, Gobswistle was hanging upside down from the perplexed looking eagle's neck, berating it soundly as he tried to untangle himself from the ropes. Myrrdin stared at the old man for only a second before turning back to Etain and Omnust. "I ... yes, we have an advantage. The Black Dogs, they were once people, but when they transformed they lost their intelligence."

Whereas we didn't, said the huge gorilla-like creature that had carried Myrrdin.

"Exactly," said Myrrdin, "we can plan, we can work together..." he flinched as he heard Gobswistle fall to the ground with a barrage of expletives.

"Whatever you want us to do," said Etain, "decide quickly. Here they come!"

Gobswistle came staggering up, one length of rope still trailing from a leg. "I know what to do!"

"What?" said Etain.

"I *do!*" said the old man. "Don't look at me in that tone of voice – get in the trees!"

"But..."

"They're dogs, woman!" snapped Gobswistle. "Ever seen a dog climb a tree?" He turned to look at the rest of the changelings. "Well ... dingoes maybe. African dogs too I suppose ..." the creatures regarded him impassively. "Get to the trees!" Then he looked at the few changelings with wings; seven creatures varying from winged lions, through giant birds to ancient dinosaurs. "And you lot, grab the dogs, fly off with them! Drop 'em in the damn loch!" He half jogged, half hobbled to the nearest tree before looking back at Etain and the others. "Well?" Around him, the other changelings were already clambering into the trees that encircled the clearing.

"Heard worse ideas," said Etain, and began climbing a nearby pine.

Omnust looked at the druid. "Do we ..?"

Myrrdin nodded curtly, thrusting his staff through his belt so that it lay across his back. "As she said," he grunted, "heard worse ideas."

"Druid, are yui...?"

"I'm fine," said Myrrdin, "don't worry about me – start climbing."

As Omnust began his ascent, one thought stood out in his mind. Myrrdin disliked the old man.

Some forty huge black hounds burst through the trees, ropes of saliva hanging down from their panting maws as they looked around, growling, their noses in the air. Some of the bolder ones moved out from under the shade of the trees, following the scent before them.

They were the first to be snatched up by the winged creatures above them, vast wings casting huge shadows as they plunged towards the dogs, their claws and talons held wide to snatch them up. The other dogs leapt forward, snapping and snarling, but could do little other than watch as their brethren were borne skyward.

As the winged creatures reached the waters of the loch they released their prey, the hounds falling into the icy waters below. The waters churned and boiled; the selkie, following the commands of their Lord, defended the waters from intrusion.

The winged changelings turned in the air, heading back to the clearing.

The Black Dogs, momentarily befuddled by the airborne attack, milled around the perimeter of the clearing, forgetting for the moment the pursuit of their prey as the sky was filled with the beating of wings.

With a scream, the Cait Sidhe burst through the trees, landing on the back of one of the hounds, its sharp teeth biting down on the spinal cord. From its back, the one armed warrior leapt to the ground, his sword biting into the flesh of the nearest hound.

From the trees all around, the changelings descended on the Black Hounds.

Etain leapt from the trees, a blazing ironfire sword in each hand as she ran at the nearest dog. It sidestepped her, narrowly avoiding the swing of her blades, its teeth clamping shut mere inches from the back of her head.

She ducked, almost kneeling in the dirt as she span round. As she span, she cast one blade at the hound, and it hissed through the air, punching a hole through one ragged ear before it shrank once more into a small metal nail. The creature yelped, shaking its head angrily, circling Etain more cautiously now.

Etain withdrew another nail from her pouch, keeping herself low to the ground as she slowly backed away from the Black Dog, peripherally aware of the screams of hounds and changelings alike as they fought all around her.

This dog seemed *different*.

The glowing red eyes were fixed on Etain as she slowly backed up, the creature keeping the distance between them even, never getting too close, as though weighing up the warrior. Etain stopped moving.

Growling, the creature stopped.

She moved to her right.

The creature mirrored her movement, its eyes never leaving her.

She moved to her left.

The creature lunged at her, driving her back once more, and it was only her trained reflexes that prevented the creature's teeth closing on her arm as she swung at it.

A torn ear fell severed to the ground, and the hound retreated, though only a little, ribbons of saliva trailing down to the ground.

She was being *herded*.

The realisation was too late. She had no time to turn as something erupted from under the trees behind her, throwing her to the ground, vast paws knocking away the ironfire and pinning her arms to the ground. As more drool pooled on the back of her head, she closed her eyes, waiting for the teeth to sink into her neck.

There was a loud whooshing sound, and dry leaves flew up all around her. The weight vanished from her back, and she rolled over in the dirt to see the winged lion carrying the hound out over the waters.

She was instantly back on her feet, another ironfire in her hand as she waited for the one eared hound to attack.

The Black Dog stared at her, one side of its face soaked in blood, its features almost cunning as it studied the sidhe warrior. Then, with a snarl, it vanished into the forest.

"Did we ... did we win?" Gobswistle held the Glass apple out in front of him, looking round at the scene. The bodies of the Black Dogs littered the clearing. Of the men of Dun Ghallain there were no casualties.

"Less of the *we,* old man," said Etain. "Threatening them with that thing ain't exactly helpin' us fight. Where was the magic?"

"They didn't get me, did they?" replied Gobswistle, returning the Apple to his pocket.

"More luck than management," she replied. "Yeah, we won, we lost no-one ..." she stopped as she saw Myrrdin making his way over, his eyes fixed on the old man. "Stay here," she said, quickly moving to intercept the druid.

"He has the Anguinum?" demanded Myrrdin.

"He has *his* Anguinum," said Etain. "Myrrdin, leave it."

"Can he use it?" He looked angrily at Etain. "Woman, can he *use* it?"

"Whether he can or he cain't," said Etain, still blocking his passage, "it ain't none of your concern."

"Do you know what I could *do* with that?" He grabbed Etain by the shoulders. "That magic?"

"Myrrdin, *leave it,"* said Etain, shrugging off his hands. "It's not yours to take."

"I could *end* this," snarled Myrrdin. "I *know* how to use it! I am not some ... *addled* old man – that Anguinum is my *birthright!"*

"Myrrdin ..."

"With its power I could end this now!"

"Like you did in Strathclyde?" demanded Etain.

The colour drained from Myrddin's face at the mention of Strathclyde. One hand flashed out, striking her across one cheek, but she didn't flinch. She simply returned his stare, still blocking his path.

"You told me once that The Sidhe took your magic for a *reason,"* she said. "Don't *think* Ah'm gonna let you take *his."*

After what seemed an eternity, the druid span, walking rapidly away.

"Ouch," muttered Etain, rubbing her cheek as she watched him go.

"What was that about?" asked Gobswistle querulously as he hobbled up. "Why's he hitting you?"

"Nuthin'," replied Etain. "Nuthin'." She gave a quiet laugh, seemingly laughing at herself.

"Want me to turn him into a frog?" he pulled out the Anguinum.

"Do that, and you wouldn't be stood here now," said Etain. She smiled. "It's nuthin', Ethelbert. Let it lie." She patted him on the arm before walking over to join Kylie.

"Why were you arguing with the warrior woman?" said Omnust as they marched along.

Myrrdin said nothing, angrily pushing branches out of his way with the staff.

"Brave, it were, slapping her," said Omnust, "or foolish."

"Bravery had nothing to do with it," said Myrrdin, his voice low and controlled. "She twisted the knife in a wound I thought long healed."

"Just ... don't be making an enemy o' her."

There was genuine concern for the druid in his voice; Myrrdin was touched. "And if she makes an enemy of me?"

"History indicates that never happens," said a voice behind them, and both men turned as the old man caught up with them.

Omnust looked between the two mirror images, one fresh and bright, the other withered and ancient. Both regarded each other with palpable mistrust. He cleared his throat nervously. "Ah'll er... go an' find Kylie, see how she's doin'."

Myrrdin watched him go before turning to the old man. "You've come to demand I apologise to her?"

"Nope. I'm not your conscience." He smiled. "In fact, many a time, that's been Etain's job."

"She overstepped the mark." Myrrdin began striding forward, unwilling to continue this conversation. "We need to move. We'll scarcely reach the castle before nightfall."

"She was always good at that," nodded Gobswistle happily, keeping pace with his younger self. "Kept me on my toes. Prevented me from making mistakes." His smile faded. "Or repeating them."

"So you make a lot of mistakes then?" the druid's voice was almost derisive. "Is this the future I have to look forward to? Old age and senility?"

Gobswistle snorted. "Arrogant little sod, aren't you? Mind, it's the purgatory of the young." He frowned. "Purgative? Prerogative?"

"You think I'm young?" Myrrdin stared at him. "*You?* I've lived so many lives, so many names ..."

"Oh be hushed, boy," said Gobswistle. "You measure your years in the hundreds. You've hardly lived! You're a ... a ... *teenager,* compared to me!" He shoved his hands deep into his pockets. "And don't think it'll be easy. You'll be defined as much as by your mistakes as your victories!" He looked at his younger self; the almost wrinkle free face, the black hair with only a trace of silver. "you want to know what one of your earliest mistakes was?"

"Gwenddolau," replied Myrrdin quickly. "Strathclyde. Eigyr. You think I don't know?"

"No, no, no, that's not a mistake," replied Gobswistle. "That's history. *Ancient* history."

"Then *what?"* demanded Myrrdin. "Please, tell me, illuminate me and educate me."

"Other than arrogance?" Gobswistle stomped ahead, not looking at Myrrdin. "Thinking it was the Daionhe Sidhe who took my magic." Something flew from the old man, heading straight at Myrrdin. Something *green.*

Myrrdin snatched the Glass Apple from the air. He was vaguely aware of Etain suddenly shouting at the old man, and understood she had been listening in, but suddenly he no longer cared.

He had the Anguinum! The magic had been restored to it, Goddess knew how long ago; he had *magic* once more.

He turned the small crystal bowl in his hands, feeling its coolness, closing his eyes as he felt for the magic he knew lived within it.

Nothing.

No magic burned within its depths; no green fire leapt up around his hands.

He opened his eyes, his face paling. Etain stood at his side, shouting at him, but he couldn't take in her words, her anger. He stared at the useless bowl in his hands, feeling robbed of the magic he *knew* should be within it.

Withered hands closed around the bowl, gently easing it from the druid's numb hands. Gobswistle held the Anguinum up between him and Myrrdin. Green fire flared briefly under his fingers, and he gazed happily at the light, then gently placed the Anguinum into his pockets.

"Now all you have to do," he said, "is figure out where the magic *has* gone."

"That was mean," said Etain as she walked by the old man's side.

"Whmm?" said Gobswistle. "What was?"

"Plying mind games with Myrrdin."

"Not mind games," replied Gobswistle. "He just needs to grow up."

"He's *you*, don't forget," said Etain.

"Well..." grinned Gobswistle, "a variation thereof. Sort of."

"Don't *start* with that mystical sh..."

"If his time line plays out as mine did, yes, he'll end up being me. You know how it works." Gobswistle shrugged. "Just because I made it this far, doesn't mean he will."

"You talk twaddle."

"Twaddle?!"

"Twaddle. Balderdash. *Crap.*"

"How rude."

"You remember any of this?" said Etain. "From his point of view?"

"...No," said Gobswistle. "Not a thing."

The thing was, Etain could *tell* he was lying.

Chapter Thirty Five

"Jean," whispered Gaira. "*Jeannie!*" she looked around her fearfully, setting her lantern on the ground.

The younger woman stirred, her eyes flickering. "What..?"

"Somethin's happenin'," whispered Gaira. She looked upwards.

The stones in the roof of the oubliette were rumbling. Gaps appeared between the vast blocks, allowing dirt and light to spill through.

"Bridhe preserve us..." muttered Gaira. Around her, the other women and children were muttering, those able getting to their feet as they shielded their eyes against the early evening light.

The blocks were lowering themselves against the side of the circular pit, embedding themselves into the wall, forming a spiral staircase that led down into the darkness below.

Three creatures began making their way down the stairway, and several of the prisoners screamed, backing rapidly away from the foot of the staircase. The creatures were large and muscular, roughly man shaped but utterly alien. Shaggy black hair hung from their unclothed bodies, and their heads, so like those of a dog, bore eyes that burnt with red fire. The lead creature was missing one ear, dried blood caking the side of its face. In its claw-like hands it carried a broadsword and a whip. The two creatures behind each carried a double edged war axe.

"Help me up," said Jean, bracing herself against the floor.

"Jean, no, yuir leg won't take it," said Gaira.

"I'll no meet mah maker cowerin' on the ground," snapped Jean. "Help me up."

With a silent nod, Gaira moved behind the woman, pushing her up from behind as the creatures reached the base of the stairs.

The one eared creature looked impassively round at the prisoners. "Climb," it said, its voice a guttural growl. "The master waits."

"There's injured people," said one of the women, "we – we can't climb; we need help, please..."

The creature stared at her, the fire of its eyes pulsing rhythmically. It raised its sword and the woman screamed, but rather than striking her, it drove the blade deep into the stone at its feet.

Water began seeping up through the stone the blade had struck as though it was no more than a sponge. More water appeared from other stones; still and mirror like, and inexorably rising.

"Climb," said the creature simply, then it turned, leading its silent companions back up the stairway.

The water was already at their ankles, bitingly cold. "Quickly!" shouted Gaira, "those who can walk, get into pairs! Carry the injured between you! *Hurry!*"

Jean was already hobbling around the perimeter of the oubliette, her bound leg dragging through the water. "This is it, isn't it?" she asked. "We're gonnae die."

"We're not dead yet," snapped Gaira. "Don't give up!"

"Ah'm no' afeared," said Jean. "Be joinin' mah boy." There was utter resignation in the woman's voice, and Gaira realised that there was nothing she could say. Jean had *already* given up.

"Here," she said, moving beside the much taller woman. "Lean on me then. We'll go up t'gether." *Where was Jason?*

The wind whirled over the courtyard, rustling the branches of the little tree, stirring the ash and smoke from the four giant firepits as they blazed and cracked, and carrying motes of soot and fire to where Jason was chained against the wall of the castle. Torches lined the wall of the castle, their light marrying with the light from the pits, savagely orange.

His face was bruised and filthy, covered in ash, soot and dried blood, his fighting leathers ripped and torn. Above him, high in the sky, storm clouds were beginning to gather, rotating slowly above the loch, slowly obscuring the sun as it headed down towards the western horizon.

He was going to *die*.

The thought no longer terrified him. In fact, it seemed almost amusing. Only a couple hours ago, maybe less, he'd held the Books of Huddour in his hands, feeling the utter joy of finally having finished the quest.

So much for *magic*.

He watched as the three werewolves (that was the only thing he could identify them as) emerged from the pit once more. He could hear the voices of the women and children as they ascended from the pit.

Huddour had deliberately placed the final step so that the first thing the prisoners would see as they emerged from their captivity was Jason, chained to the wall, utterly defeated.

He couldn't look as the first prisoners emerged, and closed his eyes, turning his head away.

"Gaira, look," gasped Jean as they finally emerged.

"Oh Bridhe Oh Mary..." Gaira felt the tears burning in her eyes as she saw Jason, remembering his vision. "Jason?" she moved out from under Jean's grasp, momentarily uncaring as Jean, robbed of her support, fell. She'd run no more than ten paces before the one eared creature cracked its whip, and a red line appeared on Gaira's cheek. She yelped, falling to her knees. "Jason!"

She saw the boy open his eyes, and their gaze locked for a moment. Then he looked away.

"Welcome, welcome one and all," cried a voice, its cheerful tone bizarre and unsettling, "welcome to this wondrous night!"

A scared silence fell across the group as they looked up at the source of the voice. Huddour stood high above them, leaning down from the uppermost windows. His black clothing rippled around him in the wind, his cape flowing through the air like some black river. His head was covered now by a silver skull cap, its widows peak ending just above his eyebrows. By his side, his diminutive pet eyed the prisoners ravenously, its eyes fixing on the red haired pech, a golden crown resting crookedly on its head. Behind them, three giant forms stood unmoving in the shadows.

"How many of you know my name?" called the black robed figure. "How many of you know my *story?*" He waited, curving one hand around his ear. "What, no-one? Surely you know the tales of Huddour?" He looked down at the trowe. "It seems they've never heard of me, Blashie. I'm *hurt.*" He looked back down at the prisoners, smiling. "What *shall* I do with them?"

"Kill 'em!" blurted Blashie instantly. "Kill 'em cook 'em burn em, 'ear them screaming,"

"Little Blashie, *so* bloodthirsty," grinned Huddour. "Let me explain, dear friends, who I am. I am a *prisoner.* Oh yes, just like you, I'm a prisoner too. I cannot travel far in the lands beyond my castle, and what people there were..." he smiled at the three wolf creatures, "served...*other* purposes." He sat on the ledge of the window, his legs hanging out over nothingness. "Now who, you ask, imprisoned me? And that is a good question. A *very* good question.

"The Unseelie Court. On Alban Eiler. Ah..." he nodded as a murmur went through the small croud. "Yes, you've heard of it. It's *today*, isn't it? You know why the Huntsman and his Court trapped me? The deviousness of a druid, bribing him with fifty unshriven souls. Nasty, yes?

"Now, and here's the thing..." he was swinging his legs like a little child, bouncing them off the wall beneath the window, "can you guess what the cost of my freedom is? Why I've invited all you dear people here, tonight of all nights?"

Gaira knew. She stared at the boy. "Yellowblade!" she hissed desperately. "Remember your magic!" If Jason heard, he made no response.

Huddour pushed himself away from the window, and several women screamed. Rather than plunging to the earth, the sorcerer hung in the air, his cloak billowing behind him, growing and stretching until it resembled a stormcloud flowing all around him.

"Fifty souls," he said, as he hung in the air, Blashie giggling maniacally behind him. "Fifty unshriven souls of the dead, as a present to the Huntsman. This buys my freedom."

Below, one woman screamed. The sound of children crying filled the air. By their side, the oubliette had filled with water, a silvery disc forming a centre point to the four firepits.

"Jason!" called Gaira, "Jason, *please!*"

"Little Pech, be hushed," hissed Huddour, one hand flicking gently.

Gaira's hands flew to her face, scrabbling at her skin, her eyes wide with horror. Her mouth was gone. Her tongue and teeth were now covered by wrinkled skin.

"Time to prepare," said Huddour, and his smile faded. He raised both hands by his side.

Five giant cages rose from the rooftop behind him, creaking as they lowered themselves through the air towards the prisoners, vast gates swinging open as they stopped only a couple of feet above their heads.

Screaming filled the air as the women and children found themselves floating through the air to be thrown into the cages. Four of the five cages held ten of the prisoners. These four cages slowly climbed into the air again, positioning themselves above the firepits.

Gaira was only vaguely aware of invisible hands lifting her as she clawed at the skin over her mouth, her breath whistling through her nose. She was aware of Jean in the air by her side, uncaring and immobile as she floated through the air into the final cage, the nine of them sealed inside as the cage positioned itself above the waterfilled oubliette.

Huddour descended to the ground and his cloak became just a piece of cloth once more. He looked up as Blashie scurried down the wall beside him. "You see? I haven't forgotten my promise to you. The pech is yours, once I've finished with her." He looked up as thunder rumbled over his head. "Now we wait."

Jason closed his ears to the screaming, kept his eyes shut against the sight before him. The clasps of the shackles bit deeply into his wrists and he could feel the blood slowly trickling down his arm.

"Oy. Sticketty thing." Something poked at his side and against his will, Jason opened his eyes.

"Leave me alone," he muttered.

"Master wants you awake," grinned Blashie. "Wants you to see." He grabbed a handful of hair, wrenching Jason's head up. "Looky there see?"

Jason looked.

Huddour stood on the other side of the courtyard, grinning delightedly. "Ah, he's got your attention then? Good. See, I have a little present for you." He put his hand behind him, bringing forth a white handled dagger. "Recognise it? Yes? No? Maybe?" he twirled the blade through his fingers.

Jason recognised it. The blade had been Carnwennan, before Huddour had destroyed it. Breaking off the handle and throwing into the waters. Now the handle was bone white, ornately carved with celtic knots, the blade itself as bright as Jason remembered. His stomach twisted; it was like seeing an old friend who'd been mutilated.

Jason.

Jason started. The voice seemed to come from nowhere and everywhere.

Jason, watch.

Neither Blashie, still gripping his hair, nor Huddour seemed to hear the voice. It was like the wind on deep waters, or the roar of the sea, and Jason, inexplicably, began to feel *hope* stirring in his breast. He'd been hanging from the chains; now he forced himself to stand.

This was what he'd seen in Carnwennan, that last vision before he'd lost her.

Huddour saw the boy stand, his eyes trained on the blade. "Ah, you *do* recognise it! What do you think of the new handle? Carved from the bone of Bec Mac Dè himself; seemed fitting somehow. That the bones of the druid who trapped me here should claim the first soul to free me." He looked up at the cages as they hung in the air. "Behold! All your prophesies of Yellowblade Crowanhawk, told by the *great* druid Taliesin," and he smiled cruelly, "come to fruition tonight! See how I *cower* before him, see how his powerful blade, given to him by the Gwyllion themselves, smites me down!"

And Carnwennan flew through the air towards Jason's chest.

Watch.

It was as if Jason was at the hill at Sowerby, watching the Medb as she was caught in slow time, inching across the field towards them.

The knife that had been Carnwennan circled lazily through the air.

Jason saw in its blade a flash of...time, different times; people screaming, running, a fiery sun, a forest, a desert, a blaze of yellow hair...

The knife twisted, and a new image filled the blade; Jason, older than he was now, his head shaved, a horseshoe scar on one side of his scalp as he sat in a dark, smoke filled room, a massive figure next to him...

Jason and Kylie, running side by side through a forest of giant redwoods, arrows thudding into the trees around them...

A desert, a teenage girl, a blaze of yellow hair obscuring her features as she stared at the group on horseback as they approached....

Jason, older still, muscled, tanned and dressed in a white linen toga as he stood on the deck of a ship, waving madly at a distant group of people on the beige rocky hillside they approached...

Jason, lying unmoving in a hospital bed, machines flashing around him, an unseen figure holding his hand, gently smoothing the black hair away from his pallid face...

And with all of these images, Jason realised one thing.

Carnwennan was still his.

Chapter Thirty Six

Huddour stared wide eyed. What was happening?

The blade he'd cast so gleefully, intending to claim the first soul to buy his freedom, hung in the air, slowly rotating on its axis, the tip of its blade a mere finger's length from the boy's heart. Above his head, the little trowe was slowly backing up the wall, its eyes wide as it watched the white handled blade.

Little coward!

Huddour angrily stepped forward a couple of paces, intending to finish the task with his own hands, the green fire of his magic already lapping around his fingers.

The boy's eyes snapped up.

The glint in the eyes froze Huddour where he stood.

There was no fear in those young eyes, nor even any anger. There was, instead, a surety. A confidence that bore down on the sorcerer like an iron fist.

"My turn," whispered the boy.

The blade whipped up, slicing through the chains that held the boy prisoner as though they were made of butter, and he stepped free, one hand held open for the return of his blade. The cuts and bruising on his face, the deep gouges on his wrists, began to heal, the dried blood flaking away, the broken skin drawing together.

Sorcerer and child warrior faced each other, smoke and fire dancing around them.

"Release them," said the boy quietly.

"The Gwyllion gifted you well, young Yellowblade Crowhanhawk," muttered Huddour. "A magical blade, the reflexes of a god..."

"I said release them."

Huddour raised his hands. Around him, five cages of people jolted as his power took control. "So you did, little boy." The people in the cages screamed as they plunged several feet, the four over the firepits halting only scant feet above the leaping flames.

"No!" the boy leapt forward, his knife held out in front of him.

"No?" Huddour smiled as he watched the cages around him, listened to the screaming of the prisoners. "But you said release them, surely?"

"Away from the flames!" The confidence had faded from the boy's face, but he still held the knife in front.

"And if I don't?"

The boy opened his hand and the blade sailed slowly through the air, halting just beyond the reach of Huddour. "I'll – I'll kill you," replied the boy.

"Really? Hmmm," replied Huddour, and around him the cages plunged lower, "two things. You've never killed. Have you? So maybe you could do it, maybe not. But, and here's the second thing, kill me, my magic no longer supports these cages." He felt a laugh brewing in his chest as the boy's eyes widened in comprehension. "My my my, what a quandary, what a *to do!*" He took a step forward, allowing the tip of the knife to press against his robes. "But of course, do what you have to."

As he expected, the knife slowly withdrew, returning to the waiting hand of the boy.

The cages rose once more into the air, and Huddour lowered his arms, marching directly up to the boy. "What now, hmm? What do you intend doing next?" He crouched so that his eyes were level with the boys. "Little boy with the bee's sting, we have a problem, don't we? I can chain you again, but you'd only release yourself. I could kill you, that'd be fun, but you'd put up a defence, something I really just don't have time for."

Thunder rumbled overhead and lightning forked across the darkness. Huddour stood and looked up. "See? The storms're brewing, the magic cast. The Unseelie Court rides out and the Corners are set and called." He looked towards the firepits. "North, east, south and west. Magic knows who calls them *best.* But I need your soul, child. So I *do* need you dead." He turned back to the boy. "So, I think the best..."

The boy was gone.

Cursing, Huddour span round. A small shadow tore down the causeway, far faster than Huddour had suspected the boy capable of. He threw one hand forward; a ball of fire roared through the night, exploding stone and brick from beneath the boy's feet, casting him to the ground. Lithe as a deer, the boy was back on his feet, racing into the cover of trees.

"Blashie!" Huddour bellowed. "Trowe! Here. Now!"

The little creature scuttled down the castle wall, timorously scampering across the courtyard to its master. "Here Sire, milord, Blashie's here."

"Trowe." Huddour glared down at it.

"You – you want me to go after the boy, no sire, no no, please, he's got strong, 'im, sodding little git'll..."

"Blashie," said Huddour, "*hush*. How many souls do I need to buy my freedom?"

"S-sire?"

"How many?"

"Fifty, sire." Yellow eyes looked up at him in confusion.

"And with the loss of the boy, how many do I now have?"

"Fo-forty nine, sire?"

"No, dear little Blashie." Huddour reached down, straightening the crown on the trowe's quivering head. "I still have fifty. Even trowes have souls." He grasped the trowe by its neck, lifting it into the air. "If I can't have the boy, I'll make do with you. *What say you?"*

Blashie writhed in his hand. "I'll – I'll go get the boy."

"Don't *get* him. *Kill* him."

If there were any light left in the sky, the storm clouds that circled above had completely hidden it. Jason plunged through the trees, slashing at branches as he fled the castle, running to...

To *what?*

He couldn't just *leave*. All those people, they were relying on him. Jean, Gaira, all the other women and children, all due to die to buy Huddour his freedom.

But where could he go?

Huddour had sunk the ship that bore Myrrdin, Etain and his grandfather. Huddour thought them dead, but he underestimated Myrrdin. He certainly underestimated Gobswistle and Etain. One, if not all, would be in the forests ahead.

He hoped.

The wind howled around him, and bitter flakes of sleet bit at him, trying to freeze him with a cold he no longer felt. A root, hidden under layers of dead plant matter, grasped at an ankle, and he fell sprawling to the ground, Carnwennan skittering through the leaves away from him. Jason lay there, momentarily winded, gasping for breath.

Something small but incredibly strong landed on his back, wrenching his arms round behind him, a bony hand clasped over his mouth, preventing him from summoning his blade.

"Gotcha!" growled an angry voice. "D'yew know 'ow long Ah've waited fer this? Sodding sticketty boy, now master, master 'e says *kill* 'im..."

Jason twisted desperately in the dirt, trying to spot his blade, trying to free his mouth to summon her.

"Wriggle little slippery fish," muttered Blashie, "on'y make it 'urt more, works for me, dunnit?" Jason's hands held firmly in Blashie's claw feet, the trowe was able to pull down the collar of Jason's leathers, exposing the back of his neck.

Jason felt saliva pooling on the back of his neck and twisted madly, but to no avail. The first prick of teeth bit down, and Jason closed his eyes.

A massive shadow leapt through the trees and the trowe was ripped from his back before the teeth had even broken the skin.

Jason turned in the dirt, muttering *return* and holding his hand open even as he did so, Carnwennan slamming into his palm.

Something large, black and feline stood before him, yellow eyes blinking in the darkness as a human figure leapt from its back, a blade glinting in the lightning that flared through the trees as it swung through the air.

Something small bounced off through the darkness, a metallic disc falling from it, rolling along the ground to strike Jason's foot.

With a yelp, Jason kicked the golden crown away.

The one armed figure turned to regard him, sheathing its sword and resting a hand on the large feline's back.

"Yui must be Yellowblade. Welcome. Ah'm Fionnlagh."

Etain looked at the castle in the distance. "It looks smaller than I expected."

Myrrdin walked down the rocky beach to stand beside her. "It's well defended. There's magic in that storm."

"Huddour, summoning the Unseelie Court," replied Etain. She watched the circling clouds. "We need to quicken our pace."

"So hungry for battle, Etain?" Myrrdin leaned on his staff, not looking at her.

"It's not battle Ah seek, Myrrdin. It's young Jason." She sighed. "But Huddour won't surrender him easily. So yeah. Ah'll battle. Ah *have* to." She shrugged. "It's what Ah do." She looked at him. "You okay?"

"All these years..." said Myrrdin quietly, still looking out across the loch. "All these years, I've blamed the Daionhe Sidhe for stealing my magic. The anger, the...the *betrayal* I felt."

"And now?"

Any reply the druid might have had was cut short by the yell of Gobswistle, and the shouting of Omnust.

With hardly a glance at each other, the warrior and druid ran up the bank, ironfire and sword drawn as they ran toward the sound of raised voices.

It was Omnust Jason saw first as the Cait Sidhe carried them into the clearing, and he launched himself from its back, oblivious to the other figures as he flung himself at the startled captain.

"You're alive!" gasped Jason. "you're alive, you're okay!" He quickly pulled away. "Where's Anna? And Myrrdin? Are they alright? Where's Aiken? Kilneuair, is it..?"

Omnust was laughing, though his eyes were bright with tears. "Slow down, wee Jason, glad I am tae see yui whole!"

A hand fell on Jason's shoulder, and he turned to see his grandfather smiling down at him. Jason found himself hugging the old man, his voice no longer working. He was vaguely aware of the old man laughing with relief.

More hands were touching him, and Jason looked up through a wall of tears at Myrrdin, and at the astonishingly big Etain.

"Wow..." he croaked, looking up at her, "you got big!"

"So Ah'm told," she laughed, kneeling beside him.

He looked around at all the familiar faces, and felt the hope and the love blossoming in his chest. "But – but what happened? The vikings? Anna?"

"We won," said Myrrdin, smiling warmly. "We got your message, Eigyr brought them to me, we would not have won without them."

Jason looked at Omnust. "Cináed? Anna?"

"Cináed..." Omnust looked at Myrrdin, who shook his head slightly, "...was wounded, but he survives. Anna's with Father Donald, she's *fine*, Jason."

"But..." Jason was looking around now. "Where's Aiken? Is he with you? Where's Kylie? Grandad, she was with you; where..?"

The group had fallen silent, their smiles fading. Jason looked at Myrrdin. "Aiken?"

"Jason, I'm sorry," said Myrrdin slowly. "We...we lost him."

"He was a revelation," said Omnust. "He saved so many people, so many *children;* he was *brave,* Jason. Yui'd ha' been proud."

"I am," said Jason, his eyes filling with tears as the loss hit him. "I am. He was my friend. My *best* friend." Memories of hot baths, fabulous stews and straw targets, of Anna and Aiken plying together, swam through his mind, and the tears began to flow freely.

Gobswistle was standing. "Jason," he said, "there's someone to see you."

Rubbing at his eyes, Jason turned to follow the old man's gaze.

The Cait Sidhe that he had rode in on was walking slowly towards him. As it walked, blue fire leapt up, obscuring it from view, and suddenly Kylie stood there, her black hair blowing around her as the fire died, her own eyes filling with tears as she looked at her brother.

"You found me then," she whispered.

Etain smiled as the two children hugged each other. She took both the old man and the druid by the elbows, walking between them as she walked them away. "Give 'em a couple o' minutes," she said. "We can give 'em that." She smiled. "Well, lookit *me*. Veritable rose between two thorns, ain't Ah?"

They talked as they walked, the castle growing ever larger in the darkness.

"I don't understand though," said Jason, his eyes still bloodshot from crying. "I *had* the books. I thought...I thought that was it, that we'd be called home."

"We should've," nodded Gobswistle, his fingers twirling in his beard, a deep frown on his face. "We should've..." he fell silent, glaring at the castle through the trees.

"See those windows up there?" said Jason, pointing, "there, that top room. *That's* where they are. That's where Huddour caught me."

"So what's the plan?" asked Etain, looking at Gobswistle. The old man said nothing, deep in thought.

"We have to save those people," said Jason. "There's forty nine women and children, he's gonna kill them all, so he can buy his freedom he says. Gaira's there, and..."

"Gaira is where she deserves tae be," said Omnust shortly.

"No...yes..." frowned Jason, "I don't *know!* She's...different from what you think, but there's others, like Jean..."

Omnust stopped short, staring at Jason. "Jean? *Jeannie?* Jason, did she have a bairn with her? A baby boy?"

"She did, but Huddour took him..." he looked up at his friend's pale scarred face. "Omnust...is she your sister?"

Omnust nodded grimly. "Aye. Praise God. Aye. Where's he holding them?"

Jason quickly described the courtyard with the firepits and the flooded oubliette, the cages held suspended above them.

"We can't just go charging in then," muttered Myrrdin. "Magic holds them. Magic must free them." He looked at his older self. "Gobswistle..."

"Don't be looking at me," snapped the old man. "I'm needed elsewhere. You're the one with Bec Mac Dè's staff."

"I don't know how..."

"THEN LEARN!" Gobswistle turned on the spot, his eyes wide and angry. "Snap out of your damned self pity, you pathetic little bogie!"

"It is *not* self.."

"It's nothing *but* self pity," snapped the old man. Etain, stunned by his anger, placed a hand on his arm, but he threw it off. "Don't try and placate me, wench! You *know* who you are, druid. You're Taliesin, you're Lailoken, you're Myrrdin! Wise Man of the Forest!"

"Do not think to tell me..."

"*You are allowed to make mistakes!*" Gobswistle's anger was palpable. "You *know* how the timelines work! You should have forseen what could happen! One world's history is *not* another world's future!"

"How *dare* you..."

"Easily! *Easily!*" Gobswistle grasped the staff that the redfaced druid held. "You *know* this, what it becomes – the Daionhe Sidhe, they've not stirred your brain yet – this night, this place, is *where* it becomes it!"

The group had come to a halt, man, child and mythical beast all staring at the two verbal combatants.

Gobswistle drove his hand into a jacket pocket, at the same time snatching the staff from Myrrdin. Out came the Anguinum, and it was burning a fierce green, brighter than Etain or Kylie had ever seen it. Green light flooded the clearing as the old man held the Glass Apple up.

"See this?" he demanded of Myrrdin. "This *magic* that you're so afraid of? The magic is *yours,* Myrrdin, it always has been!" He brought it up to the top of the staff, and the balled knot of rootwork at its end unfurled like a hand, pale fingers reaching out as Gobswistle brought the Glass Apple down. The fingers curled around the crystalline structure, pulling it within itself, hiding the glass within, only the green light now visible as it shone through the roots.

"This," said Gobswistle, shoving the staff back at Myrrdin, "is yours." As Myrrdin, dumbstruck, grasped the staff, Gobswistle leant towards him. "Physician, *heal thyself.*"

As he released the staff, leaving it in the druid's hands, the green light faded, and darkness filled the clearing. Gobswistle stared at his younger self, something akin to contempt on his face, then turned, storming away from the group.

Etain caught up with him as he reached the beginning of the causeway. "Old man, what have you..."

"What I had to," breathed Gobswistle.

"You gave away your magic," said Etain, spinning him by his shoulder, "just when we need it most."

"I did what I had to," repeated the old man as he stared up at the castle, the anger now gone from his voice.

"What d'you mean, what you *had* to?" demanded Etain. "What, was that some sort of ego trip, humiliating your younger self like that?"

"He's not..."

"Oh Ah *know* he's not you! Ah *know* he's a variation of you! And Ah know he has no damned magic!"

"Yes he does." Gobswistle turned to Etain, smiling softly. "He just needs to remember. And tonight is the night he remembers. And *forgives."* He stared at the cages of people across the loch, just visible in the courtyard. "As I must now forgive. As you'll have to in a few moments too."

"What? Old fool, you're *scarin'* me..." she tried to read his face, so calm now, so gentle. "What've *you* done you need to forgive? What do *I* need to forgive?"

"Can you remember what the Gwyllion said to me? About the books?"

"What?" Etain blinked. "They said ... they said we needed to get..."

"No they didn't."

"Ethelbert, Ah *remember* what they said."

"They were speaking to me, dear lady. *Dearest* lady. There was no *we*. Only *I*." He was looking up at the windows Jason had pointed out. "It was my mistake, thinking it was a quest for all of us. Jason, Kylie, Anna, even *you*. You had your own quests. Mine is to get the books. It's why nothing happened when Jason got them."

It made sense somehow. Etain nodded. "Okay, just say Ah believe you. What do Ah have to forgive?"

"Your own mistake."

"Which was?"

A screaming sound filled the air, and Etain, expecting to see the cages plunging into the firepits, stared instead at the skies as a huge flock of crows filled the air, seemingly descending from the storm clouds themselves, diving towards Etain and the old man. Gobswistle nodded slowly, as though this were expected.

"Trusting *me."* He turned to her. "You see, while I'm getting the books, *you're* the distraction." And before she could react, he dived into the black waters of the loch.

As the crows plunged towards her, as the kelpies churned the waters where the old man had vanished, Etain turned and ran.

Chapter Thirty Seven

"Where's Gobswistle?" shouted Myrrdin as Etain burst through the trees.

A firm callused hand slapped him soundly across the face. "Wait a few thousand years," barked Etain, "you'll remember what that's for!" She turned from him, an ironfire growing from her hand. "You!" She pointed at the winged lion. "How many of you can fly?"

Eleven, milady. Amber eyes regarded her impassively.

"Huddour's sent his crows after us!" shouted Etain, pointing at the dark shapes that were already weaving between the trees. "Get airbourne. See'f you cain't draw them with you."

Jason was already by Etain's side. "Where's Granddad gone?"

"He's gone after the Books."

"But I thought ..."

"He knows what he's doing," said Myrrdin, watching as the eagle, the winged lion, three griffons, four winged sphinxes and two huge owls took to the air. "Prepare yourselves – here they come!"

There was little time for further talk. The crows, three times the size of the normal bird, ploughed through the trees, cawing loudly. Many of them had followed the eldritch changelings up into the stormy sky, but many others remained amongst the trees, their prey now chosen.

But the prey was not defenceless. A white handled dagger flew through the air, slicing through plumage and bone, and several birds fell. Orange light flooded the ground as Etain swung her ironfire, and the grounded changelings, led by Kylie, raked tooth and claw at the attacking creatures.

Lightning filled the sky, and thunder shook the trees as aerial battle was joined. Three of the crows attacked the eagle, one landing on its back, the others attacking each wing. Black beaks stabbed down, and feathers were ripped from the howling changeling.

The weight of the birds bore it down, its wings damaged enough for the eagle to lose control, and the murky waters of Loch Linnhe welcomed it into its depths. The waters boiled; neither changeling nor crows emerged.

The griffons fared better, their sinewy limbs and claws a match for those of the crows, and the fight was equal. The sphinxes joined the fray, diving on the crows from behind, and this time it was the crows that plunged into the waters.

Omnust wiped his arm over his bloodied brow. "What now? Have we won?"

"A respite only," said Myrrdin.

Around him the Changelings had assembled, bloodied but unbeaten. Fionnlagh sat astride Kylie, his face grim. Etain stood by his side, with Jason and Omnust stood side by side, each with their blade in their hands.

"We need a plan," said Myrrdin. "There'll be more. Darrach told me of Huddour's defences. We've seen the Black Hounds, we've seen the crows. Huddour is master of transformation – all the people of the towns and villages that vanished when he first arrived, they'll be somewhere in the forest..."

"We need a threefold strategy," said Etain. "we need to defend against these ... these changelings, but we also need to rescue those people he holds ..."

"And quickly," said Jason. "He's gonna sacrifice them."

"And someone needs to go help that senile melodramatic old *goat.*" Etain looked round at her friends, then shrugged. "Guess that'll be *me,* then."

And me. The Cait Sidhe stared at Etain, and on her back, Fionnlagh nodded.

"Me too," he said. "Seems we work well together, me and Kylie."

"Ah'll stay here," said Omnust. "These men need a captain. The changelings remain wi' me. We'll hold off anything that tries tae get through."

"That leaves you and me," said Myrrdin softly, looking at Jason. "Magic holds them. Magic must free them."

"So we go across the causeway," said Jason. He looked at the staff in the druid's hands. "Will it work?"

"Get off me, get off, *off!*"

Gobswistle erupted from the foaming waters, two kelpies trying to drag him back, their mouths closed firmly on his jacket.

"Here! Have the damn thing!" Gobswistle quickly wriggled out from the combat jacket, falling to the ground and pulling himself along the paving. "And I hope you *choke* on it!"

The equine creatures, plying an angry tug of war with the tearing material, vanished under the water.

Gobswistle sat on the flagstones, gasping for breath. "Not the cleverest thing I've ever done..." he muttered. He pulled himself to his feet, looking around him, then quickly fell to the ground again, flattening himself as much as he could.

Huddour was only a matter of yards from him, his back to him as he chanted, his hands held high above him. All around him, the cages of people slowly rotated, lit from underneath by the firepits.

Scuttling crablike across the causeway, Gobswistle was able to duck out of sight round the corner of the castle. He eased himself to his feet, and began making his way down the wall.

"Door, door, there must be some sort of ... ah!"

The old archway was green with lichen, but the ground beneath was clean of dirt, obviously well used. Gobswistle peered nervously round the corner and down the torch lit corridor. There were various doorways down the length of the corridor, and at the far end was a staircase.

He needed to go *up*. The staircase seemed as good a place as any to start.

As quietly as possible he began making his way down the corridor. At the first arched doorway he ducked into its protective shadows, counting to five before peeking round the corner.

No sign of life.

He scampered light footedly to the next doorframe, feeling slightly more confident, and repeated the count. Still no-one.

He was halfway to the next doorframe when he heard the fall of feet. With a stifled yelp he froze, unsure which way to turn, his eyes wide. What he had thought was a final door to his left before the staircase was a turn in the corridor, and it was from here he could hear someone coming.

After what seemed an age of indecisive terror, he returned to the previous doorframe. One eye glinted in the torchlight as he watched.

Three lupine figures came through the arch, two armed with double edged axes, one with a sword and whip. This third one was larger than the other two, its face somehow more intelligent, its one ear facing forward alertly, the torn remains of its other ear encrusted with dried blood.

A guttural growl echoed through the hallway, and the two smaller creatures halted at the foot of the stairs.

As Gobswistle pressed himself back into the shadows, he could hear the larger creature approach.

Myrrdin had been right. Even as he and his group of two siblings and two warriors had made their way to the causeway, innumerable creatures – spriggans, Etain had called them – had poured from the trees, falling upon Omnust and the Changelings.

The sound of battle raged behind them as they peered down the causeway to the castle.

"What's happening?" asked Etain, only just able to make out the glow of the firepits.

"He's standing in the middle of the pits," said Jason, no longer astounded by his ability to see, "he's ... he's chanting, or something. Wait, there's Gobswistle!"

"What? Where?" Etain tried to follow his gaze; it was no use. Everything was black to her.

"There," said Jason, pointing, "he's just gone through that doorway."

"Right..." Etain seemed to be bolstering herself. "Right...okay, Kylie, you ready?"

"I'm ready," said Kylie, back in her own form.

"Kylie, just..." Jason struggled for the words, "just be careful. Okay?"

Kylie grinned. Jason was struck by her resemblance to their grandfather. "I've fought spriggans, sealers and changelings," she said. "I'll be fine!" But all the same, she hugged him.

"Come on then," said Etain. "Let us get across first, then follow."

Myrrdin and Jason nodded silently.

With a final nod, Etain started running down the causeway, followed by Kylie and Fionnlagh, all three crouching low as they ran.

Myrrdin looked down at Jason. "You ready?"

Jason was watching his sister. "She's done so much more than me. You know? All I've done is get tied up."

Myrrdin placed a hand on his shoulder, grasping it firmly. "That, and saving an entire town from viking attack." He smiled ruefully. "Seems we *both* have to get over our self-doubts."

"...Are you afraid?" asked Jason.

"Terrified," said Myrrdin. "Shall we?"

The werewolf passed by Gobswistle, and the old man allowed himself a sigh of relief, thinking himself un-noticed.

Then the creature stopped, its ear swivelling on its head, and it turned on the spot to face Gobswistle, red eyes boring into him as its lips curled up in a snarl.

"Oh ... poo," breathed Gobswistle, his hands fumbling blindly for the door handle.

The werewolf raised its sword, the snarl turning into a semblance of a smile, and Gobswistle grappled for the door.

The blade hissed down, hissing through empty air as the door opened, throwing Gobswistle to the floor. He scrambled to his feet, taking in the contents of the room: a large fireplace, dark and empty, a large bed, covered in moth eaten bedding, obviously unused for many years, and a few chairs arranged around the hearth, clothed in ancient dust and gossamer.

Withered hands scoured his pockets before Gobswistle remembered. Myrrdin now had the Anguinum. He picked up the nearest chair, launching it at the creature as it entered the room. A powerful arm shattered the ancient wood, the werewolf's eyes never leaving Gobswistle.

Gobswistle picked up one of the larger splinters, waving it at his adversary. "Here boy, here boy, look a stick!"

With a loud *crack!* The creature's whip snatched the wood from his hands.

"Yes okay," said Gobswistle, backing up to the bed, "that was pathetic I admit..."

A memory flashed through his mind, ancient and unbidden, of being chained up, sat in the middle of a pigsty, a whirl of dancing straw in front of him...

Almost without thinking about it, he gestured with one hand, and a wind swirled round the room, lifting the bedding from the bed, carrying it across the room to descend on the werewolf.

"Oh my..." breathed Gobswistle as the creature struggled under the dusty cloth, "useful after all!"

A sword thrust upwards through the material, and with a whimper, Gobswistle scuttled over to the door.

A large charcoal grey creature filled the doorframe, startling the old man, and he fell back into the room just as the werewolf freed itself. With a roar, the werewolf launched itself at the old man, sword swinging down.

The Cait Sidhe launched itself from the doorway, knocking the werewolf against the wall, knocking the sword from its hand. Behind it, Etain and Fionnlagh ran into the room, slamming the door shut, jamming a chair under its latch.

The werewolf dropped the whip, falling to all fours, its legs lengthening, its back filling with muscle.

Black Dog and Cait Sidhe faced each other, slowly circling each other, low growling filling the room like thunder.

Etain hauled Gobswistle to his feet. "Get up, Ethelbert!"

"What – what – what are *you* doing here?"

"Helpin' you, God knows why," snapped Etain. She reached into her pouch, then froze, her face crestfallen.

"Look out!" bellowed Fionnlagh as the Cait Sidhe leapt.

The Black Dog launched itself at the same time, the old man forgotten, and the two creatures fell to the ground, gouging and tearing at each other's flesh.

"Under the bed!" said Etain, diving across the floor. Both young and old man followed her, scrambling under the scant wooden protection.

Dog and Cait Sidhe rolled around the floor, snarling viciously. The Cait Sidhe ripped herself free, running at the wall, then up the wall, using her momentum to launch herself at the hound as it found its feet, her massive teeth biting at its neck.

It wrenched itself free, red eyes staring, blood trickling down its back. The two creatures were too evenly matched and both knew it. Slowly they circled each other.

"Shouldn't – shouldn't we be helping them?" whispered Gobswistle.

"Yeah, we should, why don't you use your anguinum?" hissed Etain. "Oh yeah, that's right, you gave it to someone who cain't use it!"

"You still have your ironfire!"

"News for you," said Etain. She ripped the pouch from her belt, shoving it at him. "Ah've run out o' nails. You got any?"

"Yui c'n hae mah sword," said Fionnlagh. "Here." He started pushing his blade towards her, but she'd shoved herself out from under the bed, dragging the old man with her. Seeing what made her move, the young man scarcely had time to move before both creatures fell upon the bed, shattering it.

Fionnlagh was separated from Etain and Gobswistle, the Black Dog and the Cait Sidhe battling between them. "*Here!*" he called, throwing his sword through the air.

Etain deftly caught it, and the room was flooded with orange light as the sword began to burn with magical fire.

The two creatures twisted on the ground, their forms merging, and Etain could find no clear target to strike at. It was only when one snarling head emerged from the mass, one side of its face caked in dry blood, that Etain found her mark.

Her blade bit deeply across the flesh of the muzzle, and a ribbon of fur and skin fell to the ground.

With a howl, the Black Dog separated from the feline, its form shrinking and changing. It returned to its werewolf form, the lips and cheek removed from one side of its muzzle, the teeth beneath streaked with red. It glanced from feline to warrior, realising it was outmatched.

Two leaps took it to the chimney, and it vanished into darkness.

The Cait Sidhe bounded to the fireside, roaring its challenge up the chimney, but it was too large by far to follow.

"Kylie!" shouted Etain. "That's enough!"

The door rattled and banged; the two other werewolves were trying to gain entry.

Etain and Fionnlagh grabbed the remaining chairs, wedging them against the door. "This won't hold them long," said Etain.

"You *slapped* me," said Gobswistle, one hand to his cheek, staring at her in outrage.

"Ah did no such thing!"

"You most certainly did!" snapped Gobswistle. "I asked you where I was and you slapped me, you damned wench!"

Etain moved away from the door. "You ... remember that?"

Kylie was in human form again, jamming fragments of broken bed under the door. On the other side of the door, creatures growled angrily. "We need to do something!" she shouted.

Etain seemed not to hear her. "You remember tonight?"

Gobswistle said nothing, his eyes wide.

"Old man, you remember tonight?" insisted Etain, grabbing him by his shoulders.

"They're getting through!" shouted Fionnlagh.

"I – I ...everything's *merging*..." said Gobswistle, his voice shaken.

"What do we *do?*" shouted Etain, shaking him.

The old man looked at the fireplace. "We go up," he said simply.

Huddour lowered his arms, shaking with weariness, the sweat flowing freely down his face, soaking his lank hair beneath his skullcap.

It was done. The Unseelie Court were summoned. Even now, from the darkness of the west, the Huntsman led the Wild Hunt towards him, riding through the night sky to fulfil a promise made millennia ago. Huddour could *feel* his anger.

No matter.

He would soon be free, free of this accursed castle, free to take control of the lands, free to take his revenge on all of the Daionhe Sidhe, the Tuatha Dè Dannon, all the fairy folk who thought to control him at the request of a senile old druid!

His magic was strong now. No mortal blade could kill him. Thanks to the Books he held, filled with magic older than time itself, even the magics of the Glowing Ones could not injure him. Only magic from the Books themselves could harm him.

And his Books were *protected.*

Smiling, he turned to the west, expecting to see, far in the distance, the fearsome clouds and riders of the Wild Hunt.

Instead he saw a young boy and a white robed druid.

Chapter Thirty Eight

"Well." Huddour stared at the two intruders, stood either side of the oubliette. "The Child of Prophecy and the Madman of the Forest." He smiled. "I take it my little friend didn't find you?"

Jason's hand tightened on Carnwennan's new hilt. "He found me." He forced himself to return Huddour's smile. "*And* my friends."

Huddour's smile faltered momentarily. "You're really determined to be the proverbial thorn in my side, aren't you? Are the books *really* that important to you?" Before Jason could reply, Huddour turned to Myrrdin. "And you, Myrrdin Emrys. I've heard of you. Running away from battle when your poor little army lost. Losing your magic to the Daionhe Sidhe. Bless." He tilted his head to one side. "And you're here to take me on?"

"You cannot sacrifice these people," said Myrrdin evenly.

"Well, thing is you see," said Huddour, "actually, I *can*. I mean, it's not really as though you've brought anything to the table to bargain with." He placed his hands behind his back, walking towards the druid. "I mean really, a staff? Oh, I can sense the Gleiniau Nadredd, but let's face it, it's not yours to command, is it?"

In answer, Myrrdin brought up one hand. Wind roared across the courtyard, twisting the flames of the fire pits, lifting the sorcerer up by his robes, throwing him to the very wall Jason had been chained to.

"*Now,* Jason!" bellowed Myrrdin, and Jason leapt up at the cage hanging in the air above the oubliette. The cage bounced a little in the air with his weight, and he wrenched at the metal gate, trying to open it. Though there was no visible lock, the gate remained steadfastly closed.

"Stop!" Huddour's voice drowned out the wind and thunder, and Jason was plucked from the cage by an invisible hand. He was held suspended in the air as Huddour found his feet, his face murderous.

Jason didn't stop to think. He cast his blade at Huddour with all his strength, every fibre of his being urging the blade forward.

Carnwennan sang through the air, catching Huddour directly in the chest, the power of its flight carrying him back and up. The blade bit through his body, the tip of the blade biting into the wall behind, suspending Huddour three feet above the ground.

Jason fell to the ground, one foot plunging into the waters of the oubliette. As he stood, the cheering from the cages filled the air as the women and children stared at the stricken lord. Jason looked up at the cages, astounded at what he'd just done, and more than a little afraid. It was almost as though the blade itself had chosen to attack, taking the decision to kill out of Jason's hands.

"Jason," snapped Myrrdin, his eyes also on the cages, "something's wrong – the cages still..."

He was cut off by the sound of laughter, low at first, then increasing in both volume and mania.

Both turned to face Huddour.

He was levering himself away from the wall, Carnwennan still embedded in his chest. As the blade finally came free of the wall, Huddour dropped to the ground, one hand closing around the white hilt. He pulled the blade free, examining the clean and mirror like blade, still giggling, before gently tossing it through the air back to the ashen faced Jason.

"Was that it?" laughed Huddour. "The best attempt of two beings of legend? Wind and a kitchen knife?" He examined the cuts in his robes. "Hmm. *Scary.*" Cold eyes regarded Jason. "What was it you said earlier? Oh yes." Both hands shot out, pointing at Jason and Myrrdin. "*My turn.*"

As lightning illuminated the black spiralling clouds, they also lit up the mass of snowy white hair that popped up from inside the chimney stack.

Gobswistle peered around nervously. There was no sign of the werewolf on the flat roof beyond, only sooty pawprints that led to the side of the roof.

Feeling a little more confident, Gobswistle clambered out, the wind lifting large clouds of soot off him. As Etain appeared, he held out his hand.

"Ah c'n manage," said Etain, hauling herself over the side. "Where's that creature gone?"

"Erm..." Gobswistle was painfully aware of his friend's simmering anger. "It-it's gone, I think. Over the side."

Etain jogged up to the side, looking down at the scene below. "Oh lord..."

"What is it?" said Gobswistle. He joined her, leaning down.

Myrrdin and Jason were raised in the air many feet below them, their faces pale and blank. Below them, Huddour stood with his hands outstretched, a dull red glow pulsing from his hands to the unmoving figures.

"What is it?" said a young voice; Kylie was clambering out of the chimney. "Is it Jason? He's okay, isn't he?"

"He's fine," said Etain quickly, moving away from the wall and frowning warningly at the old man. "He's *fine,* hun, but we need those books."

"Right," said Gobswistle, "right, then...we'd better crack on. Where's..?"

"No-one help me, will the'?" called a voice from the chimney. "It's not like Ah've only got one arm!"

"Fion, you alright?" said Kylie, and Etain ran back to the chimney, hauling the young warrior out.

"Ah'm fine, Ah'm fine," spluttered the young man, brushing the soot from his face and hair.

"We need to *move,*" said Etain urgently.

"No, wait," said Kylie. She was staring out into the darkness, walking across to the wall.

"No, Kylie, come away," called Etain, glancing worriedly at Gobswistle, but Kylie wasn't looking down. She instead looked out toward the darkness of the forests beyond.

"Sweetheart," said Gobswistle, reaching her side, "come away, what are you looking at?"

"I – I don't know," said Kylie, frowning.

"Is it that creature?"

"No, no it's something ... something I heard earlier." She stared intently into the darkness. "I thought it was ... it reminded me of Cernunnos ... I thought it was those people on the shore, but it wasn't, then I thought it was Uilleam's men, and it sort of was..."

"Kylie, you're not making sense..?" Gobswistle crouched by his granddaughter's side.

"It's getting nearer though ..."

"What is it? Can you tell?"

Kylie hesitated, then shook her head. "No, I ... no." Her eyes fell downwards, and she gave a scream. "*JASON!*"

Gobswistle pulled her away, ducking behind the wall, though the wind and thunder made it unlikely Huddour would have heard. "Kylie, Kylie, listen to me, we can help him, we *will* help him, but we need those books!" He pointed to the room Jason had indicated earlier. Kylie was struggling in his arms, tears streaming down her face as she called her brother's name.

Etain joined him, "Chile, listen to your granddad, we have to get those books. Okay? They hold Huddour's magic! We can only help Jason if we get those books! You understand?"

Kylie had gone limp in the old man's arms, and she stared up at Etain. "I understand."

"Right," said Etain, "good. C'mon. And *quietly.*"

The room was twenty feet above them, the tallest parapet of the castle. To get to it they had to clamber down part of the roof, lowering themselves into a vast corridor through a window. For Etain, Gobswistle and Kylie, it was a struggle.

For Fionnlagh it was almost impossible.

As he lowered himself over the roof to the corridor's window, he almost fell plunging into the waters of the loch. It was only the fast actions of Etain, grabbing him by his belt as he fell past her, that prevented him becoming a meal for the kelpies that churned the waters below.

Finally they all stood before the black hinged oak door.

"Locked," said Etain, rattling the handle.

"Not our biggest problem," breathed Fionnlagh, unsheathing his sword.

"What..?" Etain turned.

The two remaining werewolves were approaching from down the corridor, their battle axes raised.

Etain glanced at the old man. "You just *had* to give the Anguinum away, dincha?"

"Lailoken..."

Lailoken lurched across the barren landscape, the bodies of his men broken and unmoving. How? How could he have got it so wrong?

Rhydderch Hael was a weak man, a poor chieftain with delusions of power and influence.

Gwenddolau was a good man, earnest but honest, his treatment of his men fair and measured. When Rhydderch had attacked the borders of Gwenddolau's lands, he'd sent for Lailoken, summoning the druid warrior and his army.

Lailoken had been unworried. He'd returned from future history, knew the story of what was coming, knew of the victory of his closest of friends. It was an honour to fight beside him, and a privilege to slap down the misguided usurper.

The results of his arrogance lay all around.

Feet slipped in the bloody grass and mud, and the druid fell to his knees.

"Lailoken ..." The ravaged voice bit through the stillness, startling and obscene in the silence.

With a cry, Lailoken cast aside his battle helmet, threw down his breastplate. He staggered to his feet, bloodied and beaten.
His friend needed him.
"Gwenddolau?" his voice broke as he called out. Around him only the bodies of his fallen men, unhearing, uncaring, dead eyes staring in mute accusation.
His friend lay against a small mound, his wounds mortal. Lailoken fell by his side. "My friend..."
"This ... this cannot be," breathed the chieftain, his eyes frightened and confused. "This cannot be, Lailoken, you promised me..."
"My lord, I – I have no excuses, I thought ..."
"You led my men to their death!" A hand, robbed of strength, grasped at the druid's arm. "We ... we trusted you, trusted your guidance..."
Tears fell down the druid's face. "I'm sorry, Gwenddolau, I'm so sorry..."
"find her," breathed the dying man.
"My lord?"
"My two birds. My beloved Ravenhair."
A wave a despair washed over the druid. "No, please...you brought her here?"
"She is a warrior. It was safe," said Gwenddolau. "You said, it was safe!" He coughed; red liquid foamed in the corners of his mouth. "Find her, damn you. Find her, let her be the one good thing to leave this battlefield. Keep her safe. Please. I beg you..."
The hand fell from the druid's arm, and blue eyes stared sightlessly at the sky.
Lailoken sobbed. "I'll find her, I promise, I promise, *I'll keep her safe."*
How long he remained at his friend's side, weeping uncontrollably, he did not know. The sky was darkening when he finally stood, a new resolve in his eyes. With determination now he walked through the army of corpses, turning them one by one, each familiar face, each memory of laughter and companionship, burning into his soul as he carried out his friend's final request.
He found her finally, as the sky burnt red and orange. She lay on the ground, her long black hair covering her face, her brown eyes wide and unseeing.
"No..."
A hand plunged into his robes, dragging out the anguinum.
"No..."
He knelt by her side, lifting her lifeless form, pressing the bowl over her heart. Green fire surged over the woman. Minutes passed as the druid hugged the woman, desperately trying to will her soul back into her lifeless form. A cry broke from the druid's throat.

"No, you can't leave," gasped Lailoken, "no, I won't let you, no, not you as well..." he shook her body as the green fire began to die. "No! Come back! This didn't happen!"

The woman fell to the ground, a broken doll, lifeless and unmoving.

"No!" screamed Lailoken, dropping the Anguinum, clutching her hand. "Kylie!"

By his side, forgotten in the long grass, the green fire of the Glass Apple faded.

Huddour smiled as the druid hung motionless in the ruby light, reliving his history, facing his madness once more. He turned his gaze to the boy.

"Hurry up," said his mother, dropping the bulging plastic bags into the boot of the car.

Jason was at the trolley park, trying to shove his empty trolley into the long line of the things, so he could get his coin back. "I'm trying!"

"We've got to pick Kylie up," said his mother, slamming the boot, "and the babysitter's just texted me. Anna's creating!"

Jason finally got the trolley in place, and pocketed the coin. "She's always creating." He jogged back across the carpark, and hopped into the front seat.

His mother got into the car, popping the key into the ignition.

"Seatbelt," said Jason automatically, fastening his.

"Balls," replied his mother, effectively ending the conversation as she slammed the car into reverse.

Jason scowled. Most of the time she was cheerful, or at least so it seemed, but there were days when her mood was black. It usually followed a phonecall from his father, and an argument over money. He'd phoned while they were in the supermarket, and his mother had left him pushing the trolley while she shouted at his father, oblivious to the looks she earned from other shoppers.

When she was in this sort of mood, she wasn't a woman to cross. Jason bit down on his tongue as they pulled out of the car park, waiting for her to go from rapid boil to gentle simmer before he dared open his mouth.

She'd finally stopped gritting her teeth as they reached the motorway. "You okay?" she asked quietly.

He nodded silently.

"I made a fool of myself, didn't I?"

Jason looked at her. The redness in her cheeks was now due to embarrassment rather than anger. "Yeah," he said. "But only a little."

"Oh...I know," she said, smiling ruefully. She rubbed at her chest, frowning a little. "He just – he just presses all my buttons. Always has

done." She looked at Jason. "He still loves you though."

"Yeah, right."

"He does! You and Kylie. Look, don't let ... me and him ... affect how you feel about him."

"It doesn't," muttered Jason. And he was being honest. He'd developed his own opinion of his dad years ago. The fact that it wasn't by any means a good opinion had little to do with his mother.

"Fancy some music?" she asked in the silence that followed. "Queen?"

Her favourite band. And, he had to admit, his. He popped open the glove box, digging out the CD and pushing it into the player. And, as they sang along to their favourite track, it did indeed seem like a form of magic.

If Jason noticed his mother faltering as she sang, if he saw her massaging her chest, it wasn't until the final seconds. By that time, the car was travelling at over 80.

Jason became aware of voices. "This one's still alive! Where're the cutters?"

"Steady heartbeat, lacerations in the chest and leg."

"Where're those damn cutters? Roof panel's got him pinned!"

He opened his eyes, his lashes momentarily glued together by the sticky liquid that covered his face. He was still in the car, on its side down the bank by the motorway, and blue lights flashed around him. Helmeted and neon suited figures moved around him. He looked to his right.

His mother lay against the remains of the door, unmoving, her eyes closed. Jason wimpered as he tried to reach for her, but something was pinning him in place.

A figure was leaning in through his window. "Cut the roof! Quickly! He's bleeding out!"

He was vaguely aware of a collar being tightened around his neck, of a needle biting into his arm. A board was pushed behind him, and gently, he was eased from the car.

Then he was in the ambulance, listening to the medics radio.

"ETA fifteen minutes. Male of about twelve years, leg laceration, chest laceration, crush and penetration injuries on upper left chest, collapsed lung, responsive. Female, late thirties, head and neck injuries, unresponsive."

Jason closed his eyes. Everything hurt. It was easier to let go, to just go to sleep...

Hands moved over his neck and chest. "Boy's crashing! BP dropping, tachycardic!"

The darkness reached out to him, offering comfort in oblivion.

"He's arrested!" The voice was distant, the panic in it unimportant. "Beginning compressions, where's the damn adrenaline?" Something pushed at his chest.

Another voice now. "What about the woman? Anything?"

They arrived at the hospital, and the sense of controlled panic was almost palpable. He heard, rather than saw, the medics unload his mother, racing her in through the emergency doors, before he followed, more aware now of his surroundings, of the men and women around him as they fought to save him.

"Which operating room?" barked a doctor; the nurse stared at him like a startled rabbit. "Hurry!"

"Blood type AB negative," said one of the paramedics, "have we got any in? Clear the route!" He jogged by the side of Jason's trolley. "Which surgeon's on call? Have you reached him?"

In front, the doctor was running ahead. "Hold that lift!"

"How is he?" The voice, so familiar, was filled with pain. He tried to open his eyes, to look up, but his body would not respond.

"He...physically, he's fine. The wounds have all been closed..."

"...But?"

"You have to understand, he arrested several times on the way to the hospital. His brain was starved of oxygen." The doctor's voice was tired, weary.

"But he's going to be alright? Tell me, he's going to be alright!"

"We've done all we can. His AVPU scale hardly registers; it's really up to him now. We'll know more if and when he wakes up. There is definite brain function there, but at the moment it's just not responding to external stimuli..."

"He's my Jason, he'll be fine, just you see..."

"... but you shouldn't be out of bed yourself. You've had a major trauma..."

"I'm staying," said Jason's mother firmly. "It's only been three days. He'll be fine, he – he's just dreaming."

Chapter Thirty Nine

The werewolves were locked in battle with Kylie and Fionnlagh. If Etain had once had concerns about Kylie joining the battle, these worries had long since evaporated.

The fur was literally flying.

Etain turned to the old man. "How do we get this door open?"

Gobswistle was studying the framework of the door, flinching at the sounds of battle behind. "I really have no idea..." he sounded more disappointed than anything.

"Well you've got some magic left!" said Etain, infuriated at the eccentric old ex druid. "Cain't you use that?"

"I am not the big bad wolf," retorted Gobswistle, "nor are there three little pigs on the other side! What about your magic?"

"I need iron to work with!"

"Like the hinges?"

Etain blinked. "...what?"

"The hinges, wench! Look! They're metal, aren't they?"

They were indeed. Etain silently berated herself for not thinking of this herself. "Stand aside."

She touched both hinges, leaning to touch top and bottom at the same time. Her ironfire blazed up, the hinges instantly transforming, eating away at the ancient wood they were attached to. Etain and Gobswistle had to leap out of the way as the vast oak door fell outwards.

Etain turned to the brawling figures behind her.

The Cait Sidhe had its jaws locked around the throat of one of the Black Dogs, the dog now fully transformed, its paws pushing futilely against the Cait Sidhe's muscular neck. Behind them, Fionnlagh was locked in combat with the remaining werewolf, his sword ringing loudly off the creature's axe as they duelled.

"We got the door!" bellowed Etain as she ripped the remains of a hinge from the door frame, an ironfire sword growing in her hand. "Kylie!"

Amber eyes glanced briefly at Etain, then the Cait Sidhe dragged the Black Dog over to the window they'd entered through. The dog, sensing what was intended, began struggling harder, but the larger Cait Sidhe was too powerful. With a yelping scream the Black Dog plunged into the loch below.

"Fionnlagh!" shouted Gobswistle as the cat bounded up the spiral staircase, almost knocking him and Etain down.

Fionnlagh chanced a glance at his companions. "Yui go!" he shouted. "Ah'll hold this devilspawn here!"

Gobswistle hesitated, but Etain gave him a shove towards the steps. "Move! He can look after himself!"

"Oh wow," breathed Kylie, looking up at the vast statues, the blue fire of her transformation dying.

"Ugly critters, ain't they?" said Etain.

"The books," said Gobswistle, pointing delightedly. "Look, look, the books!"

"Ah see 'em," nodded Etain. "Kylie, you take yon horned thing, Ah'll take one eye, Ethelbert, you take that pregnant ... thing ... oh my..." Etain's voice trailed off.

The three statues had turned to look at them.

"Why," said Gobswistle quietly, "can't anything *ever* be simple?"

Omnust brought his blade down on the spriggan's head, felling the repulsive little creature, then turned to find his next mark, gasping for breath.

The Changelings had the loathsome little creatures on the run. For all the creatures had outnumbered the Men of Dun Ghallain at least five to one, the strength and agility of the Changelings had proven more than a match for the creatures.

As Omnust stared around, almost not daring to believe his eyes, the remaining spriggans were turning tail, their bright red eyes flashing through the trees as they fled.

"We cannae rest!" he shouted, attracting the attention of the Changelings, who seemed on the verge of heading through the trees after the little goblins. "We cannae pursue them! We've done our bit here – cross the causeway now, help Myrrdin!"

He watched as the creatures grouped together, acknowledging his orders, moving toward the causeway and the castle.

He raised one hand, wiping sweat and blood from his brow, then took two steps after the Changelings.

Something exploded through the trees behind him, sailing above his head to crash into the ground before him.

It was the broken remains of one of the spriggans.

Omnust turned, his sword ready for whatever was now leaping through the shadows towards him.

His eyes widened.

"You?!"

The druid and the boy hung in the air, their faces pale and emotionless as each relived their tragic past, lost in the guilt of avoidable death.

It was almost disappointing, how little fight they'd provided.

But the Huntsman approached, the black clouds already drawing in from the west, hurtling across the waters of the loch towards the waiting sorcerer.

Huddour's captivity was at an end.

All that was needed was the trade.

He walked up to the nearest firepit, looking up at the cage that hung in the air above it. "Time to die," he smiled.

As the cage began to descend, the prisoners screamed.

Etain dived between the legs of the skeletal figure as a bony hand reached for her, slicing at its legs as she passed between. But the impossible entity seemed impervious to her blows. She quickly found her feet, leaping high into the air as a leg kicked out at her.

Kylie, transformed yet again into the huge cat, was fairing little better. Powerful though she was, the horned statue was stronger, its blows sending her from one end of the room to the other, its stone lacking flesh for claws and teeth to cut into.

The pregnant woman towered over Gobswistle, her crooked mouth smiling as she looked down at him, small as a child next to her, and a lean hand reached out to him as he cringed and cowered.

A two edged axe flew from the stairwell, and the hand shattered, sharp fragments of stone showering down on Gobswistle.

Fionnlagh emerged from the stairwell, battered but whole, and Gobswistle almost cheered. "Fion!"

The youth ran to Gobswistle's side, his eyes wide as he watched the towering woman trying to gather the pieces of her shattered hand with her remaining stump, her other hand still clutching the red bound book. "Can ye no' do somethin'?"

"I – I no, I don't..." he yelped as the Cat was thrown against the wall. But the Cait Sidhe was not so easily cowed and, even as loose brick and mortar showered around it from the wall and the roof above, it launched itself once more into battle.

Gobswistle stared at the broken bits of tumbled brick. An idea burnt brightly at the centre of his mind, and with a renewed vigour he turned to the young man. "I'd find something to hold onto, if I were you," he said.

It was a slow death, lowering the cages inch by inch through the air towards the firepits and water. As clothing and feet began to burn, the woman and children screamed and cried, the women lifting the children as high as they could, keeping them out of reach of the hungry flames.

"...No..."

The voice, so quiet it should have been inaudible over the screams, still drew at Huddour's attention, pulling him round to face the druid as he hung in mid air, stilling for a moment the descent of the cages.

"Really?" said Huddour. "You choose to interrupt me *now?*"

"You will not sacrifice these people," said the druid, his useless staff still clutched in one hand.

"The Unseelie Court approach," snapped Huddour, his patience wearing thin. "Of course I will. Now be still." He gestured with one hand, almost lazily, and skin grew over the druid's mouth, silencing him. "That's better." Huddour turned away.

"You will not sacrifice these people," said the druid's voice, louder this time, the command behind it undeniable. Huddour turned, staring. The skin was gone from Myrrdin's mouth, and the druid was slowly descending to the ground.

"What? What is this? Druid, you have no magic!" Huddour marched across the courtyard, furious and indignant. "How did you do that? The Sidhe, they took your magic!"

"They did not," smiled Myrrdin. In his hand, the top of his staff burned with green fire. "I was lost to my magic, lost in guilt. I should thank you, Huddour. You reminded me who I was."

"No!" snapped Huddour. He raised his hand, looking almost as though he was going to slap Myrrdin across the face. "This is totally unacceptable! *You have no magic!"*

Red fire burst from his hand, encircled the druid, obscuring him from sight. Then a finger of green light burst from the dome of red, bright and pure. Then another, then dozens more.

Free from the red light, Myrrdin pointed his staff at Huddour. "I say again, sorcerer, you will not sacrifice these people."

"What's happenin'?" yelled Etain as she hurtled across the room, the giant skeleton only feet behind her.

"Grab onto something!" replied Gobswistle, as he slowly raised his hands either side.

"Like what?"

"Like *anything*, for heaven's sake wench!"

The wind slowly picked up speed, circling around the room, pulling streamers of dust from the ancient walls.

"You will not stop me," growled Huddour. "I still have the boy – he's cast into his past and his future – without me he shall not return!" He looked up at Jason, at the boy's blank face, the limp form.

"Crowanhawk Yellowblade is far more than you can ever imagine," said Myrrdin, his staff now shining like a star, "do not think to claim control of him."

"I claim what I like! My magic is older than yours! *I am older than you!*"

Myrddin simply looked at him. "You are a spoilt and cosseted child." He pointed his staff at Huddour. "Perhaps it is you who should be still."

"You don't scare me! I know what you want! You want my Books! You can't have them, I tell you – they're guarded by magic you can't even imagine!"

"Perhaps," said Myrrdin, "you should look up."

"OH CRAP!!"

Etain clung to the stonework of the window as the winds tore around the room, Kylie tucked tightly under one arm.

Gobswistle stood in the centre of the room; the eye of the storm. The three statues tumbled around him, the hurricane force of the winds allowing them no purchase as it carried them around, and with each crash into a wall, with each fall into the floor, their stone bodies chipped and fragmented. Around and above them brickwork was being sucked into the whirlwind, large missiles that attacked and beat at the statues, and the fragments that broke free from the three stone figures became yet more missiles.

"You are defeated," said Myrrdin as he approached the sorcerer. "Yield, and we will spare you."

"I yield to no-one! How dare you do this, you, the craven druid, fleeing from the battlefield, you dare!"

"I dare," said Myrrdin. Green fire leapt up around Huddour, solidifying in an instant into an eldritch cage.

Ignoring the now hysterical screaming of the sorcerer, Myrrdin turned to the cages, his staff sweeping through the air in front of him. As the cages floated away from the fire, from the water, the screams of Huddour became incoherent as he railed against his cage.

Creatures erupted from the darkness; vast doglike creatures, or Cait Sidhes, some apelike, others furred or scaled, muscular and terrifying.

As the cage above the oubliette touched the ground, Omnust ran across, wrenching open the door, yelling as he saw who was within.

"Jean!"

"...Omnust...?" the woman's voice was stunned, and for a moment she simply stared at her brother, then she was hugging him fiercely, sobbing and shaking.

Myrrdin ran up. "Get them out of here," he said, "Omnust, there's time for reunions later, get them out of here!"

"Druid, we've *won...*"

"We've done no such thing," said Myrrdin, "now listen to me and *move!*" He turned to face the other cages. "Do not fear the Changelings!" he shouted. Many of the women and children were screaming with renewed terror. "They're here to help! Those of you who can't walk, allow them to carry you! Get across to the mainland!" He turned back to Omnust. "*Move.*"

"Aye, aye, druid, Ah shall, but there's another come..."

"Omnust!"

Omnust nodded. There was urgency, but also fear, in the druid's voice. He lifted his sister into his arms, then, after a second's hesitation, hoisted Gaira over one shoulder.

"Jason." Myrrdin stood under the boy, gentle green fire pulling the catatonic boy back down to earth. As Jason's feet touched the ground, Myrrdin touched the glowing tip of his staff against the boy's head. "Jason. Awake."

Jason's eyes fluttered, then Jason gasped, his eyes wide and panicked. "She's alive, Myrrdin, she's *alive,* I don't understand..."

"She lives, yes," nodded Myrrdin, "I see what is in your soul's eye, but she is not in a place you can reach."

"But she's alive, how can she be, how could I *see* that, all my dreams, my *dreams,* they were trying to tell me..."

"These are questions better answered by your grandfather," said Myrrdin. "Now, CrowanhawkYellowblade, now, Dragonslayer, now is your moment. Forget the tricks played on you by Huddour."

"But..."

"Be in this moment, Jason Crowanhawk." Myrddin stood. "My magic is not strong enough yet to defeat Huddour; even the prison begins to slip."

Behind them, visible only in flashes between the fleeing people, was Huddour's glowing green prison. Huddour himself was no longer visible; a black, pulsing cloud of smoke filled the cage, slowly growing with each pulse, pushing against the bars.

Jason turned back to Myrrdin. "But – but I don't know what to do!"

"Then don't *know,*" said Myrrdin. "Just *do.*"

"Can't you help?"

"The Unseelie Court approach. I shall stay them as long as possible. Jason, this is *your* battle. God's strength... grandson." He turned, walking quickly away.

And Huddour's cage exploded.

Chapter Forty

Jason stared up at the cloud of black smoke as it pulsed ever larger above him, and he gripped Carnwennan lightly in his hand, his heart pounding in his chest as his mind tried to understand what he'd just seen, what Huddour had just forced him to see.

Something was moving within the cloud, something black and hideous, and a ball of fire shot from the smoke, roaring through the air at Jason.

He dived to one side, the fireball exploding on the ground only feet away, scouring the stone where he'd just been standing.

He got to his feet, more cautious now. Dreams or no dreams, *this* was *real*.

In the distance he could hear Myrrdin's barked instructions as the remainder of the women and children were led to the relative safety of the forests. And high above him, at the apex of the castle, a whirlwind grew, spitting out fragments of rock. And above everything, the storm rumbled and whirled overhead.

Something emerged from the cloud; a wing, vast, black and leathery, pock marked with holes and scars.

Oh no.

Myrrdin's words echoed around his head. *Dragonslayer.*

The smoke began to dissipate, the winds from the storm dragging it away from the form beneath. A huge serpentine head slowly turned, and luminous yellow orbs looked down at Jason.

And a rumbling laugh filled the air.

"Jeez, goddamit Ethlebert, *Stop!*" Etain's feet streamed behind her as she clung desperately to the remains of the window frame by one hand, Kylie hugging her as the two clung to each other like lifelines.

Gobswistle stood in the middle of what remained of the room, looking around him in bewilderment. The roof was gone, ripped asunder by the powerful winds, and the upper half of the walls were gone, blasted by fragments of rock, stone and statue. As he stood in the eye of the storm he could hardly see Etain as she bellowed at him, for so much stonework was held in the whirling maelstrom that it was almost opaque.

But he *could* see the three books as they tumbled like plyingcards around him.

"Ethelbert!" Etain's cry was desperate. "Stop!"

"I – I can't," shouted back the old man. "There's too much magic here – the storm, the books, Huddour, me, Jason – we're like lodestones! Even you two – we're all lightning rods!"

"For pity's sake do somethin'!" shouted Etain as she felt her fingers begin to slip. She pulled the little girl closer, tightening her grip on the window frame. If they were pulled into the whirling mix of wind and shattered stone it would be like jumping into a giant blender.

"I can't see Fion!" shouted Kylie as she looked around.

"He got to the stairwell," Etain struggled to make herself heard. Above her head, more stone ripped free. The stone beneath her fingers moved and she closed her eyes, knowing the whole wall would give way within moments.

"Hold on to me!" yelled Kylie suddenly.

"I am!"

"I'm gonna change!" She tried to see her grandfather through the debris. "Granddad! I'm getting Etain out of here! You need to get out!"

"I'm fine," came his voice, "bloody thing's not even ruffling my clothes! Get out of here, Kylie, if you can!"

Etain suddenly found her role with the little girl reversed. Instead of Kylie clinging to her for survival, Etain found her fingers buried deep in the fur of the Cait Sidhe.

Get on my back!

Etain scrambled onto the cat's back as its vicious claws held tightly to the stonework. She hesitated before wrapping her arms around the creature's neck.

You won't hurt me.

So as the Cait Sidhe leapt from the window to the roof below, Etain hung on for dear life. The landing was rough, and Etain was jolted from Kylie's back, skidding across the flat surface of the roof. The Cait Sidhe roared with delight as Fionnlagh pounded across the roof toward them, helping Etain to her feet.

"Where – where's Gobswistle?" he asked.

Etain looked up at the miniature storm. "Silly sod's still in there," she breathed. "Oh Ethelbert no..."

Jason leapt across the fire pit as the dragon lunged at him, spitting fire in a long stream. With a yell he threw Carnwennan, and she flew through the air, cutting with ease through a leathery wing. With a puff of red fire, the wing healed instantly.

Haven't you learned anything? The amused voice echoed within Jason's mind. *You can't hurt me! No-one can hurt me! I am immortal!*

Jason made no reply as he ran across the courtyard, his hand catching his blade as he ran.

Run little mouse, little dream boy, run all you want!

The dragon lunged at him, ivory teeth slamming shut scant inches from his back as he leapt high into the air, clasping his blade between his teeth as he flew, landing high on the castle wall, gripping at the gaps in the stone with trembling fingers.

He began climbing, not looking back as the wall beneath him vibrated as the dragon began climbing after him, its vast wings spread, casting black shadows all around Jason from the light of the fires below.

Some second sight warned him, and he jumped to one side as a rope of fire spat past him. He risked a look down, his blade scuffing the wall in front of him as he turned his head.

The dragon was within feet of him, almost within reach, and with a yelp Jason grabbed Carnwennan, casting her at a yellow orb.

As the gelatinous eye burst, the dragon roared in pain, falling back from the wall as Carnwennan flew through the air to return to her master.

Jason began to climb with renewed vigour. *I can't kill you*, he thought, *but I can hurt you!*

The dragon hung in the air, vast and dreadful, its eye already healed. Powerful wings created downdrafts that threatened to pluck Jason from the wall.

Carnwennan flew out again, knowing her target, and another eye burst. With a roar the dragon backwinged, spitting fire randomnly at the castle wall as it drew away. Jason, lithe as a lizard, sped up the wall, falling over its ramparts onto the roof above.

"Jason!"

Small arms were thrown around his neck as Kylie launched herself at him, and he hugged her back almost angrily.

"You're okay!" he whispered, almost overwhelmed with relief. He pushed her away. "You have to get out of the castle!" He looked up as Etain and Fionnlagh ran up. "Get to the forest, Myrrdin's there, he's got all the prisoners with him..."

"Jason, you can't do this alone," said Etain.

"I have to!" said Jason. "Myrrdin doesn't have the magic, he said so, and the Gwyllion, they *told* me..."

"Boy, Ah don't care if they told you squat! There's no magic can hurt him save his own!"

"I have to try!" He looked around. "Where's Granddad?"

"Up there," said Kylie, pointing at the maelstrom above. "With the Books."

Fire roared over the top of the wall, and the brief reunion was ended. "Get out of here!" yelled Jason as he ran along the roof.

"Jason, get back here!" yelled Etain. But it was no use – Jason was not listening. She looked around the roof. "Ah need metal," she growled.

The dragon breathed fire across the length and breadth of the castle walls, and the stonework became scorched and blackened. Jason's leathers smoked as he leapt from wall to wall. Carnwennan flew out again and again, slicing through flesh or temporarily blinding the creature as it lunged after its target, each time slowing it down, each time the dragon recovering within moments.

It was as Jason scuttled down the castle wall, trying to draw the creature away from his friends, that he saw the unlikely figure leaping and bounding across the causeway. Etain's words repeated in his mind, and a bold plan blossomed.

He leapt from the wall, not toward the ground, but out through the air, almost flying, straight at the dragon. The dragon, not expecting this bizarre attack, ducked briefly, allowing time for Jason to land on the back of its head.

Carnwennan bit down again and again, and though each time the savage cuts healed almost the moment the blade made the cut, the repeated blows were driving the dragon down toward the earth.

You cannot kill me! Even through the pain, the mirth of Huddour, that childish, spiteful humour, still filled his voice. *These are bee stings! Nothing more!* The dragon shook itself like a dog, trying to dislodge the boy, but Jason clung to the leathery skin.

Leathery wings began carrying the dragon higher, away from the castle.

"No you *don't!*" Carnwennan flew out, flying in a figure of eight, puncturing and repuncturing the leathery membranes of the wings. From the roof, small fiery arrows shot toward the dragon, cast from the hands of the Black Celt. The dragon began to lose air, and claws came up to rake at its neck, the short arms not quite long enough to reach Jason as he dodged from side to side.

Dreamboy, Stop! What do you hope to happen! You cannot kill me!

"No," gasped Jason, as the leaping figure reached the courtyard, "I can't. I'm not of your magic. But my friend is.

"*Aiken!*"

Carnwennan flew out once more, hilt first this time, and the blue bearded, long armed boggart snatched her from the air as his leap carried him high above the dragon, then down like an arrow, the blade held out in front of him, glinting in the firelight.

"For mah Family!"

Carnwennan bit through the dragon's skull.

"Jason?" The voice was muffled, as though Jason had a pillow over his head. "Wee master?"

The friendly voice, so warm and familiar, finally persuaded Jason to open his eyes. "Aiken..." He pushed himself into a sitting position. "Aiken!" he flung his arms around his friend. "You're alive! They said – when I saw you I thought – what..." he looked around him, "...what happened?"

"There's someone tae see you," whispered Aiken, but Jason hardly heard him as he looked around.

The body of Huddour lay only feet away, one foot in the waters of the oubliette, his limbs in disarray. Carnwennan sat proud in his forehead, buried up to her hilt.

The castle behind was almost obscured from view by the whirling maelstrom that surrounded it, and the rumble of falling stone filled the night air. Kylie, Etain and Fionnlagh stood in the distance, as though afraid to approach. Of his grandfather, there was no sign.

"Jason," whispered Aiken, "yui need tae get up."

Jason followed his friend's gaze, and was suddenly on his feet.

A figure sat on horseback before him, beautiful yet terrifying, his silver and gold armour shining with their own light, illuminating the ground him. His mount, a brilliant white, bore him on a saddle made from thousands of scales of silver, the light rippling across its surface.

Eyes of blue fire regarded Jason. *CrowanhawkYellowblade.*

Jason nodded mutely.

You know me?

"You're – you're the Wild Huntsman."

The figure nodded. *And you are the one who robbed me of my souls.*

Jason took a fearful step back, but Aiken caught him by his shoulders. "It's alright, wee master," he whispered.

He speaks the truth, little one. The Huntsman urged his horse toward Jason. Diamond hooves sparked on the stones, shards of white fire dancing upwards. *I claim a better prize. The Brittanic Lord, who thought to usurp me. The Child in Manform who thought to use me for his own purposes.*

A silver hand was raised towards the stricken figure of Huddour, and

Carnwennan wafted through the air, hovering in front of Jason. *Reclaim your blade, boy.*

Jason took Carnwennan, sliding her back into her sheath. "Th-thankyou."

The Huntsman smiled, still looking at Huddour's form. As he, and Jason and Aiken, watched, a green glow appeared over the body, evenly at first, then slowly shrinking upwards towards the head. A tiny bead of green light rose from the wound in the forehead, and it twitched through the air like a sun drunk bee to the waiting hand of the Huntsman.

He will be the least of the Spriggans, said the Huntsman, smiling down at Jason. *So shall suffer any who seek to command the Wild Hunt.*

Jason could think of nothing to say. This being, this glowing figure, was somehow more terrifying than Blashie, Lathgertha and Huddour together.

You, boy, I feel the fear in you. You are wise to fear me. But ... you have aided me tonight, by intention or fortune is irrelevant. I grant you ...one request. But only one. Choose wisely.

There was no real difficulty in choosing. Behind them, the castle was all but destroyed by the winds that tore around it.

"My grandfather's in there," he said, "please, please help him?"

You humans, said the Huntsman, *always so unpredictable. You could have chosen so much more. Very well.*

The vast storm that circled overhead suddenly dropped, the thunder deafening as it fell, twisting upon the castle in the loch. Jason and Aiken were tossed along the courtyard like leaves, powerless in the strength of the winds. The coals of the fire pits were pulled into the air, red motes that danced through the air like hellish fireflies. Lightning flashed all around them, blinding them as they tumbled along, the screams of Kylie, Etain and Fionnlagh joining their own as they too were swept from their feet.

Then, shockingly, there was silence.

The storm, the wind, the thunder and lightning were gone. The Huntsman was gone. As Jason got to his feet, amazingly uninjured by the savageness of the storm, he saw to his joy his friends and sister also rising, staring at each other in astonishment.

The utter silence was shattered by a heavy thud, and with a yelp, Jason looked at what had fallen at his feet.

An ancient, red, leather bound book.

Another thud, then another. Kylie and Etain retrieved the books, their faces as shocked and delighted as Jason's.

Where the castle had once been, there was now a single finger of stonework, reaching high into the sky. On top of this finger, less than three feet from side to side, was a small plateau. On this plateau, stood a totally confused looking old man.

"Did we ..." he called, "...did we win?"

Chapter Forty One

Morven bustled around the sickbeds, handing out bowls of porridge, stopping to chat to the more lively patients.

She longed to get outside into the fresh air. Though nearly a third of the injured had returned to their own homes over the past three days, the remaining forty people had added an odour to Gaira's home that was almost unbearable.

Finally, with the sun high in the sky, she was able to take a break, joining Bridget in the front room as she nursed the twins. Morven sank down onto Gaira's cot. "how are they?"

"Thrivin', bless 'em," grinned Bridget. "They're tough, these two."

"Where's little Anna?"

Bridget's smile faded. She nodded towards the room where Eigyr had been nursed. "She's no' happy."

Morven wearily got to her feet. "Ah'll go tae her."

Anna sat on the chair by the window, looking out across the loch beyond. She still wore the green stain over her eyes, but the sight of the fairies dancing around her, joyous once more, no longer cheered her.

They'd all left her. Kylie, Granddad and Etain, they'd left first. Then Jason, leaving her with Gaira, and Gaira, she was, she was *wicked*, and then she'd been taken. And then her big brother had left her. And finally Aiken had gone.

She was all alone.

"Anna?"

She looked up as Morven peeped round the door. "Hi."

"You alright there?"

"Fine."

Morven came into the room. "you don't sound fine. Are you hungry?"
"Nuh-uh." Anna shook her head.
Morven came up to her, easing herself down to sit next to Anna's chair. "You miss them, don't you? They'll come back, Anna. You have to believe that."
"Aiken won't," said Anna quickly. He'd been brave, they'd said. She didn't want him to be brave. She wanted him there.
"No," said the woman slowly, "no, he won't. But your brother, you know he'll come back for you."
"He left me *alone,*" said Anna, a tear trickling down one cheek.
"Anna, sweetheart, he just wanted tae keep you safe." She placed a meaty arm around the little girl's shoulder, hugging her gently. "He didn't want you tae be in any danger, did he? Didn't want you fighting vikings and such."
The sudden knock on the door made them both jump.
Bridget's head came round the door. "It's Bedevere," she said urgently. "He's asking for you. Now, like!"
"Wait here," said Morven to the little girl, leaving her staring out at the loch as she hurried away.

"It's them?" whooped Morven, staring at the grinning youth. "You're sure now?"
"The morning patrol came across them, at the other end o' the loch. They're all there! Jason, Myrrdin, Omnust, even Aiken! Aiken's alive, Morven!"
"Oh my," breathed Morven, and around her, the girls from the barracks were giggling and whispering excitedly to each other. "Oh my, we have to... I mean, they'll want ... are they alright?"
"The boggart's got a wound tae his shoulder, but they're fine, they'll be here by nightfall!"
"We're celebrating!" declared Morven. "You lot! Stop your clucking now! As far as I'm bothered, it's Alban Eiler, three days late. Bridget, settle those bairns, get tae that farm wi' the pigs."
"Aye, Morven."
"We'll need as many carcases as the' c'n spare, and see'f they've tallow candles as well. And you lot, we'll need wood for the fires, we'll use the pits we dug fer the vikings, and chairs, and tables!" She turned to the still grinning youth. "You, grinning fool!"
"Yes ma'am?" he stood to mock attention.
She swatted at him playfully. "Behave, mon. Get yui tae Aiken's place, tekk some carts. Bring some barrels back with yui."
She was unprepared for the kiss he planted resoundingly on her plump cheek, and she shoved him away, blushing but smiling as he ducked out of the doorway.

A thought struck her.

Anna!

She quickly made her way back to Anna's room, smiling in anticipation at the little child's reaction to the news. She threw open the door. "Child, your brother, he's b..."

The room was empty.

The moon, no longer full, was still bright enough to light the path down to Kilneuair. Jason stood on the banks of Loch Awe, staring down into the large village. He looked up as Myrrdin reached his side.

"I never thought I'd see it again," he said.

"You did well," smiled Myrrdin. "Young Dragonslayer."

"It was Aiken," said Jason, looking back at his friend. "He delivered the final blow. He was in the right place at the right time."

"As were you," said Myrrdin. "Shall we?"

Jason nodded, and they set off down the bank, followed by the Men of Dun Ghallain and the survivors from the surrounding villages.

Etain walked by the boggart's side. "How's the shoulder?" she asked.

Aiken eased his shoulder, adjusting the bandages around it. "Sore only. The viking, she couldnae see me properly, knocked me down more than injuring me." He looked at Etain. "You remember me?"

"Ah seem to remember you being a little more..." she looked at his beard, "ginger than that."

"An' yui were a wee bit younger."

"You know, if one more person says that..."

"T'were a while ago." He smiled. "Good memories though." As he spoke, he was looking around at the people surrounding them. Most were the women and children they'd rescued, but far to their right, two soldiers walked, a small ginger haired woman walking between them, her arms bound behind her back. The magic of Myrrdin had restored her mouth, but she had said nothing as Omnust had bound her.

Etain followed his gaze. "Have you spoken to her yet?"

Aiken shook his head silently.

"Jason ... he told me what happened," said Etain. "Don't judge her too harshly."

"No' mah place," said Aiken. "Oor king, he'll pass judgement."

"She was your *friend,* Aiken. She was misguided."

"She's no friend," muttered Aiken, and lengthened his stride, moving away from Etain.

"Granddad," said Kylie, adjusting the little sack over her shoulder yet again, "it's your turn." The weight of the books pulled the ropes of the sack painfully tight on her shoulder.

Gobswistle shook his head, a gentle smile plying on his lips as he saw the lights of the buildings ahead. "No, no, you keep hold, it's not time yet." A tear trickled down one withered cheek. "I remember this place..."

"What d'you mean, it's not time yet?"

Fionnlagh reached down, easing the sack from her, the three books within surprisingly heavy. "Here. Ah'll tekk it."

"Thanks," said Kylie. She quickly jogged up to her grandfather's side. "What did you mean?"

Gobswistle seemed lost in thought. "So many years ... so many years and I still recognise it. See, over there, those ruins? That's the old barracks – I was trapped in the chimney there you know, and over there, see, that little cottage, that's where I was banished to..." he smile faded. "Oh...yes..."

"What did you mean, it's not time?" persisted Kylie.

The old man started, as though awakening from a dream. "...What? Kylie. Oh look, Kilneuair. The books you mean? Can't touch them. Not yet."

"But..."

"My quest, remember? To find the Three Books of Huddour. To stop the Medb. If I touch them, we go home."

"Well then..."

"Be nice to be all together, don't you think?" grinned Gobswistle. "You, me, Jason, Etain *and* Anna?"

The people of the town lined the streets, and as the travellers entered the village a cheer went up, lanterns and torches raised high in the air. As Jason and Kylie walked either side of Etain, their young faces utterly enchanted by the light of the fires and the warmth of the people, the welcoming voices grew louder, welcoming the adventurers to their journey's end.

Tables and chairs filled the streets, laden with breads and steaming meats.

Music and song filled the night air as Jason and the others seated themselves around the tables, allowing themselves, for the first time in days, to relax.

Morven walked up to the table where Omnust sat, a hamshank in one hand, a pot of ale in the other. She nervously wiped her hands on her aprons, nervously fiddling with her hair. "Captain Omnust?"

Omnust turned on his stool, placing the meat and drink down. As he studied Morven's face, a slow smile broke over his weathered features. "Morven."

"Ah'm...Ah'm glad yuir safe," flustered the woman, her eyes darting everywhere but the captain's face.

"Enough of the bluidy formalities, woman!" He stood up.

"Ah'll thank yui not tae call me..." but she was silenced as he lifted her by the elbows, kissing her soundly. Around him, the men and women of the table cheered them on.

He grinned as he lowered her to the ground. "Come," he said, "there's someone Ah want ye's tae meet. Mah sister..."

"No, please," Morven hung back, wringing her hands nervously.

"What...what is it? Ah thought..."

"And yui'd be right, an' Ah'd tekk ye's tae me quarters for the next month, but..."

"But?"

"It's wee Anna, Yellowblade's sister. She's vanished." She looked across at where Aiken sat, deep in conversation with Myrrdin. "Get them two. But...be discrete."

Morven stood pacing Gaira's front room, nervously awaiting the return of Omnust. Her lips still burnt with the kiss he'd given her, and her heart bloomed with the joy he'd placed there, but now wasn't the time.

She looked up as Myrrdin, Omnust, Aiken and a one armed soldier came in.

"This is Fionnlagh," said Myrrdin as Morven looked questioningly at him. "He's a friend of Kylie, Fionnlagh, this is Morven, defender of Kilneuair." There was no mockery in the druid's tone; the introduction was genuine. "What's this about?"

"Oh, Myrrdin, Ah'm sorry, Ah did my best, Ah kept her safe, but she was aggrieving..."

"Anna?" said Myrrdin instantly. "She's missing?"

"Aye," nodded Morven, nodding. "She ran away, we've searched everywhere..."

"She's mah charge," said Aiken. "Ah'll find her. Ah've an idea where she bides."

"Ah'm coming with," said the one armed soldier. "Kylie's been missin' her; only right Ah help after all she's done fer me."

Aiken looked at him, then nodded. "Fine. But don't scare her."

"I'm coming too," said Myrrdin, but Aiken held up a hand.

"No Sire, an' Ah'm sorry Sire, but she's nae fondness fer yui nor yuir captain." He looked at Omnust. "Sorry, sir." He looked across at Fionnlagh, who was adjusting the sack of books across his back. "Ready?"

"Lead on, Aiken."

"Well," said Myrrdin, as the two left, "that's me put in my place." He looked around the room, at the various strips of material drying over chairs and barrels, at the buckets of brown water, the vast amounts of bedding. It brought home to him, these signs of treating and caring for the injured, just what had taken place in the town. "How fares the king?"

"The king is dead," said Cináed as he clasped the druid's hands in welcome. "Don't look so shocked. The townsfolk weren't. In fact it seems as though most of them were delighted with the news."

Myrrdin sat on the edge of the bed. "I don't understand."

"Oh," smiled Cináed, "I think you do. We both know the heartache I caused, the near disaster that my actions created. We both know the apology I owe you."

"So what will you do?" Myrrdin shrugged away the half formed rebuke.

"Morven and Bedevere have it arranged." Cináed sank back into the blankets. "It was announced to the townsfolk, the fact of my passing, the morning you left. Bedevere dressed one of the vikings in my battle armour. It sufficed for the funeral pyre." He winced, one hand at the wound in his side. "Morven ... she knows of an old farm a few leagues along the banks. I shall go there, once I'm healed. She will teach me to fish, she says. I shall become a fisher king!"

"So Constantine is now king," said Myrrdin.

"Aye. He is ready. He has his heirs."

"Have you seen them yet?" asked Myrrdin. "Your grandchildren?"

"No," said Cináed, "no. I haven't." He sighed. "Most think me dead – how would I have seen them?"

"I thought not," said Myrrdin. He turned to the door, and called out quietly. "Bedevere?"

The door opened, and the young soldier came in, a babe in each arm.

Cináed Mac Alpain," smiled Myrrdin, "may I present Ambrosius, son of Constantine, named for the message bearer who told of Yellowblade's visions," and he lifted the baby from Bedevere's arms, placing him on the smiling regent's chest, "and also ... Uther Pendragon, son of Constantine, named for the dragon slain by the blade of Yellowblade."

As the second child was placed on his chest, Cináed leant forward, kissing the blond hair gently. "The second name ... that is your doing?"

The druid nodded. "It seemed fitting."

Cináed inclined his head. "Names of kings," he smiled.

Myrrdin looked up at Bedevere. "Indeed."

If they were going to imprison her, thought Gaira, as she trudged through the darkness, then perhaps her old residence was not the best choice. She knew every nail, every faulty lock, every loose board of those shacks.

She'd find somewhere new. To hell with her promise to Jason. She could do *good.* She knew that now. How could she make amends if she was hung from a gibbet? She could go to Dunedin, to the barracks there, offer her services as a healer.

She paused, spinning to look behind her.

Nothing.

Yet she could have sworn she'd heard something. A growl, or a voice, wafting through the darkness.

Unnerved, she moved on, her pace slightly quicker now.

There it was again. She wasn't imagining it. Something had growled in the darkness. She was now running, ducking between some houses as she saw one of the firepits burning brightly ahead, surrounded by revellers.

What *was* it?

She could see the ruins of the Barracks ahead of her, white smoke still rising from the shell three days after the fire. And there was the training field beyond. There was movement in the field; a flash of blond hair, low to the ground, and two tall people stood there, the hair of one of them strikingly blue.

Aiken?

Something growled to her left and above her. She screamed, turning in time to see something large launch itself from the low roof, something lupine in shape, with only one ear, the flesh and lip missing from one side of its gaping maw...

"Anna?" Aiken walked slowly across the training field. "Wee Anna, what're yui doin' oot here?"

The little girl, her face streaked with tears of green, looked at him. The dawning comprehension was something wonderful to behold. *"Aiken?"*

They ran towards each other, Aiken scooping her up into the air, swinging her round. "Wee Anna, why fer yui run away?"

"I thought you'd gone!" sobbed Anna, her sobs mixing with laughter. "I thought you'd left me! Everyone else did!"

"Oh, bless yui child, the've no' left you!" He hugged her. "They're all here! Jason, yuir grandfer, Etain, yuir sister..."

"They're here?" yelped Anna. "Where? I wanna see them!"

"We'll go tae them," grinned Aiken, "we'll tekk yui now! See, this is Fionnlagh, he's a friend of Kylie."

Anna looked shyly up at the young man. "Is she really alright?"

"Aye, lassie," smiled Fionnlagh, "an' she's been missin' you somethin' sore."

"Come," said Aiken, holding out his hand. "Let's go then."

Something screamed in the distance, and all three froze.

"That sounded like a woman," said Aiken.

Fionnlagh slipped the cumbersome bag off his back, giving it to the small child. "Look after these," he said, drawing his sword. "Stay here."

"...okay..." said Anna in a small voice.

Something growled in the darkness beyond the field and the group span round. Both Aiken and Fionnlagh moved in front of Anna, pushing the frightened child behind them.

Something flew through the air, something small but heavy that landed with a wet thud in the grass.

It was Gaira.

Terrified eyes looked up at Aiken. "Get away..." she gasped.

"Oh lord, no, please..." Aiken saw the mortal wounds on her body.

"Get away," she repeated, "get the child and run..."

"Shut up!" shouted Anna from behind the two men. "Shut up! You're evil!"

"Anna..." Gaira reached out to her, fingers trembling in the air. "Ah'm so sorry..."

"You're evil! You're not who you think!"

The Black Dog sprang from the darkness, landing on Gaira, tearing at her, before turning to advance slowly on Aiken, Fionnlagh and the girl.

Fionnlagh brandished his sword. "Get her out o' here," he hissed. "Ah've fought these things before..."

With a nod, Aiken scooped up Anna.

The Black hound leapt, and Fionnlagh's youthful frame was knocked to one side with ease, his sword not even finding its mark. Momentarily stunned, Fionnlagh lay gasping in the dirt.

The creature advanced on the boggart and child, snarling viciously. Anna screamed, burying her head in Aiken's shoulder, hugging the bag of books up like some sort of shield.

Gaira twitched. Slowly, painfully, she turned her head.

Aiken was in danger.

She was dying. She knew that now. So this was her penance. No starting anew. No making amends.

No. There was one way. As the Black Dog lunged at her friend, as the one armed man got to his feet, she found her voice.

"...I love you..."

There was no flash of light, no eldritch fire or thunderous sound. Aiken, the child and the books simply vanished.

The Black Dog stumbled to the ground, robbed of its prey. This moment of confusion was all the young warrior needed. The blade plunged through the creature's neck and exited cleanly through its skull.

Fionnlagh stared down at the creature, breathing heavily. Where was the boggart? The child? He had to find the druid, tell him what happened. With a final look back at the body of the pech, the soldier ran from the field.

For a few moments the field was still, silent.

Then, from the body of Gaira, a ribbon of total blackness writhed into the air. Then another, and another. A mass of smokelike ribbons twisted and turned, and gradually a figure began to take shape.

The Medb was *free*.

Chapter Forty Two

Jason was *stuffed*. The food, though simple, was far better than any meal he'd had in the most expensive of restaurants. By his side, Kylie was laughing with Etain as they watched Gobswistle arm-wrestling with one of the children, making a huge show of losing to the delighted little child.

He looked at the men around him, the Men of Dun Ghallain, now in their human forms, enjoying the feast, but an almost palpable air of sadness surrounded them. He looked over at Gobswistle.

"Granddad?"

Gobswistle was taking a large swig of ale, and he burped happily as he lowered the cup. "Yes, young Jason?"

"The men, the changelings, what's gonna happen to them?"

"They're going away." It was Kylie who answered, and their grandfather simply nodded.

"Away?"

Kylie nodded. "They have to. They change again next full moon, so they can't be near people. They go into the Rage."

"The Rage?" it sounded scary.

Kylie nodded. "Yeah. It's not nice, but it only happens the once. So long as they're not near people, they'll be alright."

"I hope so," said Jason. "They're good men."

Etain had been listening in. "They are," she said, thinking of the bravery of Uilleam. "Some of the best."

"Some will return," said Gobswistle sagely as he chomped on a mutton leg. "Some'll go overseas."

"How do you know?" asked Jason.

Gobswistle shrugged, wiping his mouth. "Where do you think the tales of werewolves come from?"

"Wow," said Jason, thinking about it. "Wow, yeah, I guess..." They were, after all, hundreds of years before their own time. He looked up as Fionnlagh burst through the houses. "Hey, Fionnlagh, where've you been?"

"They've gone," gasped the young man, "Ah'm sorry, they've gone!"

"Who's gone?" said Kylie, staring at her friend. "Fion ... is it Anna?"

Myrrdin, staff in hand, crossed the short distance from his table. "What's happened?"

Fionnlagh quickly explained what had happened, his face pale.

Jason cursed. "We should have gone to her first! She was scared!" The food, so recently enjoyed, now set like lead in his stomach.

"She'll be so scared now," said Kylie, "Granddad, where's she gone?"

"I-I don't know," said the old man. "She could be anywhere, *they* could be anywhere..." he was staring at Fionnlagh.. "Fion...the books?"

"Anna was holding them when she vanished."

A silence settled over the group. It was Etain who broke the silence. "We're trapped here, ain't we? We cain't even use Huddour's Books to find Anna an' Aiken, to go home..."

No you cannot, said a voice, echoing through the stillness, *but neither are you trapped.*

Jason turned, Carnwennan in his hand, as he recognised the voice. Kylie was moving towards the glowing figure and he pulled her away. "Don't go near him! He's the Huntsman!"

"No," said Kylie, shrugging off his hand, "Jay, don't be silly, he's Cernunnos! He *helped* me!"

I go by many names, said the figure, shimmering in and out of reality, *but I am only ever what people expect me to be.* All around him time had come to a stop. People were frozen with smiles on their faces, their voices frozen mid word. Even the flames around them were unmoving, their glow somehow paler, less real.

"You-you're not supposed to interfere," said Gobswistle, nervously pulling at his teeshirt. The white lettering, *I deny your reality and live in my own,* had nearly worn away.

I offer only choices, my friend. See.

In the road before them, an archway appeared, a vast ivy covered archway, celtic scrollwork up its sides. Through the archway was another building, a group of figures standing outside, half hidden by a cloud of smoke.

"We can't leave," whispered Jason, "we can't, we need to find Anna, Aiken, we have to..."

"You have to do nothing."

The voice silenced them all, and Myrrdin, Gobswistle, Bedevere, Kylie, Etain and Jason turned to face the young woman who walked slowly down the road towards them. Cernunnos simply smiled as though in recognition.

The young woman was still wearing her brightly patterned yellow headscarf, her dated clothing.

"Do you know how many years I inhabited that body? That vile pustule of *filth*? Swearing allegiance to a *boggart*?"

You were given a second chance, said Cernunnos. *To make amends. But we could only put you on the path. We cannot make you walk it.*

"Spare me your philosophising, creature of magic." She looked at Jason, Kylie, the old man and the warrior. "You gave it away, didn't you? The Glass Apple?"

"I – I..." Gobswistle stared at her.

"You're not needed," she said, turning to face the young druid. "It's you I now face, isn't it?" A ribbon of blackness stretched out from her chest, reaching toward the druid. "It's you who controls our destinies..."

The cord froze.

Myrrdin, his staff half raised, became still. By his side, the young Bedevere was stilled half way through drawing his sword.

Your battle here is over, said Cernunnos, turning to Gobswistle. *Take your family and leave us. Return to your time, if not your world. Prepare yourselves. The worlds dwindle.*

"No," said Kylie. "No!"

"We're not leaving without Anna!" shouted Jason. Cernunnos smiled gently, but said nothing. Jason and Kylie grasped each other's hands.

The glowing figure turned from the children, regarding instead the young soldier Bedevere. Suddenly the youth was able to move, his blade fully drawn. *You must travel also. Your time is no longer here.*

"Ah...Ah know," said the soldier slowly, lowering his blade as he stared at the ethereal creature. "The lady Eigyr, she told me, Ah'm there at the end..."

Pass through the Gateway. The image in the gateway changed to rolling countryside, a small group of horsemen visible in the distance.

Bedevere walked slowly up to the Gateway. He stared through at the scene, his face a strange mixture of joy and sorrow. Glistening eyes turned to regard Jason.

"It's been an honour, young Yellowblade! Ah've still the mark on me ankle where yui whacked me!"

Jason nodded. He knew where Bedevere headed, and he understood that strangeness of joy and sorrow; he was feeling it himself. He knew where he'd heard the young man's name before. "Give King Arthur my regards!" he laughed.

With a final nod and a wave, Bedevere passed through the Gateway. The image changed; the pub at night now awaited them.

Jason looked up at the Glowing One. Cernunnos shimmered and

changed, one moment a bare chested, tattooed man with antlers on his brow, the next a fearful knight in gold and silver armour.

"I can't leave without my sister," said Jason, but he already knew what the reply would be.

Yes, said Cernunnos. He smiled sadly. *You can. But we will meet again, young Yellowblade.*

"No," said Jason, "no wait!" He'd realised something else. Something that, just perhaps, he'd known all along.

It is time to go for you.

"I need to speak to Myrrdin. Please?"

By his side, his companions had frozen. Cernunnos inclined his head. *As you wish.*

Jason moved up to the druid, Carnwennan glinting brightly in his hands. As he approached, Myrrdin found himself able to move. He stared at the Medb, at the frozen ribbon of blackness, his staff blazing with green fire, before looking down at the young boy.

"Jason...what...?"

"Eigyr's babies," said Jason. "Can I guess their names?"

"Jason, I don't..."

"They're Uther and Ambrosius, aren't they? You're Merlin." The name felt funny as he said it, yet somehow so *right.*

"I ... will be. Some day."

"No," said Jason. "Not someday. *Now.*" He looked over at Cernunnos. "Isn't he?"

You are perceptive, young Crowanhawk.

"So," said Jason, "that means ... that means this blade isn't mine. It belongs to Uther's son, when he's born."

"Jason, the Gwyllion gifted *you* with it..."

"They did it for a reason. It's done with me, I think. It did what it needed to do. I got the name from legends – surely it's only right it goes into those legends?" He held out the knife. "Please. Take it."

After a moment's hesitation, the druid closed his hands around the white hilted blade.

Jason moved to stand beside his sister and his grandfather. "Will we..." he looked at Cernunnos, "can we find Anna?"

Anything can be achieved by those with enough determination.

"But..."

A gentle but invisible hand pushed him and his family through the gateway. Like a stream of candle smoke caught in a draft, the Gateway rippled from sight.

Myrrdin turned to the Glowing One. "What happens now?"

You know what happens now, Merlin Emrys. Myrrdin died this night. You have knowledge of the future. The Medb shall be imprisoned in earthly form. She shall become the creature of legend once more;

Morgan Le Fay. As he spoke, the form of the young woman began to ripple, lifting slowly into the air. *There is a child. A babe that you rescued. Medb shall reside within her.*

"I have had knowledge of the Future before," said Myrrdin, watching as the Medb, her face frozen in fury, slowly faded from sight. "It has done more harm than good."

You wish to not know your future? You have railed against me and mine for our attempts to hide your more dangerous memories in your past. Yet always it has been your request.

"You have the power, Old One."

You shall live your life blind. And you will rail against us again.

"That is as it should be."

Cernunnos raised a hand. *As you wish.*

"We're back!" yelped Gobswistle, looking across at the pub. "We're home!"

"Oh...crap," said a voice from below. Jason, Kylie and Gobswistle looked down at the pile of empty leathers. Something small was moving through the leather vest.

"Etain?" asked Jason, crouching down.

A tiny plastic head emerged from the collar area. "Oh, flamin' great, ain't it? After all that and lookit me." She pulled herself free from the leathers. "Ah mean, anatomically correct as a damn Barbie doll!"

The walk through the pub was daunting. Kylie's torn jeans and teeshirt, and armful of leathers, and Gobswistle's gothic gear got enough stares. But it was Jason who held the attention of most of the people, his bloodstained features and his scorched fighting leathers silencing the people as he walked by. He looked like something out of a 1950s epic movie.

"Wot's this?" shouted one of the barmaids. "Halloween?"

It was as well, Jason thought, that the barmaid didn't hear Etain's reply as she stood on Kylie's shoulder, hidden by the girl's long black hair.

It was something of a relief to reach Edsel, whose doors obligingly opened as they drew close. Inside the magical campervan, damp footprints crossed the floor like glimmering snail trails. It took Jason a moment to realise that, in this time, no more than five minutes had passed since they had entered the Maze.

As Edsel trundled through the darkness, seemingly quite content to drive himself, the four people sat on the leather suite, silent and thoughtful.

"We have to find Anna," said Jason, breaking the silence.

"Of course, dear boy," said Gobswistle, "goes without saying."

"How?" piped up Etain, her voice having lost none of its volume despite her miniaturisation. "You gave away the Anguinum."

"The Huntsman, Cernunnos or whoever," said Jason, "he said we could do it, if we put our mind to it."

"But where to start," said Etain. She wore a toga made from one of Kylie's yellow handkerchiefs, pulled from one of the suitcases packed three hours and two weeks ago. "Where do we look? *How* do we look?"

"History books," said Kylie suddenly, her eyes widening. "No, think about it! Or – or books on legends, or mythology! Anna, she's got Huddour's Books, plus she's with Aiken. A Blue bearded boggart! Surely both're gonna stand out wherever they end up!"

"Clever girl," said Gobswistle delightedly. "Clever girl!"

Etain was looking at the suitcases dotted around Edsel's interior. "Yeah. Clever." She seemed distracted.

*

"Are they asleep?" Etain looked up as Gobswistle came down the stairs, changed now into a voluminous pink dressing gown, his hair like freshly washed cotton candy.

"Amazingly enough, yes. They're asleep."

"Did you tell them?"

Gobswistle feigned ignorance. "Tell them what? I know not what you mean, fair maiden."

"you *know* what Ah mean, Ethelbert." She marched across the coffee table as he sat down. "In Edsel, where was Anna's suitcase? Her clothes? Her *footprints*, for god's sake!"

"Maybe they dried up." Gobswistle's voice was sullen.

"Dried up," muttered Etain, "yeah right. Or, and how about this, maybe this isn't *our* world. If I went upstairs now, went into Anna's room, would I find all her things? Or would I find an empty room? Well?"

"I..." Gobswistle stared down at the irate plastic figure. "Maybe. I don't know." His voice was hesitant; he quickly looked away.

"Don't lie to me! Look under the Christmas tree!" A tiny plastic arm pointed across the room. "Where're Anna's presents?" She cursed loudly. "Ethelbert, Ah *know* this ain't our world. This is some – some parallel world, where Anna don't exist. What Ah want to know is, how did we get here?"

The old man stared at her, and for one long moment, Etain thought he was going to burst into tears. The old man finally took a deep breath, lowering himself onto the couch.

"We're here," said Gobswistle gently, "*because* Anna doesn't exist. It was the Gateway. It only sensed us four coming back through, so it sent us to a world where only us four exist."

"Great. So we're a TV show now. Lost in Time."

"We can find our way back!"

"You don't have the Anguinum anymore."

"It's still somewhere here. It's indestructible, dear lady. We just have to find it!" He smiled. "We've done harder things, you and I."

"Don't try and placate me! What did that horned freak mean, *the worlds are dwindling?*"

"I don't know," admitted the old man. "But apparently we have to prepare ourselves. So are you going to *help* me?"

Etain looked up at him. "Oh...Do you need ask? And don't be so accusing. You *know* Ah will. On one, no, *two*, conditions."

"Which are?"

"One – you find some way to get me back to my proper size."

"Your wish is my command." He smiled. "And the second?"

"*You tell Jason the truth about his dreams*. Tell him where Anna is. Tell him the rules of travelling through time."

Gobswistle's face fell. "That's four things."

"They're all inclusive."

Are you sure that's wise?"

"Will you do it?"

"...fine, okay," said Gobswistle, "but after Christmas, alright? They're going to have enough to deal with realising we're in another world. Let's get Christmas out of the way."

"Fine. But Ah'll hold you to it."

"I will, I promise, you have my word. But let's make this Christmas one to remember!"

"Yeah," said Etain. "Yeah, okay. We'll make it the best Christmas we can. Just don't you be tryin' to stick me on top of no tree!"

END OF BOOK ONE Pt 2

Characters.

Aiken Drum. A blue haired, stump-legged boggart befriended by Jason. He used to be human, but was cursed and transformed by Huddour. Not very bright, but fiercely loyal. Cursed to vanish should anyone declare affection for him.

Ambrosius, a mysterious young boy who has yet to be identified, he bore a message to the selkie.

Anguinum, the Druid's Stone, vessel of sidhe magic. Currently held by Gobswistle, who has little knowledge how to use it.

Anna Crowanhawk, youngest sister of Jason and Kylie. An innocent, able to find joy in life, but surprisingly sharp in the matters of magic. Soon to be five.

Athdara, a selkie trapped in human form, she is knowledgeable in herbal lore.

Bedevere. Young soldier in the army of Omnust.

Bernard, Ironsmith of Kilneuair.

Blashie, a sadistic diminutive trowe, or troll, servant to Huddour. Addicted to shiny objects, music, and the taste of human flesh.

Bothen Carey, a fisherman from Aneithcraig, not all that he appears

Bridget, one of Morven's serving girls. Recently with child.

Carson, Uncle to the Crowanhawks, brother to their deceased mother.

Cathal, young soldier, survivor of the doomed regiment sent to the monastery; a dangerous changeling.

Cernunnos, also Herne, powerful ancient sidhe.

Cináed Mac Ailpin, king of western Scotland, father of Constantine

Comte Dè Saint Germain; an eighteenth century alchemist, another facet of Gobswistle's personailites.

Cookiecrumb, a semi sentient renovated bungalow in the Yorkshire countryside, home to the Crowanhawk family.

Critheanach; baby girl, daughter of Ilisa, stolen by Lathgertha, then abandoned in the ashes of a fire.

Daileass, son of Athdara and Tearlach, a selkie who has only just discovered his ability to change.

Darrach Drummond, old warrior who fled from a viking attack with his daughter

Eigyr, aka Ivory, daughter of Darrach, wife of Constantine, mother of Constans, heavily pregnant with twins

Edsel, a peculiar seemingly sentient mobile home, created by Gobswistle and Etain.

Etain, ancient black celtic sidhe warrior, ironfire wielder, friend of

Gobswistle, former guardian of the Anguinum.
Ethelbert Gobswistle, grandfather to the Crowanhawks, keeper of the Anguinum. Old beyond memory, and slightly confused.
Fionnlagh, young soldier, one of the Men of Dun Ghallain, whom Kylie befriends
Firtha, youngest child of Athdara and Tearlach, only a few months old.
Gaira, a short, rotund wise woman from the village of Kilneuair. Lifetime friend to Aiken, she is secretly in love with him, and dangerously protective of him.
Golum, originally of Jewish legend, this Golum was created by Medb using the soul of Mr. McCall as a slave. A creature of clay, it can transform itself into any shape it wants.
Gwyllion. Nine sidhe sisters, known by many names, oracles who send the Crowanhawks on a quest.
Huddour, Lord. Cruel Britannic warlock, now based in Castle Stalcaire on Loch Linnhe, keeper of the three books of Huddour that Jason and his family seek.
Ilisa; a young woman rescued from the vikings by Jason
Jason Crowanhawk, aka Crowanhawk Yellowblade. Owner of Carnwennan, sidhe blade. Approaching his thirteenth birthday.
Jean. Prisoner of Huddour
Lathgertha; wife of Ragnar, vicious viking warrior, small framed and beautiful
Kylie Crowanhawk, aka Crowhaven Crowanhawk younger sister of Jason, made a changeling after an attack by goblins, she is ten. Sometimes called Ravenhair, because of her long black hair
Medb, a mythical sidhe sorceress, nemesis of Gobswistle, hunting for the Anguinum.
Miss Spence, secretary and friend of Mr McCall, killed by the Medb.
Morven, house keeper in the royal barracks.
Mr McCall, family solicitor, transformed into a *Golum* by the Medb.
Myrrdin, also Lailoken, ancient mythical druid, also a younger Gobswistle. Sharp and astute, sometimes cruel by necessity, he is the opposite of his older self. He has limited magical abilities; only slight control of the elements.
Omnust Ossian, captain of the Royal Guard of Cináed.
Ragnar, vicious viking warrior, commander of three drekar ships, associate of Huddour.
Tearlach, sealer and devout Christian, husband to Athdara, whom he 'saved from her heathen ways.' Eventually killed by Etain.
Uillaem; Captain of the Men of Dun Ghallain; a changeling.
Vortigern. Ambitious soldier of the army of Omnust. Made captain by Cináed when Omnust is imprisoned.

The Song of the Shaman

Christmas comes and goes. The seasons carry the Crowanhawk family through the next year, their lives filled with the search for Anna.

A second Christmas passes without their sister, and Spring arrives. Despite the words of Cernunnos, the search for Anna seems ever more futile.

But a chance discovery of an ancient book sends Jason and Kylie back through time, hope burning in their hearts once more.

Unable to follow, unaware of the childrens' disappearance until it is too late, Gobswistle and Etain begin their own quest, to find the Anguinum that Myrrdin left in Kilneuair.

As Jason and Kylie travel through lands of myth and legend, and as Gobswistle and Etain travel through lands of cars, trains and televisions, none are aware their separate quests are leading them inexorably to the same point…

Made in the USA
Columbia, SC
03 April 2018